BEYOND THE CRADLE

ANNE STANTON

BEAK IN HILL BOOKS

This is a work of fiction. There are a few historical facts and verifiable news stories worked into the storyline. Their purpose is only to reveal more about the characters within the story's timeline and to move the story forward.

"Each sentence is poetry. I want to savor each and every one for as long as I can." ~Kate

"Beyond the Cradle is delicious." ~Bidda K.

"This is not a 'female' only story—off limits to males. If you guys have the courage to read between the book's printed lines, I think you'll understand what I'm trying to convey. Reading it will help you be a better man (friend, father, son, husband)." ~Howard

"The writing has substance; that is to say, it is well-written! The imagery is inspiring. As I drove home (during a rain-storm) one afternoon after I began reading it, I found myself wondering how the author would describe what I was seeing." ~Noel

"This story pulled me along nicely. Samantha's words were so wise and deep. I wanted more." ~Dian

DEDICATION

This novel is dedicated to children I love. Some have grown up; others are growing faster than I can track. My hope is to spend more time together, if not this side of the cradle, then beyond it.

First and foremost my two, Lissa and Jesse, who encompass the beaucoup section of my heart, and astonishingly I theirs, even as adults, which is as great as it can get for a parent. Over the past eleven years four wonderful girls have been added to our family through them. They are (in birth order): Emily, Samantha, Margot, and Audrey.

Lastly, it's my hope this story finds its way to these students I knew and loved, while in their K-2 years of school. At present they are in middle school. Keep seeking and growing like Photogen and Nycteris managed to do in spite of the obstacles they faced.
In alphabetical order: Aryan, Campbell, Charlie, Cora, David, Donava, Elli, Gracee, Jackson, Kailee, MacKenna, Mila, Raelynn, Ronin, Sawyer, Taryn, Timmy, Trenton, and Zachary.

CONTENTS

PROLOGUE

J'm all grown up now, or as Samantha would say, "stuck in my growin'." Reaching the place where I could say, "I'm here!" involved crawling up the backside of my own story. I had to inch my way into its haze, like a caterpillar moving toward metamorphosis, unawares. When I made it through to the other side, the mysteries vanished. I stopped, sat, and wrote. I wrote to retain and to share.

Stepping back into sealed rooms, necessary or not, is a Herculean task. It takes time to face pain, pull the past up, examine the breaches we want to keep in our clenched fists, but cannot— not if freedom is to be found, life lived. For me the surrender took eight years.

It didn't need to take that long. Had the July sky not been so still or blazingly blue over the mountain that day; had the mother, who offered breast as nourishment, not been starved as a child; had certain lands not succumbed to the tyrants of history; or had vital family pieces not been sidestepped, all in the name of peace—had, had, had, and had. It's mad, but they all had, and then I had not. It's almost mathematical, the dryness behind it all. Even if one or two of the key players had not linked me into some causal ill effect, presenting grace (and they did show up), I still had not.

Catching up with the past is laborious. It requires focus; but catching up to the point of knowing you're safe enough to be found—that happens unexpectedly. That's part of reckoning's beauty. It's out of our control. And when it comes, we go on, changed. We're more aware, and grace continues to tag along to show us we don't know everything until we give up everything. That's when the crawling stops and the standing starts, because suddenly we see we're not standing alone.

I made things hard. I never wanted to, but did. It just came naturally to me. That's a fact. It's a fact for you, too. But it's not all our doing, our undoing. We've been in a long line of tumbling dominoes.

Samantha once said, "Hidin' in the dark brings the puckers down on us, the way hidin' out too long in a bathin' tub does. Only it's the soul that gets all wrinkled up 'n' ugly."

What did I learn while stretching my limits, like some would-be contortionist? Hiding doesn't solve a thing. I kept seeing myself selfishly gnawing at the fringes of Samantha, like some cold-hearted wolf, ripping apart the freedom that defined her. I couldn't shake it. I only hid all the more.

Writing wouldn't come until I could say, "Hi. I'm Robyn. I know who I am now. It took me a while, but I'm here."

Had I resurrected my own domino? No. I had not.

PART I
EARTH, OUR CRADLE

THE SHOCKER

*a*t the end of my ninth year my parents (correction: my mother) plucked me out of Manhattan and plopped me down in West Virginia, literally. At least that's how it felt—like a painful extraction—worse than having a tooth pulled, since new teeth grow in the same spot. Dad went willingly. Here's how calculating she was in what she orchestrated. We entered our new home on my tenth birthday. Wait. I'm not done. It was at the exact time of my birth: 3:43 p.m. I learned of that unknown-to-me factoid as we crossed the threshold. I waited for confetti to drop. None did.

I first caught wind of her disastrous declaration, which she described as her moving plan, one morning at breakfast. I let it pass by me, as a floating fiber or a random joke that made no sense. I regarded it as a remnant of a nightmare she hadn't shaken loose yet, since she hadn't finished her coffee when the tangled mess began spewing forth. Her words left the same impression I'd have felt, had someone said to me, "We're going to uproot the Statue of Liberty in three months and ship her to . . ." Shock. Right? When she began uttering a second round of the same, closer to my face, eye to eye, I finally responded.

"What did you say?" That's what I heard my mouth mumble,

while trying to swallow a segment of my grapefruit. The question, where, didn't matter. The mere thought of carting Lady Liberty off the Island was enough to make any New Yorker pause and put on a facial expression as sour as my grapefruit.

I chose to grumble a guffaw deep within my throat at what I thought I'd heard, because she didn't answer my question; but the insanity didn't go away. She went into repeat mode. My grunts were a form of self-preservation, a defense mechanism I learned to use, when something too crazy to understand had to be dismissed. Since my unintelligible sounds weren't fazing her, I coughed out some curt news flashes, just to be on the offensive safe side. "Flash: I have a life. Flash: I have friends and my routines are amazing. Flash: I've worked hard to score my social successes! They come with great perks." Then I said, "Mother, I was invited to the Martins' beach house in Nantucket for the summer! That just can't be eliminated, as if it's nothing! It's e-ver-y-thing!"

I tried to reach her guilt button, so that she would resurface within the modicum of insight she typically possessed. There, I knew she could dismiss the lingering nightmare clinging to her brain cells. Those bad dreams of hers sometimes tried to disguise themselves as amazing ideas, especially when she didn't grasp the whole picture—me. It was my daughterly duty to keep her on track. I glibly explained the advantages I possessed, and what it cost me to earn them. When she finally said, "All that will have to change," I laughed openly, which made her glare at me. Not good. Mother ran on ideas. When she set her mind to fulfilling a goal, only something as dramatic as a Jacobean wrestling match could deter her. Once the benefits of country living hit home, it grew like mushroom spores tucked under a forest's floor, cozy, hidden, and steadfast in its ascent.

At that point I sat straight up and held onto my seat. Who wouldn't, feeling as if a switch were about to be flipped with an *all systems go* light, flashing its own announcement? My breathing raced ahead without me. This was new territory. Usually, long before a plan solidified into law, Mother and I would talk our way through messy areas, such as misconceptions, perceived injustices, or genuine dislikes. That way we'd safeguard our existence under the same roof.

Typically, I'd be keenly invested in voicing my opinions when an exchange passing under review threatened to twist the well-secured cap off my fizz. Wouldn't you? No one wants fizz to escape its containment field, especially when it's their own. But this time was different. She never approached me. The plan crept onto my home turf before I could perk up, pick up, and load up on options. It's like she kept it under wraps on purpose. Yes! She walked around with the stink-plan under my nose, and never leaked it. I never smelled it coming. Totally unbelievable! What more could I do, initially, but laugh. I refused to cry.

Before I could sneeze ten times and die on the spot, her plan began prying loose the edges of my life. My fizz, the stuff that made me rise to the top of any situation, began popping in thin air. Nothing I tried dissuaded her. Her firm and bulldozing brainchild, the one I coined, The Rob-Fizz Robbery, the one that shook my sealed bottle, uncapped it, and let it all shoot out was in its first stage already! All I could visualize were my bubbles being kidnapped by Heather Karr, which actually did happen, once the news of my departure spread through the ranks. She began rising even before I left. That made the *Manhatties*, my best friends, angry. "Robyn, you can't abdicate your position. That'll ruin everything for the rest of us." That's when Madison came up to my face, almost nose to nose. "Got it? You just can't!"

"I know, Madison! Don't you think I know that?" My threshold of tolerance for Madi's exasperations had been crossed, miles back. I was moving on sheer imaginative energy in trying to buck Mother's reality-engine, and Madi wasn't helping. Did it bother me that my friends were freaking out? Yes, and not really. My wounds couldn't get any worse, and yet, their griping broadened the scope of my anger. Why should I be upset *for them*? They still could pop a piece of Bubblicious in their mouths and plot their next moves on Heather's usurpation. I had to forfeit the entire game.

I spent the latter part of my ninth year sulking. Father was always strolling in and out of our penthouse on business trips. He said it mattered little to him which direction his plane flew, as long as *Gypsy* brought him straight home to his girls. His spoken confession, planted with a kiss on my dampened curls, didn't reap the typical daughterly affection he'd expected, though. Dad had turned traitor to my cause. He landed on Mother's side, once again.

I let him know how upset I was by erecting a cage of icicles around me. I blasted him, once, with a double jab—the freeze, followed by a swift, fiery, verbal dart aimed at his heart. I succeeded, royally.

What I had said threw him off balance. I watched his shoulders slump. Mother's did, too. As soon as he left the apartment she said, "I'm cancelling all your social dates for the week. Everything. Period." That was her retaliatory move, which made me know she knew I was successful in my warfare. Dad deserved the payback for his vote to end my life. He allowed the sole decision of my demise to rest in Mother's hands. That made the odds impossible, because it made me the odd person out. So that's exactly how I began to behave, begrudgingly odd.

On July 25, 1985 we boarded a 747 bound for Washington, D.C. The parents spent three days being tourists. I dragged my feet and only looked at my feet. The parents sang in our rental car on the drive to *The Mon*, eventually leading to Glady, WV. I curled into a solid mute ball in the back seat, unresponsive. I seethed and grit my teeth for being forced into the worst birthday of my life.

Upon leaving the Nation's Capitol my world waned, shriveled up. I suffered the whittling-down blows of nature, as well as those one-lane ruts they called roads, which cut through a *monotonous* ever-present smear of green. It obstructed the view of my sky, the part I held onto the whole trip. I had plopped the blue backdrop into that lead role, since it remained the only familiar sight left in my life besides the parents; but I didn't look at them.

Eventually, even the sky fell into disrepute with all those green intruders stretching their way from earth to sky, like a child's simple drawing. *The Mon* redefined ennui within its vast expanse. There were no exciting highlights in the skyline, like I'd left behind in Manhattan. That one was full of history, new and old, the scene of numerous paintings and drawings, including my favorites by Peter Potter. Its canvas held unlimited shapes, and unrivaled heights. Inside those buildings were people stretching their way upward toward greatness. All the giant, needled, green things could claim were various species of birds and insects as inhabitants. Not only was there no competition in my comparison between the city and the forest, as I saw them, I recall resenting the latter for the truckload of uninvited thoughts it had laid upon my brain; but I decided to bear everything begrudgingly, while agreeing with myself, entirely.

Afterwards, I sighed, another of many sighs that day. It appeared the rest of my life would be doomed to suffering shrink-ages, all of them turning into one repetitive smear just like the boring forest, only tumbleweeds of foggy grays, blotting out its pedestrian skyline. I wanted the other pedestrians of New York City, the people, the walkers—not the boring turns I envisioned ahead of me.

Glady's skyline, as I saw it, nearing the driveway to that recently purchased piece of property, held the commonplace: trees, clouds, and the mountains. Then I conceded. Okay, trees and clouds are common to most places, but not the stupid mountains; and then I had to backtrack once again. *Okay! Okay! That many trees aren't everywhere, either.*

I always had to check myself. It was something I started when eight after I discovered how my mind popped up with new infor-mation that contradicted some old information I'd thrown out the week prior, just because it sounded good. I vowed never to expose myself like that again. So, I became my own personal fact checker. I knew mountains were only in certain places on the globe. As far as all those trees, who'd want them in any sane setting anyway?

Gangly thought-monsters poured out of me after we arrived-- for about one hour. Only one hour, you might ask. If you're surprised, consider my surprise. I never imagined my fixed-pout flipping into a wide-eyed, mouth-dropping smile within hour two. I felt like a veritable lighthouse. After one bright flash in time, I forgot about Manhattan and all my complaints. When I did think of what I'd left in New York, later in that first week, everything looked different to me. A year later I questioned how I could have thought *The Mon* boring. Unexplainable things happen all the time, I figured.

The shift of my attachment from the NYC skyline to the natural one could not be credited to nature's merits though, not then at least. Well, not ever, not fully. Like I said, I didn't dwell on Manhattan or philosophize on what was happening within me. I was too distracted to focus on the past or nature, and I was ten, newly ten. What I found and wholly embraced on the mountain that day reached higher than the architecture of the Manhattan skyline.

So, why am I taking so long to introduce Samantha, the cupbearer of everything wonderful? Is it because living life on earth is never encapsulated in one isolated moment in time? So many pieces are at play, so many dimensions; and, they're all important. *Patience.* Yes, that's Samantha's voice there.

RESIDUES OF THE UNKNOWN

*W*e arrived outside of Glady, West Virginia the day of my tenth birthday. I mention that again, because I later discovered the move had been sparked by my seemingly rapid growth—not physically, but *otherly*. This part needs a bit of explanation, so allow the French genes in me some legroom. The French don't clip thoughts, we drip like a broken faucet when there's explaining to be had.

Supposedly early on Mother noticed I was precocious, and 'something else.' That last part, back then, dangled in the breeze like a broken strand of a spider's web, one that lands on your face and feels creepy as it attaches its invisible presence onto you, fully unwelcome. Her consuming concern led to pulling me out of public school right before my seventh birthday. Mother chose to homeschool me. She said, such a platform would allow me to advance at my own pace, follow curricula and extracurricular activities according to my own bent, and be freed up from as many socially fast and educationally slow lanes as possible. Then there was that other concern. She said she'd spill its contents, when I produced a spitting image of myself, somewhere in my imaginary future, while dwelling in a place called Motherhood—in other words, never, if the choice were hers alone.

Homeschooling worked for me. There were reasons it did. Timing played a major role. My pre-school and kindergarten friends were already drifting in different directions for first grade; and then there was Mother's uncanny skill in networking. Perpetual devotion comes to mind. She organized in-home tutors, field trips, overly supervised social gatherings, and the normal grind of studies under her care at the penthouse we called home, or on various sites around the city. Dad took on the role of our field trip guide, an occasional position at best. He did introduce me and my friends to Gypsy's maintenance crew, and the operators in the control tower, without whom, he said he couldn't do his job nearly as easily. He, also, took us fly fishing for trout, *once*, in the Poconos. Everyone loved Dad and stood at attention for Mother.

I had tackled and aced a string of high school courses by the time Mother dropped *the bomb* on me. I guess you could say that's when I dropped out of high school. With all the tears and tantrums that ensued that quarter, none of my classes were officially transferred onto my transcript. No grades. Mother just pretended I was an emotional fifth grader, doing age-level work. Better yet, she announced we were on break, not just for the rest of that winter quarter, but the entire spring before our move.

What I couldn't register during those years is what Mother thought about me. What did she see that couldn't be found in a letter grade on a transcript? Apparently suspicions arose prior to homeschooling of a psyche that would prove harmful to me as years progressed. It was, according to her, an attitudinal one that germinated among my peers; and there was more. She never told me about *the more*. I discovered its makeup years later, when I overheard her speaking with Dad. That'll surface. Not pretty.

I had guessed, along the way, that Mother had not grown up entitled. I had no idea really, what the outline of her childhood looked like. She tossed hints at me, occasionally, like rice missing its mark at a wedding. She'd say things like, "Don't take people for granted. Appreciate your family, especially." Platitudes came easily to her. "Struggles are real," she'd say; or "Opportunities must be grabbed, when they surface." And one I'd never heard anyone but her say, "Every door that opens should have your fingerprints on the knob." What did any of that mean? She never provided concrete examples, and I floundered like one of Dad's fish on the end of a hook until I just stopped biting at the bait.

Towards the end of our last year in Manhattan, she lowered her eyes and looked sad after saying something about being kind to others, no matter who, and especially if others are speaking ill of them. I thought maybe she thought she had been too harsh on me of late and felt remorse, all the while knowing I had good friends and a great family life; but I never knew for sure why those disconnects happened in her, those dull-eyed aches, not then. I just assumed she'd slipped off track, because she was always blowing things out of proportion, and that she'd right herself soon.

My notion of the world was simple. Sometimes you felt good in the middle of it, other times you didn't; and where the proportions landed, well, that was pretty much up to each person to decide. I wanted to tell her not to worry about me. I wanted her to know I'd land on the softer side, that difficulties wouldn't be a part of my future. I never spoke those words aloud to her, because I was certain she knew. After all, I was an achiever who succeeded in everything I set my mind to doing, much like her. Sometimes I'd wonder, had a creepy man crossed her path before she met Dad; but that didn't seem possible, knowing Mother. She always called the shots.

Once she casually blurted out how she had to make her own dinners. That was the time I rejected her offer to teach me to cook. I didn't see either as a big deal, her cooking or my not cooking. I mean, gosh, telephones were invented before her birth, and I'm sure take outs were available, even back in the dark age. I had no clue how that grain of information revealed the tip of a mystery—

like how her parents were never around after she returned home from school. When that grain sprouted, I realized Mother never talked about her parents. That plunked me onto a momentary crossroad. Why hadn't I heard of those grandparents? For the longest time I thought all kids only had one set of grandparents, all on the father's side of the family. When it struck me differently, I let the thought occupy my mind for about five seconds, since it never seemed to matter to Mother.

The more common clichés parents used to motivate their children, Mother never used. How far she walked to school everyday didn't cross her lips, nor did the starving children in Africa. She did, however, share the antics of a mean teacher from her past. He'd whack the knuckles of a rascally group of boys with a small bundle of twigs. Sometimes he'd make the disruptive gabbers wear dunce caps, while their noses were pressed to rest and remain in a corner until released. That story never reached me. It didn't seem real, rather more in line with a far-off Dickens' tale from a work of fiction, not part of America's past. Later I discovered I was correct in one of those assumptions.

I really wanted to catch some of the rice Mother tossed my way, those silent guideposts she'd drop into my soil, but instead I found myself sinking in the immense storage bin of her sequestered kernels. There was a darkness wedged between each grain that frightened me. And so, when eight, when feeling my personal stuffing was being picked apart by Mother's character-building efforts, whatever it was she recited to herself as good in the recesses of her heart, all to dispel what she deemed unworthy within mankind *and me*, my heart began turning from her as my wisdom-bearer. She had occupied that position for so long that when the shining bits of veneer began flaking off, it was hardly noticeable at first. Even though ten was the projected year to accelerate her plan, she had already colored me, years earlier, as her personal and profound, number-one project; and she aimed to tackle 'me,' wholeheartedly.

Therefore, Mother's timeline became law. It had to land before a *hormonal shift* fell into my lap. That appearance, she believed, would disrupt my childhood emotionally, making the physical transition of moving even harder, possibly impossible. Mother wanted no additional reasons for disruptive behavior to course through my brain upon commencement. That's why she selected the seemingly safe year of ten to begin. She had no clue how to extract what she feared she saw in me, nor that I would commence *my flow* ahead of the norm. Such are the jags within well laid plans of mice and men, and even women. All things can change within a moment.

But at the time, her law held its ground. Ten remained the territory where grand possibilities could be erected, a wide place to stretch out and calculate her hopes. In her mind, it was the perfect digit to upload stimulating, new, and calming impressions as preparation for opening the tumultuous decade that would piggyback, ungraciously, onto its generous expanse. She figured my pre-teen and teen years would enter as a whisper, rather than a booming bang, if my life in that *one* year possessed the right energy and elements to jumpstart them properly.

"Ten's turned into a lure," Dad said, after listening to Mother present an overview of her philosophy in the days it first cropped up—long before I felt threatened by it. I knew he was setting up his punchline, so I waited. We both assumed Mother's intensity on the topic would wane, so when he followed his lead with, "Ten actually might catch a big *one*," I laughed appropriately. Mother shot him a look. That was the first time I saw how different my parents were. Mother wanted control and effect. Dad wanted harmony and lightheartedness. Mother figured the work behind embodying curiosity, exuding hope, and capturing the exact spirit needed to land on two feet, once eleven came into view, was more important than cracking jokes about her outlook.

When her sketched-out plan for wholeness evolved, it demanded an entirely new environment. Walking daily in nature;

running on earth's surfaces, not concrete; swimming in ponds, not chlorinated pools; and riding a bike in country air, not in polluted and dangerous traffic--all of it eliminated New York City. Dad talked of horses, which she latched onto quickly. She wanted me outdoors, outdoors, outdoors, developing my growing body, cleansing all those NastY toxins from my bloodstream, so horses fit. I was to drink in all things bright and beautiful. At times I felt like a penciled in character, traveling through a James Herriot book, when I listened to her dance around her dream. She figured, since body cells are totally refreshed every seven years, by the time I was seventeen I'd be a whole new body with a whole new brain and a whole new attitude to meet life without a hiccup.

Mother's map appeased her concerns, somewhat. If I had known what I discovered a couple years later, I'd have said, then, that Mother wanted a new me. If I had known what I discovered a bit past that point, I'd have said, I was wrong and she was partially right; but hindsight never arrives in time for us to face it in the present.

As far as country living, no one in the Thomas family knew a thing about it, other than how to cast a fly rod, and that prize went solely to Dad. If someone had asked us to draw two tails, one, let's say of a donkey and the other of a cow, we couldn't have done it, not for lack of our drawing abilities, but from sheer ignorance about the two creatures' anatomies. I'm fairly certain, if one of those animals swung its tail and smacked my dad on his backside, when he turned around to see the rump from which the tail had swung, he still wouldn't be able to identify the animal that whacked him.

Mother said that was a silly assessment, quite unfair, and then threw in the fact that dad had owned a horse as a boy, so at least he'd know that tail. She actually said, "Poop" right after I'd blurted out the accusation, which caused her to laugh as she shared dad's *tail* story. I think I made her doubt his animal knowledge, honestly, and when I didn't join in the laughter with her, she ended her giddiness by slipping back into a serious mode and speaking two words into the glare on my face: "We'll learn!"

Mother utilized something I hadn't developed, yet, the ability to project years into the future. She knew I wouldn't be at home forever, long before I did, and that my path to college would arrive way before kids my age graduated high school. She was keen on bemoaning the state of public education, and how even private schools followed the beat of their mandated drums.

In one breath she could say things like, "The current school model of snatch, catch, and hold captive is positively the most unhealthy delay foisted upon a child's natural maturation process, ever concocted by man. How do school administrators bow to invisible gods, and then not acknowledge the system's failures when they roll in, time after time, in every subject? Why they never consider changing the model is beyond me. Systems don't care that growing minds and bodies need to embrace challenges and be in motion, not when they get thousands of dollars per student per year, just by filling seats. It's all political, when bad policies outstrip common sense. No place to go with that model, but downhill; and it's not just the children who suffer."

If you're wondering how I can recall so many words, it's easy when you've heard them over and over in various ways throughout the years. Typically, an apology would follow the rant. This time it was: "Don't concern yourself with this stuff. I've got you covered. And myself, too! No empty nesting for me after you fly off to university. I'm concocting plans to open a retreat someday—for mental health professionals. I'll need to stay busy, and I know my former colleagues need relief. Two birds, one stone." And there it was again, that gray cloud over Mother's eyes. Why had it appeared so suddenly, even if briefly? She was standing in her strength when it came. Didn't the haze have boundaries?

We entered the 1902 sprawling Americana farmhouse with the assistance of a local realtor, who greeted us in the driveway with a basket of fruit. I thought my parents and I were seeing the behemoth for the first time together. Turns out, the agent unearthed the parents' secret. I mean, what parent doesn't share moving details with their kid? I don't fault the realtor one bit. Hearing the house had already been visited by both of them, independently, only added to my arsenal of grievances.

It went something like this: "So, what do you think of it, young lady?"

"Umm. I don't really know. I haven't seen it yet."

"Oh, your parents haven't shared all the photos I sent them after their visits?"

"No, they haven't. Mother, Dad? Did that slip your mind?"

My non-existent birthday cake couldn't have fallen flatter. What a notable nightmare of betrayal and kidnapping. Major. Mother had lied and Dad covered it up. Even Grandma Thomas was in on it. No recourse for my opinion, or for voicing my grievances, except to the *Manhatties*; but I'd already learned, the more I complained to them the angrier they got.

The furniture from our Manhattan apartment had been shipped ahead. How out of place it looked to me, swallowed up in the four-thousand-plus square feet it was supposed to fill. After completing the compulsory tour of the house and grounds, Mother said, "Our first project, Robyn, will be to search for antiques to spruce up the guest rooms, for vis-i-tors!" That's how she dumped her first project package into my lap. It was followed by the question, "What shall we get, first?" In other words, Mother was soliciting me, wanting me on her page, wanting me to smile, as her plan unfolded.

If I replied like the injured, solitary, and starving owl I felt myself becoming, then I'd be validating my worst fear, a complete metamorphosis into that beleaguered creature, one rising fast, as a candidate for the endangered species list. So, as *not* to support such a transmutation, I dropped the bait she longed for me to take—the one that could have solicited an, "Oh! Who? Who? Who will be coming, Mother? Let's find some wonderful things for the guest room!" That was a younger version of myself. Such a response would never cross my lips, now. My sunken heart lay under wraps. Nancy Drew couldn't have sleuthed her way through the scene with more panache.

I got the sense the old house and land regarded our presumptuous attempt to mold them into anything other than what they'd been for the past eighty-three years, a laughable mistake. But I ended up being wrong on that count, too. The house eventually turned into a showcase of impeccable taste after various restorations and renovations were carried out over the years, all by Mother. The gardens are breathtaking wonders, too.

One of the presents lavished on me that first day turned out to be a state-of-the-art, amazingly small, tape recorder. It perched atop a shoebox, full of virgin tapes. Mother said, "If Tony Schwartz can turn heads with his tapes of raw Manhattan sounds, then you can put together its counterpart, raw country sounds." Dad said, "You've got everything you need, hon. Go for it."

I thought it terribly unfair to be made to suffer loving gestures on a birthday made in hell. I knew if I had said anything to expose my feelings on the topic—any topic, probably, I would have done irreparable harm to my mother's well-being or, at least, I thought I would, since I figured I was the center of her waking hours.

My friends and I had come to the definite conclusion that our mothers were all desperate women, living vicarious existences at our expense. They were in need of our pity, yes, but never our allegiance. Alliances were ours alone. So, with a remnant of the *Manhattie*'s brand of compassion, still hovering over my cold heart, I willed myself not to sink to the level of verbal meanness toward a parent. Doing so would probably compel me to reveal the raw truth straight into her face, ugly-style, and the whole of my heart that held it. I couldn't endure seeing either close up. Nope. I hoped matters would never force me to enter that place, even though I felt the potential lurking close to the surface of my skin.

THE NOT-BY-CHANCE MEETING

*a*n hour later out of sheer boredom, I managed to tote the recorder out the door and turn it on. It opened with birds chirping; my footsteps dragging along the gravel; Dad's turning the engine of his new "Silver Fox," a Mazda RX-7, driven ahead by a friend's college-aged son, looking for some extra cash and getting the ride of his life, probably; Mother yelling out the door, "Bring home some bottled water. The tap tastes ghastly!" and me, saying, "Great." After Mother closed the door I followed it up with: "And the winner of this year's Oscar for Best Documentary goes to Robyn Thomas for her stunning rendition of *Life in the Green Prison.* Yay! Rah! Clap, clap. Thank you so much. I couldn't have done it without my wonderful mother. Boo! Boo!" All recorded. All still there.

I turned off the collector-of-great-sorrows and continued walking without purpose. None of us reckoned on the unfolding of that afternoon—not even Mother. A whirlwind descended before me. It wasn't forecasted. It landed unplanned, at least from our earthly perspective.

As I ambled upward along the main gravel road, which fronted the farmhouse, I reached a fairly level strip that dropped into a slight downward cruise, followed by another long upward stretch that continued going and going without any apparent end. I cast sideway glances, accustomed to looking both ways in Manhattan traffic, but all I saw were scratched out appendages, shooting east and west, like the stilled legs of an arched lizard, scouting its terrain. At that point, I knew I hadn't landed on my feet like said lizard—not at all. In fact I wanted to crawl under one of the scraggly trees I saw, hoping I could disappear into the ground.

I thought, surely the self-inflicted drudgery I was experiencing, walking that road-to-nowhere, only added to my depression. I vowed there and then to never repeat the mistake again, unless under total duress. I dallied, moved slowly forward, kicking rocks and pouting. An hour later, not having wandered far for lack of enthusiasm, thirst crossed my mind. Soon, it was all I noticed.

I had never walked a mountainous country mile before. Manhattan is basically flat. When you get hot, thirsty, cold, wet, or tired of walking there, you duck into any number of available eateries, seasonally cooled or warmed, and ready to provide whatever it is you'd want.

Here, with that parched lizard's back under my feet and its heat rising up through the rubber soles of my black Pumas, there were no exits to gain relief. I had gone, perhaps, a mile from home [correction: the house] when I panicked like a baby. All I had at my disposal to ease my fright was the entire Monongahela National Forest, which I considered entering, just to go *missing*. That move, I thought, would serve the parents right.

When I first took to the road, I planned on Dad rescuing me within thirty-five minutes or so. He had said it would be a quick jaunt to Elkins, and since I was on the only road to Elkins, my mind turned into his route this way: Get Mother's goodies, get back home—zip, zip, Mazda-style with an, "Ah, look! There's my Robyn!" That's when he'd stop, retrieve, and carry me back to the house. Dad never dawdled. He didn't stretch out or waste valuable minutes. Surely, that wouldn't change, *here*.

I hadn't thought of time in country terms, however, especially for a man on a sort-of vacation, seeing whatever there was to see for the first time. I didn't figure on the local color, either, the people. Instead, I wondered how he could be so thoughtless, knowing I'd be thirsty; knowing I'd be stranded on this roller-coaster ride that was totally lacking any pit stops—*on my birthday!* But then, there was this tiny detail, I realized later. When I exited the driveway in total rejection mode, I had failed to see how Dad had turned left towards Elkins; whereas, I had turned right for my walk.

If Dad had returned, as I'd wanted, if I had been swooped up in my own set of hopes and expectations, I never would have met Samantha that day, her fat bike tires zigzagging down one of the lizard's leggy side roads, trailing dust, and clipping rocks.

Suddenly the landscape shifted reality. All my discomforts vanished. The Mon had transformed itself to accommodate the vision heading my way—a dark-haired goddess, descending from the heights of Mount Olympus, from Mytikas Peak itself, with her sidekick trailing at her heels. When that sidekick, apparently a Shakespearean fool (and, yes, I used to take great joy in mixing mythological and literary references) caught up with her, their laughter filled the pulsing heat, absorbed it, and sent it out again, until they caught sight of me, and their faces grew curiously still.

I pegged the sidekick as an intruder, the boy named Scott Farley. I watched him, peripherally, while my attention fixed squarely on the girl. He seemed quiet and shy, maybe a thinker. If he stopped moving, I'd have known for sure; but he didn't. He had a delicate, ruddy face with thin lips that smiled wide over large white teeth, so large I thought his face would have to grow really big in years to come to accommodate them. His deep brown eyes drooped downward at the edge and lay partially hidden under a mop of thick, yellow hair, which he'd blow upward, periodically, to see better. His eyelashes would have been the envy of my friends, but they didn't impress me. I didn't smile back at him either, when he smiled at me. I've often wished my eyes had been better adjusted, back then.

First impressions linger, unless we want to alter them, want to know more. I thought Scott was trouble, even though the olive-skinned girl with deep blue eyes (almost violet) seemed to think differently of him. I couldn't place the ease that occupied the space between them. It was as if it had been cleared of any human tension, leaving only a familiar bond of trust and respect. I didn't like seeing it.

The goddess took the lead in introducing herself and her side-kick (my word), as Samantha and Scott. He straddle-walked and she sidestepped their bikes to join me in retracing my steps. Scott circled as we talked. I declined his invitation to climb onto the handlebars of his bike. "You're lookin' kinda tired," he said. I assured him I wasn't.

We stopped, once, to pick huckleberries. The juice quenched our thirst with the first mouthful. I chewed in quasi-puzzlement at how the berry bushes had been invisible, twenty minutes earlier. I identified the girl, Samantha, there and then, as the goddess Athena—wisdom in motion; and, just as quickly I was struck with a sudden insight, one I never imagined entertaining. I'd have to learn new survival skills, living in these mountains. I yearned to be Samantha's apprentice with every cell in my body.

When the clinging dust had been washed from our throats, I heard a slight vibrato rise in her voice. It soared into the air and then plummeted beneath my skin, sending a chill through me. Or maybe it was just my sweat, cooling and evaporating in the shade where we had landed to suck out the huckleberry's nectar. I had no clue such berries existed. "Are you sure these aren't blueberries," I asked. She smiled and shook her head.

She said she had seen a huge movin' truck in the morning from the upper ridge, saying, in the same breath, that we lived "a stone's throw away" from each other. I nodded, envisioning my Athena, astute and aware, observing her subjects from her domain's heights.

I'm not sure how I even managed the presence of mind to do what I did next. My fingers began searching for the RECORD button on the present I'd stashed in my cargo shorts. My new gadget made a slight *clicking* sound, which Samantha caught immediately. Scott missed it, of course, but since he seldom talked I wasn't concerned he'd be the first voice to mark the moment of our meeting. Samantha's words after hearing the click, was, "Are ya settin' to box up our words?" How different, I thought. Wait. Tapes usually go in boxes, if enough are made. Suddenly, the idea of recording came alive for me.

I have a wooden box of tapes, now, full of Samantha's word pictures—her voice, her simple and glorious extensions of thought. Never self-conscious in sharing, she proved to be the only person (and others *are* on those tapes), who never asked me to delete, or pause, rewind, and record over a segment of words, once they were 'stilled and surrendered, like pictures,' and that included mine.

I've played those reels so often through the years that Samantha's words came true. They became pictures, as we normally think of them—images etched into living minds. And they were coupled with other impressions I cannot shake and don't want to release— starting with those fat bike tires, kicking that fine brown haze across the trees, and Samantha arching gracefully toward me. She became so much better than the mythical goddess of my first take. That was a good rewind, because it replaced faulty thinking. Bye, Athena. Hello, Samantha, child of God.

"My name? Oh, yeah. Sorry. My name is Robyn. Robyn Marie Carol Thomas." Did I seriously blurt out my two middle names? Yes. Yes, I did. I cringed when I played that part of the tape back later that night; but, the third time, when I went further into that segment, I smiled, because Samantha sailed right by my awkwardness. She said she liked my names. "A robin is the best spring harbinger. They ground themselves. Set themselves to tillin' up the earth, always lookin' for some juicy treasures."

I had heard variations of that theme, not quite that graphic, but along the same line of the bird imagery, and nodded in acknowledgement. She didn't bring my curly red hair into the picture, as most typically had, saying something about a "red-breast," which made me totally self-conscious to hear. At that point, I'd usually wrap my sweater more tightly around my chest and fold my arms over it; but she didn't stop there. She said something new, which I had to ponder. "Looks like there might be some inner struggle goin' on in the middle of you, though. Your surname pushes on it from the end, too. Thomas means twin, which could mean, Marie and Carol might have some head-buttin' to do down the road."

"What do you mean?" I asked.

"Oh, nothin' to pin on a board, since life always has the last say." I grew more confused at that last expression. "It's just Marie sounds lyrical and all, but it means bitter, while Carol, not only sounds solid, it connects with cheerfulness. It waves and calls out for others to join in, like Christmas carolers do. People, who don't even know each other sing carols together. So, there they be, starin' you in the face. Two names, two paths sittin' side by side, waitin' for you to choose which will have the most say in you. It's like your mama had trouble feelin' her way through somethin' in her heart, 'cause those names are head to head. A bitter heart will never be a happy one. Does that make sense to you? Sometimes, my thoughts go flyin' off the rail, and I'm not sure how they'll land."

"Yep! That for sure," Scott said with a wide grin on his face. Samantha shoved his shoulder a bit and they both laughed.

"Who asked you, Scott Farley," she said, laughing. I didn't respond, because the truth was bumping around in my head and heart.

"So, Robyn, are ya bitter or happy, *right now*?" I liked that she gave me room to be in the moment, instead of asking me to commit to my whole future on the spot.

"Happy!! I'm Robyn Carol, right now." We all laughed. My laugh still held a bit of nervousness; but I was pretty sure my inner robin pulled up enough great nourishment to help me survive the days ahead. I found myself trusting that time with her would wipe out whatever bitterness attached itself to me. It did, but not in the way I had imagined. Nowhere close.

Samantha never once took credit for the good things I saw in her. When I'd mentioned her wisdom, once, she giggled and deflected. "Shucks, whatever pops outta me is recycled and passed down. Ma says that's where plucky-potential lives--in soil well-turned and nourished by others. That's what makes all the difference in the world. Whatever I got, I was given. Think of all the investment poured into a good piece of earth. How can we ever know the fullness of that kind of carin' and givin' out?"

I really had no clue at the time what she meant. I didn't understand anything about good soil or good seeds or how it all got that way. I lived in a tight little world. Even if I had, the future of some intangible seed didn't matter to me, nor did her history. All I wanted moved in a huckleberry-stained moment. My goal was to get as close to her as I could, as quickly as I could, for as long as I could.

My parents were delighted with the sunshine I brought home. Yes, I had waved Dad on after he caught a glimpse of Samantha and Scott's bikes on the side of the road. That's how he'd spotted us on the hillside. Little did I know he had been sent on a rescue mission after getting back from Elkins. If any of my wit had been operating, I would have noticed when he stopped in front of the berry patch that his car was on the opposite side of the road—as in, not facing our house; but, every part of my being that first hour with Samantha, including my power to reason or care about reasoning had been fully engulfed by the sheer delight of being with her.

Mother said my countenance had altered, as if I'd basked in some bright light. I wouldn't play the tape for them, though. "Private," I said. "Maybe, someday." I did tell them I had met my first country girlfriend, and that she was twelve. I held back her name, wanting to relish that part of her as mine, a birthday discovery—a gift to myself. And I left out the part about her turning thirteen in exactly two months. That might have scared Mother, who thought I was too accelerated for my age already.

"What about the other person I saw with you?" Dad asked.

"What other person?" I asked. "Oh, yeah. Scott."

In my room I turned on the tape. "What's your middle name, Samantha?"

"Catherine."

That night I looked up *Catherine* in Mother's old book of baby names. *Pure*. It fit, but I thought it unfair she didn't have two middle names. Maybe the other would mean something like 'dark.' I knew so little, then, especially about sufficiency and grace. Now when I put her names together, I see how they fill her being and reflect her nature. Samantha—*God heard; one who listens from a*—Catherine—*pure heart*. "The pure of heart shall see God." In that place of listening, wisdom is gathered, and that kind of wisdom sticks forever.

Mother's elation could hardly be contained, as I headed up to my room. On the stairwell I heard a bit of a squeal erupt from her lips and could imagine her doing her hoppy-happy dance in front of Dad, which always pleased him. Interesting. While I was telling them about the meeting, she did a good job of keeping apace with my concealed emotions. In my presence she hardly smiled at the mention of my secret happiness. Just a plain, acknowledging-smile broke through like the early morning sun before the fog reclaims its warmth. I assumed Dad had told her to keep a low profile, one of his favorite phrases; and, she actually listened that time. Wonders never cease.

THE QUALITY WITHIN HER

$\mathcal{M}$ore *is* better, when it comes to appreciating the gentle gifts nature pours out. A tree in a cement sidewalk is welcomed, if noticed, as are parks in the city; but vast expanses of earth, where life is bare-faced and immersions can be felt, where the ground meets in attached fellowship with trees and becomes one with them, as they sway in unison under the air's pervasive force, and then revert back to their anchored upward ascent, when the wind concedes to its cousin, stillness—that more is better. There, we're fully surrounded by nature's elements; but even there, we can still miss seeing nature, or what's behind it. We can cast away its offering and miss its moment. Intangible gifts within the natural world "mosey on up to strangers slowly," when we stand unreceptive behind closed doors.

Samantha showed me what joining and appreciating nature looked like. After long, sunrise-up mornings of perpetual motion, after tending family, land, or animals, including her 'chosen catfish,' we'd snack on our pickings of berries, apples, and laughter. That's when she'd lie on the grass near the creek and spread herself out like a four-pointed star beneath the sun's pulsing glow. She'd soak in earth and sky, and then say something brilliant like, "The sun's glory far outshines the moon's, but that doesn't keep it from blessin' us, too." Then she'd roll over and suck on a piece of grass. "Ain't it somethin' how the moon wears her twirlin' dress all the time, all twinklin' and sparkly, and still gets all her work done." That's when she'd sit up, wrap her arms around her legs and tilt her head back and say something like. "I wish I could've seen the stars when they were all tight t'gether, tellin' God's story to the ancients from beginnin' to end."

"What?" I asked.

"The stars . . . they drifted apart over generations. Once they were pinpoints of lights, all in storytellin' lines, like illustrations ablaze with truth in the dark sky. Twelve stories, all pointing' to the light of the world from the virgin birth to His second comin' as the Lion of Judah. God's hand placed each star, and each story in the sky for seekers. So many ancients got it wrong, though, like with the gods of mythology man created, and then the astrologers messin' it up, puttin' nature first and not His first comin'. But the remnant saw the true stories throughout the ages, and then we got the Book. Strange, thinkin' of a world with no writin' to read, ain't it? No Good Book in any home. That's why God gave 'em those pictures. They were visible to the whole world and simple enough for babes to see." Unlike Mother, there were no lost moments in Samantha's gazes. She remained connected.

My brain remained occupied, filtering through the *Lion of who-dah?* That was the excuse I grabbed when I blurted out, "The love of heaven makes one heavenly." Had I connected? No. Even Shakespeare fell lifeless after her mini-bursts of starlit spontaneity. Afterwards I decided not to glide into those kind of thoughts with my borrowed phrases. They felt like broken reeds, and I, just a repeater of randomness, void of glory—unless muddied messes were glorious. Samantha probably would have said, "Sure, they are," had I asked.

I found myself squinting under the light more than once that first summer, while trying to remain quiet in my ignorance. I'd heard, somewhere, how maintaining silence showed a semblance of intelligence, definitely through omission, since no one could tell whether the cogs were turning or not. When Samantha lay still on the earth in total silence, like a living sacrifice, she wasn't trying to fool anyone. Her genuine moments were only her, lifting a bit above the earth's surface, seemingly transported by the sun's pulsing waves to God only knew where. Something more streamed beneath the surface of the visible, and it formed the mystery I wanted to uncover.

I recall believing, once, that nature abhors a still child. No one I knew in Manhattan entered into stillness, even after eating, unless we were sick. Mother once said, "It's not normal for a child to lie around during the day! So, get up. I'll find something for you to do." Yes, yes, okay. I twisted her actual intent a bit and took it out of context. So, I'm fessing up. She only spoke those words, when the clock neared noon, and I was still in bed on a Saturday morning. Mother's urgency made sense to me at the time. She didn't like idleness, and as a retired psychologist, turned first-time mother at forty-five, she wanted every minute of my life (and hers) to count for something.

Samantha got up at the crack of dawn every day, which Mother couldn't even beat, by the way. Granted, Manhattan didn't have animals with udders, bursting with milk twice a day. Thank goodness! There weren't any rooftop chickens or roosters making a fuss, either. We did have alarm clocks, and sirens, and the hum of perpetual traffic, and there was always someplace we had to be; but that comparison teetered when it left behind the urgency of nature's need for us to rise and tend. At that point my compare and contrast list turned comic. I envisioned Jimmy, our doorman, shoveling cow pies off the sidewalk. It didn't translate well.

I came to an elementary conclusion, watching Samantha within her wisps of stillness by the creek. Her world loomed larger than the mountain and farther than the sun. It dwarfed New York, and even made the world feel small. It reached the truest sense of what heaven contains; and I wanted to go with her wherever she went.

But, I'm jumping ahead of myself. I didn't see her 'innards' for some time. It wasn't because she hid them from me. She didn't, not at all. It was because my eyes needed adjusting, lots of it. They had to be screwed on tighter, or loosened up—I couldn't tell which—just so I could see the fringes of life. Forget about focusing in on its greater depths. I sure did, forget that is; but that lack didn't stop me from being drawn to her instantly.

When I think or write about Samantha, my Glady voice surfaces in my head, even today. I had dropped the molasses-like drawl when I went to college. Did I toss out the region's unique color, thinking it too tacky elsewhere, or was it just me, trying to break free of my claimed failures? Both, either, neither. Don't ask. I'm still not sure what motivated me in those days. I spent years aiming for her sound, and then shed it, like a snake its skin, all within a few undulating movements forward and no concern over the loss, not at first at least. I merely stepped out of the cast off, leaving it behind for the wind to carry away or the earth to swallow.

I longed to transform myself into a better me at that time, but didn't know how. I couldn't bear not fitting in where I most wanted to be. Mostly, when I left, I felt uncertain about everything. I can say that much or that little. But again, I'm jumping ahead. I thought stepping out of the opinions of myself would require stepping out of mountain life. Someone had another thought that outranked mine.

What is it about Samantha's voice that impresses me, and why did it take years to realize I didn't want to shed it, and then understand I couldn't. When it reaches my ears, it causes me to pause and enter into a passive enjoyment. Its sappy, sticky, melodious overture of vowels cascades over every connecting space within my mind. It carries the words that live within them to higher ground. I feel open and free when they resound. I've used that gentle, slow cadence to measure time, my footsteps, and most of my routines. Her verbal pulse has become my internal rhythm.

Why would I want to be freed of someone who lived in a state of wonder more than anyone I ever knew. Nothing bore the label of mundane for Samantha, "not a lick," even the routines that looked commonplace, or worse, seemed like drudgery to me when I first arrived. Participating in her small community was embryonic, a birthday of moments, exuding firsts at every turn, no matter where she stood. She knew whatever she was doing, it was for the greater good.

My eyes began to 'set right,' as I watched her fold her palms and fingers over her goat's teats. I didn't know people actually drank goat's milk, so imagine my surprise when I accompanied her to the barn that first time. Samantha emptied Daisy's udder, full of nourishment, morning and evening. Everyday. She expressed her appreciation to the goat, as she expressed its milk, just because that's the way life worked. On and on its cycles went, without a critical eye, without measuring its effects or calculating its returns. Even homeschooling, which the Stickers saw as another part of the whole of life, called *family,* was gratefully absorbed and given back in equal measure. The Stickers never used the word, homeschooling. I imported that word. They had no word for the process. It was simply more of 'life's learnin'.' Normal stuff.

I recall one day, flies were all abuzz around Daisy. She stomped her back legs to rid herself of the pests. Samantha's presence eventually calmed her, as she moved her hands over the animal's forehead, then across her back. When she fingered her teats, it was as if Daisy had been prepared, like a fine reed instrument. The lyrical sound on the metal bucket more than confirmed my impressions.

I thought it amazing how the flies caught onto the fact that they weren't a part of Samantha's symphonies of give-and-take. They, somehow, scattered when Samantha started milking, landing on nearby posts until she left. Then they'd form their offensive position and fly into their chaos-causing activities, once again.

More often than not Samantha foiled or postponed the flies' urges to bother Daisy by rubbing a bit of a ointment she'd make every week onto her coarse fawn-colored hair, first at the top of her head, near a patch of white that dropped into each of her long floppy ears; next, behind her upper legs; and then on her chest. She'd switch the essential oils she'd use each week, so that the flies wouldn't grow accustomed to the smell and ignore the treatment. Daisy's appreciation was evident.

Animal care had been a part of my upbringing, too, but for me it was a means to an end—the end being my allowance for services rendered. The usual run-of-the-mill childhood pets in NYC resulted in runaway lizards, and a frail canary that flew into our brick wall more than once, and then eventually out a window, forever. It didn't matter or change a thing for me, when we went up the food chain of pets and got a dog.

It happened that after a pet fell from its novelty stage, it became an imposition. Even with tons of hounding (no pun intended) in the city to improve my attitude, I never got past that way of thinking. Take my dog, for example. Her name is Blackie. I reasoned, she or any other canine couldn't tell if I were thrilled or bummed when filling a bowl with kibbles, as long as the bowl got filled.

I did what I had to do to avoid verbal repercussions. I even told myself I liked my tailed critters. I mean, what kind of kid doesn't like their pet a little? I never really loved Blackie, not the way Samantha loved her animals, any animal—wild, barnyard, or of the domesticated variety. In my world, even though Blackie excelled in all things dog, I still didn't go out of my way for her, unless I saw an increase in my cash flow. Samantha never got paid for any of the activities involving her animals.

"Paid? For milkin' Daisy?" She half-giggled in wonderment at the thought of it, when I asked. I tossed out many questions like that along the way. She never made me feel embarrassed about my stumbling inquiries, though. They found entrance into her life, perhaps like those pesky flies she addressed without frustration, or maybe more like the sun on a day that's just a tad too hot. I had hoped I was welcomed along the lines of the sun, but then concluded I probably landed somewhere between the sun and the flies. It's just you couldn't tell with Samantha. Her voice remained constant. She kept the beat of life moving smoothly, unhindered.

Every so often, she'd toss a bit of her mind into the mix of my confusion, not to linger, just to pass over me like a breeze, and then she'd turn and be off to greet some other part of her day.

Her response to my question of being paid for doing her chores: "Do ducks sell the eggs they sit on?" I tossed that one around for days, since I had to waddle up to the fact that people actually bought duck eggs, let alone eat them.

THE BREAD AND WATER

*B*y the first of August I knew beyond any doubt how totally bonded to Samantha I felt. I hoped with a ticklish fervor she felt the same about me. That first week we befriended each other's families. I went to her house first, so that Mother could unpack the kitchen and regain a form of normalcy on the home front.

That dinner, which the Stickers called 'supper,' thrilled me from the get-go with its absence of formalities. Everyone's elbows rested on the table. They actually touched neighboring elbows! I licked fat off my fingers, too, after seeing Samantha's parents do it! Oh, happy days.

I remember laughing so hard, I almost peed my pants. Why? Samantha's brothers: Richard, the eldest, the twins Clem and Clay, and Jason, the youngest but still older than me all had inherited their Grandpappy Sticker's funny bone, so I was told. (His actual bones were buried in the cemetery above their barn. I can attest to that fact.) Laughing that much presented a problem for me, since the only toilet seat the Stickers had rested on some old boards in a slanted outhouse near a towering pine tree that leaned in the opposite direction. Smart tree! I forced myself to laugh less as the evening wore on. Samantha noticed and hinted that a clean, wide-mouth gallon jar could be found under her bed, and I was welcomed to use it.

She offered it, as discreetly as possible, while I scraped my plate's leftovers into the compost bucket. I think the telltale twisting of my legs together gave me away. Smiling, Samantha said, "If'n you don't wanna use the outie, you're gonna have to use the jar, 'cause my brothers ain't gonna let up with their jokin'. You're their new audience!" So, I *peevishly* submitted to my bladder's inability to handle genuine guffaws when full, and used the jar. Samantha said my bladder would grow stronger from squattin' over a jar, and I'd be able to laugh more without running to her room. Honestly, I found the jar exercise challenging and fun; and before long I was a pro.

After supper, musical instruments appeared, and soon we were all stomping our feet to the fiddle, mandolin, banjo, and Jew's harp. It was quite the jamboree. Hands, without instruments, clapped. It was either Clay or Clem who tugged me onto my feet, first, and swung me out onto the Sticker's cleared-off wooden floor. I'm not sure whose forearm accidentally brushed across my bulging, food-filled belly during a Virginia Reel twirl, but it caused a sting of embarrassment to rise in my cheeks. The flush faded as quickly as it came. There was just too much goodwill being released in that room to feel anything but sheer happiness. Not only did my curls bounce in abandon, my self-confidence perked up. The genuine gaiety surrounding me proved irresistible. (Thank you, Mother, for incorporating English Country Dance into my Civil War studies, even though I called the lessons lame at the time.)

I fell in love with both twins that evening. It's true. I couldn't tell them apart, but that didn't matter, since it only lasted four minutes. When fifteen-year-old Richard lifted my hand for a spin, my heart spun in his direction. I crushed on all four boys that summer, jumping back and forth within an impetuously voracious heart, one that only a young girl intoxicated on country air, good clean fun, and four well-mannered boys, competing and vying for attention could manage. Besides, Jason didn't remain in the running for long, since he was only an awkward eleven-year old. I even developed a crush on Pa for an hour, when I saw him help Samantha with a wounded animal. He was so kind, gentle, and patient. It was definitely Samantha, though, who continued to stand out and claim my admiration, which was totally appropriate. Mother would have said, "Young girls should have good girl-friends. Boyfriends can wait a long while." Samantha definitely occupied my heart as my best friend.

* * *

I'VE COME TO BELIEVE IT'S AN HONOR TO BE WANTED AT someone's table, to break bread even if a loaf is not in sight. Samantha shared, as we walked up the hill that evening, how Ma had put together the family's favorites, hoping most would set well with me. I took that as a green light, an opportunity to get to know the Stickers better, sort of like studying about a foreign country. Mother always acquainted me with a nation's foods before studying it. Her words: "Tastes, traditional colors, and textures reveal a lot about the lives of people. Food is one of the categories where that principle rings truest."

But, having just arrived in Glady, we had no clue about 'mountain vittles,' nor did we know if any such cookbook existed. So, I perceived my dinner invitation, somewhat as I would an archeological expedition. I couldn't help but imagine indigenous dishes, spanning generations of mountain folks, like roasted possum and pickled pig intestines. I forced my mind to dismiss those developing thoughts as unrealistic. At least I hoped they were. I was sure, if I persisted in that liberal wave of culinary thoughts, I would spoil my appetite, gag, or chicken out altogether.

Accustomed to the various quick-fix meals, provided by

friends' parents: orange juice, milk, and purchased pastries in the morning after sleepovers; cream cheese, olives, pickles, and bagels for lunch on weekends; and a ton of takeout containers from ethnic restaurants for dinner, I found myself hoping for a colloquial American fare, one that revealed the difference I had observed in Samantha. In other words, I wanted to experience a meal that wouldn't stretch me beyond my comfort zone, but still be novel enough to excite me. I wanted a blend of real and otherworldly. I wanted to relate to the Stickers, yet still be motivated enough to trek up a crazy steep hill for many future dinners, I mean suppers. Remembering to say, "Thank you for supper," rather than dinner, was my first homework assignment.

Mother had alerted me, midway through the week, to practice polite acceptance of whatever landed in front of me, even if it seemed a bit foreign. Perhaps that's why my thoughts drifted. I'm not sure if her imaginings ran along the same line as mine, and I didn't ask; but her warning proved to be unfounded. Polite acceptance would not be needed, not a bit, because the Stickers' *favorites* exceeded my expectations, and soon became my favorites, as well.

What got piled onto the gingham cloth Ma had slipped over their table, in generous platters and bowls, made me more than willing to jump in with both hands, without the slightest hint of reserve. All nine of us, including three-year-old Sue Lynn in a chair with higher legs, scrunched together in that comfortable shoulder-to-should mold I grew to love. Each of us eyed Ma's presentation with eager anticipation of putting fork to mouth; and we all did in one united gesture after prayer, which was the newest feature of the table's offerings for me.

Ma served catfish, a fresh catch from the creek. Pa pan-fried it to perfection in a twenty-inch cast iron skillet, reserved just for fish. The skill he displayed, as he maneuvered the pan over an outdoor fire provided excellent entertainment for me. In addition we feasted on corn pudding, rich with Bulla-Moo's cream, whipped and folded into tender, mashed, garden kernels of yellow and white corn; tender collards, also from the garden, plain and simply steamed, then drowned in the butter Samantha had churned that morning; black-eyed peas, dripping in hog fat, vinegar, and honey; deep fried spuds, generously sprinkled with salt and pepper; and, two heaping baskets of corn biscuits, softened in warm sorghum and Samantha's sweet butter. Yeah. Decent! Ma never made desserts—no room; but cold sweet cider from pressed orchard apples flowed the whole evening.

I had never relished a meal before or since as much as I had that one—and me, the kid food critic of Manhattan. I had opinions about numerous gourmet restaurants and ethnic delis, not to mention Mother's parade of recipes. Was it the company, the fresh air, or the virtual freshness of the food? Maybe, the thrill of newness-in-abundance, or maybe it boiled down to those two simple ingredients: food, cooked and served with love.

Only one bitter taste grabbed hold of me that evening, fear. For a brief moment, my mind fashioned a dark tunnel with a fast train heading my way. The train was called, the Unknown. I began questioning everything in my life, once the pleasure of that last Sticker morsel was swallowed, and the twins' cider ceased punching the air with its tartness. Would Mother's need for impeccable order and her flair for the fantastic, which she was accustomed to providing and serving up to guests, frighten Samantha when it came her turn to join our tiny family later in the week? Would I, and two adults, be enough to hold her interest? Would my parents probe too much into the details of her life, as if she were something to study? I'd seen my Manhattan friends squirm, roll their eyes, and turn red under such questions. I wondered if there would be awkward lulls in our conversation, should Samantha fail to choose the right fork for her salad for instance, or if she lifted a bowl to her mouth to sip her soup. I decided to ask Mother to lay only one fork out on the place settings! That would solve one potential problem, at least. Looking back on those fears, now, shows me how little I knew about Samantha, then, and equally, how little I understood my parents at that point in time, too.

* * *

FRANKLY, I WAS SHOCKED AT MOTHER'S ENTHUSIASM when I came home that night. I held back in telling her everything, once again, about all things related to Samantha, just to protect my new territory. I didn't like crossovers in my social circles at that time. Mother refrained from telling me all her thoughts, too, to protect the hope growing in her heart about Samantha and her family, as to how they might be the unique factor that would help bring her daughter back to her, the daughter she had watched disappear from view and replaced by a saucy imposter. Her hope was that the first-Robyn, the sweet green-eyed child she knew still existed under that mop of crimson curls, would rise up again, somehow, and grow stronger over time. Mother pictured me as a kind-hearted woman. Little did she know God had an even better plan and we were on track—His. How could she? Mother knew less about God than I.

When our turn arrived Mother served courses as usual—plates in, plates out. Food emerged from behind the swinging butler's door in her skillful hands, unlike Ma, who laid everything out in plain sight, only to watch the food run its course, circling the table and stopping when emptied, like a toy train on a child's electric rails. Mother created a parade of players that marched in and out in a precise and timely manner.

At Ma's table there was a solemn prayer, then elbows rose irreverently and arms crisscrossed like swords in opposition, but with goodwill always preserved. At Mother's table, we sat with our hands tucked over our napkins, awaiting the first entrée. Each plate was served by the leading lady, herself, and dinner commenced when she lifted her fork, sans a prayer from Dad—another difference that caused me to swallow hard with concern.

The first course placed before us, a delicate cream of asparagus soup with three intact tips floating over the bulk of the stalks' pureed green liquid appeared pleasant, but not hearty. I waited. I wanted, hearty. I had requested, hearty. I waited for the hidden-hearty part to arrive. The second course came--an ordinary dinner salad of lettuce, scallions, tomatoes, and parsley with lemon wedges and olive oil, all displayed in proper fashion, graced the white linen tablecloth. They were readily available with an appropriate please and thank you. I wondered why Mother hadn't served our favorites, which made me wonder if we even had any; but in Mother's eyes that may have constituted ennui, a pedestrian mentality, which I assumed she avoided in life almost naturally.

I furtively, but meticulously, observed Samantha's reactions between the soup and salad. She seemed pleasantly amused. I wondered what Mother had made for the entree. I had asked her several times that week, but she said it was a surprise. "Please tell me," I asked. "Please, pleease, pleeeease?"

"Stop with your please-voice," she said.

I wanted feedback, so that I could offer valid criticism. I hinted at Hungarian Goulash. And then it arrived; no, not the goulash, but Mother's surprise. Shrimp! Not the jumbo shrimp, the prawns you could sink your teeth into. No. These were the little shrimp, the shrimpy, scrimpy, tiny shrimp, used in shrimp scampi. She arranged them on individual silver trays, served one to each of us on an elongated white plate, alongside a single baked potato, scored and dabbed with a pad of store-bought butter, which melted demurely in the scarred, exposed center of its flesh. Ugh. Why, Mother, why? I screamed silently, as I chomped on my lower lip and breathed inwardly, my shoulders rising into a freeze.

I felt as if my own heart's veins had been exposed, like those translucent shrimps'. What was she thinking? Hadn't I informed her how much the Stickers ate? Yes, yes, I had. I hoped, desperately, that Samantha hadn't worked up a huge appetite all day, or that I had ample candy in my dresser drawer upstairs. I calculated all the bagged snacks in the kitchen cupboard that I could confiscate, while remaining politely demure, solely for my guest's sake. As I watched the melting butter drip onto the plate under the potato, I bit my upper lip.

After the scampi and some light conversation, Mother cleared the table and disappeared into the kitchen, only to call us all into the only other room containing most of the furniture at the time. There in the living room, she served us milk and strawberry short-cake with whipped cream. She glided the desserts from tray to hand in one swoop, it seemed. Flawless moves, even with protruding forks. I'll give her that much. Mother was graceful. Before she returned for hers, she positioned one of her ancient LPs onto the turntable, a favorite, which she thought Samantha would enjoy, Reinecke's *Children's Symphony*.

The music bubbled merrily over our conversation and filled the spaces between our bites with lightness that lifted us into our best selves—or maybe, the others had already been there. Dad added his genuine humanity to the gathering and, all in all, we ended up being a lively group. After dessert, we played charades until I snatched Samantha away and led her up the staircase towards my room.

My arms locked over the goodies I swept up as we made our way through the kitchen. Halfway up the stairs, Samantha stopped. I turned around to see a puzzled look on her face. She said she hadn't thanked my parents for their hospitality, which made me feel shrimpishly out-of-water and ungrateful. I watched as she flew back down the staircase and in seconds I joined her side. I listened as she praised Mother for her gracious labor and thanked both my parents for being such welcoming souls. Mother seemed so genuinely affected by those kind words of appreciation that I made it a point to repeat them someday, when I needed to soften her up.

* * *

MY OVERLY LARGE *BOUDOIR* BECAME THE PLACE WHERE all our sleepovers took shape in those years. Samantha's home was too small to accommodate the siblings' social activities with any sort of privacy. I found it hard to believe, when she told me on our second trip up the staircase that night that, "This will be my first sleepover, ever." How different our worlds were. No one would think to admit such a thing in Manhattan at her age; but not so Samantha. She beamed with pleasure.

Turned out she regarded dinnertime at my house in much the same way I had tracked suppertime in her home. It all got tucked neatly into the *first time* category of experiences for both of us. Apparently, newness surrounded her as much as it had me. Everything I took for granted, tickled her—the mirror-like sheen of our furniture; the electric stove with its fancy knobs and features; the stereo pumping out music she'd never heard; the sound system of the stereo itself; the shrimp, smallest fish she'd ever seen; and the spotlessly white toilet with its minty fragrance wafting upward between flushes. She loved it all. La, la, la! Happy, happy, I thought. The only thing she couldn't grasp, which was *new* to her as well, was leaving my parents downstairs to clean up, while we headed upstairs, to "do nothin'."

Her words *sort of* hurt my feelings, but I knew I took them the wrong way, when her enthusiasm unfurled afresh after entering my room. She hadn't meant that spending time with me equaled zilch, so I pushed my feelings into a more proper receptacle and moved forward with an explanation. "I'm pretty sure my parents want us to have some time to get to know each other," I said in all earnestness. "Consider their labor a gift of love to us." I wasn't sure how I'd come up with those lofty words, but I did assume its premise was correct, and it seemed to appease Samantha, somewhat. I still could tell, however, it didn't sit right with her.

Naturally, we sat up half the night doing nothing but 'movin' our jaws,' first with candy, then popcorn, then gum, but always with non-stop chatter and laughter. Samantha stumbled upon my huge deco hatbox, filled to the brim with my hat collection. We spent a lot of time sorting through them, picking out our favorites, and trying them on together in front of my full-length mirror—something she didn't have in her house, either—a large mirror. The only one they possessed, hung over the kitchen sink. Its tiny shape was enough for Pa to shave his face. "Why so many hats?" she asked with a puzzled look on her face. "There must be over a hundred here."

"Well, that was our thing," I said.

"Whose thing?" she asked.

"My Manhattan friends—Georgie [Georgina], Madison, Pearl, Tiffy, and me. We called ourselves the Manhatties. Get it? Hats?"

"Oh," she said. "What about the 'man' part?"

"That thought never crossed my mind," I confessed. We both giggled. It was that night I decided to record Samantha in earnest. I made a pledge of sorts. It became my secret, there, on the floor of my room amidst candy wrappers and hats, and *The NeverEnding Story* playing on the VCR as background ambience. Even though I could describe every inch of that film without watching it and had memorized parts of its dialogue, especially the scene where Artax drowns in the Swamp of Sadness, it didn't interest me that night.

I can still see Samantha trying on some of my beanie caps, looking up at me and saying, "What's playin' on your tv?" She had never heard of the movie.

"It came out last year!" I said, shocked at what I perceived as a possible failure to grasp film culture. It baffled me until my brain slid into place, making me feel badly for having criticized her world. I had hoped she hadn't picked up on my exasperation.

"I know a movie that came out ages ago," she said. "Do you have *Star Wars*? Richard saw it with some friends a couple of years ago and really liked it."

"I do!" I said. "I have all three of them!"

"Three! I'm not sure which he saw. He just said *Star Wars*."

"They're all called *Star Wars*, and then there's a subtitle. We can start with the first one, tonight, *A New Hope*."

"I like that subtitle," she said.

"Me, too!" I said, while popping the film in. "This one's really old, eight years old! It's almost as old as me!" We both hopped onto my bed, like it was naturally wired into our brains, as girls, to know exactly how to watch a movie. It had to be on our tummies; elbows near the bed's end; chin in our hands; legs up in the air with our feet twitching in pleasant expectation; and most importantly, eyes firmly glued to the television screen. Talking was optional, as was gasping, screaming, or crying.

While the player skipped through the previews, I threw my Russian fur hat at her, feeling giddy at the hope of giving her another 'first.' I wanted to give her as many firsts as possible, ones that made sense and were complete experiences with a beginning, middle, and end. I knew, even then, that's how things rolled with her. What I didn't know was how a truly well rounded soul couldn't be forced to fit into square openings someone else has designed and carved out. That night, I believed our own never-ending story was well on its way. It was. I just didn't see the middle parts.

Samantha had put the Russian fur hat on. "That Russian Ushanka actually looks really good on you, Samantha!! You should keep it. Yeah, keep it. I have more." Again we laughed, and she beamed.

The white rabbit fur hat practically lived on her head all the following winter. I wore my black sheepskin one, so I could claim Russian sisterhood with her, my *comrade in arms-full-of-fun*. I did have a third Ushanka, a faux-fur in rich brown that would have fit Scott perfectly. He'd have killed the look, but it remained in the box.

THE AMAZING FIRST YEAR

*W*hen I first arrived on the mountain, I thought the silence of nature, deafening. Strange, I know, but it's true. It wasn't until I dove into and glided through the pristine waters of Samantha's swimming hole that first summer that I could let go of my former frame of reference that made me think that way. What I had thought an environment should look and sound like, for human beings, shifted in a second. With that plunge, I'd entered a parallel universe of sorts. And I liked it, a lot.

Samantha introduced the pond to me in the middle of my second week. We were in the thick of a blistering August heat wave that blanketed the mountain in heaviness. One afternoon she exclaimed, "It's time!" I had no idea what she meant, but was about to find out. It was much more than relief from the heat, which I first thought as we approached the pond.

Diving into that pool of water, which cools and darkens by degrees the farther you go down, is not what you feel in a city pool. There's a mystery on the way down that opens wide on the way up. In a nutshell, the experience felt like an awakening. There's a good feeling breaking through the surface tension of a city pool, but popping through the surface of Samantha's pond, seemed like a bestowal of sorts fell upon me—like insight attached itself to the act. I understood nature a bit more, how it gives and gives; how it's alive. I soared into a fantasyland, not remembering the route taken, nor how I had gotten there. I just knew I landed, or took off. I'm not sure. What I had thought, the ideal habitat for humans—cities—vanished after I allowed the wonderland to wash over me, a wonderland complete with its own queen.

It's hard to express the exhilaration, the vast difference between the world I'd left and the one I'd entered. Imagine being snatched into the air, out of an overcrowded city pool on a hot summer day, and then dropped somewhere quiet. A tepid city pool is packed with bodies of every shape and size; all bumping, splashing, talking loudly, kicking, crying, laughing, and squealing randomly. Everyone stands or swims in close proximity. Fragrances merge and clash. Body applicants, like sunscreen, perfume, and deodorant wash off warmed, moistened flesh, leaving a scummy sheen floating over the chlorinated water. Not inviting, yet totally overlooked—seemingly normal in fact, but not natural.

Then there's the non-rhythmic humming, the buzz everyone hears but doesn't notice. It follows you to the pool. Once again, the noises are normalized, like any daily noise—the clunking sounds of an old fridge, or a car on its last leg, for example. We grow accustomed to hearing certain things and, eventually, ignore them; but are they gone? Undercurrents impact us. They seem nonexistent on the surface but could carry us out to sea, unawares; some can prove deadly, if we dive too deeply into one and cannot resurface. We tumble in those currents, feel the chaos of it all.

Now, what if we're extracted and put somewhere else, where such things aren't normal. At first a squinty population and its enveloping quietness might seem abnormal, until we gather data. That's what I did. I had a purpose for gathering data, though. Her name was Samantha. Not everyone gets a ready-made motivation for collecting data. When I landed in my alien territory, she had been dropped into my presence, too. All I had to do was follow her around to sniff out the land's benefits. Accompanying her to her pool was a great start.

Samantha's pool is deep and streaked with light, which bounces and vanishes in its depth's coolness. At its surface it's calm and still, but beneath, everything's in motion, swaying, breathing out life's breath, just differently. It contains secrets, histories, and untouched beauty. Exploring its depths might seem odd at first, but it isn't really, not if we pause to accept it at face value. It's the hidden that hides naturally, not out of fear, which means we shouldn't fear it.

The fish that seemed like intruders, at first, became endearing to me. All I had to do was dive in. Once in the water, they let me know I met their safety standard, and likewise I saw they'd bring no harm my way. Samantha was our bridge. She's why they swam closer to me, even though I felt flattered and startled at the same time. I left fear behind with most of my clothes. I fantasized about being *Snow White.* That's as near the sensation of that encounter as I can describe. My heart took on Snow White's words. "Please don't run away. I won't hurt you. But, you don't know what I've been through. All because I was afraid."

That's the underside of the fish's belly. The upside, or the combination of both sides was an experience I wanted to keep and repeat for as long as I could, because I'd never felt more alive. I dubbed the pool our *Sun Bowl*, since sun floods its surface, while the water rests, perfectly contained in its earthen bowl, like a cool cup of living water. Samantha liked the name, and it stuck. It was the first time she told me I had a way with words. That stuck too.

Nestled in that angelic place, I couldn't contain my desire to holler out, for the joy of it all. I tried; but why try? So, I yelled. Every part of me felt released. I yearned to live with the water, the sun, and the trees. Samantha smiled, wide-mouthed and her bright voice reflected all my feelings with words I'll cherish forever. I bellowed a huge, "Yes!" followed by another, and then splashed some of the holy water into the air after hearing her impressions of the pool's mystery. "That's it! Samantha, that's it!" In case you're wondering what she said, it's this: "When I'm here, I feel I've been turned inside out, like my truest bein' is free of its tent, just long enough to feel life the way nature does."

Watching the limbs of those majestic trees bow and extend upward in simultaneous motion, depending on the angle of the breezes that brushed against and through them, made it seem as if nothing bad or hurtful could pierce the tender veil draped over the setting. Fears vanished. It's as if nature were worshiping and drawing us into it, ever closer to the one they honored. How they did it was simply by doing exactly what they were created to do—be.

Samantha eventually shared her belief that angels occupied certain areas of nature, guarding particular regions for reasons unknown. Their mere presence carries and disperses an unspeakable quality of life to such surroundings. In them our strength is renewed, even if we're not able to see and appreciate the gift.

Awakenings are rare. Grab them, when given the opportunity. Seek them out, if no one leads you towards one. If you find out one is waiting for you to take hold, take hold, reach for it. Once entered, no one can steal it away. Only we can consciously throw away our gifts of life. What a colossal blunder, to taste life, and then say no to one of its parts. I had only crossed the threshold of understanding one of them. How were such things mine to hold? I didn't know, but I did hold on, as best I could.

I held onto the memories not recorded on tape, too, such as the one we shared at another spot she deemed a favorite. Samantha had already named that watery place, Merry Creek. It slipped through our neck of the forest, all clear and bubbly, rippling over rocks and sending its freshness into the surrounding air. Watercress lined its banks, willows, too. I recall the first time Samantha introduced me to *her* Rainbow Trout. Yes, *her* trout. They made their resting place in deep pockets at two particular junctures about a hundred feet apart from each other. They'd swim to visit each other's territory, randomly, one and then maybe another; but, no matter where they were when Samantha approached the bank's edge, they'd all find their way to her.

Samantha named them. She knew how they differed in size, markings, intensity of color, and if any had a physical abnormality from being snagged by a catch and release fishermen. I gulped at the mention of that last statement, but said nothing. Her family members, especially the boys, were under strict instructions not to touch a scale or fin on their bodies. Her fish would never be supper stretched across the Stickers' cast iron skillet. Guaranteed. Memo to self: Talk to Dad!

I was impressed at how her trout sought her out and swam up to her, even before I learned why. She had trained them since she was nine to come to her by inviting them to a feast. On that day, she had come prepared to demonstrate the activity, even though she would have gone through the motions, had I not been there.

Samantha opened her backpack, pulled out a hefty-sized tin can, and plopped its contents onto her lap, dough taken from a yeast-free larger lump Ma had made fresh that morning. She began pulling the shape apart and placing inch-sized pieces between her toes. Four dough balls hung securely from each foot, when she finished. She lowered her feet into the creek, smiling.

"Go ahead," she said. "You'll love it." I followed suit and the mutual giggles began. If you've never sat with your feet dangling in spring-fed water on a hot summer day with dough balls squished between each toe for fish to nibble on, try it someday. They don't miss a speck. Their little mouths scour every toe and gleefully examine all fleshy surfaces, tails flapping in merriment until all the dough has been fully consumed, hence the name, Merry Creek. Best part, all of us were mutually and delightfully filled up, when we turned toward home. "Girls do not live by bread alone," Samantha laughed. So much better than fly-fishing! I thought.

As we headed out I said, "You're like those fish, Samantha."

"What? Did you say, I like my fish?" she asked.

"No. I said, you're like them!"

"Well, I ain't never been compared to trout 'fore. Which one exactly am I, 'cause you know, they're all a bit different."

I was on a roll, though, and didn't even hear her question. "You're just like the creek, too," I said.

"What did you eat for lunch, Robyn Thomas?" she asked, laughing.

"Soul food? Maybe, brain food. No, really! It's just you're so certain of everything, so trusting. It's like you don't care what comes next. You think it will be as good as what came last."

"Let me swim over to your side of the creek and invite you over to mine, since it seems you're wantin' to explore my territory. Robyn, I'm not certain of everythin'. I just have hope that good will be a-poppin' up somewhere, 'cause the source of good never abandons us. What I know is that bends will be comin', some easy, some hard; but I've got a navigator I trust. You know, the only bend I'm certain about bein' all good, Robyn, will be the last one I reach."

Again, sloughing off the heavy conversation I said, "But you're always happy. You're happy right now. You'll be happy tomorrow, too."

"Nothin' to be unhappy about today, and hopefully, not tomorrow. If'n troubles head my way on the morrow, they'll be tomorrow's troubles; but I don't see any in sight right now, so all is well."

I couldn't imagine Samantha being sad. If she were, I'd lie down on the spot where she shed her last tear, and I'd wait. I'd wait for the tear to reach a seed hiding in the earth, since Samantha's crying would never go to waste. Darkness might engulf me, but I'd still wait. Those were my lofty thoughts, before I paused to think about them; then I blurted, "Samantha, promise you won't go anywhere but to happy places!" That strange eruption arrived the second I realized lying down on the cold earth wasn't my thing. I wasn't dumb enough to wait for some dormant seed to wise up.

And that's when I figured, Samantha had to be the one to make sure something like that never happened. Yeah. Magnanimous me.

She turned, cocked her head, smiled ever so slightly, and said, "Robyn, if'n a river jumps its bed and goes wild messin' everythin' up 'round 'bout, what could I do? Land would go floatin' away like whipped cream. Trees'll go a'topplin'; homes get flooded; not to mention the sorrow on the people—good people, happy or unhappy. In the end that river will find its restin' place on the earth, again. Onlookers will say how horrible the whole thing was, 'n' rightly so—all 'cause one river took on too much rain and grew bigger than its banks could hold. And then, twenty years down the road, when new families settle near those banks, they'll be sayin' stuff like, *Ain't that the most beautiful river you'd ever seen? So peaceful.* They won't connect the gravestones on the hillside with that river's story."

"Gosh, Samantha," I said.

"Hard things happen, Robyn; but if'n lives are spared, the down unders will pass. People'll find their restin' place and things'll get settled right again, just like with that old river. It all takes patience, is all. Patience is queen, sittin' at the side of content-ment, her king. Might even be grander than happiness, that queen, 'cause when she gets anchored in us, she doesn't go a-flyin' off at the turn of a screw. It's hard, though, seein' her set up her throne, though. We don't like it, 'cause she usually brings her twin sister, sufferin'."

"Yeah, I get that," I said. Lie. Lie. Lie. Triple lie. I remembered feeling like a broken teabag, when we left Manhattan. Note: Zero patience—zero desire for it, and *total* desire for my happiness. I wanted my banks intact and undisturbed, thank you. "Would you be a crazy mess if you had to leave these mountains, Samantha?"

"Not if I left with someone I loved."

"Oh," I said. Busted.

* * *

MY EXISTENCE THAT FIRST YEAR SEEMED PERFECT FROM waking to crashing. Samantha entered every conscious hour at some point or another, and even peppered my subconscious ones within dreams. Everything in the mountains reminded me of her, since she made everything come alive for me.

The waning summer mornings continued to renew my senses. Awakening to songbirds' trills, and the fragrance of flowering honeysuckle under my window made me want to greet the day. Constant city sirens and bus fumes had the opposite effect on me. They caused me to burrow under my covers in a futile attempt to escape Mother's internal alert system. Along the way, Samantha taught me to identify the feathered-ones by their songs and the flowers by their form and colors. My mind would slip into the glossary of bird calls each morning to identify the first one 'that pierced the . . . hollow of [mine] ear,' as Shakespeare wrote. When I found it, I'd whisper its name aloud and smile with satisfaction. That energized me, made it easy for me to jump out of bed, grab my binoculars, and look for the bird as a wrap up. Then I'd take the stairs, two at a time saying, "Fait accompli," because it sounded as good to me as the birds, finishing something well.

On our morning bird searching expeditions Samantha and I would eat from the same edible fruits the birds liked, including the nectar from honeysuckles--not as gracefully as hummingbirds, but just as thankfully. We also pretended to be *benevolent* birds and did things like chase grasshoppers, which remained free; catch flying bugs we'd released; help worms to lesser-soaked grounds; and rescue fallen hatchlings. (Some did live under Samantha's diligent care.) We ran as if we had wings, hand in hand in between everything. I gladly followed Samantha within the embraces of nature, but I followed her while she did her chores, too, and even helped, if able. It all prepared me to tackle my first late fall and winter on the mountain, but someone's upcoming thirteenth birthday came first.

Samantha's birthday was the highlight of early fall, since it was her rite of passage birthday from woman-child to woman-teen, as Ma Sticker let it be known; and the mountain community took that as seriously as the Jewish community does their Bar and Bat Mitzvahs. On September twenty-fifth, Ma spent the entire morning with Samantha, having given me strict instructions not to show my face until noon. Apparently, she was pouring a tad more of her usual womanly 'know-how and know-why' into her daughter's ears.

I spent the morning worrying, hoping Ma wasn't doling out too much advanced knowledge. If Samantha were learning those hidden mysteries, while I was still learning to identify birds and flowers, how would I ever catch up with her, especially with Mother as my guide? I feared such insights would leave me too far behind my friend and I would lose touch with her. I began wondering what I'd do if something like that happened. I loathed all wisdom in that moment, if any of it kept me from Samantha.

I had witnessed awkward breakups in Manhattan, when friends suddenly jumped ahead in maturity or interests; but I took comfort in knowing that I was advanced for my age, having experienced life in Manhattan; and Samantha, well, she lived a more sheltered life, which made our ages somewhat even in a way. That's what I needed to think to feel better, whenever such intruders surfaced in my thoughts. I had landed on that rationalization early on in our relationship and clung to it, especially that morning.

When I knocked on the Stickers' door at exactly 12:01 p.m. Ma's laughing face greeted me. "I should have known," she said. "Come in, Robyn!" Her demeanor was warm, so I felt safe in my precisely timed arrival. When I saw Samantha twirling in her new store bought dress, I knew my worries were for nothing.

That afternoon's celebrations commenced, Sticker-style. A warm Indian summer's breeze embraced neighbors and family, migrating onto the property. Aunt Flo and Uncle Herb arrived first. "Did you ever, in all your born days, see a face as beautiful as this one," Aunt Flo said as she took hold of Samantha's chin in a gentle pinch.

"Not a one, 'cept'n your purdy face, Flo! By gum, Sam, you're a looker," said Uncle Herb, a doppelgänger for portly old Grover Cleveland. I feared his next move would engulf both Samantha and me in one big, unwelcome bear hug, which made me step back a few feet, while keeping my eyes on him. Instead, he gave her a gentle pat on her head and winked a nod my way. I think he picked up on my apprehension and wanted to show me even crusty old goats can be gentle, if they set their minds to it.

In the next second Uncle Herb said, "Your Pa shooin' away any up starts, yet, sweetie?" The man stretched his short fat neck forward, looking here and there into the crowd. "How about that young Tribble boy over yonder, or maybe the Farley boy? Yeah. He's a good'n."

"Herb, now, that's 'nough teasin'," said Aunt Flo.

Samantha grabbed Sue Lynn's stool and placed it near her uncle's feet. She got up on it to put her arms around his neck. After kissing his ruddy forehead, she said, "Naw, neither one, dearest uncle. They're just friends. Ain't no men for me, 'cept'n you and Pa. How come you ain't caught onto that by now?"

"Awh, honey, things go changin' so fast, I just gotta check in every once in a while." His barrel-chested laugh shot over the chatter around them, and caused one of the younger Sticker dogs to tuck its tail and head for the barn.

"And, I'm glad you do. It's good for a girl to know her family men are watchin' after her," Samantha said. That whole encounter was not at all what I had expected, but then I didn't have a Grover Cleveland-type in my family, nor was I a Samantha.

Tables and chairs were moved about until everyone found a spot to their liking. Many shapes and sizes of flesh and bone, and color stood on that land to honor Samantha. Their chatter rose and fell, taking on one voice like a distant waterfall. Approaching forms dotted the hillsides; walked in; rode in on horseback; drove beaten down trucks or brand new cars slightly coated in mountain dust. The driveway soon filled up. Everyone knew early arrivals, up front, weren't leaving until late arrivals in the rear left first, and that arrangement was "plum acceptable." It was common knowledge that a Sticker gathering lingered way into the night, sometimes even hitting the wee-morning hours. I had never seen so many people come to a kid's [correction: young teen-woman's] birthday party. The guests spanned every generation and came from great distances.

"Oh, Ellen! What a beautiful cake!" I looked to see who Ellen was and when I saw my mouth contorted into a surprised twist. The young, slender woman who addressed Ellen touched Ma's shoulder. Ma was Ellen? Why did that bit of information shock me? Simple. Kids don't often think of parents having lives or even names before they arrive. I wondered about Pa's name, as the next second turned over on itself.

"Thank you, Lil, darlin'! Samantha hep'd me make it this mornin', whilst talkin' 'bout other recipes," Ma said with a wink. "Smell it, Lil. It's called Lemon Chiffon. We decided to do a recipe for a change. Just 'bout as delicate as honeysuckle on the vine. Don't it go perfect with her dress?"

Ma's eyes flit through the crowd, as she stood on tiptoe. Spotting the one she needed, she called out, "Oh, Scott Farley! Over here, Scott! Did your Maw pack that white linen cloth of hers for the big table? Go see to it, dear. We're needin' to lay it down now for the cake and presents."

"Yes'm," Scott said, like a man on a mission. I secretly wished he'd fail, but that would mean Ma's hope for 'settin' up purdy' would, too, so I scratched that thought along with others like it, since meeting the Stickers.

Pa stopped to ask if I was recording, but more so to ask if Mother and Dad were heading up. "Yes, I am; and, yes, they both are," I said, nodding. I'll make a copy of this for you, if you'd like!" I added.

Pa said, "Ya needn't bother doin' that. We don't got a 'whirly-word-machine,' and the family's kinda practiced up on pilin' up memories up in our heads. That's just how we do it." He said they'd add this one to the lot of them. "They ain't goin' nowheres 'tween me, Ma, and the kids," he said, smiling his infectious grin. And, I believed him. Still do; but for me, I remained focused on recording.

Half a cow roasted, while a shout out for a toast to Samantha's future rose above the clatter. Speeches by anyone wanting to speak were welcomed afterwards. I noticed the age-old question, as worn as the pages of a beloved book, popped through the lips of a noble face, hosting a shiny-head. The elder probably had asked it a couple dozen times with similar responses from others; but this was Samantha's turn. "How does it feel to be a teenager?" he blurted. Everyone laughed, nodded, and looked toward Samantha for her response. I did, too.

The typical answer, some of which I'd heard, myself, went like this: Not much different than twelve; or, I'll let you know after I've been there awhile; and, of course this one: Don't you remember? That last put relatives back a space or two. I wondered what Samantha would say. I knew she wouldn't be rude.

"Well, I been told I got some stretchin' to go through, in three places. My body will feel new things, my soul will struggle over those new things, and my spirit will want to lift me up from each new thing, like an observer, so that I can make wise choices along the way. Ones that will please God."

Everyone muttered an, "Amen," except for Uncle Herb, who shouted it. Samantha continued, which surprised me. "Yep. I've been told I might be pulled tight like a rubber band, as I shoot forward into life; and I can say, I'm not exactly lookin' forward to that, unless flyin' like one is easier than bein' stung by one that's a'flyin'." At that point she looked over at her brothers. "But I have to admit to y'all I've just been put into position to be stretched today, so, I'm still feelin' right loose."

Most laughed. Everyone applauded. Mother's clapping seemed the loudest. Maybe it was because I was standing in front of her. When I turned, I saw her wipe a tear from the corner of her nose, all the while smiling. "That was a good answer, wasn't it, Mother," I said.

"Oh, just amazing, Robyn," she said. "That girl . . ." She shook her head and beamed, as she looked at Samantha, who milled about interacting with everyone. Mother was speechless. That was the rich icing on Samantha's cake, and no one else tasted it but me.

MOTHER TURNED DOMESTIC SUPERWOMAN THAT YEAR, a turnover I didn't mind one bit. It kept her pleasantly busy, while my mind flew elsewhere. I found I could follow my own leads more freely than I ever had in the past. I actually thought her watchful eye had grown lazy. Silly me.

Mother rose earlier as fall progressed, to make the morning fires, which Samantha taught her how to build from the bottom up. Every step mirrored what Samantha had modeled—from clearing away the cold remains of dead embers, to crumbling newspaper and placing the kindling 'just so,' and then stacking the logs 'for breathin' room' after the starter lite. Blowing gently on the flames, until a good fire caught and leapt into the mix delighted Mother each time. She never considered it a task, nor did she mind enduring the cold before the flames warmed each room. It was a tangible enterprise with an immediate and pleasurable reward, something she sorely lacked in her professional life.

If Dad were away on business, she'd forgo lighting the fireplace in their room and slide into bed after starting mine. We'd cuddle until one of us woke again to awaken the other. Lying there, we'd talk about what tastes we wanted to concoct for breakfast. Those lolling and imaginative minutes in partnership with her were never rushed. We relished them as much as the topics discussed, our breakfasts. Once we hit upon a mutually agreed pathway to assuage our cravings, she'd sail out of bed, kitchen-bound in her massive robe, determined to pull off the creation exactly as we'd imagined.

Some dishes jumped the fence into wilder territories, like our fresh figs dipped in warmed marshmallow, and then plopped into piping hot steel-cut oats with Daisy's milk circling the chunks of delight. We called it, *Our White Wonder.* Our most succulent concoction appeared as caramelized apples, wrapped in thick slabs of bacon, and served with hash browns. Just plain delicious! It didn't need a name. Other meals were sugarless, like our omelets with three cheeses, olives, and scallions; or just a simple platter of coveted fruit flown in by the Gypsy, all topped in whipped cream. Simple perfection. Mother began abandoning cookbooks in favor of flying free with her inner creative chef. We both enjoyed the results.

The entire year, and then some, was idyllic, but not because of Mother. If it weren't for Samantha, I probably would have continued living in the form of that gnarly being who left Manhattan, as a frumpy grump—only my grunting habits would have increased in intensity as time went on, since "Practice makes even the imperfect, perfect!" Mother certainly would not be cuddling with me, wishing perhaps, but who cozies up to a grouch? I would have long since exiled her heart to Siberia, as payment for having banished me from Manhattan, especially if I had to endure the hard mountain winters, sans Samantha.

Samantha's positive influence was changing the entire Thomas family for the better. That's definitely fair to say, since I affected Mother, and Mother affected Dad. It worked in the opposite directions, too, but not so much that first year.

ENTERING LATE FALL AND WINTER HOLIDAYS

*I*n the fall and winter my heart had warmed into a constant and natural coziness. I'd become a willing participant in the unfolding of my life. Crawling into my freezing sheets clued me in on how far I'd come. I had accepted a new outlook on life in the raw. My senses no longer cried out in defiance. I didn't mind the cold one bit, knowing that in short order I could pull a new covering up to my chin and rest contentedly in the captured heat of my own body, 'lickity-split.' Mother had bought a special comforter for each of our beds from a local mountain woman the Stickers had met three years earlier, a Miss Marbella. Ma traded with her at the time—two cords of split firewood for two and a half comforters. The half size fit Sue Lynn's crib perfectly. Ma said it was "the best heat trade a body could make," and I agreed.

Samantha introduced us to Marbella, as 'the woman everyone loved to love, even without her craft.' Her name meant, 'beloved.' Samantha winked at me, while sharing that information; and then she explained how Miss Marbella made her annual rounds to farmers in neighboring counties, the day before Thanksgiving, to collect goose feathers and down, plucked, swept, and bagged for her. The next morning all those geese were laid in various ceramic or graniteware roasting pans, rubbed in salt, and stuck into the belly of a fired-up oven to roast to perfection before being set in the midst of appreciative onlookers.

She told us Miss Marbella paid a quarter for every bag of dirty feathers, which she then washed, dried, fluffed, and carefully stuffed into shaped cotton material she constructed by hand, using what's called the baffle box method, all to guarantee the stability of the feathers' fluff through many years of cold nights. She had a waitlist of names, local and across the states of people wanting to buy her goods. She sold pillows, too, if she had any leftover down.

Samantha, Mother, and I looked over her waitlist the day we visited. Folks in Colorado, Montana, Idaho, Utah, Vermont, and other New England states, even a family from Switzerland, were waiting for their big box of fluff to arrive before winter's end. In my mind Miss Marbella seemed like Midas with his golden eggs, or Rumpelstiltskin who spun gold from straw. Then I learned Samantha, whose stitching lay like parallel fences in a field of white snow, worked for Marbella in the 'approaching cold season.' The more I learned about the richness of the Mon in all its cycles of activity and community, the more I wished we had moved sooner.

When November rolled around, we made a family decision to spend it in our new *home*. Gladness soon escalated into feelings of excitement, when a surprise invitation landed at our door in the form of the eldest Sticker offspring, Richard. He extended his parents' wishes that we spend Thanksgiving together, "if'n [we] all were amenable to acceptin' the invite with such short notice." I was impressed with the big word Richard used, but found out it occupied a place within the mountain's common vernacular.

Turns out a preacher man from the north had introduced the word to locals over a hundred forty years back, when two feuding families were at the point of killing each other. It wasn't just because the preacher had plopped them all down onto the word he wanted them to live out. He did, often enough, but what made it linger, survive generations, was mostly due to another man, Nathaniel Greenly. The word got twisted up into another meaning, altogether new, and that's when it took root. Regional folklore puts it this way: Grandpappy Greenly, as he's still known in the region, came from a neighboring county and heard the preacher talk once. Just once. Afterwards, he went back to his clan and declared to all, "Preacher man say, we'z to be amenable. Guessin' that's biblical at the core. Amen-able! So, us'n bein' able men, and prayin' men, and Good Book men, we'z gonna take the high road. So be it! Amen! Cause we'z able." It became law, there and then, and has rolled off everyone's tongues ever since.

After Richard left I squeaked. Thanksgiving stood eight days away from his knock. That, *excuse me,* seemed an eternity away; but sure enough, after feeling the agony of waiting's sting, Samantha's words about patience surfaced in my head, too. That's when I took hold of time's linear line, wadded it up into a tight ball of string in my head, held onto its loose tail end, rolled the ball, and watched it moved forward. That image, watching that ball get smaller and smaller, made the waiting a bit more bearable for me—not by much, but some. And, still, Samantha's words cropped up. "Patience doesn't come from inside us. She enters like the queen she is, when she knows we get her worth." But that was too much to consider. I liked my ball.

I prepared. I wrote, *Soooooorry!* on some postcards to the Manhatties, and dashed off some other words like: *Thanksgiving, here—up the hill at neighbors. Christmas there!! Yippee! Think of me, as I'm eating a squirrel. Ugh!!!* I stuffed the postcards into envelopes after hearing how Miss Porthall, our postal clerk, read everything that fell under her nose. There was one thing I could not stand—busybodies poking about in matters not meant for them, especially when it concerned me. I figured the extra precaution could be considered a personal favor in helping her not to break the law.

After sealing and stamping the envelopes a wave of regret hung over my head like a circling crow. What I'd written troubled me. I'd rationalized, if I made my old friends think I was going to have a horrible time without them, they'd feel better; but if Samantha ever caught wind of my words, I'd have to crawl into a hole, never to resurface. I made sure the envelopes were sealed extra tight, adding Scotch tape to their defense. I wrote the words on the post-cards in light pencil, but just to ensure nobody could read through the envelope, I held each up to the light. All looked good. My lie lay well-concealed; but the thought of it and my inadvertent betrayal being found out in this community scared me silly. In Manhattan we were expected to lie. It was as acceptable as snubbing someone. After dropping the letters through the brass slot in the front of Miss Porthall's oak counter, I glared at her just to make sure she knew I meant business. She smiled at me. Her smile reminded me of Mother's tactics to disarm me.

Agonizing over my lie, and how I dishonored the good people of the mountain troubled me so much, I decided I wouldn't write anymore postcards or letters to my friends, deriding my new home like I had been. If my friends poked fun at anyone here, I'd ignore their words. I began pitying them—not the locals, but the Manhatties, which I guess meant me, too, but maybe not. I knew they'd never know or understand what I was experiencing with Samantha. Remorse grew in my heart for having fueled their ridicule, and I hoped with that same heart none of them would ever come visit. I couldn't bear it if they saw Samantha in a bad light, because of a connived falsehood I had encouraged.

Again, I found myself anxious about my worlds colliding. I'd employed that separation strategy as a safety mechanism since six. Various groups of friends remained in isolation, fulfilling their intended purpose until I solidified my bunch, the *Manhatties*.

Pearl called first. She basically expressed how she'd miss seeing me, but hoped my new acquaintances would surprise me, and my holiday with them would be extra special. Ah, Pearl, she was always the nicest of us, and the one I saw the least. I wondered about that choice for the first time after hanging up; but then Madison called and interrupted the thought. Typical Madison. Eventually, the other two *Manhatties* called, too. Everyone said they were bummed about Thanksgiving and offered their condolences. I changed the subject.

After our brief visit over Christmas, they called, too. I didn't see Pearl, which I regretted, but did have the others in sight, when we attended several of the same adult parties as their parents. Our parents weren't really friends. They just knew each other from kid-centered activities. Their social circles hardly ever overlapped, except around Christmas. The girls expressed sensing a difference in me. Point blank, or in a roundabout way between clusters of giggles, my friends, sans Pearl, asked if I had joined a cult or some-thing. It seems Madison, Tiffy, and Georgie colluded on some sort of long-distance intervention, once back in West Virginia. I told them, "Emphatically, no! Everything's good here, just different. I'm ecstatically happy, y'all," I used and emphasized the last word contraction on purpose, for effect. They stopped calling after those conversations. Shortest intervention on record, I figured.

What a far-reaching impact that first Thanksgiving had been, not just on me, but on all of us. Even Mother was "as pleased as Punch." I thought she had gotten wild bird-bones stuck in her gullet at several turns that evening, but she said she was only absorbing every part of the Sticker family, without adding her voice to it. Mother said she'd never been around such genuine people in a social gathering in all her life. That's saying a lot. Father hadn't lagged behind, either. He talked a lot, mostly to Mr. Sticker. I was surprised at how much they seemed to enjoy each other, as if they had something in common.

Once home, Mother talked. She expressed her thankfulness that I could be part of the richness she'd witnessed, especially at that particular time in my life, exactly the right time to appreciate the differences between it and my former experiences. She said I didn't have to waste time, like she had in figuring out what was crucial in life, and that would spare me from the setbacks of wasted time. She called wasted energy, *the drain,* and almost looked sad for a moment, but then perked up to extol the wonders of being ten, once again, as if I hadn't gotten the memo yet.

Being part of the Stickers' Thanksgiving stimulated and confirmed a funny suspicion I had held for a while. Life was more dynamic and flexible than most allow it to be; and that holidays, in general, had become way too cemented-in-place in our commercial culture, kind of like a synchronized production crew with a wind-up director, whose only goal was to reconstruct the same stage used in past shows, but whose audiences had disconnected from seeing its meaning, due to enduring a repetitive stupor that eliminated immediate relevance. Celebrating became a hollow shell of its former fullness, focused solely on taglines for most, agonizing affairs in the long and short of it.

Enchanting and lovely moments spring from the heart, almost spontaneously and often serendipitously. It's impossible to reproduce or force them onto people; yet every year, everyone tries. That's not to say traditions are pointless. They have great merit. It's just to say, they could deflate the spirit of the original moment, if life and love aren't carried forward in meaningful ways. Repeating any form without the right ingredients at the table will flatten them into mere patterns. They'll lose their buoyancy, especially if the cherished is anchored in discontent. I've often wondered what kind of fear causes people to hold onto the superfluous, which keeps us from exploring life's simplicity at the table of celebration.

After spending that holiday with the Stickers I wanted to grasp the simple ascent and, once there, release whatever was no longer needed—toss it from the heights and watch it fall away. I wanted to know what it was like to live as freely as one could, buoyed by the wind. First, I had to find that wind and wrap myself in it. That was harder than the action sounded, back then. There was a twist to it all, too. I wanted something else as well, something that appeared to be the opposite of that desire, stability, a firm footing. I wanted to be the salt of the earth. Dad said that's what the Stickers were.

I wasn't certain how salt came to be, but I kept its taste in my desires. Did the wind help form the salt? I wanted to know. That's why I watched Samantha move in her world. She came the closest to having both qualities as anyone I knew. Liberty and stability found their full and symbiotic expression in her. They weren't at odds. Samantha's whole family demonstrated conscious life, beating out its unique pulse, as if it were written in their hearts. In them I recognized the momentum of genuine motions, how they surge and build upon each other. It's how life unfolds best.

That evening we arrived around 5 p.m., dusk. Earlier, I had contrived a plan to divert my parents, making it necessary for them to turn back and retrieve *the long labored-over salad* Mother had asked me to carry to the car and present to Ma Sticker. Amazingly, she failed to remind me of the task before leaving and, once in the car, failed to ask if I had it. Miracles never cease. She seemed particularly distracted that night, which was unlike her. I devised the plan, because I wanted ten minutes alone with the Stickers to absorb each nuanced smell and sight, and then get my sole, attention-grabbing moments with each of them before my 'other' world tumbled across their threshold, salad and all; and, I am so glad I did. At least I thought I was.

"Ooops! Mother! The salad!" I said at the top of the hill with my head hanging like the guilty cur I was.

"Oh! Really?" Mother said on cue. "Well, we'll drop you off. Okay?" I nodded. "We won't be long. Just tell the Stickers what happened. Be right back. Ten minutes!"

"Got it," I said, embracing the secret delight of having pegged Mother's exact moves to right my mess. Mind you, I never had, nor ever would spill the fact that I had lied to get those moments. Mother's old adage, which I usually heard uttered during romantic comedies, "All's fair in love and war," did circle my head. I used it to justify my actions, if only to myself. Survival.

Mother got out to allow me to wiggle from my back seat captivity. Starting at the end of the Sticker's driveway, I crunched my way through the newly laid powdery snow. It swirled in circles over a two-inch freeze, blocking the view of my booted feet. My parents lingered until I signaled with our 'safe-wave,' fifteen seconds down the path. After waving, and watching them leave I turned into another wave I hadn't expected.

Had they seen Samantha's four brothers spill out the cabin door, without coats, and move as a fluid unit toward me, boisterous and as swift as a team of walruses excited over a catch left on the shore, I doubt if Mother would have accepted my 'safe' signal. I wasn't sure I'd have given it a pass in that first second; but that feeling shifted quickly. Soon I had gained a profound plucky pleasure in having enacted my 'lettuce (let us) plan,' and seeing its initial result. How could I not with those silly, fun-loving boys, cavorting through the snow toward me, their targeted destination?

In a coordinated flick of wrists and muscles they flung me into the air, as easily as if I were an inflatable kayak. There I remained, hoisted above their heads, protesting just enough to make them think I wanted down, when all I could think of, in actuality, was how I must have been the most fortunate girl in all of Christendom, a fuzzy term I'd heard, and recalled thinking it sounded awfully big. Within seconds I was put down, deposited on the Stickers' porch with my nose practically buried into a decoration hanging on the front door.

"At Samantha's request, my Lady" Richard said, at which point the boys ducked back into the house and headed straight towards the fire. The door shut abruptly. I backed up, noticing the object, which they obviously intended for me to see, hanging there on the door they slammed in my face, literally.

What I saw was a large piece of pinkish-yellow wood. They told me later it was Tulipwood. It had been shaped into a bulging elongated heart with several ears of last summer's colored corn, bundled up neatly and attached to the bottom of it with a piece of leather shoelace strung through a hole. The corn hung, as if over-flowing from the heart, like a new form of cornucopia.

Samantha tapped on the window. She held a note. It said: *Read the Heart*. Names had been carved deeply into the wood and then sanded smooth and oiled, family names, links of a human chain of cherished generations. Samantha's was there: Samantha Catherine Sticker. All the Stickers I knew in the cabin, even Grandpappy up on the hillside near his wife, Martha, were on it. It held their names, side by side. And, there was the name Odette. My mind flew to Tchaikovsky's sad swan, when her name pierced my awareness as different. I was told their Odette had married into the family as a teenage war bride. Her name lay right next to George's.

George was the first cousin of Grandpappy Sticker. He, as a young man strung the thick, thirty-five-foot rope onto the sturdy oak that still holds it. Back then, the oak stood upward of sixty feet. Now, the rope, embedded into its even heftier limb, is protected by it, as if the tree claimed it, in order to retain its title, the Swing Tree. Through the decades it's remained true in strength, supporting generations of dangling legs and dizzying spins, the site of secrets and first kisses.

George attached the rope and used his spare tire to create the source of summer pleasure that later amused a brood of younger nieces, nephews, cousins, and siblings, running loose on the raw earth during family reunions. It wasn't benevolence, as the story goes. Turns out, clever George did it to gain precious moments with his new bride, Odette, in a little cove he'd carved out, complete with blanket and flowers, a stone's throw from the tree and near a small creek that's since disappeared. There, he played music to her and sang the love songs he'd composed. Shortly after forsaking his spare tire, he hitched his wagon to another brilliant inspiration, and whisked his French bride up to the big city (my former city), where he pursued his passion for music. He never came home again; but their names remained, just like his rope, still present, still treasured. I figured, theoretically, I could be his New York stand-in. I liked that thought.

Samantha watched me patiently, as she waited for me to discover, yet, another familiar name. It was artfully positioned, off to one side, directly opposite hers. I looked over to see her face light up with delight upon my discovery. I lifted my mittened hand to my chest and silently mouthed, "Me?" She graciously nodded and mouthed, yes; but her eyes told me something even more affirming.

I turned at hearing my parents pull into the driveway, and when I looked back at the Tulipwood my name was still there. I ducked in quickly, so that Edward and Elizabeth wouldn't wonder why I had been left standing on the porch so long. Moments like the one I just shared couldn't be spoiled with troubling words or thoughts, I thought. They needed to be protected.

The significance of that loving gesture didn't fully hit me until later in the evening, when I lay tucked in my bed, reminiscing. *If I were orphaned, the Stickers would adopt me. Samantha had finally bonded with me. Pinch me!! I'm important to her. That means she feels the same about me as I do about her! We're sisters! Thank you, God!*

I had no idea my ten-minute-special-salad-fiasco-plan would exceed my expectations of good and cause me to voice the word *God* that night in a sort-of-prayer of personal thanks, all by myself, even if the entire focal point of the supposed-prayer lingered solely on me. At that point something unusual happened, once again, my conscience pricked my heart.

Had my parents returned sooner, I though, or had I not sent them on 'a fool's errand,' they might have relished each moment of the outside encounter as much as I; but I had aborted those memories for them before they were birthed, because I was thinking only of myself, as usual. Suddenly, that seemed wrong; but not for long.

So what did the Sticker's Thanksgiving look like? Let me say, it didn't center on food even though the natural and abundant food excelled my expectations. Those traditional white-feathered turkeys, fattened in confinement and shipped frozen to grocery stores, only to sit on millions of American table's a week later, didn't sit on theirs. The meat we ate was richer, fuller, darker and juicier. It was my first, wild, iridescently feathered turkey, bagged that morning along with a pheasant, which was brought to the table, too. The rabbits and quails were put on ice for suppers to come. It was the men's 'huntin' morn', and they hit the jackpot.

The table Ma laid was void of store-bought cranberry jelly, the one sporting those telltale marks, ridges pressed into their jellied form, molded by captor-cans. Ma served fresh cranberries, picked the day before, chopped, and simmered for hours in honey, sweet orange juice, and mint leaves. Missing, as well, was the typical display of cooling pies, off on a side table, or stovetop, or some kitchen counter. The Stickers reserved those treats for their Christmas morning breakfast along with a slab of green ham, and black coffee or milk.

After eating, there were no leftovers. Every bit of meat; stuffing; cooked greens; various salads, hot and cold; smoky, spicy, black-eyed peas with bacon; garden yams and potatoes; roasted chestnuts; and biscuits from scratch had been consumed; nor were there any overstuffed stomachs. Ma said she couldn't bear to see lazy feet or sloppy fingers on the dance floor or on an instrument, respectively, so she made 'just 'nough,' which brought ample satisfaction to everyone. How she knew what *just enough* looked like, has remained a mystery to me to this day.

Prior to eating, a quick prayer was uttered by Pa. Not knowing what my parents' response would have been to a longer one, and not wanting them to feel uncomfortable to the point of hatching new plans-of-concern for me along the way, I was relieved when the brief prayer held the food in place for only a few seconds.

Never wanting my new friends portrayed in a bad light, either,

I felt a sense of relief that all was flowing smoothly. I had calculated that a short prayer before dinner was an acceptable American tradition for Thanksgiving, one that could slide in nicely without a critical eye cast over it. So, I began to relax. Concern number one had been eliminated. Just so I'm clear about this—hoping to eliminate something good in order to safeguard against something one imagines bad is a sheer waste of time, and crazy hard on the nerves.

After the meal I waited in excited anticipation for the instruments to fall into appropriate hands and the spirit of play to rise up in our hearts. Safe territory. The table had been cleared quickly with the help of everyone. Even dad pitched in. I was glad to see Mother sit back in her chair, afterwards, chatting with Ma, while Samantha and I set the dishes to soak.

Then I heard Pa's voice soar above the chatter. "Come to the fire, everyone, please." Around the hearth soft and hard seating had been arranged—enough for all of us to present ourselves comfortably near the fireplace. Once we were all in our seats, Pa said the words that deflated my smile. I cringed, took a deep breath, and felt my face freeze into an awkward pinch. My wide eyes landed on my parents. "We usually take time at this point in our celebratin'," he said, "to give thanks to our Creator God for whatever it is we recognize as His provision. And we invite y'all, Edward, Elizabeth, and Robyn, our good neighbors, ta join us in doin' so this year."

I sat like a cardboard cut out, incapable of moving or breathing after that last deep breath. I felt my mouth drop open for about three seconds, and then willed it shut. The Stickers settled in under the warmth of their love and recollections, apparently oblivious to my reactions. I needed to calculate my parents' responses to know what action I needed to take later to dispel their prejudices of my friends. When Mother grabbed my dad's hand and smiled a smile, one I don't recall ever seeing on her face, my eyes grew even wider under my arching eyebrows. As I dropped my brows a long breath was released, the one I didn't even know I was holding in. I finally realized I could relax about them; but then my focus fell upon my own disheveled mind. Should I say I was thankful my parents didn't just get up and walk out? No!

What in heaven's name am I supposed to say to God, though? Variations of that sentence shot through my mind. Unaccustomed to prayer, I felt like the proverbial 'stranger in a strange land,' even more than when we first arrived on the mountain. I swallowed hard again, waiting and knowing I had much more to lose now, than I had before.

To my utter astonishment my dad began and Mr. Sticker nodded in approval. "God," he said, "we've been estranged for a long while now. My fault, of course, all mine. I find I'm more sorry than I can express. I know I've neglected you more than I've neglected my wonderful wife and daughter. I want to thank you for not giving up on me, because honestly, well, I'm thankful for that more than anything. The extensions of that thanks are all around me, now. Right here. Thank you for bringing us to this place; for meeting the Stickers; for keeping our hearts united as a family through all our years together and every transition; for the job I still enjoy doing; for the few old friends we have, and the new ones; for our family up north. Thank you. My hope is that we, ah, I mean, I . . . I won't be such a stranger in the years to come. Amen."

I could only stare in bewilderment. *Okay, where did that come from and who or what replaced my parents?* My dad's word choice, *stranger*, stuck in my throat. I swallowed hard again. Mother held her peace. Sue Lynn, whose voice filled the spaces with her constant murmuring piped up. "Mama, me next. I wanna fank God."

"Go right 'head, sweetie," Ma said.

"Happy Fanksgiving, Jesus! Fank you for horsie, my baby, God, Mama, Papa, big brovers, Z'manda, and new fwends. Ahh-men."

For a short spell we delighted in the little person named, Sue

Lynn. No one spoke. Mother wiped one side of her face. Only the sound of crackling fire and the kitten, purring on my lap filled the room. Richard prayed after our focus returned. He impressed me with his brevity, warmth, and to-the-point prayer. Samantha prayed after her brother and said this: "Everythin' is right, with you in the middle, God. Your presence is sweet and good. Thank you for family, friends, the land under our hearts, and everythin' made by your hands, but mostly for you with us. Thank you for unscramblin' things and settin' them straight. Thank you for the peace we get inside when you are rightly settled in us. God, thank you for Ma kickin' the bug day-fore-yesterday in short order; for the Thomases bein' here with us tonight and always in our hearts; for Bessie Jane still bein' steady on her pins—give her safe travel back from her daughter's; for Pa gettin' a new outlet for his carvin'; for Richard's advancement with Mr. Guise; for Clems' new friend, Greg, who plays the fiddle as good as Clem, or maybe better. (I watched as she paused and peeked up at Clem with a crooked smile of mischief on her lips.) God thank you for lettin' Missy-My take honorable mention at the fair this year. Ya done a good job in makin' her purdy, Lord. Oh, and thank you, again, for Trumpet's easy foalin' last week. What a beautiful colt you added to us. Finally, thank you for the humor and laughin' you put into your children, but most of all, for your love. In your Son we come. Amen."

Clem and Clay began praying at the same time. They eyed each other. Jason laughed. The younger, by two minutes, allowed his elder to pray first. Jason followed up. Ma Sticker slipped in a short beaming prayer of motherly contentment, wifely love, and neighborly kindness, allowing the woman I had grown to know and love spill out her big heart in a "just 'nough' way. Her warmth gave me courage to speak up.

I looked up at Samantha. She smiled and winked at me. I watched her bow her head again. Her raven hair spread over her fire-rouged cheeks like a veil. She waited with everyone else. How did they know to wait? I swallowed. The fire snapped at me, or was it laughing at me? I recalled Samantha's prayer. Humor. It was laughing, not at me but with me. The kitten purred. The fire laughed. "Thank you, God, for laughing fires and purring kittens." I peeked at Samantha. She was smiling, head still bowed. "And for the love I feel here." Sue Lynn hugged Pa. "Thank you, God, for now. Amen." It was all I could utter before my throat felt as if it would close with a well of tears trying to rise up from my heart. I had no idea until that moment how a wall of fear had surrounded me. When it fell, I breathed deeply, feeling released, but just as quickly apprehension arose with its wagging finger, preparing to shut me out, again.

After my prayer, I noticed Pa looked up at Mother, and without words asked if she wanted to participate. Mother declined within the same silence. Pa wrapped up the prayers, and within a hair's breadth of his amen, instruments were dislodged from shelves, music stands, and bedside tables. In a flash we, who weren't making music, were clapping or dancing or enjoying the evening's feast of joy and love.

I wondered about Mother's lack of sharing a prayer and if anyone else, beside Pa and Dad, noticed. I wasn't able to read her face afterwards, but she seemed content and pleased to be in community with the Stickers. I decided to let my curiosity pass, as one of those uncertain things I would never understand about her; but more so, because the festivities captured my whole attention.

DISCOVERIES

"*W*anna go dragon huntin'?" Samantha asked one spring morning, when cloud clusters gingerly sailed across the face of the sun. It was as if they were in cahoots with the wind to dissuade the fiery orb above them from warming the earth too quickly; rather follow their lead in alternating the temperature between waves of coolness and warmth. Combined, they harmoniously blanketed all of life with the winsome call of, *Come forth*. I asked if I needed to bring a sword. She replied, "Nope, just your senses and a readiness to appreciate what they take in."

Approaching a pond, I was struck by glistening movements punctuating the air, patches of pastel light that vanished as quickly as they appeared. An out-of-the-ordinary sound impregnated the stillness, like dozens of spinning pinwheels, or rotating water sprinklers, furiously turning, 'round and 'round incessantly. The logic of that assessment fell short, however, since there were no pinwheels in sight, nor any droplets of water landing on our flesh. "What's that sound?" I asked.

"Dragonflies," she said with the biggest grin on her face. "They're out!"

The closer we got, the more enthralled I became with the revelation. There before me, darting, hovering, turning in angled dives, after split-second directional shifts were hundreds of dragonflies. "What are they doing!' I whispered.

"Lookin' for lunch, I 'spect," Samantha laughed.

I'd never seen such precision in motion. They were uncanny, going up as fast as down. Their movement appeared more striking than a lightning bolt's. They traversed the pond as easily as the wind, and under the sunlight their four translucent wings glowed. Each wing moved independently of the others, causing every transparent and delicate surface to be exposed to the sun. The brilliance captivated me.

They continued to zoom about effortlessly, landing on reeds, only to leap off a split-second later. When colors merged, a light show emerged, a veil of bouncing pastels, sheer, infused with light. They ignored us as we gazed in awe. I found myself thinking how we moved more like boulders, compared to their agile stunts, which were nothing more than their common ground maneuvers to catch food on the wing. What I found most fascinating was— not a single collision occurred with all those insects, moving randomly at the same time.

"Where'd they come from?" I asked.

"Below the water. They lived there as nymphs for around two years!" Samantha said.

"Two years! Without those wings, right?" I asked.

"Exactly," she said.

"And they're already so skilled in using them?" I was baffled.

"Yep. Built in instincts. Genius, ain't it? They looked totally different in their darker phases of life, too—like pint-sized 'gators. They had smaller eyes and bigger jaws, juttin' out like pinchers. They were really ugly." Samantha laughed. "But, that's how they caught their unsuspectin' prey, with those jaws. They ate a lot down there, 'cause they changed a lot."

"Changed?"

"Ummhmm. They were bein' transformed, becomin' like new creatures, kinda like butterflies and ladybugs in their various stages. I think they shed their outer bodies, more than twice, to grow bigger. That's like snakes do, too. All that happens in the water's underworld, for them, 'cept'n for that last sheddin'. That's when they crawl up on a reed and spend about half a day becomin' a dragon that flies away. I love these guys!" She twirled, arms stretched upward, beaming and watching.

"Even when they're out of the water, their new parts have to get ready for flight. Their wings spread open for a good dryin. Like taken the laundry out of the bushel and hangin' it in the breeze. That's when they wait for their thorax to function, too."

"Why?" I asked.

"It's what makes their wings flutter. Amazin', huh! Even after they finally fly off, they go somewhere to be still some more, while their newest outer body hardens."

"You make learning easy, Samantha."

"Pa taught me those things a couple years back, even though I've been watchin' them take wing for years. Ma taught me somethin' 'fore then, though—a thought to open up beauty, I 'spect. She came up with it, when we were up here, together, years ago."

"What?"

"Oh, how, if the light settles upon our transparent beings, like it does on those dragonfly wings, we'll glow, too, 'cept'n we don't get to see the beauty of it all. Only God does."

Samantha stood up in a wiggle, pretending to be a dragonfly nymph, trying to figure out its next move, and falling to the ground out of sheer frustration. I'd never seen her act so silly. I could never outguess Samantha, and that made me happy.

"That kind of transformation is beyond a dragonfly's will, and ours. Ma said what has to happen with humans is just the opposite of what has to happen with dragonflies to reach maturity. They have to harden on the outside, while we have to soften on the inside." Samantha paused in reflection. "Strange thinkin' 'bout that day. Seemed somethin' was troublin' Ma 'round that time. I remember, now, it was the time her stomach began growin' with Sue Lynn." '

"Sue Lynn's three. Were you around ten?" I asked.

"No. I was around eight. Now, that's confusin' 'n' strange. I know I had the thought her tummy was swellin' 'cause she was with child. Thinkin' on it, now, that's probably why she wanted to walk with me that day. She seemed heavy of heart. The dragonflies made her smile, and that's when she told me what I just told you."

"I wonder what was wrong," I said.

"I have my spectin' thoughts, since you brought it up. I aim to ask her, now, since I'm a woman and all." Samantha smiled. "Accordin' to her say, that is." She giggled. "I gather she won't mind talkin' with me 'bout it."

Suddenly, the topic shifted like the wind and the dragonflies. It became Samantha's turn to ask me a question. "So, Robyn," she said, skipping a stone across the pond, "what makes a pond a pond? Is it the water, or the earth it sits on?"

"Oh, gosh," I said, feeling a bit nervous. "Ummm? The water?" I proposed.

"If'n I got a big vacuum and sucked out all the water, then put the water in a big tank, would the water still be a pond?"

"Why are you torturing me, Samantha?"

She laughed. "Wanna stop?" she asked.

"Of course not!" I said. "Besides, that's not a fair question. You could have said the same thing about the earth the water sits on, if I said it was the earth. Yeah, you could have," I said, when she smiled. "If I brought truckloads of dirt to fill in the earth after you sucked out the water, would the area still be a pond?" I chimed, thoroughly satisfied with myself.

She only grinned, again, and said, "There's no rush, if'n you wanna think more on it," which I knew was my cue to do just that. And, then she said, "How did I not known Ma had a miscarriage?"

"Don't you think it's kinda natural for little kids to skip over timelines on those kinds of things," I asked.

"You're right. I 'spose Sue Lynn's comin' along, shortly after, must 'ave filled the gaps I didn't even think to question, but still."

That's when I discovered there was something similar about Samantha and the dragonflies: They're both impossible to capture; but, if you're very still, one just might land on an extended finger or a bare knee.

* * *

When I arrived at the place of marveling at the Stickers' garden, I imagined years of labor poured into and onto that fenced-off piece of ground. After voicing my admiration of the decades of labor put into it, Samantha thanked me and added, "It's more like a century and a half, though."

The soil was as rich as her hair—black, soft, and yielding, but it wasn't the soil or the wealth of knowledge Samantha possessed that impressed me the most when it came to that chunk of earth. It was her way with it, the dedication I saw on a daily basis. It's what she did for the soil and with the knowledge passed onto her. That's what captured my heart, the 'goin's on' within that fence.

In no uncertain terms I knew, if I sensed a chill within the hush of a spring night, I'd pull my blanket up higher and curl up more, hands tucked between my legs. I'd feel the warmth of my breath hit my blanket and return to sleep. That same cool sensation would cause Samantha to rise up, dress, go outside and stack her wheelbarrow with bushel baskets and quart jars. She'd push that load up the dirt pathway to the garden, dogs trailing in low-headed silence, all the while wishing they were still strewn across the porch against each other, asleep; but duty bound to the one they loved, they followed close at her heels. Within the boundaries of that fenced piece of earth, she'd work out her commitment to the land, unseen, unsung, and definitely, not paid in the ways most would want to be paid.

I would watch her fuss, countless times, over individual plants during daylight hours; turn cucumbers, so that all sides would receive a share of the sun's warmth; pick aphids off overturned leaves, one by one; and aerate the soil around sickly plants with a gentle twist of a hand fork.

I have a running recollection, not fashioned in words but with feelings, the deepest kind, which the Sticker family brought to my awareness most vividly, especially Samantha—around the art of caretaking. The Sticker women exhibited it differently than the men. There was no higher honor or glory in how any of them labored out of love for their family. It amounted to a careful consideration of the whole by way of the smaller parts. There was no boasting in the men folk or pride in the women over how they served and extended unspoken love to each member of the family. They just took the place that came most naturally to them and worked it. No one competed, complained, or envied. No one entered their territory confused, or moved around others, while in it, in a controlling or begrudging manner. They were all solid in the knowledge of who they were and how they fit together.

I learned the delicate realization that women are the gentle nurturers, even when strong. Ma never had to prove her strength. It was known, just as Samantha's was, and even baby Sue Lynn's. She, at three, shared in the household tasks for the good of all. Whether that love was spilled out to a spouse, children, animals, or rooted plants, it unfolded in the same manner—lovingly and well. Even when the overflow wasn't visible, it was there. It was their inner strength that made others feel at ease.

Samantha once said, "A self-centered person ain't no better than a castrated bull." She said, "If'n we cut off the natural cycle of givin' and receivin' in ways we're able, whatever that might be, we'll be wagin' a cold war within our own soul and suffer grave losses down the road."

This conversation illustrates it: At the start of an early July morning's heat, she said, "Here's a baseball cap for you, Robyn!"

"Don't need one, Samantha. Head's not hot, yet."

"Oh, you'll be needin' it, alright. Make sure your hair's tucked into it!"

"What?"

Samantha relished surprises. I hated them. I noticed she held three boxes in her hands and began running toward the garden. "Wait for me," I called.

"Come on poke," she replied.

Sue Lynn was already at the garden, jumping up and down in her cute knee jerk way, never really getting off the ground. With my hair swept up into the cap I entered the garden. Samantha extended one box to me. I read the small typed label, and my eyes widened. "Seriously!" I exclaimed, "Oh, my gosh!" We all squealed. Sue Lynn squeezed her box.

"On the count of three, we open them, all at the same time! Okay?"

We nodded.

"Ready?" Everyone counted. "One . . . two . . . three!"

I heard Sue Lynn say, "Free!!" on the last count, which I thought was her way of saying *three*, but maybe it wasn't. We opened our boxes and within seconds nearly one thousand, confetti-sized insects, three-hundred and twenty-five per box, all shipped overnight, swarmed before our eyes, their black undersides sailed upward like little boats on a blue sea, all hoisted up with their orange exoskeleton sails, polka-dots and all.

My arms and legs erupted with goose bumps, when the delicate wings under those numerous upraised hulls flapped vigorously near my bare flesh. Released from their temporary captivity and bent on satiating their hunger, they immediately shot forth toward their objective—aphids. Once that lid opened, three tangerine clouds merged upward and away, as if they had never been contained in our hands; but the thrill didn't subside.

"Ladybugs! Come back," Sue Lynn called out.

"It's okay, Baby Sue," Samantha said.

"They all go 'way, Z'manda?" Sue Lynn asked.

"No! I betcha lots stayed," Samantha said. "They're just playin' hide 'n' seek. Let's look for 'em." Samantha spread apart the leaves of various plants, exposing their bottom side. Sue Lynn squatted nearby and looked. Eventually, her pudgy fingers caused the several she found and wanted to pet to ascend, but they descended just as quickly. They had found their food in the Stickers' garden and no one could interrupt their quest for long. "And, there are more still hidin', baby girl. I'm happy for our neighbors. How 'bout you? They'll be gettin' garden visitors, too! Won't they be surprised! Oh, how strikin' when they set off, findin' their way."

"Absolutely!" I said in awe.

Sue Lynn nodded. "'Zalutely!" she added.

Samantha looked up at me, smiling. She stood and took hold of one stray piece of my hair, while gently extracting a misdirected voyager.

"And," Samantha said in a half-whisper, "next week two hundred lacewing will be comin' in the post. They love the mealy bugs and caterpillars just as much as the aphids. Nice thing is, they're settlers."

"Settlers?" I said.

"They won't cloud away, when released. They'll just settle down almost immediately, like freshly fallen snow." She turned her eye to the littlest among us. "Two hundred more visitors a'comin', Sue Lynn. Can you count that high?"

"One hundred, two hundred!" she exclaimed.

Samantha laughed. Both Sticker girls began imitating the ladybugs' flight. They weren't quick to let go of the exhilaration that flowed through them. "We have ladybugs, lots and lots of 'em," said Sue Lynn, as she flew up the garden's three stone steps, climbed onto the top one and jumped with opened wings into Samantha's arms.

PART II
CONCEPTION, OUR BEING

PERCEPTIONS WE RETAIN

Mother changed the celebratory salutation of my second birthday on the mountain by saying, "Happy Ten-One, Robyn!" Was she trying to prolong my tenth year? I honestly didn't know. I wondered if my subsequent birthdays would follow course with a, "Happy 10-2; 10-3; 10-4." You get the picture. "Mother," I said, "I'm eleven. I know you can say it, if you try," which she did, of course, after tossing a party hat at me.

That summer Samantha and I spent a bit more time with Scott. People got used to seeing the three of us on our bikes flying by them. Word got back to us that some of the locals draped a nickname over us—*the flag*. "Why the flag?" I asked Dad who had heard about it.

"Ummm, I . . . I think . . . yeah, I heard it had something to do with the color of your bobbing heads."

"What?"

"I'll ask around next time I'm in town," he said.

Turns out I was the red, obviously; Scott who was a towhead from birth was the white; and Samantha, whose raven-colored hair appeared blue when the light hit it just right was, yes, the blue.

Voila: red, white, and blue—Old Glory. My thoughts: Lame. Didn't they understand Samantha had to come before me in everything? And Scott couldn't take center stage, not even in a color scheme. Sidekicks don't matter. If they needed a name, why not the storm, or the bullet, or better yet, the peregrine falcon, since we pedaled so fast we were hardly visible. They should have given us a name that's always in motion, not some flag chained to a pole. Yes. It upset me.

I tried to switch it up, eliminate Scott entirely from the picture, fold the flag and put it away, neatly in its triangular stored shape, respectfully and all. Not the flags fault. I brought our eyes into the equation. "Samantha," I said, "with your blue eyes, I'd say you're the sky, and your hair, it's . . . it's a dark rain cloud. We need rain clouds in the sky. Right?" Now I sounded rather lame, but Samantha seemed to like the game. She said, "Robyn, your eyes are green, so, you're the leaves on an apple tree full of red apples." Again, she left the robin redbreast on green grass in the dust.

"Nice," I said. "I'll take it."

"What about Scott?" she asked.

"What about him?" I asked.

"What's he?" she asked, waiting patiently, as if an answer had to exist.

"I can't think of anything to go with Scott. I don't even know the color of his eyes."

"Oh, that's easy. They're brown, a sweet 'n' gentle, light brown. I'll do his," she said. *Oh, this should be good*, I thought. "He's the good earth, covered in pale spring jonquils." *Ugh. Ugh. Ugh. Why did I bring this up?*

"Let's do something!" I shouted gaily, trying to awaken Samantha from her vision of the good earth.

"Let's walk and explore," she said.

We walked a lot that summer, paths new to me but familiar to Samantha. Our walks were more like explorations. Most of the time they seemed to disband all the mental gnats that plagued me.

My concerns vanished in the summer breeze after I focused on what lay before or around me. That day was no exception. I forgot about Scott. I drank in nature. In my more humble moments, which flashed through me as swiftly as mini-bolts of lightning, present and then gone, I lost sight of knowing what I thought I knew about most things; rather, I felt known. It was a bit creepy at times, especially when I wasn't at my best. In those moments I felt exposed, out of joint with the surroundings; but after being zapped by several more non-frying bolts of inspiration, I'd drop even that opinion of myself. I began feeling more like an empty journal, waiting to be written upon, rather than a book. That I could accept, because Samantha blazed the trails.

One of my favorite places to walk and then sit, a half-mile or so below my house, was in an old grove of sweet magnolia trees. Settling in, upwind of their seductive fragrances was a must. Their pure white flowers, bejeweled with honeybees trying to draw forth nectar, while coating their back legs in pollen, proclaimed summer to my senses like no other collaborated effort within nature. Those hard working bees and yielding flowers made me feel like an insignificant clod in the cycle of life's give and take. But that clod felt warm and content, happy to be a humble observer amidst such beauty.

The exchange and rhythm, there, reminded me of the strange little poem Mother had dropped into my lunch tote, when I was nine. Blake wrote it. Something about a clod and a pebble. I hadn't understood it then. I remember sitting on the edge of the Bethesda Fountain in Central Park, under the angel's face, when I unfolded the small piece of paper and found its puzzling words written in Mother's hand.

> *"Love seeketh not itself to please,*
> *Nor for itself hath any care,*
> *But for another gives its ease,*
> *And builds a Heaven in Hell's despair."*

> *So sung a little Clod of Clay*
> *Trodden with the cattle's feet.*
> *But a Pebble of the brook*
> *Warbled out these metres meet:*
>
> *"Love seeketh only self to please,*
> *To bind another to its delight,*
> *Joys in another's loss of ease,*
> *And builds a Hell in Heaven's despite."*

I tossed my reflections of the poem aside, once again, as we walked on and came upon a mud hole where the water had dropped significantly in volume over the hotter summer months. In May the little pond's water level reached the upper bank where we knelt. Mud puppies continued to swim in it, however, along with flipping and leaping frogs and their more crude-looking cousins, the toads.

The amphibians captured our attention until a painted oriole and some bobolinks, followed by a darting scarlet tanager, shook us free of our downward focus and lifted our gaze off the earth into the heavens. Even their less colorful cousins, the warblers, mockingbirds, and yes, the robins with their sumptuous symphonies grabbed our attention and secured it. Later, Samantha helped me spot a coy white-tailed deer, hiding behind a broken limb that angled in its resting place. Its foliated tip touched earth, while barely remaining connected to the Sugar Maple, its life source; but it provided security for the deer. We found the tracks of a great black bear and a wildcat that day, too, along with several occupied habitats—a fox's den, a mole's burrow, a raccoon's den, and hares peeking out of their warren, only to turn and show us their tails, posthaste.

"I used to hunt with the boys," Samantha said, unexpectedly, ". . . till I didn't anymore. Maybe, I should say—till I couldn't. I just discovered, one day, I wasn't a hunter down deep. Some folk are. Some ain't." I understood her heart and was happy it spread across the same horizon as mine. She said, "God made men and women hunt in different ways." I wasn't sure what that meant, exactly, and since the thought made no sense to me at the time, I tucked it away with the clod and pebble poem. They fit nicely atop the duck eggs.

* * *

It's the Thomases' way to want and pursue. The Stickers taught me, "I shall not want." They showed me through living their lives. It didn't mean they stopped working to move life along. Desires didn't cease, neither had the refining moments within any process, where we think we're reaching goals. It's just an umbrella perspective, where we come to see our needs are not met merely by our own efforts. It's a realization that we're part of a greater circle of dispensation. Samantha explained it this way: "The wantin' that gnaws at us, along with the fear of not havin', they have to move aside, play second fiddle to trustin' the Giver. Knowin' who's first chair always matters, both in orchestras and in life." I grew up hearing Dad sing, "Whatever Lola wants, Lola gets." Lola was Mother.

Mountain walks with Samantha taught me, in unique ways, about the pitfalls of wanting. My first lesson came from the birds. They helped me see how knowing the way to get something on one plane didn't transfer, necessarily, to another plane. It reached my understanding while watching Samantha walk among the wild critters. The same ones that came up to her would scatter when I approached them. I tried every technique she employed: slow movements; a tender endearing voice; and cheat-treats *she* never used, but I brought just in case. I even sat or stood absolutely still for a crazy amount of minutes. Nothing worked. Every attempt failed. Everything failed, even my version of good thoughts. I sang, and then tried chanting "Om," complete with the pose a friend showed me before leaving Manhattan. Again. A bust. Samantha's eyes widened upon witnessing my last method, and then asked me to drop it from my repertoire, forever. We laughed. I admitted I thought it was lame when Georgi showed me. Basically, the fact remained, what I wanted I couldn't get.

"Samantha! Pssst. Hey, Samantha," I whispered, while stuck in one of my unproductive tracks. "How did you make that Canada Warbler eat those berries from your hand?" It flew away when I opened my mouth.

"I didn't make it do anythin', Robyn. It chose to do it."

"I get that!" I said with my grump-voice. "But, why don't they ever choose to do it with me!" My frustration had become obvious even to myself.

"Maybe 'cause your wantin' has built too thick of a barrier for them to fly through?"

Bam. Another unseen boulder rolled over me, another one I'd have to push off someday, if I ever could get my fingers around intangibles.

"Gotcha," I said. I let her think I understood, often.

* * *

IN MID-SEPTEMBER WE PLANNED A DAY HIKE WITH OUR parents' permission. It was Samantha's idea. She said, "You've been here over a year now, Robyn, and I ain't introduced you to our most honored neighbor yet. I'm 'shamed to say so; and I aim to rectify that, right soon. It's a two-hour hike up the mountain. Would you be up for that tomorrow?" I nodded, excited by the mysterious destination.

We both packed food, extra clothing, more water than I thought we'd need, a compass and pepper spray (Mother's ideas on the last two items), and headed off early in the morning, early for me, that is—a respectable 8 a.m. departure. Samantha even walked down to walk me back up, but mostly to assure Mother that there were homes all along the road, if you knew where to look, which she said she did.

The climb in altitude zapped the strength from my body after forty minutes, but Samantha seemed undaunted. We crossed over a gushing river on an old narrow bridge, which I wished hadn't been there, because it meant we'd have to encounter it again on our way back. I never liked the idea of falling into a river full of rocks. Call me crazy, but . . .

Samantha said Pa checked the bridge each fall to make sure it remained foot-worthy and secure, even for the occasional light load of store bought supplies, which had to reach the people up higher by pack mule or small vehicle. She said, "He came up last eve, knowin' our plans." That sort of reassured me. I did trust Pa, but the relief I felt as my foot set down on solid ground, again, surpassed that trust.

A wide path had been cut into the forest and appeared well kept. Samantha told me neighbors took turns keeping it cleared for the one I was going to meet. "You're goin' meet Bessie Jane, Robyn. That'd be Mrs. Grover Stoddard, properly called. She raised ten whelps, all boys. She didn't get to raise her one daughter, though. She flew on home, when just a babe. Her grave was the first to be dug behind the cabin. Mr. Stoddard was laid alongside the little one, near sixty years ago. He died young in his late thirties from a felled tree.

"They've got mountain goats wanderin' over their green-grassed graves, now, in that pastured valley, an ancient valley, where no river runs through, no more. It's a bit of a hike, but I heard tell it was much frequented in Bessie Jane's younger years with her boys all in tow. They never tried to shoo the goats off the gravesites or plant flowers atop them, 'cause the deer would just eat 'em up. Just left everythin' natural. Visitin' was the only thing on their minds. Spendin' time in the valley became their storytellin' time 'bout both restin' lives; and even though the little girl's stay was so short, it stirred the hearts of those boys to rememberin' and bein' grateful for what they still had—the whole of the land and the life they'd been given to live on it, off it, and beyond.

"People from old have passed down stories about how 'mazin' Bessie Jane's homestead used to be, not to mention her—a wild beauty, smart as a whip, they'd say." Samantha continued in her narrative, knowing we'd reach Bessie soon. "Her boys all growed and scattered like wind-blown seeds, and their child'en's child'en got child'en of their own, now. Bessie's a great-great grandma. They come, most of 'em, and keep the place up for her, paintin', trimmin', plantin' plumbin'. They scattered, but not terrible far. They always loved their maw." She's told me some of their stopping places—Virginia Beach, Nashville, Charlotte, Washington D.C. and the Shenandoah Valley.

"Her boys tell each other that it's for their families' comfort, when vistin' to make the place look nice; but each son knows they do the groomin' for her pleasure. The son who lives farthest in Kansas City and comes the least—that son sends boxes of foodstuffs from specialty stores, thinkin' she'll delight in new and strange things, but most of time they never get unpacked. He'd know if he visited more. No one has the heart to tell him that it's hard for Bessie to open packages with her achin' fingers, and she's pretty much on a simple diet of goat's milk, honey, apples, prunes, cabbage, potatoes, lamb 'n' fish, now. Neighbors bring a fresh supply every week, knowin' those are foods that agree with her."

Samantha stopped talking. We'd arrived. Before my eyes sat the mountain's honored inhabitant, propped up as properly as a lady of ninety-seven could manage, a slender form with waxen limbs wrapped in moss green and brown shawls, rocking in rhythm to the swaying pines, conforming perfectly to the inner and outer beauty of her hills—hills that seemed more demure than other slopes, having shared in her history. The flecked brown bag skin, hanging in folds on her cheekbones, rounded like papier-mâché magic into a smile the moment she caught wind of Samantha's presence.

"Come here, chil'. Come here," she waved. "Ah, dear, that's a dear. Sit right here. I was just a lookin' out yonder." She paused, squinted, and then, as if wanting to scratch off her last thoughts to catch up with her special guest, but unable to do so, said, "Out here . . ." her pole-like arm gilded slowly in front of her face in a semicircle, "Out here the young sprigs grow straight up from the fallen ones."

Samantha joined in, "Out here, not a lick of life is wasted."

Bessie smiled. "Yaa-ess," she said. Instantly, she no longer inhabited the woods, but locked onto Samantha's eyes. Upon first breath, they were connected, one mind bouncing off itself as gingerly as the gleams in both their eyes. Samantha's exuberance fueled Bessie. Her soul awakened and, if she were a bit younger, and only a bit, she would have risen and shuffled her feet in a dance of joy. I surprised myself by seeing that image. Perhaps in such places veils are lifted a bit higher. I figured, probably all the recent seeing I'd been experiencing helped form its edges; yet on the heels of that unexpected view and assumption, something else rose up that blocked me from entering into it more, and what I had seen faded.

The two reached for each other. Samantha crouched near Bessie's rocker. Their hands formed a circle. I couldn't tell if Bessie's clasped Samantha's, or if Samantha planted hers deeply into the thin-sheathed grip of surety, which she tenderly kissed.

"Samantha, it's fittin' ya come."

"Why fittin', Bessie? It's been way too long 'tween my last visit and now."

"Ah, cherub-girl, my boys are a-wantin' me to part with my mountain 'n' go with Wille to Harrisonburg. That'd be in the Shenandoah," she said. "They says, 'twon't be far, Maw. We'll be takin' ya back for visits, Maw; but, far 'twill be for me, Sam. I knows it. I feels it."

Samantha listened.

"My youngest, Willie . . . my William Tucker Stoddard, well, he's learnin' kids at that there college named for a president. Oh, what is it? Oh, ya-ees, that James Madison school. He got himself a PD, or some such thing, makin' him professor of somethin' or another. I think it'd be for a language. Do they got such professin' for our own language, 'cause I thought I heard it be English. Ain't that the funniest thing. I didn't say such or nothin', but 'magine all that schoolin' for just talkin' English."

I couldn't help smiling at that point, even though I was fully impressed with her and feeling more awkward in her company than I had with the birds. I wanted to tell Bessie it was a PhD, and that it was way cool for her son to be a professor, teaching English, but I couldn't find my footing into the conversation and my offering felt like it would have fit as much as a toadstool on a *Better Homes and Garden* lawn.

"Bessie," Samantha said, "your boys love you so! I'm guessin' they want to see more of you. Maybe, they have concerns beyond the point of bearin', thinkin' of you out here, alone for so long. How have things been goin' for ya, lately?"

"Good as winter frost," she said, laughing a bit. Samantha smiled and grabbed Bessie's hand with both of hers again.

"Winter frost has its place," she said.

"That it do; but, Sam, it's fittin' that ya come, 'cause I have somethin' for ya." Bessie dropped her hand under her shawls and into her dress pocket. She pulled out a yellowed piece of paper. "I want ya to read this in 'bout two moons. Can ya do that for me, dear?"

"I sure can do that, Bessie." Samantha took the paper and put it into her overall pocket. She asked no question and slipped her hands into Bessie's once again.

The look on the old woman's face melted into calmness, as if an important transaction had been made, a burden lifted from her shoulders. "Can ya 'magine, dear, livin' between thousands and thousands of people in one place?" she asked.

"No ma'am. I sure cannot; but I'd try."

"Hmm. Would ya now?" Bessie said. Her voice trembled a bit. Samantha soothed her by changing the subject.

I never held Bessie's hand that day. She never reached for mine, even while I helped her up by her elbow, when she needed to stretch her limbs. I couldn't extend mine either, because for the most part Bessie's eyes were either on Samantha, or wandering off to trace the familiar lines of the jagged woods against the cornflower blue sky, or resting on the boards of her cabin. Later it struck me that she was saying good-bye to old friends, over and again—just to make sure every element knew how difficult her parting would be and how her heart was awash with gratitude for being a part of them all those years. She was stroking each in her vast love, all within her limited ability. I'm sure if she could, she'd have risen, taken Samantha by the hand, and run into the open field like a graceful gazelle, spreading her good-byes in an entirely different way. I was stung into silence at getting to see the end of her history in the place I was just beginning to love, the last remaining moments of her love affair with a part of earth's truest reflection.

She wasn't unfriendly to me, and we did chat briefly, but a connection never happened. I did feel a tinge of jealousy and alienation drift over me like a rainless cloud. It's just I had lived among millions and millions, something neither of my porch-fellows could imagine, but something I considered ordinary. That made me feel different, and different was the last thing I wanted to feel.

On the way down, Samantha never spoke, except once when I asked her a direct question. "Aren't you curious about that paper she gave you?"

"Not thinkin' 'bout it, Robyn," she said.

At that moment I felt even stranger. A thought brushed my mind that perhaps I didn't belong on the mountain, that my people were city people, that Mother had made a huge mistake in bringing me here against my will. My 'ten-one' mind felt trapped, unwanted, and out-of-place. I know, now, it wasn't really my mind dumping those foreign and uncomfortable thoughts onto me; but it was me who let them linger. I had no defense. I was completely ignorant about how darkness moved in this world and into people's thoughts.

I rationalized later that night that Samantha had known Bessie since birth. "In fact," as Ma Sticker reported upon our return,, "she was there at eighty-three, boiling water for the delivery and calming the men folk." Samantha buried her face in the folds of Ma's sleeved arm. It was the first and only time I'd seen her cry.

It wasn't clear to me why I felt I had to justify their relationship—make it fit, even though I knew I didn't fit into it. I remember trying to look at ease. My mind turned over on itself, seeking ingress. I sucked my lower lip and played with my fingernails, waiting for the moment that never happened. I couldn't sum up the division or subtraction, when all I wanted was addition. After all, I was me, an entire entity.

I didn't tell Samantha the day was a bust, seeing how she maneuvered her way home in sadness. It wasn't everyday that someone like Bessie Jane left the mountain. I was glad I understood that much at least. Losses hurt. I thought—*finally I know something Samantha doesn't*, which helped me feel a bit better, until it seemed absolutely wrong to think that way.

UNAVOIDABLE CHANGES

A couple of weeks after meeting Bessie Jane, a thorn punctured my relatively smooth surface. Discomforts began flaring up on every side. For one thing I was forced to steal from Mother. I had no choice. I found a red stain on my underwear, which I carefully washed out and hung on my towel rack. It's not that I was fastidiously clean. I only wanted to rub a strange sensation away—that my body had stolen a piece of my personal freedom.

The object of my thievery was one of Mother's sanitary pads. Later that day, I went back for more. The first had been saturated in a matter of hours, which shocked me. It turned out Mother used ultra lights at that time in her life, and I needed the big guns. I lightened her big box even more, not knowing how many I'd need. I ended up stashing twelve more pads under my pillow.

I hoped I wouldn't have to return to the scene of my crime again, and that the curse would end quickly, but my hopes were dashed along with my desire to keep my 'flow' private. Mother found out. I have no clue how, since I'd wrapped each used pad carefully in toilet tissue and sunk each down to the bottom part of various wastebaskets and receptacles in the house, just to avoid any conspicuous differences in their usual bulk.

Mine wasn't a happy entrance into 'womanhood.' It wasn't at all like Samantha's, which Ma celebrated with her. I didn't like the cramps. I didn't like the blood, especially on my underwear; and, I didn't like the fact that I had no clue what any of it meant in the bigger scheme of things. I did manage to capture a shred of thankfulness, though. *It* didn't happen in public, and *it* didn't happen in New York City, where I would have gotten an ear load of its meaning, whether I liked it or not. "Stop!" That would have become my favorite word in no time. Of that, I am sure.

Something even more major plagued me that eleventh year, though, and continued through my thirteenth. It threw me off in ways I'd never anticipated. A shift I couldn't hide. I couldn't pretend it was something else, like I often did with my period—stomach flu or muscle cramp, for example, or that it would be over quickly. My body began changing in ways that mortified me. My limbs and in-betweens grew in bizarre outcroppings.

When those changes started showing up in November, I kissed the ground beneath my feet, snow and all, knowing I was safe from the ridicule I would have experienced had we remained in Manhattan.

We *Manhatties* had a definite way of reducing the sum of our parts, if the total package did not add up to our liking. We were friends, who didn't know the meaning of walking with mutual respect for each other. Not to ridicule others, even each other, would have been like tossing out an opportunity for fun or advancement. We grew tough exteriors, since the final thunking sound of those horrid boomerangs we threw, generally hit one of us, the one who sailed it off, elsewhere. We learned to suffer in silence, though, to maintain our cool, some better than others. Sometimes, there were complete meltdowns. At least that's how we operated, when I was there. I figured nothing had changed and, perhaps, the pressure had gotten even more intense. Maybe their bodies were changing, too, but I doubted if the changes were as drastic as mine, knowing their parents were all of normal height. The only one of us who wouldn't go low to gain ground was Pearl. I wondered how her body and mind were doing.

No one on the mountain, young or old, seemed to notice the distortion overtaking me, at least at first. Even if they did, not a one commented in a negative way, not even when my neck lengthened into a thin, giraffe-like shoot, which made it difficult to balance my head. Seriously. I took comfort in knowing my curly shoulder-length hair fell softly around my neck as filler, a perfect camouflage until my hair went straight. Yep, believe it! All my curls uncurled! That change came in stages over three months, until one morning every strand on my head lay as flat as spaghetti before it's cooked. Without my bounce-thing in place, I felt like a bonafide pinhead.

Those recessive genes Mother had thought were being passed down to me for a more average height—likely thinking a mid-to-upper-five-foot range—were fading fast into the dominant pool lottery pick. Mother's six-foot stature was dwarfed by Dad's five extra inches. The cards seemed stacked against me; yet I had never figured on that house of cards tumbling down and giving rise to a *Ms. Frankensteina* disaster. What a gene pool that was. I thought I'd be different from my parents in most ways. Turns out Mother had a similar experience, when she was eleven. I guess that's why ten had become an obsession with her; but that didn't matter one bit to me. She should have told me my fate. That's what bothered me. She could have prepared me for this stage of non-proportional limb-shock! After my first growth spurt my hands nearly reached my knees, standing upright. I felt like a four-wheel-drive chimp. That's when I began sitting a lot more and tucking my hands under my thighs, mortified.

The only solace I found was in knowing that no one who loved me saw me as critically flawed. I never let my appreciation for that support show, though. That would have been compounding my awkward life.

"Robyn, you're a lovely girl who's going through a growing spurt. That's all," Mother would say, when I lingered too long under my comforter.

"I agree," Dad chimed in as he passed my room in the hallway on his way to somewhere else. "You'll even out. Look at me. You don't think I got to where I am all at the same time, do you?"

"Gee, thanks, Dad. That's really encouraging. All I have to do is wait a dozen years or so for all my parts to get on the same page, right?"

Half listening, he said, "Right."

"Edward!" Mother said. I peeked out from the edge of my comforter to see her shaking her head and closing her eyes. Mother was quick to extend an unnecessary reprimand and rescue, not knowing I found Dad's responses hilarious. "You're beautiful, right now, and you're only going to get more beautiful. That's my final word on the matter," she said.

Meanwhile, I grew into a freakish semblance of the future me, inch by surrendered-inch, year in and year out, never knowing what area of my body would be hit next. At least I had hopes that nature would eventually triumph, since both my parents were physically pleasing, for the most part, I supposed. I dared not ask about generational relatives.

Samantha slid through those years like a seasoned ballplayer slides into second on a steal, with grace, minimal effort, and fun. Swoosh. Just a bit of dust kicked up and brushed off. I never begrudged her that gift.

Like I said, when we met she was almost thirteen, looking proportionally athletic, perfectly petite, and packaged for whatever activity she chose to undertake, all without an iota of concern about stumbling over her own limbs or staying awake at night with growing pains. After her fourteenth birthday, I had no fears she'd morph suddenly into someone totally different. I felt sure any altercations, if they were to come, well, they'd come unnoticed, like things in nature do. Does anyone ever see a bud unfurl into a flower? No. Not really. One day it's a bud, the next it's a flower.

What made my nose wrinkle was the thought of *that other* change I saw approaching Samantha. It moved like a slow and steady train, scheduled to reach the depot at some upcoming time. It had nothing to do with anything biological, well not directly, as far as I knew, and what I knew wasn't much. I supposed rightly that hormones did play a part in the process, but I chose to call it a *heart matter*, which didn't involve that vital organ in any physical way. It was my opinion that Samantha could avoid, sidestep, refuse to get near, if need be, that train, for sanity's sake—mine.

December hit me hard. I was glad we weren't going anywhere outside our mountain-territory for the holiday. The aches in my shin bones produced almost two more inches of growth that month. My arms hadn't stopped either. They resembled a corn-field's scarecrow, constructed on the fly by a kid in a hurry to get to football practice or something. My favorite pants didn't fit anymore, which wasn't half bad, since Mother and I liked shopping for clothes. She seemed astute in making this trial as fun for me as humanly possible. All the appropriate relatives were called, too. They, already fully aware of my growth potential, were informed that the season was in full swing and all clothing gifts were to be extra long on all possible fronts.

I was thankful I didn't have to put on a swimsuit, shorts, or tank tops, and thought how much harder it would have been to hide my appendages in hot weather, not realizing how I was sticking my head in the sand to think I'd bypass the next two summers, being a robin without feathers.

My legs were sticklike and shapeless; but the scariest part of my jump toward adulthood came with two bumps, which appeared out of nowhere, one on each side of my chest. Instant breasts would have been nice, but my torso didn't have dibs on things coming in easier, I concluded. I just hoped in the midst of the drastic shift that the bud-to-flower mystery would hold true for the chest bumps. Please? Overnight would be good. News flash: It didn't. I did draw a bit of comfort when my first suspicion, regarding my chest turned out to be wrong. It wasn't cancer. That relief passed quickly.

"Robyn, what did you do with the tapestry I had draped over the table in the hallway? I didn't move it. Your father said he hasn't touched it. It had to be you, unless you're hiding a stranger in your room."

"It was me," I said.

"You're getting into décor splashes?"

"No, I'm eliminating my waves of nausea."

"Robyn, are you aware that your conversation is lacking clarity?"

"Mother," I said, "I can't look at myself in the full-length mirror anymore. I put it in the closet. The tapestry is hanging over it, just in case."

Mother tried not to smile, but I knew one lay across her face as she walked away. I knew it, just as she knew how my eyes rolled upward in years past, when my backside was all she could see leaving a room after we had a disagreement.

She'd say, "Get that facial attitude straightened up, young lady!" That night I felt like saying, "Get that smile off your face, old lady!" But, it sounded rather lame, so I let it go. I was tired of lame.

It was at that juncture I knew my worst enemy was going to be me, now and forever. Amen. I had to let up on the attitude stuff, at least try to find some enjoyable places within the whirlwind. If I had held to the belief, then, that I was under construction by a divine being who loved me, perhaps those awkward years would have been transformed into an accepting surrender. But I fought the lack of control I felt over my own life. It wasn't in my nature to submit. It's not in humanity's nature, period, but it never occurred to me that was the reason we needed another nature at that time, one to hang over ours like a rich, colored tapestry.

Even though the breadcrumbs Samantha put on the paths we walked together in those years stretched all the way to heaven, I could not retrieve them. I watched her toss them before me. I even had some inkling as to where they would lead me. I mean Samantha put them there after all. I imagined myself picking them up, as I followed her trail, but I was too preoccupied creating my own destiny, too focused on me, and what I wanted to pick them up. I did catch most of them on the reels of tape I'd collected, as a consolation prize to myself. I packaged them up neatly on polyester ribbons and stored them in that big box I shoved under my bed. I even stuffed some in my shirt pocket near my heart, but at the time of our movements on the mountain, most morsels ended up being neglected by my wandering mind and desires.

I am thankful they weren't entirely lost on the wayside, though. They weren't hoisted away on the darkened wingspan of blackbirds, never to be found again. They remained in my possession, waiting for my surrender. Forgive me for taking so long to understand the way of life, Samantha. My body wasn't the only part of me that needed to grow.

JONQUILS IN GOOD EARTH

Samantha knew. She knew Scott's heart. I often wondered what she thought of me in those years when I avoided him or thrust verbal lances his way whenever the itch to be cruel surfaced. I felt like King Saul, spear always at the ready and aimed at David. Samantha never sided with me against Scott, just the way Jonathan never joined his father's side against his friend, David. She never smiled at my barbs, not once, even when I applied thick layers of humor over them. She could tell.

The Farley family stayed off my radar for obvious reasons in those early years, but living there after a while, one eventually begins hearing things, lots of things. Scott and his parents lived off that lizard-leg-road where I first saw him, maneuvering his way down with Samantha. She'd often ride her bike to fetch him for one adventure or another. Approaching 'the good earth' began one year after she met him at an annual ice cream social. Families took turns hosting them on their property. When Scott was six, it was the Farley's turn. Samantha's sixth followed on his heels. That's the first year Ma allowed her to ride her bike "ta visit that kindly boy, Scott."

Scott's father, Jeb, entered the mountain community as a

single, itinerant preacher a year before he put money down on the lizard-leg property. He rode a horse named Bits in and out of various pockets of mountain communities that didn't have a local church. Our mountain was one of his stops. The second time in our area his eyes fell upon a delicate young woman, a grown child with white, long hair, and amber eyes that slanted upwards like a wide-eyed kitten's. People say he was smitten to the quick in a second and wasted no time asking her Pa for her hand in marriage. Her Pa put a condition on Jeb. Well, two. He had to wait until Dawn turned sixteen and, when he did set up a home for her, it had to be a short horse ride from her "upbringin' family." Jeb agreed; he was a man of his word and he made good on his promise.

In those seventeen months young Jeb, only nineteen himself, set to work building a small log home and installing sturdy fencing in a clearing alongside an old barn. The existing structure had stood on the land long before Ma could recollect. He set to replacing the missing or rotting boards and reconstructing a proper door as diligently as he had tackled all the other work in his life, "as unto the Lord," folks said.

He planned to use the fenced off area for a pig farm venture, to earn a living up in those foothills, since preaching brought nothing in but pocket change. He dreamed of constructing a small church, one day, to house and guide the good people of the mountain in their spiritual growth. The latter never materialized, but pig sales flourished and Jeb built an additional room onto the little house after marrying Dawn.

She became pregnant eight months after saying her vows and carried the baby boy full term; but it was a stillborn child, dead in the midwife's arms after delivery. Dawn held him for an hour, not wanting to let go. Jeb made a marker for the boy and etched his name on it, Samuel.

The young girl never quite got over that affliction on her soul. She couldn't understand how God could request such a thing from a mother, especially a firstborn; and she spoke those words often to Jeb. He never responded, knowing she didn't want theology. She wanted comfort, so he put his arms around her and drew her close to his side during those days. She resented him, however, for not providing an answer, being a man of God and all, even while lying still in his arms. If he had done the opposite, spoken only theology, she still would have resented him. It was her own soul's pain that pulled her into such a state of malcontent; it had nothing to do with Jeb. Deep down she knew it, but couldn't overcome it.

The next year Dawn conceived, again, and delivered a healthy boy in August. They called him, Scott, after Jeb's grandfather in Richmond. When Scott was five months old, his mother was caught in a freezing rain while walking home from visiting a church friend. Jeb had been called to a funeral in a nearby community and the friend had no transportation. She urged Dawn to spend the night, but she insisted all would be well and left, only to discover the air had grown colder. A northerly wind dropped from the mountain in brisk, penetrating spurts. An icy rain formed and slapped against her pale flesh. She took off her wool coat and tucked it completely over her son to shield him from the violent pelts. He lay against the warmth of her chest, content and unharmed. When she entered the cabin, still smelling of fresh pine from the new addition, she lay Scott in his crib, removed her wet sweater and cotton dress, donned flannel pajamas and curled up under her covers to chase away the chill that had found access to her bones. As she fell asleep her lips remained deep purple for some time.

Dawn Lucille died four weeks later of pneumonia. Her 'upbringing family' blamed Jeb for her demise, said all sorts of things that made no sense, whatsoever. Ma Sticker told me such. Ma never gossiped, but she held a sorry eye against Dawn's Pa, who cast those surly remarks across the mountain. Ma said, "People can be mean, when they be hurtin'." I lowered my head, knowing all too well that her words were true.

The impact of having to care for a newborn, enduring his wife's death, and the accusations of his father-in-law sent Jeb into a tailspin. He took to drinking the cooking sherry Dawn had put above the cook stove, and then he started buying a bottle of whiskey each time he went to Elkins. Scott grew up well loved by a functioning alcoholic his first three years. He was no worse for the experience, since Jeb's heart was a kind one, even though lost in pain. Perhaps it had marked him, though, someone once said—by forming a more sensitive and compassionate side in him.

Three months before the third anniversary of Dawn's death, an old friend of Jeb's family, Prudence, paid a visit. When she saw the state of their living conditions, it grieved her. She set her focus on scrubbing, and rubbing, and tidying loose ends without a word of chastisement on her lips. She took lodging in Elkins and every morning returned with the proper material for the day's chores; fabric for temporary curtains; pine soap for the floors; steel wool to scour the cookstove; and something other than pork to eat.

Honest folks whispered, "Brother Jeb would be a fool to pass up askin' that carin' 'n' sensible woman to marry 'im," which he did, proving he was no fool. Prudence essentially raised Scott and instilled godly qualities into his heart. He watched her minister to his Pa and him, day-in-and-out, without ever uttering a cross word or complaint. Within a year Jeb had laid the drink aside and never picked it up again. He began preaching in the open air in spring and summer and teaching serious students in his home in the colder months. They all huddled near the burning hearth, where Prudence hung a pot of soup to boil at the start of the study, and they all ate at the end. Scott heard every word of the lively discourses, while resting in his new mother's lap.

It was a happy family, gentle and rich in mercy and grace. Scott seemed to carry that spirit as naturally as his mother's smile. It was no wonder Samantha was drawn to him. He embodied a soul that complemented hers in every particular. I think I must have known it all along, which is what infuriated me the most. I had no chance of being first in her life. Even during that initial year when I thought I was her best friend, I probably wasn't; and I certainly fell short of occupying that spot in her heart after I entered my bitter stage. That year, however, I did learn there's no room for a competitive spirit in relationships, no matter the angle from which you enter them. There's room for everyone to receive and give. I learned it in theory, but something kept me from making it walk on two legs.

Ma Sticker showed me a poem Scott had given her after her miscarriage—the loss Samantha vaguely recalled, when we walked among the dragonflies. Ma wasn't sure how Scott knew, other than figuring, like the other person I'd mentioned, that his first three years made him keenly aware of unspoken feelings. Then she paused and said, "Unless he was just endowed with it." Either way, he had observed Ma's sorrow, and probably the tummy that had decreased in size without a baby to explain it. Scott was seven when he wrote it.

> *Did a child make the print,*
> *A child in the snow?*
> *Or did a holy one come down*
> *To make the dint,*
> *To lie down, still and low?*
>
> *Then when human eyes turned 'way,*
> *And left them all alone,*
> *Did they lift and play together,*
> *Making silhouettes all day,*
> *Singing to the ungrown?*
>
> *"The spring is gone,*
> *The fall is past,*

Winter's in the air.
Child up to heaven,
Play with me there."

When ma slipped that poem into my view, I was eighteen. I wept and placed my face in the same sleeved-crook of her arm that had held Samantha's head, when she wept those many years before after we left Bessie's home. We can do nothing more than weep for lost moments, or for our ignorant refusal to love someone, like I had Scott.

AN INTERLOPER

*E*veryone knew about the Ryan ST-A. It had been the talk of the mountain when it appeared in Old Man Gunther's potato field back in the summer of 1936, when Gunther was but a boy. The pilot had been a young man. Information filtered back slowly about the lad, Michael Fitzgerald. He was the only child of a married steel tycoon. Both parents were renowned philanthropists. Reports claimed a jolt to his brain upon impact caused him to fall into unconsciousness, and then death followed soon afterwards from internal bleeding. "Too much pressure under the skull," they said. "No proper care to relieve it." Apparently his body had just stopped working in that moment, just the way the Ryan had stopped functioning, unexpectedly. One could say there were two crashes that day.

The fact that the ditching hadn't even been noticed when it happened, troubled many. It occurred at the rear of Gunther's field. Some motorists finally spied the plane. They parked their car and crossed the isolated road to take a closer look at the oddity. When the couple saw the young man, the woman gasped, covering her mouth, and the man shook his head for the pity of it all.

The pilot appeared beautifully normal, except for two trickles of dried blood that ran from his right nostril and ear. The couple marveled at his cold loveliness, and held each other, having been made suddenly aware of the fragility that travels alongside those living life out upon this earth. Without those slight traces of mishap, he would have looked like a weary sojourner, taking a needed rest. "He looked like he was a'sleepin'. His skin, white like chiseled alabaster. Such a prudy young man," the woman muttered, head lowered as she recalled the image.

The plane, itself, had been ditched perfectly—not as in a perfect landing, but all in one piece and virtually without a scratch on it. There was a mystery surrounding it, as to how it sat in that field, stately and shiny and altogether wonderful in appearance, just as its pilot; but when stories surrounding it broke, ones written on site, experts began piecing the information together, and three facts emerged. First, they learned that the Ryan ST-A was an aerobatic, lightweight craft. Secondly, it turned out, Gunther's Pa had sunk two large, triangular-shaped cement blocks, embedded with D-rings into that field to tether his goats, decades past. The blocks had been camouflaged from the air by the over-growth, and the Ryan cruised straight toward them, according to what the reporters noted.

The young pilot had ditched with gears down, without choice, since down was the standard position for gears on the Ryan. Spec-ulation was, the plane flipped when its wheels hit the angled incline at a high-speed glide, resulting in a complete somersault. It must have been a perfect circle of grace, for everything on the plane remained intact; and young Fitzgerald's head hit nothing hard or sharp, since there were no contusions. A possible reason: the cockpit was generously and painstakingly trimmed in thick red leather.

The third clue put all the locals' minds to rest. It's why folks came to think of it as a flipping accident, rather than a plane crash. These words did it, "the matted grass, showing the entry tracks leading straight toward the blocks." Gunther's field had revealed a forty-some-odd-foot-swath of compressed or uprooted grass and slightly upturned earth, which speed-producing-friction could carve into the earth. It lay in front of the triangular cement structures, but after the structures, nothing. The earth lay undisrupted beyond the cement tethers for around seventy-five yards. That space is where the plane lost touch with earth and reentered the air, just long enough for grace to appear then fade away. They probably noticed how the Ryan's landing gears had been thrust deeply into the soft, rain-soaked soil, too, obviously from direct impact. Gravity is merciless, when objects or people fall without a safety net.

Even though light for an airplane, the nearly 1,600 pounds of metal hit hard. I can only imagine the exhilaration the young man must have felt as he spun forty to fifty feet above the ground, much as he had in the higher altitudes, like a silver swallow, twisting and turning with ease. His mind probably grappled with the thought that he had gained an upper hand on the mishap and would not, in the final tally, crash into the copse of trees ahead of him, which is probably what he thought when he first put down. I doubt he even considered the possibility of death in those brief moments before his craft leveled off and began to descend—right before it slammed into the solid field and his neck snapped or his brain hit his skull with equal force, if he were still alive. I remember asking myself, when I heard the story, did people think that particular part, the suddenness part, merited a slice of blessing over the whole thing? I couldn't find a positive takeaway on the tragedy and thought people who did were only fooling themselves. Another thing I wondered, did his undoing happen as soon as the Ryan's wheels hit the cement tethers? I think storytellers liked imagining he had more time for his hopes to surface. It gave everyone room to breathe. It allowed Michael Fitzgerald those extra seconds of grace in their minds, something everyone wanted.

The tragic tale grew into a legend during the '40s, when new details of the young man surfaced. People talked about it, incessantly, as a way to forget the war that was swallowing up other young pilots from their communities, near and far. Some considered the Ryan a bad omen. They wanted Gunther to dispose of it —not even use its part for the war efforts. Others shooed away such fears, as nonsense; but the senior John Gunther would never release the goldmine that fell into his lap. He recognized when an ace-up-the-sleeve appeared in his field. It bore perennial fruit. That had become his positive takeaway on the tragedy.

The pilot's background eventually revealed more details about his family. Those who regarded the Ryan's presence as a charm, and those who saw it as a curse had to lay their opinions down at the dividing line of Gunther's property, for that *is* where it landed; and Gunther claimed it, even before he legally had permission to do so.

The history of the aircraft swelled and shrunk, depending on who told the story. A reliable, levelheaded source told us it had been a high school graduation gift from the boy's parents. They had watched their son fly toy planes for years, engines powered solely by the sputtering motor of his flapping lips and vocal cords. He pushed himself to carry all his planes to their charted destinations, which pleased his parents, since most of the flights were aided by his legs, scurrying across wide expanses of lawn. With a balsa plane firmly anchored in his hand and his arm extended and positioned over his head, his mother knew every step he ran helped boost the strength of his smaller right leg, weakened from Polio when two.

The boy would fold and pitch countless paper planes all over the house's interior, too, especially from the landing over the winding staircase, often hitting his mother's flowers in the crystal vase perched sweetly on the entryway's marble table, for which she mildly scolded him; however seeing him sail down the stairs to retrieve those planes, and then run back up, again, arms full of future flights, fueled the more lenient side of her heart.

Outside, the youth built cockpits from fruit crates he begged his father to bring home, gluing on buttons for control gauges and using a baseball bat his father sawed short as a control stick. There were various wires he rigged for effect, shiny pots in various places, too, for the sun to bounce off and catch his eye, allowing him to feel as if he were in motion. He seated himself on cushions he confiscated from the back porch couch, knowing the sofa cushion, in the family room, were off limits. Something he learned through displeasing his mother, once.

Eventually, his parents splurged after realizing the boy's passion would not subside. They bought him an authentic leather bomber jacket and flying cap, goggles, and a red silk scarf when he was thirteen. Before his high school graduation they signed him up for flight instructions, which he faithfully completed, earning the seal of the highest standing. His parents thought it a novel idea to own a family plane with their own family pilot, so naturally, the Pittsburg socialites' next move was to purchase an aircraft and build a runway on their property for Michael. Aside from being practical in their approach, the love they held for their son wanted nothing more than to please him; and what pleased him most was the handsome and playful Ryan ST-A.

We never figure on the thing not figured on, being the thing that doesn't figure in, or work out. Those things arrive incognito and get entangled into the orderly elements we do figure into the equation. That's how the Ryan became a mountain tale, weed-locked and anchored deep into the earth. "Lookie see, over yonder!" A bit of history rendered, as heads turned towards it in those initial years, still all shiny and maintained well; people stared shocked or saddened, tsk-tsked, bit their lip, then cast their eyes elsewhere, signaling to the more sedentary observer that it was time to move on with their day.

But when Scott Farley saw the weather-beaten aircraft, his eyes pictured it flying, not destined to be a stationary marker, commemorating a death in perpetuity. Scott saw it as an air-worthy craft in need of redemption. The Fitzgeralds' desire was conveyed simply to the senior Gunther: "Maintain the Ryan as a memorial to our son." They never wanted to see it again, but they'd send someone to inspect it, once a year. In return for a good report, they paid the elder Gunther a nice sum of cold hard cash. John Gunther kept his word for over forty years, until his death. He left his son, the new Old Man Gunther, with the responsibility of the Ryan; but that man rarely stood in its shadow in the far off field, let alone bother with its upkeep. Inspections ceased around the time of Gunther Senior's death. Fact is, both Fitzgeralds had died and were buried in the earth near their son's gravesite, even before the elder Gunther died. Old Man Gunther Junior continued getting and pocketing what turned into checks with a formal statement of gratitude. Those checks came regularly from the Fitzgeralds' estate for five more years. Then they stopped, too.

Periodically, as a younger child Scott would scamper near the Gunther property, just to delight in something as grand as the Ryan. As he got older, his boldness grew. One year in late August he came alongside it and peeked into the cockpit. Nothing was the same after that brush with fate. He had just turned fourteen. Samantha would be fourteen the next month; and I had turned eleven the month prior. We were all over the map in our desires and growth, and what we thought of the Ryan.

That fall Scott began approaching Mr. Gunther, first by cleaning up the words that came before his surname. "Mister, mister, mister. . ." he muttered as he approached his house, ". . . not Old Man! Mister!"

"Mr. Gunther," he said aloud in an assured voice, as the recognizable form shuffled toward the front screen door. Scott put on his best smile and drew closer. Flies in various stages of decay were splattered on the screen door and left to drop onto the threshold inside. Scott wondered why all the flies were on that side of the screen and not outside where he stood; then he wondered if Old Man Gunther were stepping into any crunchy corpses, when he drew close enough for his nose to hit the meshed wire. He quickly laid those thoughts aside.

"Yeah," the man inside said, scratching chest hairs under a threadbare, sleeveless undershirt that hung like a wet paper towel over him.

"Sir, I come to talk to ya 'bout the Ryan."

"What 'bout it?" he asked.

"I wondered if'n I can take it off your hands, sir."

"Not on my hands. On my land. Not botherin' me none. Just sittin' where it's been sittin' since I was a bit of a boy, younger 'n you."

"Yes, sir, I know. I was just wonderin' if'n you'd like that field opened up, sometime soon. Maybe planted even. I can do that for you, sir. I could haul off the Ryan, too, and plow your field and plant it, if'n that's amenable."

"Not amenable. Now, gid' off w'ya."

It went on that way with slight variations for months. Scott sucked in courage; laid out the benefits of his plan; offered new appeals, like how great it would be if tourists "stopped pokin' 'round your field," actually parking and getting out on his road, as they drove by in their huge RVs, making more potholes, which were harder on his own truck's suspension. It was true, the patch of road that bordered Gunther's property had more potholes than anywhere else, but no one connected the dots back to the Ryan. Scott created that image right before knocking, because *it could be true, if'n one considered it a bit more.*

That next summer, a month before Scott turned fifteen, Mr. Gunther agreed on the deal. He wanted a field of strawberries planted next spring, and not only planted, but harvested too. Scott quickly replied, "Deal," and then, he set to figuring out how to haul the Ryan over the terrain to the barn his Paw said he could use, "if'n it don't upset the pigs." That occupied his thoughts until the week before he'd planned to plant Mr. Gunther's field. That's when he'd move the Ryan, and invited Samantha and me to *the grand event*—his words.

I asked Dad to buy a bottle of sparkling cider for me to take, so that it would seem as if I were in a celebratory mood. In my gut I still looked at Scott sideways, when it came to Samantha. It's not like I thought my friends shouldn't have other friends. The *Manhatties* and I equaled five—a five-pointed star, lighting up the city, is how we saw ourselves. We were an undisputed team. Maybe, it had more to do with the fact that he wasn't like anyone I'd ever known, not even Samantha. For one, he was a boy; and something else troubled me, but I wasn't sure why.

It was this: There was a solid conviction of reliability anchored to his bones. Samantha had it, too, but not in the same way. She felt more malleable to me, open to ideas and new thoughts, sort of like a willow tree, while Scott was more like an oak. Maybe, it was because I couldn't compete with the magnetism he created, when he stood near her. I feared that mutual attraction, slowly brewing between them, drawing them ever closer until whatever space someone else could occupy was eliminated. Just try pulling powerful magnets apart, and you'll get the picture.

Maybe, it wasn't *just* that he was a boy, but a very handsome one, and he already knew he was Samantha's boy, just like he knew the Ryan was his plane. I envied him for the certainty he possessed.

THE BURLY BEAR

"*Robyn*," Samantha said in a distant voice, as we walked in the chilled stillness of a late October afternoon. We were making our way back to her house after gathering dry kindling for the cook stove, when a mist began to rise.

"Yeah," I said.

"What would you do, if'n a burly bear with a twinkle in its eye came ramblin' up to you, unexpected like? Would you look it in the eyes; play dead; or run faster than you thought you could?"

"Gosh," I said. "For real? I mean, is there a right answer here?" I asked, while looking around just in case and sucking harder on my big jawbreaker. I waited for Samantha to give me a clue. When she didn't, I said, "How big's the twinkle?"

"Just the tip of a twinkle," Samantha whispered, as if not wanting to wake the bear.

I remember stopping to watch her. She moved slowly forward. I'd only seen her that pensive once before, when walking down the mountain after leaving Bessie.

"Is Bessie Jane okay?" I asked, suddenly.

"I 'spect so. Why? Did you hear somethin' I didn't?"

"Nope. Just wondered."

Her slender form, erect and sure cast a stunted shadow that appeared, then vanished in quick spurts as the sun's rays poked through various clouds and peepholes in the foliage, trying to pierce and overcome the gray patches of mist that followed us. I felt a chilling sensation form under my skin, as the gray form jumped into view near her, then thrust itself flatly onto the decaying debris of fall, only to rise up and repeat the grotesque dance, once again.

"Samantha!" I called out in anxious appeal, as if my voice could snatch her up and disconnect her from the antics of her own shadow and thoughts. She stopped in a shaded area. I spit out the jawbreaker, wanting my voice unhindered if I needed it, if Samantha needed it. Stepping to her side I asked, "What's this bear stuff all about?"

"Oh, nothin', I s'pose," she said looking down at her feet. "At least nothin' I can rightly think to mention. It just sort of wanted to be asked."

"So, there's nothing wrong, and you're okay?" I asked.

"If'n I ain't, I will be. If'n I will be, I am. Just, sometimes . . . Oh, it's nothin'." She turned toward me and said, "Turnin' cold, ain't it."

"Uh huh," I said, looking straight into her eyes. "It is." She didn't seem to see me.

In those upcoming months, Samantha and I spent more time together. Scott was in the planning and preparation stages of figuring out the ways and means to transport the Ryan to his parents' property, and then into the barn, where he'd restore it. Samantha and Scott saw little of each other that fall and winter. That night I had wondered if she missed him in a way she hadn't previously thought she could. I already knew Samantha never had to deal with much separation. Bessie was one thing, but day-in-day-out people, they could hit home even harder.

I didn't want to focus on Scott or the possibility of the two of them drawing closer in mind or heart, so I welcomed those days when their activities didn't mesh. I liked thinking of Scott as only having eyes for the Ryan, but always followed that thought up with one of my self-corrections, knowing the misguided declaration was a mere bandaid I placed over the inevitable. I couldn't deny or hide the actual sense I felt—the one Scott had already scripted.

I knew Scott had his priorities straight. The Ryan didn't amount to a relational division. It was a momentary diversion, and he'd use it, somehow, to get closer to her. I knew it. I dreaded it. For Scott the path always led back to Samantha; but Samantha was becoming harder for me to read, and that produced feelings of insecurity in me. Let's not forget, my own general state of dissatisfaction still existed. My body, my longings, and my misplaced sense of being were never out of reach. I was starting to wonder about life in general. It seemed too random, too full of tension and angst. I began to sense that control was key, but I wasn't sure, yet, how to approach that evasive concept.

It wasn't until one early spring day, when crusted-over mounds of snow still clung to places the sun couldn't reach that two strips of plowed snow began looking sinister to me. They lay along the road's shoulders, all dirtied and black with cinder. When they started melting and diminishing in size they took on the appearance of dark snakes to me, curling their way up to Gunther's property. That's the day I saw something else, too—the twinkle.

I'd never seen it flash between their eyes before then. It was foreign to me, but that day it became too obvious to miss. Scott and Samantha seemed unimaginably pleased with it. I recognized it in that split second as the overture Samantha had seen in Scott's eyes, the burly bear come-to-life, the one Samantha entertained and considered in earnest that afternoon in the woods. I knew it involved Scott, yet it wasn't Samantha's bear that startled her. Her bear was known territory. It was the twinkle she'd never entertained. The form, the bear, merely held the twinkle. She wasn't unsure or afraid of the bear. No. Her bear was Scott. What she contemplated and was hesitant to entertain was another life. That was new ground. At least it had been.

It was my bear, however, that startled me most. I stared it down for a brief second, as it followed closely on the heels of Samantha's bear. I had hoped it would never show its face to me, but there it stood, tall, broad, its head rolling back in a defiant roar. Its teeth, like an opened cage, surrounded its roar and equaled the terror found in its protruding claws. Neither of us saw that bear coming towards me, but there it stood. Had I not given it cause to be there, it might not have come for me. There was no reason for Samantha to have invited it in. I wasn't in her field of vision. I was like the shadow, bouncing along near her side, there, and then not. That was the nature of my bear until that moment, a shadow that came and left. When that twinkling linked their hearts in an unspoken bond, that's when my bear came to life. It became flesh and bone, mostly fierce muscle. I invited it in. How unthinkable!

Samantha, you asked me what I'd do, if I ever met up with the burly bear. I know, now, you were asking me to help you figure out your own heart, as if I could. As impossible as it was for you that day, it was doubly impossible for me, especially after my bear appeared; and, your question became my question, too, because I loved you.

I sensed, even then, I wouldn't fit. I wouldn't fit, just like I wasn't fitting in my own body, which, by the way, any intelligent bear would have refused to consider as worth its effort to pursue as food, mostly bones, large bones and little flesh. It had to be obvious that I couldn't fit into my own head in ways that were good for me. Hadn't you noticed? I recall vividly how self-loathing thoughts kicked in and filled up those years. I avoided looking at the desperation I felt in losing your friendship. I wasted countless slivers of time, allowing those lost days to consume me in lies. I could have sucked up the pain, I suppose, created a side story and made an effort to remain as close to you as our previous year had been; but I absolutely refused to be a part of a quirky love triangle, to compete for your attention. So, I began letting go of you.

Would I look into the bear's eyes? Of course I would, because they'd reflect your eyes. At least I thought they would, since you were always in the picture. Would I play dead? I had to. Would I run? Eventually. I tried all three. Nothing worked.

Samantha and I accompanied Scott several more times in March to chop down the old, woody vines and tendrils, securing the Ryan to the earth. We cleared the matted, overgrown grasses around its wheels and attacked the path that led to the road. Finally, we stomped and trampled down the disrupted ground, making a solid pathway for the Ryan to move over it, unhindered, once again.

Jeb Farley and Samantha's Pa had come by twice to help; once when unearthing the thatched grass, leaving us to stomp for hours, and again, when we hauled up three truckloads of gravel to lay down upon the flattened clearing. Stomping turned out to be fun, which redeemed that day for me, a bit. It's hard to emit twinkles, when engaging the earth so vigorously.

Scott promised to pick every last piece of gravel up from the field before planting the strawberries, but Old Man Gunther liked the feel of it. Said he could tote a lawn chair out and sit there in the midst of his pretty red berries after the sun had been denied access to his house from the mountain's shadow. It seemed, as time went by, that Scott could do no wrong in Mr. Gunther's eyes.

And, then the day came to tow the prize out of its graveyard. Unwrapped, like Lazarus after his resurrection, the Ryan was given a second chance by two souls who saw more than its wreckage. Yes, Samantha had begun a love affair with the noble, downed wings, too. She thought it "the cutest form to ever surround a motor." I suppose I did appreciate its compact and elegant design, once it got polished up, but not then, not at first. Everything Scott liked, Samantha seemed to like instantly, which upset me and made me want to dislike whatever Scott liked. The Ryan was at the top of that list. In my mind Samantha would never be put on that list, which meant Scott had to go. I had no clue how that would come about.

I tagged along at first on their Ryan venture, just to monitor Scott's contacts with Samantha. I believed he couldn't like me, since I had been rude to him far too long. That made me suspicious of how Samantha would regard his dislikes, especially the one I conjured up concerning me. If they rubbed off on her, as much as his likes did, I'd be in trouble. At least that's what I surmised. I had to track the situation, monitor it, and warn her if I saw it tilting off balance. Self-preservation runs high in the Thomas family. I wondered, then, if that was why we'd all grown so tall, and then I wondered if that's where our tendency to control came in.

The towing took place, one early evening in late March. Scott, mounted high on his Pa's tractor with Samantha waving wildly in the open cockpit, rolled into view. A silver dollar moon loomed large in the backdrop. It rested there like a giant white gumball on the mountain. Samantha's black hair tossed as she moved with glee. The moon captured every strand, etching them across its fat face. I hated to admit it, but I couldn't have felt more impressed with them and the whole project they were undertaking. That image stuck firm and evolved into a reference point for my real life hero-heroine fantasies. A thought trickled in and accompanied the image. It wouldn't leave my head, like a song you don't want to sing, but do, again and again. It ran unrestrained. I couldn't stop it. Yes! There it was. Here it is. I thought they outshone Hollywood's brightest stars. Those two occupied center stage, right before me. I wanted both the image and thought out of my head, because it produced a constant source of depression and jealousy in my soul. It remained, however, since a part of my soul knew it was too perfect to trash.

Scott parked the Ryan in the barn he had rearranged. Maw had raked and swept it clean in anticipation of its arrival, and then

Scott walked away from his prize. He set out to work Gunther's field the next week, once the weather warmed some. He stuck to his promise of preparing and planting in the spring in spite of the all-consuming itch to begin work on the Wes-Ginny, the name he and Samantha had chosen for the Ryan in honor of the state that held claim on her for so long.

Was I consulted on the name? Nope. I wasn't. It wasn't as if the newly written script for their movie with the moon shot included me. I really wasn't in that inner circle of intimacy. I was just an 'extra' the studio hired for a few shots in a budding teen romance; and I wasn't going to get a paycheck, only an exit ticket, as the movie progressed. Eventually, Wes became Scott, and Ginny, Samantha, in their coded language. That truly irked me. I guessed I was the hyphen.

Once Gunther's field had been completed, plowed, planted, and supplied with drip irrigation, Scott began looking over the engine, what I dubbed the 'WGI,' or the 'Dub-Gone-It' to see what he could see. Trouble shooting the engine would come first, and then the bodywork. Those were his plans.

Scott was about to begin dismantling the engine in June. He started his look-see inspection of possible parts, jotting down names in his grease-stained journal; but something happened before he could get his hands on it. His mother, Prudence, became dizzy and nauseous. At first she thought she had the flu, but the odd feeling persisted, without a fever. Then her ears started ringing and her head ached. When she took to her bed Scott's plans changed overnight. All the cash he had saved for new or used parts and put into a metal box he dropped under a loose floorboard in his bedroom, he gave to his Pa. His words, "Whatever she needs. I got the money, Pa."

"But that's earmarked for the Ryan, son."

"I know, Pa. Don't fret 'bout that. Maw needs help, now. The Ryan can wait. She comes 'fore 'nythin' else. Right?"

His Pa wept with pride, humbled by the love he witnessed in

his boy. "It's good for a man to be feelin' what you're bringin' out in my heart, Scott," he said. "Thank you, son. God's gettin' the glory. Surely is." The two men embraced.

The work on Wes-Ginny was delayed a good portion of that next year; but, the other labor of love, the one I dreaded, accelerated. Had I eyes to see, I might have recorded a tribute to the purest possible expression of that state of being, love, but I stood in the midst of it as a slighted player. My reality, visions, and discoveries didn't line up with the story God knew existed apart from me.

I could gloss over the 'me' of those years, leave myself out of the picture entirely, refashion history to focus only on the good parts that happened; but in leaving out my foibles and the stark elements of my role as foil, I'd be contributing to a type of lie. Such a lie could not be tolerated, because Samantha stood squarely in front of my face and wouldn't back down. "Not tellin' the whole truth is the same as lyin'," she said, once. That one rubbed me the wrong way, but I got it.

Since I know what I thought in those days, and what she thought, I'm going for truth and placing myself onto a stack of stubborn donkeys with every other 'ass' found in some literary, historical, or film archive. Check it out. I'll be there somewhere. I've learned it's the honest tales (no pun intended) about self that lift truth from the dust, because when pride decreases, pain heals, shame is transformed into glory, and truth becomes the rising star. But that came later. I was definitely just entering my Eeyore stage.

What happened, first, was summer. It burst into a wider scenario of 'Samantha possibilities,' since Scott's thoughts were focused on his maw. Doors of adventurous opportunities flung open before me. *Goodbye, Scott, old boy. You're a good boy, Scott,* I thought. In my excitement I ran all the way up to Samantha's cabin on a late June morning. Richard greeted me.

"I've come to see Samantha, Richard!" I declared, out of breath.

"Did you run up here?" he asked, and then added, "She's not here."

My heart sank. "Let me guess. She's at Scott's."

"Yep. Helpin' with stuff, while his maw is down."

"Of course she is," is all I could say.

"Ya wanna come in?"

"No, I need to run back home," I said.

Richard laughed. "Why all the runnin'?" he asked.

"Why not," I said, without even thinking. Truth is I don't recall even seeing Richard. That's how blindness works.

I turned and slowly jogged back down. Since the day was young, I decided to make my way to Scott's, just because. Once there, I didn't knock or seek anyone out. Everything lay still in silence, except for an occasional pig squeal or trill of a songbird. I wasn't paying particular attention to nature that morning, though. Nancy Drew had surfaced.

I peered through a red-trimmed window on the north side of the Farley cabin, having avoided loose porch planks that might have squeaked out my presence. The white muslin curtains were pulled back and a clear view of Samantha lay before my eyes. I tensed up. I realized I had never spied on her before. It felt wrong. I had spied on friends in Manhattan, like at the library. The trickier and more exciting kind were the 'street-to-interior' ones. That's following someone from store to store, unawares. That spelled sheer fun and I delighted in those ventures; but I never spied in such a personal way, through the window of someone's home.

I watched as Samantha hand-dried a bowl and piled it atop others on a shelf. Several pork chops lay on the counter near two plates, one contained raw eggs that had been whisked and the other, some sort of fine bread crumb. A skillet was heating on the stovetop. Samantha wiped her hands and prepared the chops for the pan—dip, pat, sizzle. Repeat and repeat. I turned away and sighed. "What a wasted day," I said under my breath.

I tried her cabin again the next day. That time I came prepared with an invitation for a movie and sleepover. Richard answered the door, again.

"Gone again?" I grumbled.

"Yep, same as yesterday. You best resign yourself to it bein' a thing, Robyn. Samantha's got Ma's full approval to help out. Ma's even pickin' up a lot of her chores, and tossin' others onto Jason. Mrs. Farley's feelin' poorly, and Mr. Farley is rightly concerned, 'specially considerin' his painful loss, while back. But," he finally said, "I'm thinkin' Samantha would like seein' ya. Go visit her."

"Okay, Richard," I said—once again, not having heard anything he said past the first six syllables.

"Sure ya don't wanna come in for some of Ma's cookies, first?"

"Cookies? I'm not in the mood," I said in a daze. I'm sure that red-blooded boy wondered what kind of mood someone had to be in NOT to want to take hold of some freshly baked cookies.

When I arrived home, I slumped down into the couch, plopped the throw pillow over my head, and anchored it with my arms. I wished it had worked in shutting out the world, since it felt that way to me under its cozy darkness. Fat chance! Mother zoomed in on me, and alarms went off in her head.

"Robyn," she said. "I had an idea the other day and wanted to pass it by you. You know the front-facing room off the mudroom that no one could figure out what it was used for, originally?"

"Umhmm," I muttered.

"Well, I thought, I would turn that into an art studio, more specifically a sculpting studio with a front-loading gas kiln."

"Okay," I muttered.

"For you!" she said.

"For me! What do I know about sculpting? Mother, I don't want to sculpt. I don't need to sculpt. I'm not going to sculpt."

"I'm doing it, and you're going to sculpt until you figure out what it is you do like doing."

"I like doing things with Samantha."

"And, how's that working out for you, lately, Robyn?"

"That's not fair, Mother. Not fair at all!" I said, as I stormed out the room and threw my useless pillow onto the table.

The 'sculpting studio' opened in August. I, being deemed a thirteen-year-old sculptress-in-the-making, was required to heed the art teacher Mother had employed for the entire month, the esteemed Ms. Archer from the junior college in Elkins. She actually moved into our home to avoid the long commute. Mother's clever ideas never stopped. I spent most of my waking hours with her, listening to her go on and on in the areas of her expertise, which was good, because I didn't have to think of Scott's sixteenth birthday picnic with just Samantha in attendance.

I caught about half of what she said, which left me wondering how half-knowledge worked when firing up a kiln. Would clay pieces that weren't hollowed out properly explode? I imagined a smattering of epic proportions, making the interior of the kiln take on the appearance of a flat rock covered in sea barnacles. I wondered what would happen if I set the clay directly on the floor, too; but I left those thoughts behind after Archer packed her bags and moved out on the first of September. That was my cue to get down to business. I had to produce busts, full figures, modern art pieces, or whatever my heart desired, as long as it resembled statuary. My reply: Bother! Double bother!

As the month moseyed forward in a quasi-blur, I produced several large pieces and dozens of smaller ones, all monstrous looking in form, part human, part alien; some grouped together in triangular or circular shapes, others stood as solitary figures, altogether formidable. The lot of them would have given any normal child nightmares.

Samantha came over after I removed my latest piece from the kiln. I made it clear to Mother I would not see Samantha in the studio, so after she knocked on the door, opened it, and announced Samantha had arrived, I feared she'd forgotten. "Mother! Make her wait in the living room, while I wash up. Please!"

"I know, I know," she said, as she bowed and exited the room backwards.

"Very funny, Mother," I said in a huff. I knew she wanted to hide my state of mind (a la statuettes) from Samantha, as much as I did.

Samantha had come down to explain, once again, why she'd been absent from life (not her words) so long. Turns out, it wasn't really an explanation, as I came to see. In her mind she was sharing her life with me. As she talked, she slipped in gems like: "Scott's as skilled as a beaver when it comes to woodworkin'. Did you know he could do just 'bout 'nythin' with his hand, even metalsmithin'? Come on up and I'll show you the bedside table he made his Maw to keep her water pitcher on. She'd probably love a new visitor, too."

"Thanks," I said, thinking Richard had suggested this invitation, which made me cringe inside.

"I find helpin' Scott with stuff strangely fun, no matter what it is. He doesn't even have to be in the room," she said. My estimation of Samantha's brilliance crept narrowly close to toppling and crashing forever. If it had, I knew something in me would break, forever too, so I kept the thought at bay. Mouth shut.

Perhaps that's why, after she'd left and I reentered the studio, I began knocking over every kiln-dried piece I had on display in the room, including my teacher's. Mother was entertaining several of her psychologist lady friends over the weekend, giving them a taste of what it would be like when her retreat ran like clockwork. They were just commenting on how lovely a girl Samantha was, Mother nodding the whole time. She didn't plan on me, however, at least not in the way of the revelation that was about to fall over her like hail and brimstones.

From that back mystery room, turned studio, words erupted, which I won't write down, as well as mixed outbursts of screams, sobs, and booming sounds of heavy clay being hurled with subsequent crashing noises, as they broke into fragmented chunks on the floor. I had made sure Samantha was well on her way up the hill, knowing the pace of her steps and counting: one, two, three, four—all the way to twenty-seven—before letting myself spin out of control. I had totally forgotten about Mother's guests.

The ruckus upended her gathering of delicate finger food and latest news about friends; gossip, I believe it's called. Dad was in his study wrapping up a business order, or whatever it is he wraps up in there, whenever he's actually home. I had forgotten it was one of those rare days, when his presence was actually upon us. Truthfully, my only thought was the depth of my own disappointment in what seemed like Samantha's complete shortsightedness.

Immediately, Mother and her friends vacated the drawing room and, as if entering one superglue-moment, came back together again as one entity before the closed door of the studio. There they clumped, listening. I could feel their presence outside it, but could care less. They slowly opened the door, afraid it seemed that perhaps a statue or a harsh word would be hurled their way and their form would divide into separate pieces once again. *Strength in a united front,* I thought.

There they stood, door ajar, watching me with all sorts of grimacing stares on their faces, ranging from disapproval to pity. Several leaned forward, open-mouthed, bringing others with them like a cresting wave. Incredulity gradually spread across each face, as an unbearable realization sunk into their minds. I was living proof that their profession bore no fruit. How could it? I, the child of a peer, was an utter failure.

That notion quickly altered and shifted, so they could bear it. That's when the burden of fault landed squarely onto Mother, as a parent, not as a professional. I saw it take hold, and for a brief second it provided a moment of satisfaction at the surface of my thoughts; but the white noise of their thinking grew disturbingly loud. In defiance of their self-righteousness, and all their circling judgments, I cast down whatever kiln-dried clay remained standing.

Then I felt outside myself. I watched me, watching them. There I felt impervious to any ill thoughts, or concerns, or where my hands fell next. I abandoned all thoughts within that present reality about me, or Mother, or anyone else, good or bad. I found the entire moment turned in upon itself, as my lifeblood spilled from my heart, flooding my brain. I sought desperately to make the outer world reflect my inner one, but found no relief in doing so.

Finally, I fell to the floor in the midst of the shattered pieces. The strain of standing weighed too heavily on my frame. My energy had been sucked from me. My bones had been replaced with gummy bears. No, just plain hot rubber. Gummy bears were too sweet. I marveled that my humor hung on, even if morbidly. My muscles had been stretched into uselessness. I felt like a rag doll, stuffed with filthy, uncarded wool, still bearing pieces of briar twigs and dirt. When I looked up, I saw Dad had joined the group. He stood at the rear, easily peering over every head in front of him. He didn't feel like a part of the clump they formed. He seemed to remain separate, his own person.

Then he spoke, "Good," he said, looking about the room. "I didn't like any of them, anyway."

Mother's professional friends weren't quite sure which entity, within their observational scope, they should gasp at more—father, with his obvious cavalier attitude and total ignorance of the situation, even when exposed in severest bloom, or me, paused in action, apparently within a complete mental and emotional collapse on the floor.

All the women, including Mother, chose dad to crucify. I could only imagine all those eyes with their beady focus afterwards, since backs were turned to me in a quick about-face. They probably, I thought, shot in unison one particularly stinging dart upward at his laissez faire face in an attempt to demolish his outlook. All were on cue, aiming very unprofessionally, since they weren't on the clock. I have since wished I could have beheld the spectacle from Dad's height and perspective; but my limited angle, coupled with my dimmed wits, but still functioning imagination proved quite sufficient in the moment.

I pictured the shortest woman in the front, nearest me, standing at approximately five-foot-one-inch, having to bend her head back quite far, so as to reach Dad's eye level, if her aim were to be successful. I relished the possibility of her either tumbling in the attempt into a teetering free fall and joining me on the floor with a thud, or discovering that her head had been stuck in reverse, never able to alight atop the straight, albeit, squatty pillar of her neck again. I knew a thing or two about awkward necks at that point and felt relieved to find I still possessed a remnant of kindness in hoping the outcome would not be the latter.

Those simple thoughts, though, caused me to burst into laughter, which then flowed quite naturally into uncontrollable sobbing. The noises that poured out of me caused greater alarm within the ladies, who promptly refocused on me. I imagined their former stares at the man in the rear would turn to me in short order, but at the same time, I dreaded the thought of all of them rushing to my aid with their makeshift psychological bandages. My pleading eyes caught hold of my dad's.

And then, this happened. Dad simply said, "Excuse me ladies, my daughter needs me." He, then, walked straight through them, like Moses in the midst of the Red Sea, finding a way that opened without any striving on his part. The dense force before him yielded, split apart, and he walked through all of them to reach my side, unscathed. He bent down to where I had fallen and wrapped his long strong arms completely around me. That was the first time my father held me within a tender, openhearted hug that wasn't a greeting, a goodbye, or a goodnight. He had never held on as long either; and, this part was equally remarkable to me. I believe he knew it, as much as I. It was the first time he took the lead in parenting me. He acted of his own volition, made a fatherly decision and followed through without consulting Mother. Better yet, seemingly, at that point, in opposition to Mother. I melted in a quiet surrender, sensing some mysterious shackle had been unlocked and lifted off my being.

I wept within his soothing embrace longer than I thought I would or could. I know he felt the same freedom in our shared experience, and wasn't about to let go. The world vanished in those moments, as he rubbed my back and rocked me in his love. We sat unconcerned of the eyes that watched what they could not see, except for Mother. She finally got it and joined us on the floor, not touching me, for she knew I was fully covered, but laying her hand on Dad's shoulder, as a display of solidarity with his familial decision.

"You'll get through this pain, Robyn." Even though I recall the feeling of those words down in the marrow of my growing bones, I don't remember Dad saying them. The words were sent into my heart within a masculine voice; and they've never left me—not once. *I'll get through the pain*, I thought, *but, when?*

WHEN LOVE WALKS IN WISDOM

*D*ad came into my room the next morning and sat on the edge of my bed. He waited for me to open my eyes, as if he knew I'd know to awaken. I wondered how he could know such a thing, or if I were wrong in thinking it. Maybe he just wanted to watch me, as I lay still and quiet, a rarity for sure; however, neither of those possibilities, the uncanny knowing or the quiet watching was what struck me most. It was the first time I sensed my dad saw me, inside me.

Maybe my wondering was foolish, based on the drama of yesterday, and what I thought wouldn't play out in the days ahead, even in the minutes at hand. Maybe, he came in to say he'd be gone again, for another week, but looked forward to seeing me soon. Maybe. Maybe not. Maybe it was wishful thinking for me to imagine he'd actually want to spend another day at home, since he was home yesterday, and what fun *that* day must have been for him.

Stretching that thought into imagining a day at home *with me* seemed unrealistic; but still, I couldn't shake the feeling that something had shifted. I couldn't eliminate the possibility of turning sensibility on its head and wishing for the impossible. I mean, Dad even sat on my bed differently. I know. That must sound lame, but it's true. He sank into it more, like he was finally home and could relax—like he discovered what it meant to walk in his body, and he liked it! It struck me how he felt a little like Samantha does, when she takes her star position under the warm sun and sinks into the grass, comfortably at one with her surroundings. It was that kind of sinking, a good sinking. We both sensed something had shifted, but didn't speak of it. Speaking of it might make it disappear, and I began to see how neither of us wanted it to go away. It probably startled both of us, too. What if we didn't know how to act with each other anymore? Was that possible? I thought so, at first.

"I'm due for a great vacation," he declared after I stretched and yawned. "So, as head of my company, I'm giving myself one. It starts today. I'm going fly fishing. Would you like to join me? Whatever I catch, I'm going to bring home to gut and fry. No more catch and release. How 'bout it, Robyn? Does that sound like something you'd be up for, this morning?"

I smiled and stared at him. *Who are you*, I thought. *I like you. You feel like Samantha, but, also, like me on my best feeling days.* "Do I have to gut the ones I catch?" I asked.

"Not if you don't want to. I could do yours, too; but if you wanna do it, I can teach you. My father taught me, so it would be an honor for me to pass it down to you."

"Yes!" I said.

"Oh, that makes me happy," he said. "Mother is cooking up some grits for breakfast. No, not really. It's waffles. I'm going down to help her pack our lunches. I'll see you when you're ready. By the way, good morning, honey," he said, planting a kiss on my forehead. He actually waited for a response.

"Morning, Dad," I said. As he was leaving the room, I asked, "How long is your vacation?"

"Six months," he said nonchalantly.

"Six months!" I exclaimed.

"Yeah, I've got some really cool things I wanna do. We can talk about it while we're out."

"Okay," I said, giggling and feeling genuinely giddy for the first time in longer than I could recall. I'd almost forgotten how good it felt to feel good. I wanted to check my enthusiasm, though, thinking there had to be a catch, an unforeseen hook that would puncture my heart, somehow, but I couldn't. I couldn't hold back the feeling that swept through me, even if I tried; and I didn't really want to try.

We caught five trout between us, enough "eatin'" for two meals. Dad began unraveling his thoughts for what he called his working vacation.

"Working?" I asked.

"Don't panic. It's totally unlike what I do for work, and it's all outdoor stuff! I have a feeling you might be interested in helping me pull it off. Maybe I'm wrong, but you can let me know."

"Did you think of this, or did Mother?" I asked, point blank.

Dad laughed. "You tell me after hearing it. Let me see if you know your old man." I smiled at the expression he used to describe himself. Dad was surprising me at every bend, and I liked it, a lot.

"All right," I said.

"So, here it is. I'm thinking of getting a contractor out here to build us a small barn. I wanna design it and get an architect to give it the once over before starting construction, just to make sure it's all structurally sound. I plan on hiring a small crew and helping them with some of the nail pounding, here and there, just so I can say, 'Look what I built.'" He snickered. "You could help me at any stage of this project, if you'd like. I figured I'd ask Scott, if it's okay with you, and Richard, if either are available and interested in building us a fenced corral to the west of where the barn will go up in that green spread. Can you picture it?"

"Scott," I said blankly, since that's the part that stuck out the most to me.

"If it's okay with you. I'd like to hire local, especially young men I know would do a good job."

I was so concerned about Scott's presence in the picture Dad had just painted that I overlooked the part about what he'd be building. I paused. "Dad," I asked, "what's the barn and corral for?"

"Oh, that's the part I love most. Did you know I used to ride as a boy?"

"Horses!"

"No, cows."

"No way! You want to get horses?"

"I do," he said, chuckling. "Mother must have mentioned my horse as a boy, a Chestnut Paint, named Chief. I wanna find two Paints and start riding, again. The second horse could be for guests, or you, if you'd like to learn and join me."

"No way!" I said, again. "That would be awesome, Dad!" I actually felt myself jumping up and down, causing the three fish I'd caught to slap against my thighs. I didn't care that I looked like a happy little kid. That's how I felt, and I liked it. Then it crept up on me—I'm a kid! Whoa. Life just got real for me on the positive side of the spectrum—fishing, horses, dad, and me, a real kid. Wait. Scott. I considered it for a whole two seconds. "Okay."

"Okay, what?" Dad asked.

"Okay, on Scott."

The more I thought about Scott helping out Dad, the more ingenious the plan sounded. Scott down here with Richard, and Samantha up there, helping Scott's Maw, well . . . the possibility of more time with Samantha opened up before me, again. Then a strange twist happened. I knew I'd rather be down here building with everyone, so I contented myself with the fact that if Scott were here, he'd be with Samantha less. I giggled, again. "Scott could earn more money for the Ryan," I blurted.

"That's just what I was thinking," Dad said. "I like helping neighbors out that way. They'd be welcome to help with the barn, afterwards, too."

"Yeah," I said. I actually stood on tiptoe and gave Dad a big kiss on his cheek. I decided, there and then, that I would stop thinking about Scott, and just let Dad fill in all his details. He was doing such a good job, after all.

"So?" Dad asked.

I stood looking puzzled.

"Tell me who thought up these things for me to do."

"Definitely, you! They're just too much fun to be Mother's."

Dad laughed again, and for a moment I wondered if he tricked me.

That night I had an urge to hug Dad goodnight. I walked the hallway toward my parents' bedroom. Their door, slightly ajar, allowed me to hear their voices before I knocked. I heard intonations before words, but when I drew closer I clearly heard Mother say, "She actually jumped up and down!"

"Precious," Dad said, as he lifted his nose from a book and adjusted his glasses.

"Well," said Mother, as she took down her hair, "you certainly were the missing piece in this family's equation."

"Missing is right," said Dad in a sorrowful tone.

"Oh, Edward! Don't berate yourself. I think the timing is just perfect. She needs you, now, more than she needs me. I think you're the essential key for uprooting those narcissistic streaks I've seen in her for years."

"I wish you wouldn't say things like that about Robyn, Elizabeth. She's just a normal adolescent, finding her way through tough changes. She'll turn things around, when she gets her footing. I was the same way."

"Oh, no! You were never as self-focused as Robyn."

"Elizabeth, you didn't meet me until I was a young adult. Please, you have to stop thinking like a trained psychologist and start thinking like a mother, first, when it comes to our daughter."

"What! That's totally unfair of you, Edward!" Mother said, as she slid into bed, flipping a light blanket over her chilling form.

I stood in the hallway, holding back my tears. I made my eyes open wider and wider to allow more room for the liquid welling up, until I blinked and a stream from each eye plopped onto my red pajama top, bypassing my cheeks entirely. I watched as those two dark spots spread outwardly in ever-widening circles, reaching for new fibers to hold their volume. I wished I could be that free, just to drop off into soft fabric like that, hide in the least expected place and spread out unnoticed. I wondered why the brain made tears when our heart hurt. Was it so people could tell a really deep wound from a surface one? What happened if we cried alone in dark hallways? What good were our tears, then? Maybe they came to show us what's happening inside our hearts; otherwise we'd try to fool ourselves into thinking nothing happened or mattered. Tears aren't us. They expose us. That's why I vowed that night never to cry again.

At that moment I felt orphaned. I didn't like the feeling. I wanted to feel included, but it seemed I was always the cause of some turmoil, or unwanted plan, or bedroom talk, or--and this is where it got difficult--trips Dad took. I wondered about every conversation my parents must have had before the words I over-heard that night were voiced in that stale and rehearsed way—hardened offerings, hashed out countless times and apparently going nowhere but back into their mouths, once again. The words fell into my ears as zestless syllables. I was a stale topic, like the trash that hadn't been taken out. My confusion brought me to the place of questioning how I had never heard such words spoken before, being they were so old and worn. Why hadn't I known I was an iron wedge seated firmly between my parents? I pondered the new information I possessed until remnants of yesterday's gritty clay dislodged from a crevice in my tooth. I crunched it into powder between my molars and went to bed.

Within this time of crisis, though, I resolved to remain

perfectly silent. I wouldn't knock anything over, *Mother.* I wouldn't jump up and down, *Dad.* I wouldn't breathe; but then, I knew Samantha would be breathing and would want me to breathe. I ran to my room, buried my face in two pillows and screamed for the sheer ache of seeing imperfection's face show up, so unexpectedly. All the perfect knots Dad and I tied together were undone.

The next morning Edward and Elizabeth seemed completely 'normal.' They smiled. They talked. They tried to engage me, but I wouldn't play their game of make-believe. I was wise to their theatrics.

"Mother," I said, "You really should have been an actress. And, Dad, you could have been her understudy." I wouldn't look at them. I ate. My stomach hurt. I left the room with most of my cereal still in my bowl.

Dad followed me. "Hey, kiddo, I'm going shopping for contractors in town today. Would you like to come along?"

"Nope," I said.

There was that shift I'd seen earlier. Dad didn't budge. Normally, if I clammed up, he'd just continue on, pursuing whatever it was that pressed his mind to distraction. Not today. "Come outside with me, Robyn?" he asked.

"No thank you," I said.

"I understand it's not what you might feel like doing right now. I'm asking you to respect my request in spite of your feelings though, because it's for our good, our mutual good. Can you get behind that request?" He extended his hand to me. I brushed by it and went outside ahead of him. I walked to the Mazda and sat against its hood, arms crossed, legs crossed, mouth pinched tight.

"So," he began. "You seem mad at me. Are you?"

"Not just you." Immediately, I regretted having given him even that much information.

"So," he said again, "if I asked you, right this second, if you still wanted horses on the property, you'd probably say, no. Right?" I said nothing. "Okay, I'll just sit here with you until you're able to tell me what lie has penetrated your heart." That was a new approach. What did he mean by a lie getting into my heart? I heard the two of them talking. *That conversation was real,* I thought. I felt completely justified in my anger.

We sat until my stomach growled. I wished I had eaten more breakfast, but then remembered why I hadn't. "This is ridiculous," I said.

"No, it's not, Robyn. You're my daughter, and I love you."

Wait! Dad doesn't just come out and say things like that to me.

He continued. "I don't mind investing my time into you, one bit. I don't care if it's fishing, or shopping, or horseback riding, or helping you with Trigonometry, or waiting for your heart to open up just enough to let me know what's troubling you."

"Mother hates me!" I blurted out. "There! Are you happy!" I'm fairly certain he wasn't expecting something like that to emerge. "And," I continued, "you don't really like Mother either, but you keep telling her things, private things about me, about us. So, where does that leave me? She takes everything that's wonderful and turns it into an impassable concrete wall. And all you do is tell her not to do it anymore, but she keeps doing it and you keep telling her everything anyway."

"Whoa," he said, as if riding a horse he wanted to stop. "That's a lot," he said, "but I am hearing it all, Robyn. I just need a moment to take it in."

I didn't expect that response. I thought for sure he'd get on his steed and gallop towards Mother's defense.

"You're absolutely right in thinking things have to change between your mother and me, but not in the ways you imagine. May I explain?"

I nodded my head once, dropped my chin to my chest, and listened closely. His words came slowly. It was, rather, his heart that reached me first as I watched him from the corner of my eye. He stood up straight, took a deep breath and exhaled, only to put his hands to his hips briefly, circle one-hundred and eighty degrees, stare out toward the road and then run his right hand through his light brown hair, which I'd noticed was graying around his ears. Then he swung around again, and said, "Robyn, your mother's my wife, and I love her more than you're probably capable of knowing at this point in your life. Maybe, you'll never fully get it, because you'll never fully be in our relationship. That's okay. I just need you to understand, I am committed to her. Yes, sometimes, she'll do something or say something I don't agree with, and I wish like crazy she wouldn't have or won't again; but I don't stop loving her when that happens. She's shown me things about life I'd never have known without her; yet—and you'll need to grow into this part to understand it—I shouldn't have given her the final say for everything pertaining to this family from day one. That place should have been given to someone else all these years, someone I should have been listening to more closely; and, I'm finally coming around, seeing where I've fallen short. That's what I can change. Not her. I can change myself, what I do and don't do."

"What's that got to do with her hating me?"

"Okay. Fair question. I have to say you're not correct in that assumption, even though you don't agree with me right now. Remember how I said earlier that a lie can affect us deeply? That's one. It's just not true; and I can say that without a doubt in my mind or heart. Your mother loves you so much, Robyn. She just, well, gets carried away trying to snip the loose edges she thinks are sticking out and hindering you. She gets so taken up by it all she forgets what life is like outside of how . . . how she pictures it. Her wanting to control everything for you puts her in a place of missing out on what's most important, seeing you for who you really are, right now. She needs help getting past that point; but all of it, whatever it is she's scheming for you, it's exactly that, Robyn. It's for you. It's how she loves you. Hate wants to harm, exclude, or use people for their profit or gain. Love provides and protects.

Think of your mother. Do you honestly believe she'd ever wanna harm you, out and out harm you?"

"No," I said begrudgingly. "But, why does she think I'm something . . . so terrible? Why does she think that about me?"

"What do you mean?"

"I heard her last night. I looked up the word, narcissist. She thinks I'm one."

"You heard us last night in our bedroom?"

"Yes." At that point my dad looked like I did last night in the hallway. His eyes widened. He looked like he might pass out and leaned against the car with me.

"I am so, so sorry, darling. You never should have heard that conversation."

"But, Dad, why does that kind of talk happen if we're all loving each other? Why did she label me? Why did you tell her about our time together? That was our time, Dad. I felt so embarrassed, when you told her how . . . you know with the horses. You two talked behind my back about my reaction, my happy reaction, like I was something amusing. Like I wasn't a real person. "

"Robyn, you're right. Your feelings are totally valid. I shouldn't have described your reaction to your mother. My only excuse is, well, it was so adorable I thought she'd love hearing about it; but you're right. She can have her own moments of joy with you to cherish, forever, and we can find them together as a family, too; but, from here on out, whatever happens on that emotional level, when we're together, stays between us. That's in my head, now. I get it," he said, tapping the gray hairs at his temple.

"But, you have to know this, too, Robyn. You are your mother's favorite topic, and I am her favorite sounding board, which means we've always talked about you—from the time you were in her womb. That's what parents do. That won't ever stop. I wouldn't want it to. Neither should you, because if it stopped . . . think about it, Robyn. If it stopped, that would mean you're not part of our life anymore. That would hurt so badly. I don't even wanna think about it. You're stuck with me, and your mother, kiddo. You're part of our marriage vows, in a way, for better or worse, you know? Do you understand?" he asked.

I nodded, again. "Am I part of the better?" I asked.

"Oh you bet you are. Honey, will you forgive me?"

"Yes," I said. I remember hugging him that morning and feeling the same secure warmth I had in the studio the day before. My dad was with me and for me. Mother wasn't an obstacle between us, anymore. She was just Mother.

"Do you think I should talk to Mother about this?" I asked.

"Do you want to?"

"No," I said.

"This is what I've got for you, off the top of my head. If you understand why she uses clinical terminology, as something she's been trained to use in her thinking, then covering you lovingly with one of her words won't seem as overpowering. Think of it as sort of her starting point to organize her thoughts around your needs, all with good intentions. Remember that part, then you might begin to see why she goes in those directions; and remember, she's learning too. I have to remember that stuff, too; but if it still bothers you, we should talk more about it. Definitely. Maybe even as a family."

"No, I'm good for now, but maybe sometime later. I don't know. It just feels too much to think about right now, Dad; but, you've helped," I said. I remember directing a small warm smile his way at that point. He took my hand and we strolled toward the white *New York Daisies* Samantha had planted after our arrival. He picked one and handed it to me.

OPENING WINDOWS

*I*t's odd how one tilt from normal can change things across the board. A wild mountain goat uproots a plant growing in a crevice between two rocks. The tugging dislodges one rock. It tumbles, disrupting other small rocks around the base of a large boulder. The boulder slips an inch and rearranges other rocks, which in turn causes the boulder to slide and slam into loose rocks of various sizes. Gravity takes hold, and voila! People are scattering on the road below the mountain.

Seemingly, these things are out of our control. Such abrupt turnovers can change the entire face of existing terrain, and affect lives living nearby, not just once but again and again. We can live from glory to glory, or merely from dust to dust.

When I turned thirteen, a recurring thought ran through my head. It was, "Earth is one big graveyard." I never shared that perspective about our spinning cradle with anyone, not even Samantha. It faithfully surfaced, though, whenever things felt uncertain to me. Not sure how it evolved. Maybe, it felt like an unavoidable truth to me at the time. I needed truth. Even the simplest spread comfort over me—a sure finality; but then what? I didn't want to think that far ahead.

When my boulders and rocks went sailing that day in the studio, there was no way they'd have made a dent toward a better outcome. They wouldn't have clipped another boulder just right to stop an avalanche. They wouldn't have stacked up, so that I could climb *my* Everest in victory. It was a free fall mess, not far-reaching for others or myself, but even though temporary in scope and lame on my part, that action changed my life. Not because of me. That day would have been a disaster if Dad hadn't crashed through the granite amassed at the doorway, threatening to hit me at a most dangerous angle. He averted an avalanche that September, and helped extract me from the graveyard that ran through my head.

Dad and I became a team, but he desired a family trifecta. His goal was to extend our victory ribbon to Mother. His approach was systematic, one step after another. "We have to reel her in first," he'd say. Dad chipped away on her stone surface for a couple of weeks, which was tricky. I mean she was in the business of analyzing minds, so he tread lightly yet firmly. The other thing is, Mother never liked talking about herself. Dad said that had to change. He began advocating for an appropriate amount of transparency trickling down to said child, me.

It took time before she was able to step up to the edge of our victory circle. When she stuck her toe into it, I finally began to understand my mother, somewhat better. Not completely, but more. Dad said not to worry, "She's had a long road," and that made sense to me.

I used to think Dad saw Mother and me clearly, because of some emotional distancing he held, not that he didn't love both of us, but because he hardly entered into our day-to-day exchanges, therefore he got less entangled in the tensions that built up between us. I thought that distance gave him the advantage of neutral ground, so to speak.

Even when we arrived in West Virginia, he only exposed his face to us around twice a week for the first three years. When that all changed, I began seeing Dad as the grand mediator of our family. Some would call it being the head of the household, and in its truest sense that meant he was a servant. He led us by laying down his life for us.

When he completed his six-month vacation, Dad actually transitioned into an early semi-retirement. That's when he became a full-fledged insider. He switched it up by showing his face at work on those two days, and then giving us the gift of himself the rest of the week. That outside flip matched what was happening inside him. Mother and I both saw it.

The other shift in our terrain began about two weeks after our driveway conversation. Dad dubbed it, the Thomas Family's Meaty Monday Meeting, or TFMMM. Later, it morphed into just, Triple-M. They were designed, originally, to keep the family informed of thoughts and feelings, a way for us to uncover stuff we didn't know about each other. We were allowed secrets, but there had to be a good reason for them, like birthday planning, or things just too personal to toss onto the table, if the timing wasn't right. Most importantly, keeping the secret couldn't create a rift in our unity. Dad had made two Fess-Up rules. One was the 'do' rule, and the other the 'don't.' Rule Number One: Do share anything to help the family understand you or your circumstances, thereby creating a sense of togetherness; and Rule Number Two: Don't share anything, if it's out of meanness, spite, or pride. In other words, drop the mean bundle outside the front door, since we don't ever want words to hurt a loved one's feelings intentionally. He made sure I knew there would be times when conversations could produce pain, but if it fit into the first rule's intention, it was allowable.

The topic scheduled for our fourth meeting got serious: Mother's past. I wondered what could be so crucial to our family to go all the way back into Mother's past, especially her childhood. Surely, she must have thought such conversations unprofitable, or she would have brought them up by now. I saw her eyes widen and then narrow into a piercing stare, directed at Dad, when he approached the topic at breakfast, but he didn't back down on the agenda. I sensed he was onto something juicy, which made me actually want it to happen. If there was something I couldn't see, and Mother didn't want me to see, I wanted to see it.

He and I walked into Mother's favorite room, the one she had modernized into a symbiotic relationship between the old and new. She aimed for peacefulness. Old architecture had been gracefully touched within her vision to unite its established worth with new vitality, a blending of generations, sort of like what Dad hoped our meetings would become. We paused from our activity under the coffered ceilings. Dad was silent, as he entered, pensive. My eyes scanned the Greek-like columns edging the fireplace, as we waited for Mother to enter. Ornate molding faced outward in its new coat of rose-tinted paint. Its sweetness bordered the new wall lath and its plaster, covered in a warm cappuccino glow. Whenever I looked about the room, the expansive beveled mirror, trimmed in ornately carved wood and stained in gold caught my eye first. It spanned the length of the fireplace mantle and rested in its posed position just below the crown molding. The whole effect promoted calmness and a pleasing sense of wellbeing. Frankly, it made me think of how well it would fit in one of Marie-Antoinette's gilded chambers. It was the room in which Mother chose to open her life to me.

Mother entered and sat on the edge of a cushion, as if fully prepared to bolt. At first she hemmed and hawed and then chatted casually, alerting us to her latest checklist of improvements for the house and garden. I waited for her verbal notes of solicitation to enter my unwilling ears. I never enjoyed her projects and felt relieved when she didn't mention me in any role. I tried to suppress the frustration welling up in me from the diversionary tactics being used after she joined us. Dad had warned me this meeting would be extremely difficult for her, which made me wait as best I could. At one point I did get up to roam about the room.

I approached the three, floor-to-ceiling windows at the far end of it, to see if anything interesting stirred on the horizon. On my return I veered toward the baby grand and slid my fingers across some keys. Dad called me back. He rose from the arm of one of the two oatmeal-colored couches, facing each other, and moved to the one where Mother sat. Dad waved me over to join him, and we three ended up occupying one couch.

As I sat down something happened. Mother had sensed Dad's persistence in motion. She scooted back a bit, dropping her elbows onto her thighs. I'm sure they had talked about the matter without me, as well. I recognized how she was switching, going into a deeper space to share; but when she lowered her head, looked at her hands, took a deep breath, and said, "These hands buried my little sister, or at least they tried," I gasped, "What?"

I froze. Thoughts tumbled. I heard myself say to myself, How could *that* just have happened? Isn't there some sort of rule about easing into that kind of talk? Did we really go from plans of burying black iris bulbs in the garden to burying a sister? Really? My mouth hung open and my hands rushed to cover its gaping silence.

"I'm sorry, Robyn. I don't know how to do this." Mother's eyes shifted to Dad.

"Tell her your story, Elizabeth," Dad said, as his hand reached out toward her shoulder and rested lightly upon it. She nodded.

"I wasn't born in America, Robyn," she said. "I was born in Germany in January of 1930, three years before Adolph Hitler became chancellor. You've heard of him. You've read, *The Diary of Anne Frank—Het Achterhuit*." That last part sounded unfamiliar to me, especially Mother's accent. "The diary of a young girl," she said under her breath.

She looked at me and said, as if it were a mere bit of common knowledge, one as simple as the freezing point of water, "Anne was one of the daughters of my parents' friends, the Franks. I met her when I was three. Of course, I don't remember the day, outside of a photograph. She had turned four a few months earlier. My mutti, my mama, took that photo of us girls all playing sweetly in the apartment with our dolls and tea set. Our apartment and my family were lovely," she said drifting off for a moment. "The baby, my little sister, joined us when she awakened from her nap. Mutti threw open two small windows, so that we could enjoy what she said might be the last days of freedom's air. I'm not sure how I remembered her words, other than them being directly tied to the reaction they caused on my papa's face, a direct link of cause and effect impacted my young mind. Papa's skin turned ashen. That's what I remember most. That and her words, drifting across him like a shadowed whisper of death. Anything that meant a lot to either of my parents meant the world to me, especially if it involved their feelings. I didn't have to understand the particulars. I just had to sense their hearts. My papa looked . . ." Mother paused. "He looked as if he'd begun to die after Mutti spoke those prophetic words." I don't recall ever being more still and attentive as Mother talked. I had been captivated, breathless in a type of suspended reality I'd never felt.

"There's nothing lovelier than living life as if no evil lurked about to swallow you—nothing ominous following your actions or spreading lies. There's a joy in living as if nothing mattered but the sweet voices of four young girls with their parents nearby, their every syllable void of restriction, rising and falling in a natural, unaffected cadence and inflection, all ascending upward and out into the air of an opened window." Mother paused and from her place on the couch glanced out the large windows she often stood near. I felt she was gazing into freedom.

"Anne's older sister Margot struck me as a wonderful person," she continued. "She attentively fussed over my baby sister, Freida. We never saw the Franks after that afternoon in Bonn, but that didn't seem unusual. It wasn't our habit to visit them. Papa knew Otto Frank before he married Mutti. They were boyhood friends. As it happened, Otto Frank said he was on his way to Aachen to visit his wife's mother, before they traveled to his jam factory in Amsterdam. That's what he said to all of us, but there was more he only told my papa, and even more that history bore out. Herr Frank was fleeing Germany. His first stop was where he had said, but that was only a decoy of sorts." Mother arose.

"Do you need a break?" Dad asked.

"Fifteen minutes? Walk with me in the garden?"

"My pleasure," Dad said, as he took her arm. He signaled for me to stay behind.

Timing had its perfect way with us that day. The moment my parents stepped out, there was a knock at the door. Samantha stood smiling at me. "Hi," I said. "What's up?"

"I have something to ask you."

"Okay. Can you ask it in ten minutes? We're having a family meeting, and my parents are taking a short break." I realized in that moment what I had just said. I actually turned down more time with Samantha to be with my parents. I wasn't sure if that was a sign of approaching maturity or insanity.

"I think so," Samantha said, as if it were a perfectly normal request. "So, this is what I was wonderin'." I noticed she talked a bit faster than usual. "When it's time to tear apart the Ryan, and that won't be for a bit, probably late spring, would you be willin' to be our recorder? I'm thinkin' we'll need all the parts drawn out, where they sit now, how everythin's connected 'fore they go trailin' off 'round the barn. Some color-codin' and notes would be helpful in gettin' us to remember how everythin' fits t'gether for the next reassemblin' part. We'll need to put everythin' in its proper place. If'n we don't have great diagrams, it'll all go haywire midstream. Scott's good at it, too, but he leaves a trail of greasy smudges behind; and if'n the notes are hard to read, it'll be impossible for us to rebuild it. I know this task would suit you. What do ya think? Are you up for it?"

"Hmmm. Would everyone be there?"

"Would you want us to be?"

"Well, I thought it would be more fun with just you and me. We could do a test run. Right? Afterwards, you could explain the things I've jotted down, 'cause we'll probably talk about them, and Scott can inspect the drawings on site, too, to see if they make sense. That's what I'd like."

"Oh, good, Robyn! That sounds fine and doable. I've missed you!"

Wow! Two base hits with Samantha and in less than ten minutes! I wondered why I didn't feel more triumphant.

"Oh, and we finally went to a doctor who thinks he knows what's happenin' to Scott's Maw. Some fancy title sits behind his M.D. letters."

"What title?"

"Never heard the likes of it 'fore today. It's got a researchin' sound to it. Wait. Yeah. It's clinical somethin'. Ummm, oh yeah, Clinical Ecologist."

"That sounds weird. What did he say?"

"Basically, she got some bad stuff into her body it can't handle. Maybe rodent poison, decades of mold, or rat droppin' turned into powder—maybe all three. Happened when she raked and swept out that ol' barn to make a place for the Ryan. Timin' is spot on. Scott feels terrible bad 'bout it. Said he should've done the sweepin' up; but honestly, he never would have thought 'bout cleanin' that barn out. That good deed was all his Maw's idea. She did it for him, never thinkin' it would hurt her."

"Oh, gosh! Will she get better?"

"Not sure. She's gonna 'liminate and avoid, like the doctor told her, and substitute with natural products. That might kick in her immune system, but maybe not. How she feels will get lots better, but it might not be an overall cure. Relief is good, though. She feels all normal, when the air is good. So, yep, changes goin' on up there; totin' off the bad 'n' bringin' in the good. I s'pose that's where the word ecologist comes in with the environmental stuff in the air. We got a list. Stuff like disinfectant sprays 'n' mothballs gotta go. Did you know mothballs are nothin' but volatile pesticide in solid balls? They're always leakin' out poisons! And so many bar soaps brands have formaldehyde in them! It's crazy! Then the obvious chemicals, like the bug spray canisters under the counter, and the unused weed chemicals in the shed and barn, all gone. Mr. Farley ain't never needed chemical fertilizer with the pigs, though, so that's good." Samantha smiled. "Those are just some of the things. The list goes on. The doctors said, learning' new routines will take time and might feel hard at first, but they'll start seemin' normal soon 'nough, and everyone, no matter if'n you feel the difference or not, will be better off for it.

"There's a phrase used for her sensitivities—a canary in a coal mine. Imagine. Why, the other day, she reacted to wood smoke, so, Mr. Farley's gonna rewire the cabin to get electric heaters up 'n' runnin'; and that beautiful propane cookstove, it has to go. But, you know those pieces don't matter much, if'n we get pieces of her back. We see it, already. It makes my heart happy, knowin' how the community is steppin' up, too, collectin' funds to pay for some new appliances. We'll be providin' all the organic milk she can drink and vegetables--as much as she wants. That's it, in a twirlin' nutshell," she added, smiling.

As soon as she finished, I heard Dad call my name. "Coming!" I called out. Prudence left my mind; but I did remember to tell Samantha I'd let Dad know about the collection for the Farleys. It did bother me how she had used the 'we' pronoun, "we finally went to a doctor'," instead of "they," but other than that I didn't mind hearing what was going on in the Farley household, one bit, and I did feel sad for Scott's Maw. Then I thought, perhaps Samantha had earned the right to use that inclusive pronoun, with all the help she'd been giving Prudence; but that's as far as I wanted to go with my generosity. Samantha and I touched fingertips before she headed out. I turned toward the house, wondering what would come next in Mother's story. When I entered the room, only Dad was there.

"Your mother isn't feeling well, Robyn. She wants me to share some of the facts she can't seem to find her way to share, today. Would that be okay with you?"

I said, "Yes." Actually, I preferred it. I was having a hard time believing Mother's story about the Franks was real. How had history fallen in Mother's lap, all tied up with feelings and mental images like that? I mean she was just a little kid! I wanted the bare bone facts Dad could provide. I missed the whole purpose behind the revelation, too. Perhaps she sensed as much, and it was why she declined to put herself through the strain of reliving more of it for me, her unappreciative daughter. But then those thoughts shifted. Maybe, something else would have happened, had she continued telling her own story—something neither of us expected. With that last thought I resented Mother for skipping out on the hard part. So, by the time I added, "That's fine," to my "yes,' I wasn't quite sure it was fine.

"Let me say, what's ahead isn't something to dwell on, Robyn. It's the epitome of evil unleashed on man by their fellowman. It's unthinkable, and that's why it's so hard for your mother to bring it into her mind, let alone talk about it in front of you. She's lived it. It's buried within her brain and nerves. It causes a lot of discomfort, when those shadows drift over her. Can you understand that at all?"

"When you put it that way, Dad, yeah, I probably can."

"Okay. I'm just going to lay some events out. Stop me if you need me to stop." I nodded. "I won't go further into the Franks. You can read about them in history books; but, you have to realize, Robyn, when Anne Frank visited your mother that day, there was no notoriety attached to her name, yet. She was only a little girl, like your mother. I will say, though, that their visit was an important one, because Otto Frank's words to your Grandfather Jakob sunk in."

"Wait. Grandfather Jakob? What was my grandmother's name?"

"Johanna."

"Jakob and Johanna. It works! It's like Edward and Elizabeth."

"Yes, I suppose it does," he said. My dad stopped to watch me grasp my maternal grandparents' existence, with actual names, for the first time. I saw his head bob slowly in approval, and his lips tighten a bit, as if holding in emotions. He breathed in deeply.

"Your mother has said this, more times than I can count in our first years together: 'Oh, how I wished we had left with the Franks that day.' See, they had additional years of freedom in the Netherlands, and had they tried to leave there sooner—had everyone tried to leave Hitler's ever-expanding Europe sooner, things could have been different for so many. But in day-to-day life, we don't pick up on warning signs so well. It's human nature to hope goodness wins out; no one expects evil to descend so quickly. Okay," he breathed in, again. I could tell this story wasn't easy for him, either. "So, your mother's little sister's name was Freida Lea Koppold. She turned one, shortly after the Franks left."

That's when another voice entered the room. "And my name used to be . . ."

For some reason I was exceedingly happy to hear and then see Mother. I actually cut her off mid-sentence, when I blurted, "Mom!" I had never called her mom before that day. I rushed to her side and took her hands. We walked to the couch together. Dad stood to open up more space on it. He shot a smile at his wife. "Your name used to be what," I asked?

"Elisheba Miriam Koppold," she said. Dad beamed. He saw something he had longed dreamed would happen, but I'm sure he would not have imagined my immediate response to hearing my mother's birth name.

"Miriam!" That's what struck me. It lassoed my Marie and bound me to her. What Samantha had said about its meaning loomed over me, making me miss the next beat of my mother's heart, entirely. "Oh!" I whispered. Then I realized it was I who had drifted. I came back as quickly as possible. "What happened, Mother?" I asked.

"My papa wanted to leave, Robyn," she said.

"Jakob."

"Yes, Jakob." Mother smiled, looking up at Dad. "But my mutti was afraid. She seemed more terrified at the thought of leaving than staying, which puzzled my papa. Her only thought was making sure her girls were safe. Papa worked around mutti's fears and denials as much as possible, without her blessing. He took all the preliminary steps he could to sketch out the first draft of an escape plan for us. He'd been a professor at the University of Bonn, and . . ."

"Professor of what?" I asked.

"Physics," she said, happy to answer that question. "There were so many brilliant Jews on the faculty then. All were dismissed when Hitler came to power. Papa got all our passports secured with our new names on each one. That's when my name became Elizabeth Cooper. That's how I met your father, as Miss Cooper."

Mother put out a series of emotionless factoids, as if she needed to avoid what was coming. I stopped wondering why she just didn't tell me about the baby. Instead, I listened, thinking those parts must be important to her. She seemed to be remembering everything, as if it were yesterday. I wondered if she'd planned on passing the history of my heritage down to me one day, before Dad strongly encouraged it, or if her plan was to hold it all in, never to reveal anything, hide it, relegate the responsibility of revealing it to Dad through some cryptic paragraph in her Last Will and Testament, along with my other inherited things. I dared not ask. Would I be the new bearer of her history, now? Would I be the generational vessel with less pain, better able to speak it clearly? Would I pass it down, or would I neglect it? I didn't consciously ask myself those questions then, but somehow, I knew the answer. As she spoke I realized I had never seen any photographs of her parents. That felt wrong, which made me listen all the more.

"My mutti was tall, a half-inch shorter than I am," she continued, "with dark blue eyes and sandy blonde hair, a beauty, and a talented artist. She was a Gentile. Jewish customs allow the mother in a mixed marriage to decide what religion a child follows. Papa was Jewish. Mutti chose the national religion of her ancestors, Christianity."

It was the first time I'd heard those words uttered by Mother in the same breath, Gentile, Jewish, and those religions. In fact, I never heard her speak any of those words, even alone, ever. And then there was that singular word that had always been in the shadows, ancestors. In the same way she avoided speaking of her parents, she avoided her heritage, altogether, around me. Mother never laid claim to an ethnic background, nation, or religion. All I can recall, when she made reference to herself, were the words *modern American*.

"Papa didn't like the idea of his girls being christened," she said, "but he allowed it for Mutti's sake. He cherished her. She had faced severe opposition from both sides of the family when marrying him in 1928. I'm sure he must have felt he owed her that support." Mother paused and caught Dad's eyes. I became aware of the depth of love a good husband has for his wife, yet it struck me that leadership within that kind of love could be hard for most men to pick up and carry well.

"Do you need something to drink, Liz?" he asked.

"I would like some water, Edward," she said in the dreamlike state that crept back into her expressions. Mother had nodded her head up and down while responding to his question, but the nod didn't stop when he exited the room. She appeared stuck.

We sat in silence. Mother didn't look at me. The past had overtaken her, again. The nod ceased. I finally understood all the blank stares I'd seen in years past. I watched my mother shrink in stature before my eyes. She had always been larger than life, an unstoppable force—but today, she seemed small, as if she'd have to look up at me, if we stood in that moment. I felt an uncanny sensation well up in my chest. It whispered to my heart: *You must learn about this woman.* I felt protective of her for the first time, not in a condescending way, but as one who loved her.

When Dad returned, she sipped some water. When she finished, I took the glass and held onto it in case she wanted more. I sat in the silence of hesitancy, afraid that if I spoke I'd shatter some fragile fragment, an image that hung before her. I waited, wondering if she'd recapture the past, slip into its form, return with it fully pulsating to offer me more of it. When she spoke, again, I smiled, for she had done just as I'd hoped. "You inherited your grandfather's red curls, Robyn, or . . . at least you had." She paused. "But the color is still the same as his."

I placed my hand over hers, but instead of embracing mine, her fingers remained limp in her lap. I looked at Dad, pleadingly, not knowing if Mother would return. He nodded and said, "Elizabeth, do you want to go on, or is that enough for today? We have time. There's no rush."

"Oh, no," she said. "I need to continue and be done. I need to."

"That's fine, honey," he said.

Mother's narrative carried us back, once again. "A year after the Franks' visit, my papa began letting Mutti know how uncomfortable he was with the political climate in Germany. He didn't believe people should be imprisoned for their religious or political views, as the Jehovah Witnesses and the party members in opposition to Hitler were. He feared the increase of strict regulations upon his people would lead to distress beyond enduring.

"He lamented the fact that Jewish physicians were being barred from their practice, especially the women. First year medical students were replacing them. That fact irked my papa greatly. He added how Jewish youth were no longer being admitted to medical school. When my papa's good friend, Hermann von Simon could no longer practice law, a dark cloud emerged and overshadowed his gentle features. Not only was he grieved for his friend, but since it was von Simon who had signed our important exit documents, his signature would be worthless, now, as would the documents Papa struggled to obtain.

"I began feeling tension form under my papa's clothing. His muscles tightened into knotted ropes. His arms and legs had lost their playfulness. They didn't extend outward in play anymore. He paused when he walked, wondering which street to turn down. He became a man possessed with one thought, saving his family from imminent harm. The thought and its details wrapped around him like a chrysalis. In it he hoped for new life, for the evil to be exposed and sucked out, an evil that made men and women think of us as worms to be plucked and destroyed; but he remained confused as to how we'd escape their clutches and how evil fed on the cooperation of the willfully ignorant. Both saddened him.

"My parents didn't know I could hear them talking at night. They thought I was too young to understand even if I had, and they were right. As far as my cognitive understanding, I didn't comprehend the political muddles of the movement afoot on the streets of Bonn, which stretched into all of Germany and Austria, but I felt the fear it struck in the hearts I loved more than life, and I remembered the overall image of good and evil at our door. It lingered on my papa's breath. I could feel it fall on me, when he'd tuck me in and kiss me goodnight. His kisses had become hard.

"I loved my papa so much. It wounded me to see him burdened with fright and pain. I wanted to take him away, force Mutti to come, too; but she would not. She could not entertain the thought of an atrocity occupying a position in her world on the scale and magnitude Papa painted. 'Never,' I'd hear her mutter in the cold night air. 'Not in Germany.' She thought there were cracks in the current regulations, but surely, they wouldn't last long. 'Things will be restored,' she'd say." I extended Mother the glass of water. She shook her head. She didn't look at me. Her eyes remained lowered.

In a minute she continued. "As weeks passed my mutti could

no longer deny that the Nazis had begun attacking groups beyond political opponents or the Jehovah Witnesses, and what she called other dangerous elements of society; however, she remained firm in her belief that even the portions of life they were altering for the Jews would be restored, as they were part of the fabric of Germany. She said things like, it would make no sense to disrupt a whole people group, entirely. After all, they've held positions of great honor. They're invaluable citizens. Our nation's infrastructure would suffer sorely. Chaos would result.

"On and on, my mutti went, saying such things, until her thoughts on that issue started to unravel in a way she never anticipated. Her favorite screen actors and actresses began to disappear from films. Such a silly thing to turn her head, but it had. Dora Gerson, Joachim Gottschalk, Paul Morgan, Max Ehrlich, and more, all vanished from the screen. Unbeknownst to her they'd been sent to concentration camps.

"Peter Lorre, the odd little man who talked funny, made his way out via France and England, and then landed in America. He succeeded in Hollywood. And I read what had grieved Mutti, once, finally made her happy--the fact that her beloved Marlene Dietrich had sidestepped all of Hitler's strong-arming. She left Germany shortly before he rose to full power.

"Faces erased from films seemed unthinkably more perverse than faces being exiled from universities, hospitals, or businesses. She wrote about this, along with many of her impressions around that time in a journal she'd hidden for her girls. She placed it in a hollowed out history book she packed in a suitcase that stood ready for my sister and me. Two photos lay between its pages, too, the one of us girls, taken on the afternoon the Franks spent with us, and her wedding photo. As often as I read her words, I could not understand why the film industry affected her more than other areas, but I never really got to know my mutti. She must have been a romantic."

I wanted to share with Mother how idolizing celebrities probably had something to do with it. The glittering illusion they're wrapped in, one other mortals acknowledge as true, elevates them above the common man, even professors and doctors. Apparently, the fact they could be touched didn't shatter the illusions surrounding them in my grandmother's mind; it just made the darkness all the more dark.

Mother leaned forward. "My mutti fell ill once evil became an inescapable reality in her mind. It's as if she resigned herself to a fate she couldn't fight. Her family had migrated from Flanders before the turn of the century, so she understood migration; but once she realized the obstacles in her path, the ones that could pluck stars from their places, she quit on herself but not on us. When her eyes had been opened to our danger, the dangers Papa had been trying to convince her were happening all along, that's when my parents began planning our escape as a team. If Mutti hadn't awakened, I wouldn't be sitting here. I know that, because I knew how much my papa leaned on her for support.

"The Germans had ramped up confiscating Jewish property. Undertaking personal matters, once so easy to maneuver in the public sector, became impossible for them. Restrictions, written to be insurmountable challenges for the Jews, closed doors everywhere Papa turned. They weren't just extra steps. They'd become signposts, designed to lead the enemy to our doors. Arranging passageways grew more unattainable as 1935 loomed into view. Our private lives were closely observed. Papa had to go underground often, only to resurface with more information. He heard rumors from Jews, who still had loyal friends in government positions, that an identification patch would soon be issued for them to wear; but other tactics, to create hate toward them, had to be undertaken first, or else the citizens might resist. The plan rolled out in systematic order.

"Existing marriages between Aryans and Jews began to be disavowed, and future ones forbidden. That step meant they were targeting my parents' sacred vows. Soon the Nazis would burst through our doors. Papa grew desperate. Mutti's frailness increased. Fear reached my heart. My sister was a plump, adorable toddler when Mutti said we must leave—just us. I said, "No!" Papa said we must. Mutti cried. They both held us for what seemed an hour. Frieda grew squirmy and broke away. I tried to draw her in again, but Mutti said, "Let her be. I want to watch her playing in her world of make believe, as long as possible."

"Papa took me aside. He explained that a whole Jewish family could not escape; but fair-haired kinders with Aryan friends, posing as their parents could. It was 1936 when the chancellor lowered his onslaught of anti-Semitic propaganda. The Summer Olympics were to be hosted across the country in Berlin, but tourists would be everywhere in Germany before its opening day. Hitler did not want to provide any opportunity for vicious slights or attacks upon his Reich's platform. No uninformed opinions of his vision for the Motherland were to cross the threshold, especially by tourists.

"Wording on posted signs, constricting Jew or casting aspersions on them, were to be removed from cities. Overt criticisms by Aryan citizens were prohibited. Anything that could be construed by prejudicial eyes or heard with uniformed ears by outsiders, so as to equate their platform with human violations, must be removed. Everyone knew how to play his or her part on the world stage. That, Papa said, would be the time for them to escape, when integrity was being feigned. "That's when you'll be most safe to travel, my darlings. Shhhhh. Say nothing of this plan," he said. We had no idea whom we would tell. We seldom stepped foot outside our apartment, but we nodded our heads to please him.

"With the upcoming influx and outflow of tourists, our camouflage was secured. Papa smuggled a letter to a former colleague, Mr Goodchild, a physicist friend in England, to finalize the details they'd been discussing. His friend and his wife would appear to have arrived to attend the summer Olympics, buying four tickets both ways to throw border security off their tracks.

Our passports, which Papa had arranged, were in hand. We were to be the fortunate Cooper nieces, which the childless couple from England would bring with them to the games.

"The entire time Papa had feared for our lives, Hitler had been constructing the Olympic Stadium, an arena that would hold one hundred ten thousand people. Those sport's enthusiasts would come to mean a great deal to us. They could not have imagined how being Hitler's focal point would occupy his mind and provide a window of escape for the Jews. I heard Papa say it more than once. We hoped many other Jews had seen the opportunity, too, but we never knew.

"Papa's friends, the Goodchilds, had purchased tickets for several events of the first day's program, which they never attended. Instead, the day before the games started, they feigned an emergency, while in Bonn, one that required an immediate return to England. They stood in the streets of Bonn, peddling their tickets, just to gain attention, which they did. The tickets sold; their story was broadcast. Success in the initial stage boosted their confidence. Even friends in England, stood by, if called to confirm the emergency. No one thought anyone would call, but the extra attention to details made Mutti feel better about the plan.

"I recall every step I walked with Papa toward the park that day. He held my hand tightly, too tightly. While carrying Frieda, he continually whispered reassurances into her ear. The air even tasted different. Mutti watched from the window, which she opened one last time to thrust her white handkerchief forward in waves. She threw multiple kisses at us with her other hand. I remember how she closed the window abruptly, as if she could no longer bear watching us walk away. Papa kept telling us in low tones, mingled with heightened fear, 'Don't talk. Not a word. You speak German. You're pretending to be English. Don't talk, darlings. Don't talk. Verstehen?' We nodded, as practiced, to show him we understood.

"As we sat on the bench under a towering Beech tree, we

waited for the plan to ripple through our lives, wash us out of Germany. As we rehearsed multiple times, sitting on our living room couch, Papa stood and walked slowly away without a word. Mutti had pretended to be Mrs Goodchild in our rehearsals. So, when practicing, as Papa left, Mutti approached us, just as slowly without a word. I felt my mutti's absence most painfully in that moment on the bench, when it wasn't really she who walked up to us slowly, but a stranger. We hadn't practiced that part. We were not told about the overwhelming grief.

"Frieda did look back and called out, "Papa!" Mrs Goodchild's quick response was planned. She provided Frieda with a piece of hard candy, to fill her mouth and soothe her troubled heart. She then helped her to her feet, took our hands, and hummed a song Mutti had taught her, so sweetly—one we loved so much that we walked to the public transport within a sequestered veil of peace. We rode to our waiting train at Bonn Central Station, where Mr Goodchild awaited us. From Bonn we traveled to Calais, France, spent the night, and the next day ferried to England, as if we were on a lovely holiday. All the while my heart was breaking."

I watched Mother crank her neck from right to left, chin up, then left to right, chin down, several times. I joined her. I even stood and stretched. The palpable heartache, even when the words had ceased, filled the room. Dad, who had heard the story before, perhaps multiple times in bits and pieces, maintained his composure. He stood at the ready to help either of us in any way he could.

One thing occupied my mind. How did Frieda die, if they got out; and why did Mother have to bury her if they were with caring adults who risked their lives for them? I waited, knowing it was coming. Mother's skin had grown quite pale. I didn't think she could withstand more conversation, which emboldened me to ask. "Mother, what happened to Frieda?"

A LITTLE CHAPTER FOR A
LITTLE GIRL

*M*other sighed, determined to answer my question, even with exhaustion's handprint pressing on her whole body. I think Dad was a bit annoyed with me for pushing her that far, but she assured him it was better for her to go on, than to begin afresh another time. So she continued without hesitation, as if she'd entered the story outside herself.

"We made it to London," she said. "Papa's plan was flawless. Flawless. One thing bothered us, though. We wondered why Mutti, a Gentile, could not pretend to be Mrs Goodchild, as we pretended to be the nieces. We didn't understand the bond between my parents at that time. How could they explain it to their children who wanted both of them, but would settle for one? I had read in her journal that he begged her to go, but she would not leave him."

Mother went on to unfold the story. "The Goodchilds kept Frieda and me with them in their lovely home, all the while proclaiming that our parents would join us, soon. *Any day, dears* became the common refrain on the good lady's lips. We lived with them for nearly five, mostly happy years, every day hoping for what seemed but a dream at times, for the war to end, for our family to be reunited. Instead, we saw more and more Jewish children stream into London from Germany, Austria, and even Poland.

"Shortly after the start of our fourth year in England, the words so often spoken in our ears ceased; however, they remained hidden in our hearts. I was ten, Frieda, seven. I had read Mutti's journal aloud to Frieda so often we almost had it memorized; and the precious photos within its pages took on a more flimsy feel over the years. The constant touch of our fingertips, tracing the forms that bore the names of our parents had its wearing effect. We lingered over their faces, time and again, and kissed them each night and morning. That September, four years and three weeks after the closing of the Summer Olympics, Hitler made his way to England, not like he had in Germany, but from the air. The bombing of major urban cities began. It was called the Blitzkrieg. Of course, I knew what that meant, when most children did not. It meant, *the lightning*.

"The merciless attacks lasted eight months and several days. Our house remained standing until the sixth month. I was already eleven; Frieda, still seven. The Goodchilds were not home when the sirens blared. Our nanny called us into the house to access our safe shelter under the stairs. We were accustomed to riding out the shrill sound by that time; but that evening the outer disruption felt closer. Our world shrank. Frieda called out for the puppy, Dutchess, which the Goodchilds had given her over the summer, but the dog was not responding. Her crying prompted the nanny to exit our shelter in search of it. Frieda insisted the puppy did not like Betty and wouldn't come to her if she called, especially if she were already afraid. After declaring such, loudly into my face, she pried her arm from my grip and ran through the house. "Frieda, no!!" I screamed. The next thing I remember I was running after her and then awakening among the rubble and someone shouting, "Here's another one! Over here, quick. It's a child."

"Every fuzzy voice was unfamiliar. No Frieda. No Goodchilds. No Betty. No barking Dutchess. No close neighbors. Nothing surrounded me. "Take them to the orphanage. There's a doctor on duty tonight," one voice said. That gave me some comfort, as I was sure 'them' meant Frieda and me."

"Did it, Mother?" I asked.

"Yes, but Frieda had been seriously injured. When she had regained consciousness, she began begging for one of the four beings she loved and missed. Any one of them would have soothed her. She and the other children on the little cots, all in a row, cried in whimpering spurts. The room had purposely been darkened. The windows, all-too-commonly crisscrossed in tape and covered in paper, let in no light and only added to the coldness surrounding us. Nurses sailed between beds with one hand cupped over the flame of a candle they held. Every darkened element withheld what the children needed most, a sweet warm light they could follow.

"I'll never forget what Frieda kept muttering, over and over. The order never changed. Mutti; Papa; Helene, which Mrs Goodchild allowed us to call her; and Dutchess. She never called my name. I didn't understand why, then, but now I think it was because she knew I was near and wanted me to fetch the loves her heart yearned to hold again." Dad nodded.

"Her relentless requests stirred me to action. I had to go, seek out her desires, which meant leaving the orphanage for a while. I departed in the hope of finding at least one of the most possible requests on her list, Mrs Goodchild, or the puppy. I'd even bring Mr Goodchild, if he were home. I felt sure the nurse on duty would take care of my Frieda.

"I made my way back to the house, as the first and most sensible place to look. I wasn't aware of what had happened to it, but my curiosity was piqued. I wanted answers instead of confusion. Nothing was making sense. Perhaps, the Goodchilds had returned and wondered where we'd gone. There was no thought in my mind that Frieda wouldn't mend, once her request was satisfied and she could rest. God would never take a child's life, whose heart only wanted to be loved, or to lavish love. That's what I'd assumed. Surely the man on the cross knew pain, died for children, and would not want Frieda to suffer. That's the hope I carried in my mind, when I snuck out that night.

"When I returned with no puppy the next morning, or news of the Goodchilds, or home to call mine, I found Frieda's bed empty. I asked where they'd taken my sister. The night nurse I recalled said, "Come with me." She led me down the hall to a large room, filled with gray filing cabinets and bare metal shelves, where fewer cots were set, more closely together, in a row, maybe twelve in total. Sheets were draped clear over their heads. I thought it was to keep them warmer, surely, while waiting to be released to a loved one. Frieda and I often pulled covers over our heads for more warmth. The nurse knew exactly which cot Frieda occupied. I was glad to find she cared enough to remember we were sisters. "Are you sure you want to see her," she asked me. "Of course!" I said.

"When she pulled back the sheet, the nurse then realized I had not grasped death's face. Perhaps she had thought I was older, being tall and responsible. I spoke to Frieda, saying, "I'm sorry, my darling, I couldn't find your puppy. Frieda? Frieda!" I touched her arm. Its coldness startled me. I withdrew my hand immediately, and stood quite still, taking in the beauty of my sister's face, like I had never done in all the years she lived. When the nurse finally left me, as I had asked, I lifted Frieda. I didn't know how the strength came. That startled me. I didn't know where I would take her. I couldn't figure out why nobody stopped me. I thought they would. I thought some adult would redirect me, pull her from my arms. I began to feel invisible, like a shield surrounded me. I found a chair with wheels and put her onto its seat, covering her to her shoulders with the sheet. Her yellow hair lay against it, short golden wisps.

"I walked north. I didn't know why. Our home had been southward. Maybe I thought, after seeing it earlier, it was no place to be. I wheeled her down one long street, around rubble, past areas we had never walked. I pushed forward towards what I thought would be the countryside, miles and miles of unending countryside. I came to a green space with two opened, metal gates, held in place by stately brick columns. The undisturbed order of it beckoned me. In my fatigue I tripped through its entryway. It was a cemetery, a Jewish one. The sign read, Hoop Lane Jewish Cemetery, both in English and Hebrew. I sensed it was right that she should be buried with our papa's people, since the crucified man my mutti worshipped had failed her twice already; but that justification only existed before I learned of my papa's fate.

"I wrapped the sheet tightly around Frieda and laid her near a tree. I had found and snatched up a broken brick and a bent metal rod, earlier, in the rubble we passed. I used them to open the earth. I picked away, but tree roots hampered my progress. We were at the western border of the acreage. I mentally marked the location. I dug outward from the tree, scratched, and pushed the soil for what seemed a deadening hour with little progress, but I wouldn't stop. Stopping would be worse than what I was doing. Burying my sister there seemed the only right thing I could do, which made it the most important thing in the world for me to do.

"I worked for another hour, pounding the rod with the brick. One strike crumbled it into chunks. I used the fragments to scratch with both hands, like a dog with long nails. The progress was pitifully slow. My fingers began to blister and bleed. I sat down and wept for the first time since the sirens blasted that fatal warning the night prior. It was then I realized my world had crumbled like the brick, mere clay, dust to dust. I cried, remembering those words from somewhere, and how they carried doom in their breathless sweep. Someone overheard me. Someone gasped and wept softly with me. I looked up to see an elderly woman, leaning on a tree nearby, watching me with eyes of grief greater than my own."

PART III
DOORS, OUR FOREVER

CONSTRUCTION AND
DESTRUCTION

*J*never knew the leader inside my Dad until I watched him move among the crew of men and women he hired to build our barn. It had nothing to do with micromanaging them. Most were experienced carpenters. It's what he brought into the everyday mix, a sense of goodwill, which made everyone perform well in what they did best, unhindered. His ability even affected Scott and me, or maybe I should say, me with Scott.

I began regarding Scott as a partner. His focus on the tasks-at-hand, even when Samantha came to visit, impressed me. At first I wasn't sure if his work didn't slack when she arrived because others were around, watching. I soon realized that wasn't it. Scott was a goal-setter and worked hard on reaching the mark he set. When I liked his goal, I liked him. He and Dad bonded; and I grew strangely relaxed in his presence. Richard became more of a family friend during that time, too. He started standing out as an individual in my eyes, apart from his family or Samantha, that is.

Mother puttered about on the fringe of the activity, in quiet contentment, fixing large pots of chili or soups to supplement the crew's bag lunches with something warm that winter and early spring. She supplied hot coffee and cookies we baked together every evening, nibbling through many each night before they were set out on the front porch in the morning.

Samantha stayed busy with her academic studies, which Ma piled onto her in the cold months of November through mid-March. The rest of the year was for "doin', outdoor learnin', and readin' whatever ya please." That routine seemed brilliant to me, almost like paradise regained. Samantha handled the intensity of the 'winter jam' sessions, abounding in textbooks and assigned lessons, as well as she did the relentless 'fall jam' days, when jars were stuffed with nature's pickings.

Scott went out of his way to help me on certain projects. At first I wondered if he thought me incompetent, but as with every other positive that surfaced in those hours under the sun, seeing him just as a good guy popped into my field of vision, too. Sawing boards with his weight on one end became twice as easy; whacking nails was more fun when we raced, but never at the expense of a poor job. Sometimes, he'd say, "I lose," just to make sure my nails were going in straight after I pulled out a few bent ones. I think he wanted to be friends, because he knew that would make Samantha happy. That made me happy, in that setting.

None of those relational perks would have happened, though, had the working environment not been one of cheerful cama-raderie, which Dad set in motion. He never called for overtime. He proclaimed the days surrounding holidays, free, knowing the value of family first. He provided a turkey on the Tuesday before Thanksgiving to each member of our crew, and a type of stuffed stocking in December. The latter gifting arrived in the form of backpacks, filled with cookies, ground coffee (not mine), cakes, candles, and Dad's favorite Christian book of the month, incon-spicuously packed at the bottom.

"Thanks, Ed" was often heard, which made me smile when my back was turned. I wasn't used to hearing Dad called by an abbre-viated name. I liked it. I became tagged with the nicknames, "Birdie," or "Little Edbird," preferring the one that aligned me with Dad, not a robin, more; but I smiled at both. Mother, however, never became "Liz" or even Elizabeth to the crew. Forever the more dignified member of our family, she respectfully remained Mrs. Thomas throughout the entire project.

Even though her name didn't get lightened, I could tell a burden had been lifted from her, ever since she told me her story. My heart not only connected more to Mother's, but in general, to humanitarian deeds of mercy. Learning about that Jewish woman in the cemetery, who observed Mother as a strangely disheveled little girl in dire need affected me for the good. Mother said the woman would have been like a great grandmother to me, because after she took her hand that day, she took her home, promising to arrange a proper burial for Frieda next to the gravesite of her husband. He had been a longstanding member of the cemetery's board of trustees and lay buried in a sweet area within a hedged-off courtyard. "There is plenty of space," she said. It turned out the woman's adult children and grandchildren had been trapped in Austria, and like Mother's parents, executed. That one hard distinction in both their lives formed an inseparable bond between them.

The woman grew to love Mother, as if she were her own granddaughter. When Mother turned seventeen, the woman sent her abroad to America to study at Harvard. The two had planned the venture together, but eventually only Mother sailed into the other life. She became one of many groups of European Jews to enter the renowned university, recovering from its major weak spot at the time—its antisemitic enrollment prejudices. The walls of that bias continued to crumble ever so slightly until it no longer existed after Mother graduated. She had enjoyed poking another stick through its already collapsing wall, though.

Mother's own prejudices were partially combed out in her confessed unburdening that day in her special room. Light trickled through the slightly opened door, and with it came a wider understanding of life, past and present. Mother and Dad laughed a lot more in those days, and we felt more like a family than I could ever recall. When she'd call out, "Edward?" from a distance, invariably he'd respond, "Was that 'Bird,' or 'Ward,' dear?"

"It's the one who captured my heart long ago, dear," she replied. I'm not sure why, but that made the men smile and the women smile bigger. It, also, made me wonder if the crew carried my parents' warmth home with them to spread its glow upon their own loved ones on those cold winter nights.

Those months slipped by too quickly. I wished we had a dozen more projects with the same crew, the same smiling faces and helping hands, all working together as a team; but the barn got built. The corral went up, and the horses showed up in May, the same month Scott renewed his all-consuming focus on the Ryan with Samantha at his side.

I was the first to be called into the Ryan project. I had agreed to my part months earlier, but truthfully, the moment I arrived and threw open my sketch pad I sorely missed my other group, the fresh wood, the sounds of saws and hammers, laughter, food smells, the fresh open air, and Dad's cohesive cheerfulness. In Scott's old barn, which smelled strange and unwelcoming, I drew old parts with chilled fingers. The stale air retained the night's cold hand. A stagnant stillness found its way through those battered walls, sucked out any beauty and never returned it.

Scott had asked if I would arrive before nine, which didn't seem a problem, since I had gotten used to popping out of bed at seven to be at work on our barn by eight, however, it wasn't long before I noticed I no longer popped out of bed. I lay, covered and cozy well past the ringing of my alarm, several times, bringing Mother's questioning voice to my door.

"Yeah, yeah! I'm up, almost. It's okay."

"I don't appreciate double talk. Are you up or not?"

"Not really."

"Well, really get up, Robyn. Your friends need you."

When she put it that way, I said, "I'm up!" but the motivation never stuck, when the next morning arrived.

Scott and Samantha liked my drawings, even though I thought them stiff, like my cold fingers. "Well, I like them," Scott said.

"Bolts are s'pose to look stiff," Samantha added, while rubbing the side of my arms. *There's that one mind, again*, I thought. I wondered if young love took a bit of exercising to feel natural enough to see that two minds are better than one, even within their interdependence; or maybe I was just letting my own prejudices surface, once again, and seeing bad where nothing but good stood. Maybe it was as simple as the wire, bolt, and gasket drawings, accurate enough for the next stage to commence, and that's what excited them.

So, I set myself to following the order of their repair plan. I laid each section on paper, down to the last threaded cap. Samantha never left my side. She knew I hated the barn and tried to make it as pleasant as possible for me, while there.

I won't deny it. There were some good times in those weeks. I still loved being with Samantha. How could that ever change? I only wanted us somewhere else, somewhere on our mountain, somewhere open and fresh, and full of wonder—places where she could lead me into the truths she captured in her heart. I missed those times. They were nowhere in sight; but her outpouring soul kept churning even though its references changed, somewhat. Her expressions took on mechanical overtones. She dipped into nature's wellspring less frequently. For example, here's one unnatural truism I recorded: "Every positioned nut and bolt, every connective wire has its story, 'cause even *things* are placed where they are by someone's hand for a reason." See? It all surprised me, but it made sense, too. Her center remained on point. It was just the allusions that shifted.

When I had completed all the drawing, neatly labeling each section, I laid my pad and pencils down and asked Mother if we could go somewhere warm and bright for my fourteenth birthday, as a family. I said I'd like to return fresh to help Scott and Samantha with the Ryan. She loved the idea, and began planning our exodus. She chose two weeks in San Diego, California.

Samantha and Scott agreed to muck out the horses' stalls, as well as feed, water, and exercise both of them in our absence. Richard was asked to stay on as our house sitter and take my role as official caretaker of Blackie. He liked the idea and accepted it readily. My parents didn't hold an iota of concern for their homestead, while under the supervision of those three mountain teens, nor did I. We pulled away within the same time frame we left New York, four years earlier. It was a longer trip, but this time at my request.

When in San Diego, I met a boy. I thought it terribly strange that a good-looking boy, three years older than I, found me attractive. That's what consumed my head. He actually liked me! My parents didn't approve. They questioned his motives and his character, which I resented. "You don't know him like I do!" I blurted in front of Dad's face one morning, as I walked by him abruptly.

"Oh, I see," he said, turning to watch me head toward the beach, which made me stop, but not turn. "You spent, what, four hours with him yesterday? Your mother and I had twenty minutes with him, and that makes you better equipped to read his unvoiced and veiled intentions? That makes perfect sense, Robyn." My thoughts ran along these lines: I never imagined my dad would use sarcasm on me, nor that he would be so unfair and judge someone from surface appearances, especially so quickly. So what if Mark had some tattoos and long hair! "It's a free country!" I blurted in defense of his appearance. I could understand Mother being hypercritical. Hints of it had already cropped up in New York, but Dad? That threw me. Mother chimed in, "Attitude reaches farther down than one's surface, Robyn, and his is infecting yours. Stop and look at yourself."

So, once more and just like that, I felt my parents ganging up on me; but it didn't matter. Why should it? This was *my* vacation, and I'd spend time with Mark if I wanted to spend time with

Mark. It was easy, really. I simply wandered off toward the beach, while they lounged poolside. Everything they did seemed boring to me. Mark, being his charming and cute self in those baggy shorts and encircling friends, excited me. I could see other girls cast sideways glances at him and then at me. That, along with the fact he obviously favored me, threw me into a new type of emotional tailspin, a good one, or so I thought.

I mean, realistically, I already knew I'd have to forfeit his friendship almost as soon as making it. We met on our fourth day there. So why, I asked myself, were the parents so upset? Going to California was specifically for a fun, carefree, non-thinking time— a birthday gift to me, not to please my parents and cater to their prejudices. That meant, casting Mark aside *before* our departure was unthinkable. There was still a week and a half left of the vacation. And, if I liked him enough, I might even keep him.

It was only when I snuck out that last night and found myself at an extended beach party three miles away that they blew various fuses. Yes, I got back two hours past my 10 p.m. curfew, but I had a great explanation. We lost track of time, because dancing around the bonfire was so much fun; and all the cars were blocking us from leaving anyway. Really, we were lucky to get out at midnight, since we were parked way toward the front of the lot. "Can't you just be happy I'm here," I finally blurted out, which only sent more sparks flying my way.

"Sneaking out, Robyn; and we not knowing where you were, is that how you want to treat us? And by us I mean our family," Dad said. That's all he said. He turned and walked to his bedroom with his hand extended to Mother. She took hold of it and left, too. His silence tortured me. Her silence baffled me.

All in all, the vacation flopped. I longed to be with Mark all the way home, and hoped to see him again soon. He promised he'd write and come visit. I hung onto his promises, golden sun-filled threads of hope. Those expectations lasted through the week, including the long weekend. By Monday I knew he'd never write or call. Disappointment loomed. My failure list seemed complete. I hit another low point in my relationship with my parents. It all felt crummy. After Mark's deadly silence, I began suspecting Dad and Mother might have been right about his character. How could they know stuff like that about someone right away? It was beyond me. I couldn't even complain aloud. No one was in my corner. I thought of calling Georgi, but didn't. Blackie, she listened.

To make matters worse, in my two-week absence, Samantha and Scott had solidified. They became synchronized. I hardly recognized either of them. They were a new entity, transformed into one from two, yet obviously still two. Talk became minimal between them as they worked, more like a verbal shorthand, all to further production. I did hear chatter during their breaks and at meal times; but, basically, body language overtook talking. Facial expressions followed their almost unnoticeable physical touches. Those types of affectionate micro-movements happened within seconds of their eye contact. Even though such encounters occupied the breath of a raindrop's visible descent to earth, they seemed to fill each hour, for hours on end with a heavy, never-ending goop, until I felt as if I were drowning in a vat of syrup. It clung to me, entered my bones. Soon I felt the chill of exclusion slip in.

I brought my sketchbook with me that first day back home and drew them. When I looked at the sketch later that night, my heart sank into a forlorn state. It wasn't envy. Jealousy wasn't even in the picture any longer. It was, as if I had resigned myself to being the outcast, the third-wheel that got no grease. I lost my footing, my function, my place of being. I shed no tears. I felt like dried dung, still attracting bothersome flies. Bother! In that place of isolated resignation, I began planning my future.

I had one more semester of high school to complete to be accredited and graduate with high honors. My ACT scores were great. The world was my "oyster," as they say; but I didn't like oysters, so I said, my piece of cake, which I intended to consume, whole, with my fingers, and have it, too. I began looking at college brochures Mother had been collecting for me, spreading them across my bed like pastry on a bakery shelf. I twirled and rubbed my hands together, as I had imagined Silas Marner doing when standing over his gold. I could almost feel myself salivate until I remembered Samantha's compassionate feelings for Silas. They mushroomed into expressions I couldn't understand. I wished I had never suggested reading it with her. She said the title could just as easily have been, Solace Mourner. I sloughed her thoughts off and returned to my pressing questions: What would I do next in this big world? Where would I go to school? Who would I meet? What delicious things would happen from this decision? The speculation almost drove me wild with excitement and I bound downstairs seeking food.

Mother was in the kitchen, fixing a fruit salad. I declined her offer to share it, politely, which she noticed, and made myself a fat ham and lettuce sandwich with extra mustard on a poppy-seed bagel. I dropped it on a plate along with some potato chips, poured a tall glass of ginger ale, and headed back upstairs with the same enthusiastic speed. Mother called out, "What are you doing up there?"

"Looking through college information. Can't wait!! Thanks for getting all of them for me, Mother. Talk to you later about it."

Dad walked into the room at that point. "What was that bolt of energy I just saw dash upstairs," he asked.

"I think that was our daughter on her way out the door," she said, looking gravely concerned.

GOING, GOING, GONE

I had to get into a school before I could sail off the mountain, so I focused on my exodus by spending the rest of the summer assembling the most winsome and winning application packets possible. I labored over each essay question until every word fit, and then I worked it again, stringing lines together into what I thought were shimmering turns of perfection. The words eventually danced; and so did I—across my room, several times. I did allow Mother to proofread each application. She approved of my choice to include her in the process.

I didn't stop there, though. When I mailed my first-pick applications to Yale and Princeton, I included two non-Ivy packets, state colleges of reputable standing. One claimed the journalistic award for excellence: the University of Missouri in Columbia; and the other, held an enticing allure: the University of Pennsylvania's English and Writing Program. Those latter two, however, fell into the just-in-case portion of my brain. "Back ups are good," Mother said. I wasn't at all concerned that I'd need back ups after dropping the first two into the mail slot at the post office.

The pressure had been released, but my joy seemed to flee with it. My dancing feet dragged themselves home. Something about all of what I was doing landed in the territory of strange. I was pretty sure my destiny would show its face to me, even though *how* remained a mystery. So, I waited, read novels, and tried to set my mind on being open to the obvious. It would be obvious, wouldn't it? I asked myself.

Weeks later, Dad said, "You've got a couple of large envelopes from two colleges, Robyn—Yale and Mizzou." I paused, wondering which I should open first, and then chided myself, ripping open Yale's. "Of course, Yale's," I yelled. Dad walked aimlessly around the kitchen, sporting a goofy smile. "Dad, stop," I said, "you're making me nervous." I opened the envelope.

"Congrats, daughter," he said after seeing a telltale glow appear on my face. "Pretty sure tomorrow's mail will bring the same," he said; and it did. Four applications turned up four acceptances. Suddenly, the decision-making task sat like a rock between my eyes. What had seemed a fantasy in the possibility stages had morphed into a greater burden than the application process. Four paths mushroomed into an atomic cloud before my eyes, blinding me in its sheer energy.

"What am I supposed to do with this mess!" I uttered in complete dismay. My parents gawked at each other, stupefied at my misnomer. "Mess?" they asked at the same time. It seemed they intentionally stayed clear of voicing an opinion. "You don't think this is a mess?" I wailed. No input.

That evening I went to Dad and asked, specifically, what he'd do, and then he asked me something I'll never forget. "Robyn, will any advice I have for you in your immediate future depend, solely, upon you wanting it? Will I have to wait for a checkered flag to wave before I can offer you advice on things you race ahead on, just hoping I can catch up to you and you'll hear me above your own engine's noises? Or may I feel at liberty, as your father, to offer my counsel, unsolicited? In other words, will you listen to me, if I think you need to hear something for your own good, or have I been relegated to being merely your personal sounding board, whenever you're confused?"

"You're talking about Mark, right?"

"Yes, I am. I'm not happy with how you snubbed our advice; and afterwards, how you ignored us, zooming ahead into the universe of your making once we arrived home. I'm proud of your mental abilities, Robyn. I'm impressed with how hard you worked on your application packets. Truly, I am. I stand in awe of how you've captured the attention of four outstanding campuses. And, yes, of course, I will give you my opinion on which I think you should accept, as you've asked; however, I'd like to know if you'll hear me in the future, when you feel adamant on going your own way, and you're not soliciting my advice. Will my opinion be welcomed at those junctures? After all, child-of-mine, you've only recently turned fourteen. Most students applying for admission into these schools are between seventeen and nineteen. You do realize how wide a gap that small, but significant age difference is, don't you?"

"Yes, I know, Dad, but . . ." He lowered his head, glaring at me, briefly.

"But what?" he asked.

"But, I think I'm mature enough to handle it."

"So, that would be a no, then, on offering unsolicited advice?"

"No, not exactly. Just let me get there and spread my wings a bit, is all I'm asking."

"Fair enough. I just don't want you to fly too far from our reach at your age. Robyn, my choice for you would be the University of Pennsylvania."

His response surprised me to the point of speechlessness, since Yale was closer to home than Penn; but somehow, I felt he had chosen my destiny. Later that night I planted a kiss on his cheek and thanked him for making my life a bit easier. I, also, said, "Don't give up on me, Dad." That response surprised him.

I left that winter to start my first day of college, mid-January, long before the Ryan had undergone its full dismantling and received only a partial reassembling. Samantha had begun polishing sections of the outer shell, which they detached in sections and carried to the workbench near the potbelly stove Scott's Pa had installed. It was a tall order for a stove to warm an uninsulated barn, but no one figured on them working through the winter.

Eventually, Scott nailed up some tar paper to keep the wind off Samantha, but the chilling force found access around it and through the layers of outerwear she wore. Still, they refused to work less, even during the severest winter on record. Both persevered, only to collapse over the holidays. Afterwards, they started up again.

That month my dark imaginings tumbled into my head afresh. All the good I had learned about Scott started to peel away. I figured he had to be obsessed in an unhealthy way with work, since Samantha was getting sucked into the dark hole of his intense preoccupation, and that the best thing for me to do, with such an impossible scenario, would be to leave them both alone to figure it out on their own. I refused to see how fond Samantha had grown of the Ryan project, independent of Scott's passion. It became a challenge for her, one she'd never tackled before, and the possibility of extending that work out into the heavens, into uncharted beauty, excited her as much as the mountain had me under her eyes. In a way, Scott had become her guide, the way she had been mine.

I spent one brief hour with Samantha the Friday my parents loaded up Mother's SUV with all my college-bound boxes, new and old things I wanted near. We walked in silence mostly, both a bit overwhelmed with the changes in our lives, and even though we both welcomed them, we sensed our paths had split. It wasn't a pleasant feeling. Seeing the burning fire and hot cocoa Mother had prepared in my honor, when I returned home, comforted me some, but those two bandaids were not a remedy. We three relished those closing moments before the fire, knowing we were a family under change, too.

Father stayed home to tend the beasts, as Mother and I set out for territories unknown. An hour into our trip, an unexpected gust made driving hazardous. We pulled over to search the map for an exit, indicating a motel. That's when the snow began to flutter across our view, first in flurries, then in big wet flakes. They slapped onto the windshield under the force of the wind. Thankfully, we only had to drive two miles. Once in the motel we learned no one was on the roads, and all flights had been cancelled due to some storm's premature arrival. "No!" I cried. "I'll be late for orientation."

"You, and a few hundred others. Don't worry. The storm's early. We don't have to be. We'll get there; and when we get there, we'll get there safely." I laid my head on my mother's shoulder as we leaned against a stack of pillows on our king-sized mattress, watching an episode of Seinfeld. I felt happy to have her at my side and on my side.

College's initial weeks flew by. I revisited Sir Gawain and the Green Knight, and other notable characters in the stories that peppered my childhood, all from new perspectives and with stimulating input. My classes provided a welcomed shelter of intellectual acceptance. Socially, I was the odd duck out, though. Boys were attracted to me, but shied away after catching wind of my age. I wondered about the fixation on age, a mere number. My age became even more awkward, when I was encouraged to test out of several freshman classes by a professor who saw my potential, thereby furthering the possibility of being admitted into one of his classes. It was held in the fall for sophomores and he wanted me in it. Doing so would allow me the advantage of applying to a fledgling study program abroad during the summer, too, a pilot program Penn hadn't officially announced, but one, which the same professor suggested I take, so I did. After my first semester of college, I was a sophomore. Whirlwind.

I made a friend, Petra, an international student from Germany. I wondered what Mother would think of me having a friend from Germany, considering her past. When she wrote back she was delighted, I was relieved.

Petra and I both registered for the summer program, an intensive to be held at King's College in London, England. Literature was the main course, sprinkled with theatre for artistic diversity, probably to get our bodies up and moving, and to help walls fall more quickly. Excited for the opportunity to visit places Mother had known kept me alert and happy with anticipation.

Toward the end of our fourth week, when Petra and I were cleaning up theater props, I shared my mother's story. Hearing it made her remorseful and apologetic. She swept a hooded cloak around her form, covered her head with it, and slumped down onto a short stool. The cloak engulfed everything. I told her it wasn't her fault, what happened in the political arena of her country's past, and added how Mother would truly enjoy meeting and getting to know her.

Those weeks in London rolled away quickly, and the summer snapped back upon us, leaving little room for reflection. Petra invited me to spend the rest of our break in Germany with her family, which frightened me a bit. My parents thought it a good opportunity, but when Petra still noticed my hesitation, she leaned into me, saying, "My mutti would so be pleased with your company. I know it. Father, too." I perked up when I heard the word, mutti.

"That's what my mother called her mother!" I said.

"Yes, it is the common way," she said. "Please, say you will come to Neubrandenburg with me. It would honor my parents." When I saw the tears form in her eyes, I felt there was a story behind them, one of great compassion. I told her I'd love to go.

"Where am I going, exactly?" I asked.

She inhaled quickly and exhaled slowly. "Oh, so good you come!" she said. "You will be going to the northwest part of

Germany. You will meet my brother, Hans, too. He is sixteen, but does not get underfoot. He has a motor scooter. It is fun, when he offers rides. Oh, I forgot, you will be turning fifteen, soon, so he is not so young, after all, to you. Never mind. I ramble." I felt a momentary dizziness and sense of being overwhelmed by her summation, but her accent and the way she formed her sentences accelerated the warmth I already felt for her.

The first night in Petra's home Hans showed up mid-way through dinner, apologized curtly, and sat like a bullfrog waiting for food to come his way, which it did. He did jump up, once, to snatch a small bowl hidden from everyone else's view. He, also, shifted in his seat once, to acknowledge my presence with a nod.

I questioned why he impressed me, not physically at first, exactly, but in the way emotions get thrown off balance by an unseen soft punch, for reasons unknown. The impact didn't land on me like Mark's had in California. Mark made me laugh. He worked hard, in a playful way to draw me into his circle of charm. When he tried to steal a kiss from me that last night, it terrified me, which is why I ran back to the motel room and presented myself in a defensive posture to my parents. I already knew I shouldn't have stayed out that late. Guilt masks itself.

Near Hans I was aware of how much I missed my parents' input. The seemingly unaffected boy drew me in without so much as a second glance. I was sure he'd never try to kiss me, yet I felt more terrified of him than I had of Mark, which baffled me to the point of distraction. I began feeling utterly annoyed with myself.

In the days that followed, his interest in me had not improved. He was serious and dignified. His sandy blond hair, cropped short, made me strain to imagine how much more adorable he'd be, if it were long and fell onto his upper cheeks; but, he was already oddly handsome shorn, so its length was probably a good thing for me. I say, oddly, because his looks didn't complement his manner. Grace did not accompany the chiseled form he inhabited.

Petra's parents had taken me to see their bakery the second

week after my arrival. They wanted to tell me a story that involved the store and their delivery truck—more so, the story of the grandfather, who drove the truck during the war. Their business was called, *Brot des Lebens*, Bread of Life. It had released its fresh baked scents into the streets of old Neubrandenburg for the first time in 1925. Petra's Oma and Opa baked and worked the shop, but it was her Opa who delivered the bread to the restaurants and grocers. I was told, standing there near the truck, how Opa Otto had delivered not only bread, but on six separate occasions twelve Jewish children to other Christians families, who strongly opposed Hitler's persecution of them. He and that truck, now restored, brought life to those children, when they were secreted out of Germany into other nations. Opa Otto's route was the first leg of their escape, and the most dangerous. It was said of his children years later, "They smelled as sweet as freshly baked bread for hours after leaving his truck." They were called, *The Risers*, because their bellies were full of his warm sweet bread.

I nodded as the familiar staging and drama of the story swept over me. Hearing it caused me to miss Mother. I thanked Petra's parents for sharing it, knowing such stories were only spoken before ears that could hear. They sensed I had, and I sensed their satisfaction in finding a kindred heart.

Afterwards, in a moment of awkward silence, Petra's father addressed Hans, "You take our guest to see sights, now."

"Me, Papa? She's Petra's friend."

"Petra's friend? Why not you, too? Are you so bashful?"

"I'm not bashful!" Hans said. "I'll take her."

I looked down at my feet. The grace revealed in the family's past had flipped into an embarrassing present. "Okay then, we'll be off," he said, when no one offered another suggestion, "but don't expect her back in two hours," he said. He took me by the hand and motioned me towards his scooter. I welcomed the shift in activity and waved goodbye to Petra and her parents. "Save us some supper," he called out. "I'm taking her to the tree."

Hans drove north thirty minutes to show me his "favorite tree." I never heard of anyone having a favorite tree. I loved my magnolia trees, but their beauty was connected more to the wafting fragrance they produced, coupled with the enveloping hum of winged ones' compelled to enter each flower, thereby covering en masse the entire grove with their sight and sound. Yet, the exhilaration I felt, while holding onto Hans made me believe that a favorite tree was a normal thing everyone should have.

"Hold on tight," he said, and I obliged.

As the small town of Stavenhagen appeared, so did the cobblestone. A beautiful baroque castle, drenched in warm colors, popped up on the horizon. The area felt enchanted. "This is home to one of our great authors. We could visit the literature museum on our way back. I know Petra likes it," he shouted back at me. "Oh! Yes!" I said. As we drove through the village and beyond, I began wondering how much farther we had to go, since I thought Stavenhagen would be our stopping point; but, since I was in no hurry to get there, I let my curiosity drift away. If I were on my own, I would have felt lost after the village, but not with Hans. He knew exactly where he was going, just the way Samantha had in the mountains. A chill crossed my back as I thought of her, still in that dark drafty barn, hunched over metal and grease. I wondered if she would like Hans. I decided she would. "Not much farther," he called out.

When we arrived, he parked the scooter and gave me his hand to help me step through. It struck me that my parents would regard Hans in a better light than Mark. I ruminated a bit on the shortsightedness of a girl's eyes and heart, when smitten. Dad spoke his mind about boys after we got home from California, which seemed so long ago. One of the things he said, "I want a young man to treat my daughter with the dignified respect she and all other young ladies deserve. If he doesn't know how, he needs to go off and learn, but not around my daughter." I wished Dad were in Germany with me, waiting for me to return to the Ottos' home in Neubrandenburg, if only for a day, so that he could meet Hans and take home a glowing report to Mother. I thanked him, secretly, in my heart for picking the university he had. If I had gone elsewhere, I wouldn't have met Petra, which meant I would not have met Hans.

"Here we are. This is the Ivenack Zoo, and there stands the oldest and largest oak tree in the world," he said. We walked the pathway near a wooden railing, bordering the tree. The massive oak leaned to the right. It looked healthy and imposing, anchored as a solitary attraction. Its base resembled the foot of a mammoth mastodon, complete with toes, only a hundred times larger. I figured it spanned the linear breadth of nine broad-shouldered men, if standing side by side. I wondered if its circumference would beat out the biggest Redwood tree in California. I thought for sure the person in front of me had beat out a certain boy in California, but I estimated the Redwoods were taller, and probably some were wider. For sure I knew all of them were in better company within their unique forest of kindred trees. I kept those thoughts to myself, though. Apples and oranges, I figured. I tucked them away with others labeled 'not for sharing,' even if true —Dad's wisdom.

"So, would you like to sit at this picnic table or walk around?"

"Walk," I said.

"Oh, you don't like my tree?"

"No. It's not that," I said, hurriedly. "It's just I've been sitting most of the day. We could walk backwards and look at the tree, if you want," I said to lighten the mood, once it turned sour.

"What?" he said.

Did he really not get my humor or was it just a language barrier? Surely, it couldn't be the language. He spoke English better than Petra. We stood by the tree, not walking or sitting. I suppose he thought stagnation constituted a compromise of sorts, or maybe he was just plain stuck and needed help out of a predicament he hadn't wanted. Maybe he really was bashful, but that didn't seem possible.

I wondered how so many unanswered questions could pop up that fast, more so, why? I had acknowledged his tree, pleasantly; but another tree begged to take root inside me, one that would provide a silent insight I sorely needed. This is what struck me to the core that afternoon. I needed to take more time to get to know a boy before placing my heart in his back pocket.

"I'm kinda confused, here, Hans. Being away from home, this long, isn't easy. Could we try keeping things simple and upfront this afternoon, especially since neither of us imagined we'd be put together or end up here." He shot me a look of irritation, as if I were unappreciative of his efforts. I was only trying to let him know I didn't want to decipher his hidden thoughts, especially when they seemed rooted in an unattractive childishness. "Why don't we just do what you wanna do?" I finally said, waving my arms and turning in a circle, like we learned in a theatre workshop to release tension.

"I'm too distracted to think about doing stuff," he said softly. My ears perked up. My eyes opened wider, and blinked quickly three times in an uncontrollable flutter. Was that his strained attempt to connect with me? No, that's silly, I thought, as he looked everywhere but my way. Couldn't be. Besides, boys seldom pick up on what girls want. Dad told me as much. "Girls want us to read their minds sometimes, but they can't turn boys into mind readers. So, be straightforward, as much as possible," he said. I was sure Hans knew I wasn't smitten by his tree, and pretty sure no lines of romance would be dangling on a summer breeze under said big tree. Hans had no clue I'd been crushing on him, but I decided to probe a bit on that distraction he mentioned.

"You are?" I asked. "About what?"

"Yeah, I can't believe my parents told you that sob story. I apologize for them. I think they wanted you to know it, so you'd carry some sort of goodwill message back to America. They want people to know there are do-gooders everywhere in the world, even in Germany."

His words felt like hot pebbles being tossed onto my already-warm flesh, pebbles I needed to shake off. "What do you mean by do-gooders? Don't you think your grandfather did something good?"

"He risked his life, and for what—a few Jewish kids?"

The strength in my legs failed me. I sought the edge of the picnic table and sat. I'm fairly sure he thought I was bending to fulfill his desire to sit. How thankful I was that Petra hadn't shared my mother's story with him. "I mean," he continued, "if his escapades had been uncovered, Petra and I wouldn't exist today. My oma and papa, even his two siblings would have been killed along with him just for his foolish acts of bravado. It was all in the name of looking good and courageous in the eyes of some pious friends. Imagine the loss, if caught!"

His words dropped into my ears, "Imagine the loss." My mouth turned dry. I put my head between my knees, feeling faint. But, he wouldn't stop. "I'm sure you, as an American, can understand how too much bravado can harm others. It stirs things up. Look at your former President Kennedy with the Cuban Missile Crisis. All braggadocio. Also," he added, "I have a football game tonight. Or, should I say, soccer. It's a big night. I'm kind of anxious about it."

"I see," was all I could utter. I'm sure he didn't understand why.

"Do you play any sports?" he asked, as if the transition were a normal leap.

"Not really. Horses. Hikes," I mumbled with great effort. I wanted to say, I swim in a Sun Bowl, and rescue old airplanes from decades-old potato vines, and plant flower bulbs with my Jewish mother, whose family was killed here, in Germany; but, I didn't. I wanted to say, I want to go home now.

"You have horses?"

"Yes, two. Can we go now? I don't feel well." He had no clue what loomed larger than his old tree in my eyes. It was what he'd put on display in broad daylight—his *naked ugly puckers*. I'd never seen any so clearly before then. Those twisting wrinkles cut deeply into his outer form. I no longer saw Hans as attractive. He had lingered in his own biased brine too long. Grace was lacking. Merit had been cast off. I felt pity for him, but could not be near him a second longer. I groaned quietly inside myself on the ride home.

The first thing I did at Petra's house was call Mother. "I can't believe the difference between the two siblings. One is so precious inside, and the other, even though pleasing outwardly, oh, his heart. It's like a cold rock. I wanna come home, Mother. I can't stand it, here, anymore. Do you know it's illegal to homeschool in Germany? What's wrong with people who support a law that forbids what's good for children, and then deride what an elder has done on their behalf, like Hans! Oh, what he thinks about his grandfather's brave deed is monstrous."

There was no time for comfort in Mother's economy, especially when this prejudice showed its face. It was a call to immediate action. "I'll make reservations as soon as we hang up," she said. "I'll call you right back and give you the flight information you'll need. Say your good-byes to Mr. and Mrs. Otto and to Petra. Call a taxi. Avoid Hans. Your father and I will meet you at the Dulles."

I arrived home on August thirteenth—more than enough time to buy Scott a birthday present. How thankful I grew, flying home to my people, knowing I could spend three whole weeks with everyone before the new semester started up. I yearned for the simple—for Scott's birthday celebration. It didn't matter what it would be like, or where. If he wanted to celebrate in the cockpit of the Ryan, even in the barn, it would be fine with me. I just wanted to look into the eyes of good souls.

THE INVITATION

*W*hen I landed, Samantha wasn't home, neither was Scott. The Farleys had taken their first vacation as a way of celebrating Scott's eighteenth birthday. They all wanted Samantha with them. Naturally, she accepted. I could see how the disconnect happened. No one, not even I, knew I'd be home. Disappointment fell into my lap, once again. My timing always seemed off with Samantha, when Scott was in the picture. I corrected myself--except for the day we met.

When I called Mother from Germany they were already in the air on their way to Aruba for two weeks, which left me with one week to squeeze some precious moments in with Samantha before I left again. I'd hoped she'd want to spend a large chunk of that time with me, but things didn't work out that way.

Seems my behavioral patterns were still intact, when it came to all things Samantha. How was I to understand the sheer volume of space a boyfriend occupied in a girl's life? I'd never had one. Zippo. I had two infatuations kidnap my power of reasoning, briefly, but I'd no clue what happened to a brain in love, or was it the heart? I hoped it wasn't both.

I'm home! Wish you were here! Yeah, I can hardly believe I wrote that on a postcard, let alone mail it; but I did. I scribbled those words, not really. I scripted them in my best handwriting on a picture-perfect Elkins' postcard for the whole world to partake in my insanity. Oh, how Miss Porthall probably chuckled over it, while sharing my lunacy in the café the next morning. Who said reversal-postcards couldn't end up being a thing? No one. So, we're good, Miss Porthall. Besides, it was my way of letting Samantha know I was home, so that she could send me a proper postcard.

I asked Mother to drive me to the airport, when I found out her arrival time. She said, "No." She'd been watching me, again, and didn't like what she saw. "Robyn, you're absolutely obsessed, when it comes to Samantha. You need to relax and see her as a separate being from you. Give her room to breathe."

"Are you kidding," I said. "I haven't seen her in like seven months!"

"And, how many times have you called her?"

"What? Calling a friend is a crime now? I don't get it. I just wanna get together with her. What's wrong with that?"

"Honey, Samantha is going to be eighteen next month."

"Yeah, so?"

"She's not a girl anymore. She's a woman."

"And, I'm a girl. Is that what you're saying?"

"Yes, Robyn, that's exactly what I'm saying. Her relational outlooks differ from yours right now. That doesn't mean they'll always be different. Down the road, you'll both be on the same page, again, because you'll both have grown into women. Your friendship is undergoing a strain, sweetheart, especially during the initial years of her first love. She'll always love you, though. You know she will." Mother took my hands. "But, you need to let go, some, now, Robyn. Later, three years won't matter as much, just like it didn't matter, when you were both younger."

"By the way, it's only two years and ten months," I said.

Even though Mother wouldn't drive me to the airport, she

couldn't stop me from parking myself on the Farley's front porch to read a book. An hour and a half later I croaked out a greeting. "Hey, cough, cough, clear. Hey! Samantha, Scott. Hi!!" When I jumped up, my thigh, which had fallen asleep, began tingling. I threw *Gone With the Wind* down on an upper step and limped to their car.

Slowly everyone emerged wearing a warm, reddish-brown glow with smiles that stretched the scope of a double rainbow. I could feel the envy monster surge through my veins. I actually looked at the veins on my wrists to see if they were turning green. They were! *Nah! Can't be*, I thought, but I rubbed them together just in case, until they reached their bluest blue. "How was it?"

"Oh, Robyn!" Samantha called out. "It was so wonderful! You're hilarious, sendin' me a postcard, by the way. Only you'd think of such a thing. Thank you!"

Happy to be acknowledged and see how my postcard had been spun into a unique place in the universe, I felt my inner monster crawl off into the shadows.

"It's absolutely spectacular down there, Robyn. I didn't think any place could win my heart over so quickly. What beauty! All that light blue water, and unobstructed sunshine, and those beaches, oh, Robyn, the soft, warm, white, never-endin' beaches were. . . ." She twirled with arms wide open. I knew in that second, she'd carry that image all the days of her life. I also realized the bug of a true adventuress had been awakened in her, more so than any under my pale skin. But I also detected infatuation in Samantha, which amused me.

"Maybe, we can visit the West Indies together someday," I said. "I'd love to see it." I couldn't figure out why my words drifted outward, sounding empty and pathetic.

"Oh, that's the best idea. Scott and I plan on travelin' lots, once the Ryan is up and flyin'. And, Robyn, it's almost there! Probably another two months. Maybe even sooner. Well, I'm positive Ma is waitin' on me. Do you wanna walk up with me?"

With you? I thought. *I'd go anywhere with you.* "Yes, I do!" I said, sounding more like myself. "I'll help you carry your things."

"Oh, no need. Scott'll be drivin' up my stuff after he helps his parents get unloaded and gets some chores in. His Maw ain't feelin' so great, but she wanted me to scoot on home, knowin' I've been missed."

Right, I thought, another narrow window with you. The fire I'd felt dampened, but I decided to put on my Scarlet O'Hara attitude, and blow on the dying embers. The walk up was fun. I had missed going on walks and hikes with Samantha. She said she had been "sittin' so long," first on the plane, then on the ride home that "my muscles are scoldin' me." I could relate. Ah, brief commonality, but as we went on I felt the walk unfold bits of sharpness within its steps. It projected forward, making it contrived, rushed, and too purposeful, not at all like our walks of yesteryears.

I wanted, no, I needed the "down and moseyin'" moments with Samantha to reach the place I longed to revisit with her, the one I knew possible if we could just bend time backwards for a minute or ten. The surroundings still offered the invitation, welcomed us in; the enchantments remained accessible, the ones where unbridled life walked with us, but my guide found her new adventures more captivating. My soul craved the past, but she was bent on reaching her goals, telling her family all about the tropical island and helping Ma with the fixings. Samantha was focusing on the future.

"Scott will be eatin' with us, too." Of course he will. Why even say it, I wondered with a sigh. And then it struck me. Maybe I was wrong. Maybe life had swept her up fully, just differently than when she was younger. Maybe it was I still standing outside its flow, disconnected once again, merely looking in like I had at the window that day. Maybe Samantha was showing me another phase of life, one I'd enter in my future. Maybe she was blazing a trail for me, one I should note and remember. Maybe, Mother was right.

Never a pleasant thought, Mother outthinking me. My Eeyore was on the rise. I tried hard to bridle it.

"Do you want to share supper with us, Robyn? I'm sure my family would love seein' you for more than a few minutes. Everyone will be home tonight to say boo to me." She chuckled. Such happiness flowed from her.

"Sure," I said. "That would be awesome." And, it was.

I hadn't seen everyone in the same room in so long. Samantha's small home seemed even smaller with numerous bodies occupying larger forms. When Richard walked into the cabin, I actually stammered.

"Richard! You . . . you look . . . so grown up!!" I exclaimed with my hand over my mouth.

"Guess that's what happens when a body turns twenty," he said with a half-grin on his clean-shaven face. "And, look at you, the same little neighbor girl, who's finally got all her parts fittin' t'gether." He took my hand and gave me a twirl. "What are you, sixteen, now?"

"No!" I said, punching his arm. "I just turned fifteen, since you're asking."

"Ahha. Still a baby. What's happenin' with you these days, neighbor girl?"

"I'm leaving in a week for UPenn. I'll be a sophomore."

"A sophomore? What? I'm a sophomore!"

I laughed. "Well, you started late and I started early. Guess being able to learn is an area where age doesn't matter so much, once we're past five, Mr. Smarty Pants," I said, gloating. "Where do you go? What are you studying?"

"Well, after years apprenticin' with Caleb in Elkins as a drafts-man, and then working on construction crews in between, I figured it was time to take my passion to another level."

"Your passion? I didn't know you had one." That's when I got hipped for the first time in my life. His hip swung over to mine, bumping it briefly and gently, but hard enough to push me off balance. Just as quickly, though, his hands were there to keep me on my feet. "What was that!" I exclaimed.

"Oh, I keep forgettin'. You're that Miss No-Siblings girl from New York City. Ask Samantha. She's had her fair share of brother-moves."

"Are you saying I'm like a sister to you?"

"Somethin' like that, my little neighbor. So, do you wanna know where my passion's landed or not, 'cause there are things to do and people to see. I'm an important man in this circle."

"Right, right! You know what, I'm not sure."

"Okay, fair 'nough," he said, turning away.

"No, no, Richard! Stop! Tell me!"

"Ya sure?"

"Yes! What school has captured your passion?"

"I'm a UCLA man."

"Seriously! Impressive, Sticker!"

"Yeah! I've parked myself in their School of the Arts and Architecture. It's a great program. And, there's no snow!"

"Hmmm. I never knew it snowed in other arts and architecture departments."

"Oooh! You're a quick one. I better watch out," he said. We both laughed.

"Hey," he continued, "ain't it cool 'bout Samantha and Scott?"

"You mean that they went to Aruba together?"

"No, that they're engaged."

"Oh . . . that. Yes," I said, stalling, while trying to think of an exit plan. I found my feet. They were still standing on the floor. I hoped the hands that had balanced me a minute earlier would still be around to scoop me up after I exploded into a million pieces, when I lost my footing, so to speak, but how could they, if I never let anyone know how those pieces were cracking inside me.

I didn't want to stay, but couldn't leave graciously at that point. I struggled swallowing Ma's delicious food and feigned conversations, mostly by nodding and smiling at appropriate intervals or when others did. I acted my way through the meal; but the festivities I knew were coming would surely uncover whatever acting I'd managed to muster up at supper. The scarlet embers I had carried into the cabin had grown cold. Smoke began to ascend into my eyes, darkening them. My time to depart had come, all too prematurely, but all too necessarily. If I hadn't gone I would have startled everyone with the terror that gripped my heart. Death has many strangleholds, and its face has no place among merry hearts, well-loved.

The engagement hadn't been spoken in public. Samantha didn't have a ring. The news was meant solely for the family; therefore the deduction was simple. I hadn't been told; ergo, I was not family. I wondered, as I said my goodbyes, if Mother knew about the engagement. I wondered if I should take a chisel to my name on the Thanksgiving heart to make room for Scott's. Clem offered to walk me home, since it was dark. I declined. "I'll make it fine," I said. I made it, but I was far from fine.

"Why so glum, chum?" Mother asked when I sat down.

"Did you know Samantha was engaged?"

"No. When did that happen? That's wonderful!"

"I have no clue," I said abruptly. Mother watched me shuffle off to my room like a wounded warrior. "Robyn, give her time, honey."

"Right," I said, abjectly.

We walked up the hill together, and she said nothing. I couldn't wrap my head around that type of self-control between friends. Did Samantha know I had less than a week left before leaving for school? Richard might have mentioned it. Would she apologize, fill me in on every detail? No. She probably knew I couldn't reach the caliber of her joy. She never called me, and I didn't call her. Change seemed an ugly thing that week. I thought my life would continue in looped disappointments until all the tangles choked the breath out of me. I left for school without seeing her.

Monday, October 1, 1990 had surfaced on the calendar. My classes, although many and varied, had fallen into order by then. I had gotten back on track. My mind cleared and I enjoyed being in my element. Petra and I shared our meals together in the dormitory cafeteria, but other than that we didn't see much of each other. I wasn't sure why. Our classes didn't connect like last year, but back then we found time to meet somewhere to chat and compare notes about campus life. That waned. She attended more church functions, which didn't interest me. I didn't mind. Seeing her reminded me of Hans. Even though I knew she didn't share his outlook, the two fused together in my head. I wanted that unjust connection to dissolve, and tried to dismiss it, but it persisted.

Along the way, Petra told me how Hans had been adopted as a toddler, but that didn't change my opinion of him. In fact it made me angrier. He had attacked Opa Otto's bravery as an inconsiderate act that jeopardized his future life, his very existence. How could a fabricated story about a capture and execution of Petra's grandfather be regarded as a threat to his life? I wanted to shout at him, "You weren't even his blood relative!" But, all I did was kick a stone in front of me. Besides, even if he were blood-related, he was old enough when we met to have known what genuine goodness looked like. Children can form emotional misconceptions, if they feel threatened, ones that can cloud their minds, trick them into believing what's not true, but he was sixteen! I asked my inner audience what the expiration date was on childhood silliness, and it remained silent.

That's when I caught a glimmer of what Petra was doing. She was avoiding me, for my sake. She saw the connective threads around my troubled soul and let me go. It was the same kindness and sensitivity that filled her heart for Hans. *No! That can't be possible*, I thought. But when the realization solidified, I knew the insight was true, and I grieved that she felt the need to extend such compassion my way, too. My lack hampered our friendship.

That first week in October had already proven to be emotionally difficult. I began doubting myself, again. By the second week, hot coals lay under my feet. I couldn't seem to find my place on earth's ruptured surface. I began wondering about the transfer of knowledge, ad nauseam. Why did we pursue it? Nothing held my attention anymore. I asked myself how smart it was to skip four years ahead in school. I got no answers.

I checked my mailbox everyday. On the ninth I found a large handmade envelope with Samantha's handwriting on it. I froze, thinking it was a wedding invitation. I carried it to my room, leaving it on my desk for two days. It lay in plain sight. I must have looked at it a hundred times, and examined the folds and writing half as many. I questioned why I hadn't been a part of her wedding plans? I would have flown home, whenever she needed me, if only she had asked.

On the night of the second day, I opened the envelope while alone. I don't think I've ever opened an envelope more slowly or carefully. I waited for some telltale sign to pop up, specifically the word, 'wedding.' Nothing showed on the outside, which forced me to open it all the way, and there it was, the sketch I had drawn of the Ryan before I started drawing its opened guts. It had been copied onto the front of the card. A Kodak photo of the nearly completed plane with Samantha and Scott in the cockpit lay inside. Printed, in a fancy font, were the words:

Join us, Scott and Samantha, in celebrating the completion of the Ryan, our amazing aircraft, on Friday, October 26, 1990. Family and friends will meet in the back pasture of the Farley Farm at 10 A.M. RSVP

In her own hand she wrote: It's so exciting, Robyn! Thank you for helping us make it to this point! We couldn't have done it without you, dear friend. I look forward to exploring another of God's beautiful places with you—the one sitting above our mountain!! As Reepicheep says, *Come further up and further in!* Imagine where we can go together. Did I tell you I got my pilot's license, too? Yep. Love forever, Samantha (heart).

I felt relieved it wasn't a wedding invitation, but that fact only made the strain of her secret harder on me. I did the worst thing I could do, without thinking it through. I chose to avenge my pride at the cost of her joy. My actions fell directly into Dad's calculated and malicious acts category. I had never done anything like it in my life, and I hoped to relish a satisfying reward from it, even if brief. I did not RSVP, nor did I go home to see them fly away together. I believed I had witnessed events similar to it several times already, and I wouldn't subject myself to it again, especially while standing in a cold mucky field as they basked in all the glory together. "Big deal and good riddance," I said, as I tossed the invitation into the trash basket.

That's when I felt my heart harden, just a bit, which I didn't like; but the alternative, another round of disappointments, seemed more painful to me. Two weeks later, I dropped a postcard in the mail that read, "Break a leg! Got tests." It would arrive at the post office the day before their virgin voyage.

A VOID

*O*n the twenty-sixth, I got a call. I figured it was Mother, wondering why my face hadn't been where it should have been that day. I thought I'd hear about the extra money she'd deposited into my account to cover my flight. I told her not to do that, but she insisted. "Thomas, phone!!" the girl called a second time. My dorm room was the last on a long hallway of rooms, which is why my name had to be belted out. "Coming!" I shouted back.

On my way to retrieve the phone, I braced myself for conflict. "Hello," I said, nonchalantly. Mother was crying. "Mother, it's no big deal," I said. "I'll see them flying around some other time." That made her cry all the more. "Okay, okay. I'm sorry. I'm sure you probably made a lot of food and had other cool things planned for the weekend, too, but I . . ."

"Robyn," she said. "There's been a terrible accident."

"Is Dad okay?" I asked, immediately.

"Yes, yes, your father is fine. It's Samantha and Scott. Oh, Robyn, it's bad. Come home."

"Come home! You're going to leave me hanging, there? Tell me what happened, Mother!"

"The plane. They towed it to the community airstrip, yesterday. They must have gotten married in Elkins, yesterday, too—eloped. Today, as they flew over the Farley field, there was a huge banner streaming behind the Ryan with the words, *JUST MARRIED*. No one knew, not even her mother. Samantha was up there, waving with such abandon. Even though we couldn't see her face, we all knew it was beaming. She tossed red rose petals at the start of each wave. Hundreds made their way down to us, fresh red love-petals—such a spectacle. The joy was palpable. Scott thrust out his arm, once, with such gusto. Such happiness. We simply were in awe of them; we about jumped out of our shoes waving back. I'm sure they heard us cheering through the sounds of that motor. Our kisses were sent along with our clapping and shouts of congratulations. We had to hug each other, because we couldn't contain wanting to hug them."

"And . . . then what, Mother!"

"The unthinkable, Robyn. I . . ." She cleared her throat. I could picture her standing up straighter in that minute. Standing straighter helped her go forward. I gave her that moment, but it was good she started when she did, because I was about to bark an order at her. "The engine sputtered, Robyn. It sputtered as Scott was circling to make another pass toward us. Then it stopped sputtering. We didn't hear the engine anymore. At first we thought it was some kind of stunt, but the petals stopped falling." Mother drifted, but continued talking in a whisper. I strained to hear her. "We watched them glide, like a beautiful bird out of sight, and then we heard the horrible sound, a muffled thud that echoed in the mountain. Mr. Farley calculated they were about a mile out. We all piled into our cars to where we thought they'd be. And that's where we found them.

"When we got there, we saw the Ryan in the trees on the east side of the mountain. Scott was thrown to the ground. Samantha's body draped over the cockpit a bit, her arms were reaching out, downward. We had hope for her, that she might be alive, up there;

but we had none for Scott. He fell so far. I think Scott must have tried to throw himself over her. There's no other explanation, as to why he would have fallen out and not her. Robyn . . ."

"Mom?" I said.

"Samantha died. She's gone. Our sweet one is gone. Scott's in the hospital, in critical care."

I dropped the phone. I couldn't listen to Mother crying. Every sound filling the hallways of the three merging dorm wings, thronged with warm and clueless bodies, going about life as if everything in the universe were normal, vanished into nothingness. Even Mother's voice, calling out my name, faded away into the void. I stood still for a moment, realizing how I chose to study the works and words of Spenser, Milton, Shakespeare, and Homer, when Samantha's story had stopped, ended—to what end? How did their wisdom and rightly fitted words matter anymore? Who were they that their stories should go on? Why were their names and works going to be remembered throughout history, and not hers? What value were they to me, now? Wherever good existed, it lost all meaning.

My *Faerie Queene* had died; Paradise, indeed, had been lost to me. *Hear MY soul speak*, Shakespeare! Homer, *any moment might be our last*, but not for her! Not at the beginning of her journey! I exhaled into my thoughts. Studying literature suddenly plummeted into the growing void along with everything else. Why speak of love and life? The last, ill-fated chapter of the greatest friendship I would ever have, ended—with me being a fool, once again. I failed her. I disrespected her work, her dedication, her passion, and her love. My lack of moving in love, fueled by my own self-will, ignored her. That's worse than hating, ignoring love; but in my heart I knew, someday, I would make it right. I would send her name out, as if she took wing within it. I just couldn't think about it then. Everything faded out. My own body disappeared.

The elevator took me down to the main floor. I had gotten outside, moved, as if in a vacuum, as if every molecule of life had been sucked from my being. The one thought, bobbing up to the surface of my sealed, lifeless container, one that would not sink or fade away, was: How could I go home to her funeral—me, the least worthy of friends this world could roll out? How could I watch her, being lowered into a black hole, when I pitched her invitation into a trash can, belittling the plan and joy she wanted to share with me? How could I, after willfully missing the most amazing duos' last triumphant scene, ever go anywhere near either of them again? I helped clip her wings. How could I even imagine restoring them? I hated myself.

I watched my feet move into the woods behind the dorm, the area we were warned to avoid on campus. I touched tree trunks, picked a leaf from the ground, a gold one, tipped in red-orange with scrimshaw patterns of fading greens, a dying leaf, so full of beauty. The sky opened wide, inviting me to look up; but, I cast my eyes downward, uniting them to the things of the earth, the dying, the dead, since it was there I found an uncanny connection and some inexplicable solace. I lay among the dead.

I went back to my dorm room, picked up the first suitcase my hands touched in the dark recesses of my closet, lifted and thrust sections of clothes, still on hangers, into its opened mouth, and then buried them under a stack of dirty sweaters, waiting to be washed. Random bottles of things, within reach, laced the bag's edges. Some bottles fell from the heap and remained on the floor. I sat on the lid's hard surface, snapping it shut. I never wanted to open it again. I didn't even want to carry the burden, but some-how, I knew it was necessary. I knew I had to use the phone again, too, to call a cab. The thought made me feel nauseous, as if Mother would still be there, crying or calling out my name.

When the cab pulled up, Carly Simon's oldie, *You're So Vain*, spilled from its opened windows along with a hint of cigarette smoke and bad cologne. Even though my mind muted the words, I still knew them well enough to feel their truth. They stuck to human nature, everyman, not just one. They stuck to me. A grating static tried to muffle the truth, as it traversed the airwaves. The cabbie stepped out after turning off the radio to stretch. "Where to?" he asked. I wanted to say, "Nowhere," but didn't.

In that back seat I stared blankly at the world reeling past me, images of life in motion, but eerily turning into stagnating blurs. All the roads began melding together, seemingly merging in the direction of the airport, as if to say, *be gone*. Inside, I bought a ticket to Manhattan, using that extra money Mother had deposited. I almost fainted, thinking about the switch I was making.

I arrived in the dark under a cold rain, wearing only the light jacket and scarf I had on in the dorm. I dropped two dimes into a dirty payphone that smelled of urine. "Madison?"

"Yeah, who's this?"

"It's Robyn. Can I crash at your place tonight?"

"Robyn!!! Roby, as in Thomas! Wicked!!! Totally, girl; but, we moved. Got paper and pen?"

"Uhhh. Yeah. Just a sec."

"How utterly gnarly. Did you run away?" she asked.

"I guess. Kinda, yeah."

"Well, I always knew you wouldn't be able to stick it out with those hicks. Here's my address . . ."

"Okay."

"Ha! I am going to collect my wins tonight," she said in a sing-song voice. "Tiffy thought you were a goner. Man, I bet your parents are going crazy. I mean, your mom must be nuts with worry."

"Yeah, I imagine so. See you soon. I'm really tired, Madi."

"You're not high on something, are you?"

"No, no . . . just tired."

"Okay. Maybe you can catch Georgi's party after you chill a bit, get some jiggy time in. After all, it's the weekend!"

"Right. No. I don't think that's happening, for me, Madison. I'm *really* tired."

"My bad, but, never say never, girl. I'll leave a key under the mat and alert the doorman to let you in, 'cause I'm outta here soon. Just rattle the bars at the door. Jezreel will hear it. He's got hawk ears. Parents aren't home till Tuesday, so the place will be all yours. Ummm, probably, if things go the way I hope. You'll see me tomorrow, late morning. Glad you're here, Roby! I'll let everyone know."

I hung up, thinking, *what am I doing?* But, I was too stripped of energy to forge another thought into existence. I hailed a cab. I remember doing it countless times with Mother. It seemed like second nature. "Cabbie!" My voice continued to sound alien to me. The night loomed in darkness. I heard prowling voices, and two pops, like fireworks, but not. Then the sirens came like clockwork.

When Jezreel let me in, he smiled. "Get in here, girl," he said. "Young girls outta not be out alone, these times bein' these times." I nodded. I found the key, let myself in, and fell asleep on someone's bed. Slept twenty straight hours, probably would have slept longer, but Madison tramped in. Her time out had gone longer than her highest hope. I pulled one of the pillows over my head, thinking maybe she'd leave me alone; but then I sighed. The Madison I'd known never considered others' needs. All of the Manhatties were with her, along with two unfamiliar boys' voices. They all piled onto the bed, shaking me.

"Show your face, girlfriend!!" Tiffy said.

I groaned, feigning sleep. Wishing for sleep. Wanting sleep. Wanting them gone.

"Come on, get up, Rob!" Madison said. Do you know how long it's been since we've seen you? We've all changed our plans for you. We're skipping school in your honor." They all laughed or snickered after hearing that last declaration, and I realized, *Oh, gosh, they're all still in high school. Sophomores!* I groaned, again.

They grabbed the pillow from my head. "Wait. Her hair is straight. Girl, you're damn beautiful!"

"Does she quit?" someone else exclaimed, as several of them pulled back the covers I had thrown over my clothed body.

"How tall are you, girl?" Tiffy asked.

"It's her parents! I remember them. Remember! They're both giants," one of the shorter boys said. I still couldn't place him, but apparently he knew of me. No matter. *Go away, short boy*, I thought. And, I thought this too: If they only knew how not beautiful I am; but I smiled and thanked them for their generous appraisal. Honestly, any other time, any other moment in my recent past would have had me laughing at their antics; but even so, even within the pit of my numbness it was good to see their funny faces, again. We all hugged.

"So?"

"Yeah, what's up, Roby?"

"Spill it. We want all the dirt."

"I quit school. I just wanna work here in the city."

"You can't quit school. You're only fifteen!" Tiffy said.

"Yeah, well, about *that* . . ."

After telling them I was a sophomore at UPenn, up until I quit yesterday, the room's atmosphere shifted. The warmth of our shared commonality dissipated, leaving everyone but Pearl in a cold, blank stare. Sweetest Pearl—why she hung with us had always been a mystery to me. Pearl, the quiet one, never fully entered into our antic-mania, even back then; she harmed no one in word or deed, and no one dared attempt to slight her. It must have crossed our minds that we'd all probably feel undone if we ever wounded such pure simplicity. Something about her made us want her presence, even if only as a shadow on the wall, or was it a light? Pearl looked at me and smiled more warmly than I'd ever seen anyone in New York smile. I smiled back.

On the third day I moved into Pearl's home on the Upper East Side. She was the one who encouraged me to call my mother on the second day. Father flew up in *Gypsy* on the fourth. We met in the café, where I'd hoped to be hired, having just submitted my application right before he arrived. I liked the down-to-earth simplicity and caliber of the place, *The Quint-S*. They served five things and only five things in total perfection, as far as I could tell: Sandwiches, Soups, Salads, Shakes, and Smoothies, three subcategories within each category. New York was turning a new leaf in the culinary arts. Ethnic restaurants and everything-anything diners, even though still prevalent, had been pried open. A new cultural wave was sticking its toe into the eatery biz, a small toe.

Me, why I liked the place, had nothing to do with embracing culture's ever-changing waves. I needed, simple. If simple came packaged as perfect, then all the better. Everything else was too complex, fussy, over-the-top, or fell into the baser presentation of plain. Plain wasn't simple. Plain lacked class. I wanted to be surrounded by the mind that created a simple, non-pondering menu of excellence, quickly ordered and delivered within the ambiance that supported it well. I wanted to survive without losing my mind, and *The Q* seemed like a good place to start. I liked the 'no surprise' element and the efficiency that worked 100 percent of the time. I liked the thought that what I offered people would be sure to please them—everyone, everyday—no punches pulled, only faithful customers who knew what they wanted and got what they wanted, and knew when to go home. *The Q* closed at seven. Something else I liked about it. Pearl worked there.

I ate one thing from all three categories before Dad arrived and before submitting my application. I had to make sure my impression, and Pearl's nod of approval, were correct. They were. And since Pearl's parents dropped her off at four-thirty and picked her up at seven-thirty three days a week, my transportation was covered. I learned how an eight-minute subway ride to Midtown was too risky in 1990 for a young girl. New York, it seemed, had grown darker since we left. I wondered if Mother knew its forecast. Probably.

It was strangely good to see Dad. He downed the Greek Salad and a glass of filtered water, and then scooted off the deep-green

Naugahyde seat of our booth. "Come on," he said. "Let's walk." Walking is what we used to do, when together in Manhattan. Our thoughts flowed better after long sticky separations, when we had to find our footing with each other again. I wanted to know what he thought of the salad, but didn't ask. I liked that he finished it and seemed pleased.

"Where are we going?" I asked, wrapping my wool sweater more tightly around my body.

"I thought we'd go back to my hotel room and talk, more private."

"Sure. You at the Hilton?"

"No. Too much construction going on right now. I selected the one that jumped out at me."

"What do you mean?"

"I'm at the Penta across from the Gardens."

"Ah, I see, Penn Plaza. Got tickets for anything?" I asked.

"I'm not here to take in a game, Robyn. I'm here to talk, and then to bring you home."

"I'm not going home, Dad. Besides, who's to say I'm not home already? After all, I was born here. You weren't. Mother wasn't. I was." We walked the rest of the way in silence, both unusually unanimated.

I didn't want to push Dad away. I did want to let him know I was safe and had plans, but I wasn't sure if he'd hear me out. I gave him the benefit of my doubts.

As soon as we got to his room, he ordered-in, a large pizza, coffee, and two cokes, saying he was already feeling hungry. I had to admit my three category-spree of discovery felt like it had left my stomach already, too, having eaten over an hour before Dad arrived; but eating had lost its appeal on the twenty-sixth. Typically, when stressed, I ate a lot, so I wasn't sure what state I was in anymore--other than New York.

We both watched the stream of people from his eighteenth-floor window and decided the hotel didn't rate visit-again stars. We ran out of small talk quickly, since we weren't up for it. The small pizza was nothing more than crust ends, forming a pattern on the cardboard box when Dad asked if I'd join him at the small table. It sounded so formal. "It's not the coziest spot for a chat, Robyn, but sometimes we just have to make do."

"I agree, totally," I said, seemingly surprising him.

"Robyn, Samantha's funeral is tomorrow. Everyone wants you to be there. Scott can't be there. He's still in a coma. I think . . ."

"Dad, stop, please!" I felt the lump I had tried hard to destroy, resurface, the same one that appeared when I dropped the phone on Mother. I tried to take a breath, but my lungs didn't fill up properly. I tried to breathe deeply without success. "I can't go." That's all I said. Dad saw my stress, but continued.

"Can't or won't? There's a difference, honey."

"Can't or won't? The end result is the same, Dad. I'm not going. I'm living with Pearl and her family. I'm sharing a room with her in her parents' amazing apartment. They're practicing Jews, Dad. You remember Pearl. Right? She's so sweet and such a good influence on me. That's what you used to say. She works at the Naugahyde Café," I said, not knowing why I called it that name. "That's where I put in my application, today. I wanted you to see it, to eat there, so that you'd know where I *will be*. I think they'll hire me."

"What about school?"

"I can't do it, now. Maybe sometime in the future. It's not exactly like I'm behind. My friends are still in high school."

"And, with their parents," he said.

"If you want to think that, that's your choice, but they're not, not really. I mean, there's not much parental supervision with the *Manhatties*, Dad. They're pretty much out there. I'm not sure why Pearl still hangs with them, really. It's gotta be her one fault, when it comes to them—loyalty. She has a real family thing going on, a caring family, like ours. I want you to meet her parents, Dad, to see for yourself. Pearl is different."

"That's good to hear, and I agree, Robyn, I'd like to meet them. Tomorrow before I take off? Maybe we could invite them to breakfast, somewhere."

"I'd like that. I'll call and ask. Her mom works at home, but her father leaves at eight-thirty, same time she does."

"That's doable, if they're amenable."

And there was that word. The lump surfaced, again.

"Okay, Robyn. For some reason, I'm very tired right now, but I still need to put a call in to your mother. She needs to know what's going on. I don't want her to be wondering. I'd like it if you could stay here tonight, in case we need to talk more in the morning; and, it would be great if you could talk to your mother, too. She needs to hear your voice."

"Soon, Dad. Not now. And, yeah, I can sleep here. Less trouble for the both of us."

I slept, pleased with how everything went, yet heavy of heart, thinking of Mother's reaction. In the morning I learned of her disapproval; but Dad seemed to understand, and that gave me hope. Everything hinged on Pearl's family.

NEW WAVES

"*H*ow did we get two identical orders, Pearl," I whispered as we hung our tickets. "What are the odds?"

"I'll have to calculate that, later," she laughed. "Shouldn't be hard." We both smiled knowingly.

In my third month at *The Q* I had eaten everything we served too many times. With a total of fifteen selections, that's not hard, but we had steady patrons who kept a checklist rotation, alternating salads, with soups, and sandwiches in a very systematic way. Eventually, the owner added coffee to the menu, since requests for it never ceased. Even the coffee was simple and good, straight black java, served in an off-white diner's cup.

Everything remained in the status quo plus zone, but I still knew I walked in the negative zone. My brain couldn't grab hold of substance. It seemed intangible. But I felt safe. My life had order and simplicity at every turn. Pearl's parents helped dissolve any concerns on that level. Nothing was too much to ask. Privacy in my great room was allowed. I couldn't face my lack, so courage drained out of me. I felt robotic.

Somewhere around that time of feeling annoyed with myself,

especially when alone, I began letting the past trickle in, a drop here, maybe there, maybe not. It all condensed below the surface of my daily routines, unnoticed. I hadn't returned to the mountain for any of the holidays. Christmas wasn't celebrated in Pearl's home, but we did Chanukah, which was a first for me. I imagined myself creating new brain cells. I clung to that idea. *I want a whole new brain for Christmas, thank you very much. Chanukah could provide the heart.*

Pearl was an only child, like me. Her parents didn't fuss over her, though. They invited her into their adult world, which was full of good things. I missed the epic dimensions larger families spill into their home life, but remained thankful that the Greenburgs had taken me in and treated me like a daughter. Pearl and I grew close; yet, she never asked me why I hadn't gone back home, or why I quit school. I liked how she didn't pry, but was always ready to listen.

It struck me when I looked at my work schedule that I'd be spending the first day of summer indoors. It wasn't a monumental disappointment. It sort of made me feel like an adult, even though I kept casting my eyes out the window towards what little I could see of the sky. Did it beckon me? I couldn't tell. I had no plans or desires outside my routine.

I told myself it was good to slide through time and space, to keep moving and living in the present. My life had no projections, no plans, in other words no long-range goals. I couldn't see how the mental detachment I enforced upon myself, religiously, engulfed me, tied me to my pain. My days bordered on the shadowlands, skirted the overpowering void I allowed to walk before me; and the strange thing was, no one seemed to notice. One thing I could do well: hide; but at what cost?

I had no interest in anything other than taking orders, placing them before the cook, and then walking them to tables, all in a painless environment I thought I could control. Being at *The Q* pulled no punches. The unexpected didn't happen. That, plus being wrapped up in the contented lifestyle of the Greenburgs provided all the dragon scales I needed. Simple, uncomplicated traditions, precise schedules, and a friend's warmth defined my days until Lea Chan walked into one of them.

Lea couldn't have been more than four foot eight in her bare feet. Her stylish platform sandals probably added two inches. By that time in my life I had reached my full height, six-one. Lea had reached hers, too. She was twenty-six. I recall her popping her head into the door and sniffing the air a bit. Well, at least she raised her nose and moved it back and forth. After she sized-up our culinary offerings, she turned to reenter the flow of sidewalk traffic, when something drew her eye back into *The Q*. Me. I don't think anyone noticed the catlike finesse she executed in that doorway turnabout, other than me. I concluded we were both aware of each other, and that caused me to feel extremely wary.

I watched her. That action on my part hit me like a sandbag thrown at my chest. The fact that I bothered to observe another person meant I was breaking one of my scales off, thereby making my dragon-suit a bit more vulnerable. I immediately cast my gaze elsewhere. I figured, since *The Q* hadn't met the satisfaction of her olfactory scrutiny (spices did not dominate the place) *she* probably lived in a complex, dangerous world; but when I realized she didn't exit *The Q* because of me, I began feeling freakishly uneasy.

She had cast more than a glance my way. Her dark eyes traced my form the way an aloof, but focused doctor would examine a patient. In a split second the staring shifted into another type of encounter. We engaged in an eye-lock moment. I'd been watching her on the sly, near one of the swivel seats at the counter. Her height and delicate beauty fascinated me the way an encounter with a rare bird would; but no bird I knew gave off her energy. She seemed like a panther on the prowl, and I was her prey. Her straight black hair fell gently over her brows, near enough to her upturned eyes, that hiding them, whenever she deemed it convenient, presented no problem.

Eventually she made her way to a booth out of sheer necessity, as regulars were waiting behind her to get in. It happened to be one of my booths. I breathed in and straightened my neck, while pushing my shoulders back, and then I walked toward her with my eyes on my pad. The first thing she did was to apologize, but I wasn't going to make it easy for her to switch gears. She explained her prolonged pause of intrusion on 'my space' had provided her time to take in my height and, what she called, my 'bold beauty,' which she said she felt I had trapped in a net of my own making. Whatever *that* meant, I thought.

Lea came in everyday that month and sat in the same booth, when available, all to make me feel more at ease in her presence. Since I didn't know why, I remained distant. She ate, almost as if it were a trial of endurance, which in my mind detracted from any credibility she could have offered me in words. I felt her eyes on me, constantly watching my movements between nibbles. That was another thing about her I did not appreciate. Once, she threw out, "You're endowed with a natural grace." What? I felt like saying you don't know me at all, lady; but instead I laughed and replied, "If you only knew the person I've known, you'd have seen what natural grace really looks like."

"Don't compare," she said. "Just be you. That's more than enough."

In the second month she warmed up to our soups and salads. "Not a sandwich person," she said, when I first suggested one. That's when I began to relax some, and she became some-what less straightforward in voicing her opinions. We entered into the customer-waitress relationship on one of those days. Two weeks later we found common ground. We acknowledged we'd become acquaintances. We actually smiled at each other, when she sat down. She seized on the moment while drinking a smoothie and laid out a proposition she probably had sat on for weeks.

"Robyn," she said, "I'm flying out to California tomorrow. I'm a talent scout and agent." She slipped me a business card. Its simplicity impressed me.

"Of what?" I asked.

"Models, film actors, game show personalities. I have connections both here and in LA."

"Cool." I said.

She looked at me, trying to detect any spark of interest. When she saw none, she said, "Okay. Look. I know you're young, but I've placed sixteen year olds in some prime spots before. If you're ever inclined, call me." I felt nothing that resembled an inclination, and so I said nothing. Her offer was extended on July twenty-second, three days before my sixteenth birthday. Surprisingly, my birthday hung low in my awareness. It never surfaced for air. I don't think the Greenburgs knew about it either, which was fine by me; but Mother called that weekend to say she and Dad were flying up on the twenty-fifth to celebrate my Sweet Sixteen. "A day trip, a show, anywhere, anything you want." Sixteen. What did that mean to me? I could start working full time, if I wanted, jump out of my blue papers and into the green. Green meant go. Sixteen sounded good, I thought.

On the twenty-third of July, though, something else happened —the heart of the city broke. An unidentified four-year-old Hispanic child was found on the side of Henry Hudson Parkway. She had been brutally tortured, starved, sexually abused, and then killed. Her small body had been tied, put in plastic, and cruelly stuffed into a blue and white cooler with frozen soda cans. The perpetrator of the unspeakable crime upon the unidentified child, who came to be known as, "Baby Hope," was never apprehended.

Mother heard about it the same day I had. Friends called her. The first sentence she spoke to me after our embrace was, "Robyn, please leave this city. I took you out in '85 for a reason. I never imagined you'd be here, again, in your childhood. Honey! You've been here nine months. You've succeeded. You've carried on. Come home. Please!"

Father put his hand on Mother's shoulder. "Elizabeth," he said, "let's get to the hotel and freshen up. You've put out your plea. Let's focus on Robyn's birthday, for now. Okay?"

"You're right," she said. "I'm sorry, Robyn. It's just, she was just a little girl, and . . ."

"I know, Mother," I said. "Come on. We can talk about what you have in mind for the day."

"First, tell me what's on your wishlist?" she said.

"Nothing," I confessed. She probably had no idea how much it took for me to recognize how that word had grown in me, let alone speak it.

One month hadn't cycled on the calendar from the birthday visit, when some other friend called Mother at home to report another New York City tragedy. It shook Brooklyn to its core. The news rang out across the airwaves as a first in America. I could only imagine what ran through her mind, when the news struck her sensibilities.

Dad had already called me two weeks earlier, saying he didn't like seeing the downturn happening in Mother. Her anxiety over my safety had caused him concern. What, I wondered, would the news of America's first openly anti-Semitic riot and murder do to her, especially since I was upwind of it, in its backyard?

It happened over a three days period in August. Three days, and the course of my life started to veer off course. If Samantha were here, would she have mentioned another Jew, nailed down onto a wooden crossbeam and lifted to die an ignoble death as an innocent man? Pearl never mentioned the man. The thought of him didn't comfort me, or offer any recourse I could follow, unless I were to hide in a cave, hoping another world would materialize three days later—one without Mother's dreaded concerns. I suddenly grew agitated with myself for having spread Samantha's voice over this event and twisting her faith into a type of satirical escapism to satisfy my anxiety, not to mention the criticism I plastered over Mother.

Each time I tried using Samantha's voice, the grave injustice of my failure would crush me. Maybe I projected and thrust broken splinters of her truth into my head to cover all things ugly, hoping against all odds I'd find some of the fragments forming a structure where I could hide and feel secure, the way she typically made everything feel better with one glance my way; but each time I failed her, I sank lower in my estimation of myself.

I even argued aloud with that botched version of her in my mind. "Seriously, Samantha, not every bad thing becomes good, and even if some find some good, somewhere, somehow—not everyone does. You of all people should know that. Scott lived. You didn't!" When I spoke those words, alone in Pearl's bedroom that night, not only had I started to sob, I saw fear's face surface in my presence. It slipped over me like a piece of soft silk, and burned as it settled in place.

In my attempt to free myself, I latched onto any living and fearless memory of Samantha I could. Scott materialized in my thoughts. He was in a cave of sorts, lying in a room in a deep coma. He didn't have to deal with any of the madness. His nineteenth birthday, and the timing of the riots didn't escape me. I would have envied his deep sleep, had not resentment toward him overtaken me.

But then, Mother surfaced, and her soon-to-be reaction to what was erupting—a frenzied retaliation within a black community, embittered against another persecuted minority in the same neighborhood, one they thought possessed unfair advantages. That's what triggered the anger and resentment. It wasn't the horrible accident, which came first.

Thinking the Jews secured favors; thinking the Hasidic lived lives of privilege; not thinking the common dust and scents in the streets and shops; the waves of heat that brushed over everyone in the community alike; the searing pain of injustice each group bore in their hearts and minds, whether behind tattoos or tefillin—not thinking such commonality could defuse the tension of the first evening and night's rage, or the three days of hateful rioting that followed, something raw and vile erupted.

How does hate escalate? I sat on my bed mulling over news articles I'd read. How a two-car accident, involving a black child and an Hasidic Jew had become the first two pieces of a vast universal puzzle of hate stymied me. It aroused questions within me. I wanted to unravel it all. The child who died had been playing on the sidewalk with other children. *That's innocence in motion.* A car going north, hit a car, going west. The driver of the westward moving car was a young Hasidic man. *That's innocence in motion.* When his car was hit, it leapt onto the sidewalk, where the children played and slammed into the building's brick wall. The Jewish driver got out of his car, wanting to help the child, who got hit. *That's innocence in motion.* The black community rushed upon the Jewish man and beat him. *That's not innocence in motion.* The Hasidic community managed to tear him from the rage to safety. *That's mercy in motion.* And, that's where I paused. Got stuck. The vengeance that arose from that horrible, yet innocent accident made no sense to me. My world turned upside down that night; but the pile, pouring out, grew larger.

The rioting in the black community continued. It culminated in the murder of a young man that night, and this is where Mother was probably pulling her beautiful hair out. A young man, who was not from that community, not even an American citizen, but an Australian, out walking the streets of that community, when several teenagers selected him as their target—all because of how he looked. The teens had been walking the streets as predators, streets in the predominantly Jewish quarter of their community. The twenty-nine year old Australian possessed all the markings of a Hasidic Jew, because, indeed, he was. He had come to the city as a student in pursuit of his doctorate. That night, as he walked, twenty black males surrounded what they thought he embodied. They beat him. They stabbed him. They fractured his skull. He died later that night after identifying one of his assailants. Mother would not be able to survive this news, seeing I was a stone's throw away from the blood assault—even if it were a long stone's throw.

The mood of the city shifted after those incidents. It got darker. Most felt the injustice. That night I called Lea Chan. I remembered what she'd said about not comparing myself to Samantha anymore. I decided to dive deeper into the dark pool. Maybe in California I could break the surface of the water, feel more refreshed. I'd settle for different, if it carried a tinge of freedom with it. I tried to sound nonchalant, but my voice trembled. "Anything in LA I could do?" I asked.

Thus, my life skipped over the heartland. The middle of my life got left out, again. The nearness of friends, family, everything I once called familiar, I forsook. Don't tell me people don't interconnect, that we're not interdependent. Don't talk to me about how some butterfly wings flapping in the Brazilian rainforest change the atmosphere thousands of miles away, when there's so much pain from the motion of people's flapping arms in our own backyards. Talk now. Talk here. Talk about that.

When I told my parents about Lea and my decision, I averted a crisis by creating another; but the latter would be temporary and one that only held sunshine in Mother's mind. Therein lay my tinge of freedom, I thought.

It was decided Dad would fly out to LA with me, commercial flight; we'd search together for a decent place to live, and he'd remain to scope out where, and with whom, I'd be working. That all felt wonderful to me, and it calmed some fears Mother had. I wasn't prepared for the enormous challenges drifting my way under the moon's gravitational pull upon the Pacific waves, because I couldn't imagine any outside of some teenage flirts, like Mark. But that kind of teenage insanity, I thought I could handle. All I knew at that point was I'd miss Pearl, *The Q*, and the Greenburgs.

BIDING

*W*hat I didn't know until we landed at LAX on September sixth came as pleasant surprises. Dad said, "Okay, let's drive to my real estate agent's office."

"Oh, yeah, they do rentals, don't they," I chimed in.

"Actually, Mother and I wanna find an investment property in Venice Beach, near the water. One popped into view in our price range the day before we left, a two bedroom, one bath bungalow, built in 1920. Sweet, huh? We thought you might look adorable in it."

We toured the bungalow. Dad made an offer on it, and off we went to a used car lot for my second surprise. The way Dad moved during the barn building process, delegating tasks into competent hands and then trusting it would go well, surfaced again. He reminded me of a bee-on-task, unwaveringly efficient. Zip, zip. How he leaned into every new endeavor, as if he'd done it a hundred times impressed me. If something or someone landed in his care-package, it was covered. I was glad to be a top priority in that bundle of goodies.

We drove away from the lot in a slightly rusted out 1970 Malibu convertible, which Dad said he'd like to restore, when visiting. "I want you to know Mother and I are planning on crashing at whatever place we land for you—at least one weekend a month. Good by you?" he asked.

"Good by me," I said.

"I think it'll be fun," he said. I smiled, not knowing what it would be like until it happened, but remained thankful for being in the center of Dad's benevolent whirlwind.

"Great! We got the bungalow on Rialto!" he said the next morning after hanging up the phone. I hardly had time to respond before he said, "Now, we're gonna focus on getting your learner's permit, so we can get those driving lessons started. I think you'll pick that part up quickly, honey, the technical side, at least. It'll take a bit more time to feel the whole of it out; but there's nothing like time in the saddle to learn how to ride a horse or drive a car, especially in sunny California."

I liked the way he thought, but had to add, "I hope it happens as you envision it." I did pass the test with flying colors, and later that week logged in my fledgling hours behind the wheel, first in a parking lot, and then in quiet neighborhoods, while kids were in school. I learned to be in control of a moving vehicle, going twenty-five miles per hour and stopping outside of crosswalks, perfectly.

"Lots more to go, but we'll get there. No worries. I'll make trips out without Mother." Within five weeks the full 120 hours, which included the required night hours, were accomplished. I loved driving, especially along 101. How expansive and fresh driving the coast felt, especially with the top down.

Warming sunshine washed over me. California earned a big golden checkmark in the months that followed. The sun bathed me with its constancy, providing a sorely needed respite from hiding indoors. I was utterly amazed at the steadfast beauty of its presence through the fall and winter. California seemed like the perfect haven, a sunny harbor. That's how it felt before my ship came in, at least.

Toward the end of winter someone in the movie industry contacted Lea. Apparently, he had seen me in the '92 Ford Mustang GT ad in Cars Gap Magazine, and according to Lea, he was duly impressed and hoped I could act. Lea set up a screen test audition for me.

"So, what's the gig," I asked, trying to sound professional.

"The man is affiliated with Kidz Entertainment. I can't imagine anything more perfect for you."

"If I land all the preliminaries, you mean," I said.

"Oh, you will." Lea always voiced more confidence in me than I ever could.

"Do they have a film in mind?" I asked.

"You ready for this?"she asked.

"I think so. What is it?"

"There's a small part, but it has some dialogue. It's in the next Batman movie!"

"Hmmm."

"That's it?" she balked.

"It's all I've got, Lea."

"I know. It's just a small part, but you'll gain so much experience from it. It's an awesome opportunity."

"Oh, it's not that, Lea. I'm really happy for the opportunity and that you arranged a screen test. Really. It's just . . . oh, never mind." I was getting flashbacks of Mother's excitement preceding mine, and most of the time mine never caught up to hers. "When do I . . . Where . . . Who . . .?" I muttered.

"I'll arrange everything and get back with you! You have a car, don't you?"

"Yeah. They come in handy here."

"They sure do! Coasts are quite different."

"So are the mountains," I said.

"What?"

"Nothing."

"Okay, Robyn. Get some rest. I'll call soon with all the details."

Apparently, the moving film 'liked me.' I went forward in the process. The next step was a live audition before the casting director. That rolled up four days later. In the queue, waiting my turn to read a script, which only arrived the day before, I overhead other girls practicing the same lines. They were focused, confident, competitive, and good at what they were doing, like they'd done it many times. They read the lines with intensity. I read the lines differently. At the studio, I repeated the scene's dialogue quietly to myself the way I had on my couch the evening prior. I didn't feel the pull to join the others for advice, or feel slighted at not being invited. I couldn't relate to them, even though I knew the energetic tension they broadcasted, all too well.

I read the character as a lost soul. She hadn't been in Gotham City long and seemed uncertain how to move in it. (Gotham city, basically, is New York City at night.) In truth the character, peeled back, was me--a girl uncertain of herself in a new environment. I decided to use the obvious parallel and infuse my own out-of-context feelings into the lines. I let the character flounder some, hesitate, expose her vulnerability, my vulnerability. I wanted her to be honest, to expose her soul, not hide it. I was being offered the perfect relief valve and yearned to take advantage of it. My mind raced to Samantha. "This one's for you, girl," I whispered.

Lea told me I got a callback. "Wear exactly what you wore at the last audition. Act out the script in exactly the same way, too. Don't change anything, unless they ask you, which they probably won't. Again, get . . ."

". . . some rest. I know," I said.

The callback differed from the first audition in that the girls in the waiting room had been reduced to three, counting me; and the adults in the room behind the door doubled. I have to admit nerves factored into the equation more the second time, since I never thought I'd get the first nod. But as I read over the lines, again, I felt myself drift into the character as I had the first time. A gentle identification settled upon me, and the takeaway of Samantha's philosophy on life trickled in. I asked myself: *Why be nervous over something I can't control? If it happens, fine. If it doesn't, fine.* I told myself something more: *Those people can't change my life, for better or worse. They're only doing their job. My task, right now, is to do my job, and right now that's to lift this character off the paper and bring her into the room.*

My life remained in a quasi-sheltered cove of contentment with spot photo shoots Lea set up; beach walks with my new Golden Retriever puppy, Rusty, brought to my doorstep one weekend by Mother; enjoyable solitude in my cozy bungalow; and those occasional weekend visits from Edward and Elizabeth, which turned out to be welcomed and enjoyable.

In that season, I painted every wall of the bungalow, scrubbed out the tub and its surrounding walls till they sparkled, watched two men install new wood floors, and a roof, and thought how the air in Venice Beach smelled salty-clean. I knew I had become a local, when the steady sunshine streaming through the windows got too warm and forced me to drive to the beach or sit on the shaded part of the house, the front porch. I'd never noticed how the steady flow of traffic ramped up, and then subsided until those days, when I sat much of the afternoon in the gray zone, reading books from the library and wondering if I'd return to college sometime soon. Nothing penetrated my covering and nothing grabbed my heart.

Lea called after all the auditions had been held for the movie. "You've got the part you read for, young lady," she said. "Be on the set a week from tomorrow, 9 a.m. sharp. That's Wednesday, next week. Just use the ID Pass I'll be mailing you to access the set. Looks like the movie will be shot, entirely onsite. It's going to consume all seven of their large sound stages! They'll direct you once you're there. Got it?"

"Yep," I said.

"Yes! It's true. You've got it, Robyn Thomas! I knew it, the moment I set eyes on you. So proud of you, girl!"

"It's really nothing, Lea."

"Okay. I can go with humility. It's refreshing in this day and age. Oh, I forgot to mention. I'm back in New York. Gotta run, now. Call me, if you need, whatever. I'm dashing off to the Federal Express, as we speak, and to a late luncheon at Alidoro with someone I just met. Their Italian heroes are the only sandwiches I'll eat, if you're wondering," she said, laughing.

So, just like that I was offered a part and soon found myself on the expansive Burbank sets. Mother and Dad smiled from the east coast to the west, when I told them. My role in the film consisted of a two-minute walk-on-and-off, halfway through the film, and then, a five-minute scene that actually required me to speak eight words to a stranger; but it was all I wanted. Nothing more. Nothing less. It paid my living expenses for the next four months, which, in my mind, was the highlight of the whole endeavor in a strange and satisfying way.

When my seven minutes on film (which took two hour to capture with other cast members' retakes and a couple of my own) ended, my thoughts returned to the application I'd requested from UCLA's admissions office. I considered acting classes, but scratched that off the list quickly. I wondered why. I put the papers aside on the kitchen counter and, once again, like my beloved Scarlet, decided to sort my thoughts out tomorrow. At that moment I leashed up Rusty and headed to the beach on my bike.

Living that life created a new way for me to divide time. It fell into work project segments, rather than months. There was: the Mustang ad; the Dr. Martens' (grunge boots) ad; the Hot Pockets ad; the Batman role; and then the UCLA course catalog. Dad understood the mental process, when I told him. I knew he would. Mother gave me a creased-brow stare. "How do we fit in?" she asked. "Like the stars and the moon," I said, which made her smile.

In the thick of reviewing classes, I remembered thinking, when driving to the studio on the 405 and passing all the exit ramps for UCLA, how close those ramps were to the Rialto bungalow. It took me by surprise. I wondered at that moment how things, which seemed unreachable or bigger than life for a long time, once they appeared in plain view slid into place as if normal in only a few seconds. It's as if humans cannot live in a constant state of excitement. I wasn't sure why that campus seemed unattainable in my mind, as if it were part of a fairytale. Perhaps, it contained that element of the California-glow that was out of reach for a Manhattan girl, even a mountain girl--that *I-wish-they-all-could-be* glow. I still found it hard to believe Richard was there and, if he was, that I hadn't gone to see him yet. Surely, I had no foothold on reality in that time of biding under the sun in Venice Beach.

That week, and its reflections turned out to be the last ones I could claim as normal for some time. I heard from Lea that I'd been *discovered*. She quickly added, "In a small way, so don't panic." It's odd, thinking of people being discovered, as if one is lost in Hollywood before a producer or director arrives on the scene, acknowledges the person, puts her onto a set, under their selected stories, attire, moods, almost as if the person has become an entity, a living fixture or investment. Perhaps the term, discovered, is appropriate when people don't seek success, but others seek it for them. If success comes without any striving, just easy follow throughs, coupled with other elemental pushes, which compel us to be where we are, then maybe we are discovered. I wondered if Lea felt she discovered me. Maybe I discovered her, or maybe all of it was a preordained path to take me somewhere else, entirely.

I pictured Samantha speaking up at that point, nodding at me, and saying something about the art of being. Would she ask, "Does being discovered feel like a threaded cap that's missed a rib on its way down, makin' it sit a bit crooked over its own stuff, or does it feel like a completed process, wanted 'n' good all 'round? Why sit anywhere, if'n it's not quite right? Maybe it's good to start at the top, again, and go down slow 'n' easy. That's when we'll land right." I told my imaginary *her* that sometimes *right* is hard to find, when wrong butts in line ahead of it once too often.

That was the last week I'd wondered if I'd bump into Richard, if I walked the campus near his department. I wanted him to be there, still. Just the thought of his friendly face, nearby, gave me a good feeling; but it was more. His was a familiar face, even more, one from home. I didn't go further into the 'more' speculations, since nothing else surfaced. I had planned on making my way to the campus the following week to talk to a counselor, but that never happened. I got sidetracked, because someone discovered me before I could discover myself. All the possibilities on that side of the horizon didn't happen. I began thinking of myself as the girl in a magician's disappearing act.

I got a call from Lea. Kidz E wanted me to audition for a movie under consideration. Everything began happening so quickly. The company landed the movie. I got the part, a big role. A contract was signed. When rehearsals began, the Gotham City character's feelings surfaced in me. "Hello, lost girl," I said.

I found the director of the film unfriendly. Forget about being kid-friendly. He was inept at being friendly to all sizes, which seemed strange, considering Kidz E's supposed platform. I wondered how he could get anyone to do what he wanted. Then he began drilling down hard. I came to see he was a perfectionist, and that many actors considered it a privilege to work under his direction. Not me.

He blocked out scenes on location, even before giving us the script. We'd sit, stand, repose; pretend to pick up things, hold something, eat something, turn, bend, reach, smile, cry, laugh. He made us repeat the gestures and actions fifty times or more. Then he had us repeat them again, with script, another fifty times—all before the camera crew set up its gear in streets, buildings, or at the studio. He never once spoke about what we were to feel or think during those exercises. When we had everything down pat, the way he wanted, when the skeletal structure fit together, he said, "Forget everything we've done for the past six weeks. Go home. Take a vacation. Do whatever you want next week. Just don't think about the film, or your lines, or anything you've done with me. I'll see you one week from today. I'm off to Barcelona. When I return, I'll be in touch."

When we came back, he said, "This week think about your character in each scene you're in, and then in ones you're not in—not your lines, just the character and what he or she feels about the lines. Here's a breakdown of the characters, inside and out." He handed us a two-page description in his nearly illegible hand. "Get into their shoes. Wear their clothes. Wardrobe will provide each of you with your character's garments. Get comfortable in them. Wear them. Wash them, if needed. Break in their shoes. Appreciate the time period. Do your research. Go to a vintage clothing shop. Shop for your character. Get wardrobe's approval after you buy something. If you don't get it approved, shop again. Find a whole ensemble that gets Anthony's okay. Got it? Get it done ASAP. I want to see you decked out for next Wednesday's read, lines ready for the first scene."

That Wednesday we had one dress rehearsal in our chosen outfit. When the day ended, we were told to rest the next. The day we returned, filming began, cold turkey, take after take after take, or one take. We never knew what he was doing. He kept us off balance. The days didn't end after the filming started. Weekends no longer existed. The devilish pace messed with my nerves and then my head, faster than I could have imagined. Even the seasoned actors felt the gut punch. The guild was concerned about the child labor laws, but the director always slipped in under the restriction limits, somehow. It's as if he had a sixth sense, telling us to go home or take a long break, but return at such and such an hour for more.

I commuted forty-five minutes to an hour, each day, sometimes four times a day. That made me consider Rusty in a new light. His behavior had shifted. He became mischievous. I didn't connect the dots at first, but then realized my absence affected him. Dogs are dependent, affectionate, and loyal animals. None of them deserves abandonment, and Rusty let me know that was true for him. His resentment grew more and more obvious.

He started by knocking potted plants over and leaving them for me to find and rescue. Destroying them came next. Then he graduated to ripping apart my stuffed furniture. Initially, it was the cushions on an older couch, then the couch itself. When he completely mutilated my favorite new armchair, I froze in my tracks. My eyes darted across the living room. I called for him to no avail. He never surfaced that night. Apparently, he'd found a great hiding place, and in a way, I was glad.

The final straw happened when he peed on my bed, the second time. The first time it saturated the topper, which I threw out. This time it soaked the mattress itself. And, the weirdest part of this final straw is that Rusty didn't hide. He stood near the bed, slightly wagging his tail, while looking at me.

I finally realized, being locked up in a house all day, alone, even if an adorable house, day after day, no matter if food were accessible or how many toys were strewn about, a dog will feel abandoned. Since they cannot rationalize the abrupt change in relationship patterns, or create another world to replace the one they'd lost, their feelings will spill out in ways that will get noticed. They'll become sick or, if one of them has enough spunk, try to rip their way out of their cage, even if it's the owner's home. Yes, they feel neglect, sorely.

I came to the place where I figured Rusty was just entertaining himself in the only way he could. I dropped the thought of him being vengeful, especially when those eyes looked at me in complete dejection upon seeing how I finally understood the meaning behind his mischief. My face was totally honest, typically, and my voice did not hold back disapproval until that moment. I turned to him in my newly found compassion. "Come 'ere, boy," I said. "Dogs just wanna have fun, too, don't they, sweetie." I ran my hands over his head and lifted his front paws to dance. I sang the song I always played when he romped with me as a puppy. Within seconds of connecting with Rusty, the kitchen phone rang. I dropped his paws, and chatted with an acquaintance for twenty minutes, tops, while the dishwasher hummed its way through a cycle.

When I came back into the bedroom Rusty wasn't there. The sun had set and darkness closed in. The opened windows admitted a fresh cross-breeze. I was struck with an odd feeling, when I made my way to the living room, like something was amiss. Rusty was gone. On the floor a picture frame lay in pieces. It held my favorite photo, the one Dad took of everyone at the Stickers' Thanksgiving, 1985. It was mauled and wet. That's when a bit of my heart broke, and I didn't know how to pick up the pieces. That's when I learned, dogs do exact revenge.

After a week of searching, news of Rusty reached me. He had been welcomed into a family with kids. They found him roaming in the foothills near to where they lived. I knew he'd found his home. I didn't tell Mother. Two weeks later I moved closer to Riverside. I didn't tell either parent, but knew I'd tell all before their next visit. My days were filled with filming, my nights with parties or moshing at concerts. I still could pass as an ordinary person in the mosh pits, especially wearing the costumes I created to transform my looks. I spent a small fortune on those glad rags.

I rented my parents' bungalow out to a fastidious tenant, assuring Mother all was well. The lease was month to month, just in case she didn't like the school secretary, who offered me herbal tea before I handed her my keys. I didn't look back. My new apartment had two great master suites. One of the bathrooms even had a dry sauna. "You'll love it! It's on the water with huge picture windows!" I was in the middle of my fourth film, while sliding into my eighteenth year.

I never shared my feelings with anyone at the studio. After shoots, exhaustion would set in, but I kept spinning like a top. I twirled to retain the tier I'd attained. I told myself not sharing my personal stuff with my parents was for their good. I knew they wouldn't rein me in. They couldn't. I knew they knew it, too. I did know, however, that they'd stand guard over me, if anyone or anything threatened me; and that's what I did not want. There was something else I had to admit to myself—I carried an emotional block inside, a heavy one. It produced a fear, a fear that if I fell off this show horse, I'd never be able to get up on any other horse again. I felt something in me would die, if I failed to complete another endeavor or cycle. I didn't want to expose myself as lifeless; but I couldn't find life in my head or my heart. So, I continued hiding, when not acting. I poured myself into my acting. It seemed the only place I could be real.

My peers in the industry tagged me with a nickname that summer. After joining them at a handful of their notorious teen-parties, they pegged me, *Gelee Enflammee'*. French. Why French? I wasn't sure at first, but eventually I figured out the troubling tide of their thinking.

"S'up Gelee," the boys would slur, walking past me in their affected strides. Some purposely grazed my shoulder with a ninety-nine degree lean into me, and then cast a look backwards to see if the contact threw me off. That's when their female groupies, those who globbed onto the boys' puffed-up inflatable forms, like ribbons on a kite string, streamed by in wiggling flutters, giggling and mimicking, like mere shadows, slightly glowing under dimmed party lights. "Hey, Gelee. Tee-he-he." Hands flipped over their fake smiles, while their eyes, dark and sultry, drilled holes in me.

None of them had a clue about the *burly bear* I'd met as a young girl—the one that stood before my face, nonstop, exposing the center of my soul's entrapment. They knew nothing of the promise Samantha and I had made to each other on that cold day, when we crunched our way, a lifetime ago, through the new fall leaves resting atop the rich humus of an ancient forest floor, all still so crisp in my mind.

No, 'Flaming Frost,' wasn't applied to me, because of my red hair and pale skin tone, like I thought at first, naïve me. And it was in French, for a specific reason, not because the German translation, 'lodernder frost,' or the Italian, for that matter, 'gelo flammeggiante' sounded stilted, which they did. It was because the French language translates into raw sexuality within the American mind, not all minds, but the ones that go there, probably as a byproduct of the movie industry. Oh, the irony of it all.

Those people began commenting openly about my virginity, jamming it up against what they termed, my physical appeal, as they saw it. How did they know I was a virgin? Perhaps, they took note of my disinterest. I wasn't interested in lingering later at parties, once the action started. I wasn't interested in joining in their tell-all-tallies about the number of hook-ups each had that week. I wasn't interested in dating. I wasn't interested in taking acting roles that compromised my values.

Maybe they felt slighted. How was that my doing? How could I tell them *I have cassette tapes? They're in my home in a carved box my dad made for me. The box is tucked away, high on a shelf in my closet. There's one tape labeled, The Burly Bear. It records the pact a special friend and I made with each other. We pledged to remain virgins until we forged a deep love relationship with someone special, and then we'd marry that person. I know she kept it. That was her style. Now, it was my turn. So, fade away, boys and girls, because nothing you say or do will make me break my promise to Samantha. Nothing, because it's all I have left of our friendship. It's all I have left of honest integrity. It's my promise, because it was hers.* They'd never understand, though, even if I were that blunt. Why bother trying to say it was the last thread connecting us, since they probably never wound such a thread around their hearts? So, I just turned the flame and frost up higher.

When others, living within the shadows of life surrounded me in those years, I recognized them as the people I'd once considered in the abstract as *those people.* They had thickened into forms with names and voices, and fluttering eyes. I worked with them. Our world's connected. After a while I saw how they wanted more than my virginity. They wanted my chair on the set; my roles in movies; the trailer I used as my hideaway; and the increasing fame surrounding me. They wanted me gone, or converted; conformed, or less than. I knew I wouldn't surrender to their desires; but willfully walking away, making it my choice, my decision, for my good--that thought began forming inroads.

It was around that time I started calling Mother to hear news of the mountain community. I had avoided the tales for two whole years. I specifically insisted Mother and Dad never speak about any of it to me. Now, I wanted parts of it. Sharing my feelings about Samantha was still off limits, but finally, I could hear about her and the community's heartbeat, whether concerning her or not.

Mother eased into it, first telling me that she finally did what she'd been telling me she wanted to do for a long time. She changed the retreat into a normal, but special, bed and breakfast. "Oh, what a relief to discard those professional biddies," she said laughing. "Give me some regular, good folk with wildly ordinary lives, the kind that just want to enjoy what nature and we can offer them without judgment."

Dad enjoyed taking 'her new people' up the mountain on horseback. Crossing the bridge was always the highlight. Dad would stop short of the valley, where Bessie Jane, her baby girl, and Samantha lay, side-by-side. He'd linger on the hilltop above it, letting the horses nibble, while riders stretched their legs. He didn't tell the special story of the three honored women, below. He reserved that journey, as a precious and private one—land meant to be left undisturbed, the land of love and dreams, the land passed down from woman to woman, when a worn, folded piece of paper, an old title deed the color of Bessie Jane's skin, slid out of her warm garments, one day, and was tucked into the hands of a most trustworthy soul. No, that story and the land belonged only to the community family, not strangers. I'm positive Bessie Jane never imagined Samantha following her beyond the cradle, as quickly as she had; but willing her property to her wasn't for naught.

Happily Mother told me how Samantha had set up Bessie's gift, the cottage, as a reception hall to express her love for the community and celebrate her marriage with them. "No one's taken anything down," she said. "No one's dared. Everyone agreed on it. It would be like taking down an elaborate tapestry that celebrates life in a house of worship—one created to remain and give pleasure to every eye that looks upon it." The party decorations Samantha had created for that special day in October still hung, or rested in the exact spots she had put them.

Her family and Scott's came up regularly to dust and keep everything in order. They knew, one day, they'd have to take the decorations down, when Scott awoke and returned to what would, then, be his cabin, even though he had never spent a single night there. Everyone thought being there would be in his best interest, to be somewhere where memories didn't follow him through the door to knock him over at every turn. They thought it would be the perfect place for him to recuperate after learning of his greatest loss, somewhere serene and still, where wisdom and love had dwelled in abundance. There he could gain his full strength.

Naturally, Scott awakening was considered a future fact by the mountain families. How could it be otherwise? The doctors were uncertain, but that didn't matter. Loved ones knew he'd come around, and that's when the decorations would come down, when absolutely necessary. When he said so.

Mother filled me in on all the little things Samantha had done. The miniature model aircrafts she crafted of balsa wood and painted silver, dozens of little Ryan ST-As, were strung across the cottage ceiling. Each had a banner of trailing paper attached to emulate the bigger picture of that day. The words, "Just married" produced a bittersweet flush that stirred up images of her in the air, casting those rose petals out upon them. "If only a moment could

be frozen, strung in time like those little planes," Mother said, "but
. . ."

Those who believed in heaven's reality saw Samantha even
higher, I thought, casting praises in some eternal celebratory mode,
shining brighter than any model or even the original Ryan. I
wondered for the first time what had become of the Ryan, but
couldn't ask.

So, the little planes stayed, as did the flowers, which they
refreshed every week. The cottage had become a memorial to
Samantha; yet prayers went forth that a part of Samantha's life and
love would return to it, to live within the world, again, and soon.
Until then, the cabin remained frozen in time, linking a wedding
to another reality. Samantha had alway been a bridge, linking life
to life, while living. It seemed appropriate how she left behind
pieces of her joy that day, so that onlookers would look to life.

Mother began sharing news of Scott, whenever weather was
friendly enough for her to visit him; but in winter, when snow-
tinged winds swept down the mountainside in icy sheets, a sweet
rest fell upon its people. Most sought solace, indoors, in much the
same way they imagined Scott had. In that waiting period they felt
a kinship with him and his undisturbed repose, where no foot-
prints, tears, or missed conversations could enter, just the rush of
wind, outside, going nowhere in particular.

I was grateful to be able to hear those stories after living two
years in another reality. The distance and shift in tempo and reflec-
tive contemplation allowed a buffer to slip in, so that the pain
surfaced less and less. In the opening months of my third year, I
began asking Mother to tell the stories to me, over and over, like a
small child would ask for her favorite storybook. They comforted
me. Mother asked if I'd ever step foot on the mountain, make it
home, cross the bridge, go to the cabin. "Someday, maybe," I said.
I asked how the bridge was, these days. "Oh, totally renovated,"
she said. "Not scary at all, anymore. Just thrilling."

My parents came out every other month after I turned eighteen and stayed a long weekend, Friday through Monday--not too long or too short and at welcomed intervals. It felt right to me, as it did to them. They filled me with home-cooked meals, chapters of books I bought and never had time to open, and those Dad-prayers I never rejected.

Mother and I remained distanced from Dad's confession of faith, but we tolerated him, because we loved him, even when he laid it out before us as a path he deeply yearned for us to enter. At times I felt uneasy that I wasn't by his side in the way he wanted, but I couldn't enter places my quest hadn't opened to me yet— marriage and sex, or religion. They all lay outside my beating heart.

Dad respected that stand in me, especially the marriage and sex part, but he prayed I'd come to see the difference between religion and relationship someday. "Relationship is what makes the heart beat its truest song," he'd say, "not religion."

"Yeah," I'd say back, "Samantha would say stuff like that, sometimes, in her own way. But, I still don't get it, Dad. I can't hear what you want me to hear, anymore than I could hear what she wanted me to hear. I know neither of you are upset or trying to force me into something against my will." I puckered out my lower lip, and he smiled at me.

"Fair enough," he'd say. "We'll leave it there, for now." Then he'd kiss me on the top of my head to say good-bye. It never failed. That's exactly when he'd speak of Jesus, each visit, right before leaving for the airport. I grew to expect it, and because I respected his right to speak, I heard him out each time, just as Mother did, but each time he'd finish, we'd wink, smile, and nod at each other, when he'd stoop to pick up the luggage.

HOME

*W*hen my eighteenth birthday showed up on the calendar, a thought surfaced, which I didn't share with my parents on their weekends with me. I wanted every part of it to be my decision, even though I knew they wouldn't object. My Kidz E contract was set to expire the day before *the day* society tells us we're supposed to be adults. I decided not to sign with the parent studio, as an adult actor. Instead, I chose to set my sights on modeling, again, just for a while. I figured it would provide the break I desperately needed from the film industry and, somehow, everything would go back to the easy days, like when I first arrived in California. I thought, with my child-star status, I could be more selective with the jobs I took, and I was right. That seemed like a great bonus, high pay and with less intensity.

The hook into the fantasy world's glow that I imagined, lasted around three months before the strings of paid servitude formed its web around me. Once again, I found myself being in high demand and trading my life away. For what, I asked myself. When I cast my gaze outward, I didn't like what lay in the box with me; and when I looked inward, I felt even worse. That's when I called Lea and said, "I'm going home, Lea."

"You mean, you're on your way to Manhattan? That's wonderful, Robyn. I'll start lining up some shoots for you. What are you thinking? Lauren? Armani?"

"Lea!"

"What?"

"Not New York. I'm going home to the mountain."

"What mountain?" she asked. That's when it hit me. I'd never let Lea in. She knew nothing of what made me tick or, more so, who. It was time to reconnect, not with Lea, but with the chapters of my life I had ripped out.

I returned to the mountain in February of my eighteenth year. Strange, going home when most people my age are leaving the nest, to go off and do *whatever*. Most of us have no clue about the *ever* part, which stretches out beyond the nebulous *what* part, complete with its own shifting horizon. We just go, because it's expected or planted in us, somehow, to go. We follow an itch to conquer a fear, explore a fantasy, or just experience what *different* feels like. I was going home to face my *whatever*, leaving acting and fame behind for the unknown, even if it came wrapped in the familiar. Mostly, my timing on going home hinged a lot on Scott. Mother called toward the end of January in tears, saying he'd awakened. When I arrived home, I was the age Scott last remembered himself being.

Turns out, the little planes didn't have to come down. Scott awoke blind. When everyone heard I was coming back, they decided to leave the decorations up for me to see. They wanted me to catch up on the reference points of our community history, perhaps finally say goodbye to Samantha. Fat chance. Since Scott needed to use his visual memory to navigate his environment, he couldn't be at the uncharted cabin as everyone had thought. It worked out for the best. He arrived home before me. I got to the cabin before him.

The possibility of incurred pain from the visual past was considered for Scott, even before they knew he was blind, but not for me. I wondered why. He was spared being jarred into old memories of love's ascent. That was wise of the community. The cabin would sit in its preserved limbo state until I got back. All would be cleared out after I had seen how Samantha arranged everything. Only then would the rejoicing be boarded up, so that animals couldn't get in, unless I wanted to stay there.

The whole way up the mountain, I asked myself if I should spare myself the jolt that awaited me. A thought about the community surfaced, too. Had they wanted me to go, so that I would feel sorry for not having gone to the take off? No. That couldn't be. No one played God in our community. I realized I carried a bit of LA home with me and saw I had a ways to go before feeling the mountain's overwhelming serenity fold itself around me again.

Mother hoped I wouldn't choose to stay at the cabin, even though she said she'd understand if I did. I said I had no desire to stay there, and wasn't even sure why I was going to spend any time in it at all. Even when I walked through the door alone, I wasn't sure of why I opted for the self-inflicted sorrow I'd probably encounter.

When I saw the dozens of mini-Ryans, rocking back and forth from the exchange of air as the door swung open, even the prepared and warming glow of the hearth's fire, which greeted my cold cheeks and finger, didn't help stay the chill that rushed through my body, landing over my heart. Let's just say, I was thankful no one else had crossed the threshold with me. Maybe I had to have that memorial cry, a renting of my heart, again, in the midst of sensing her life-touches around me. Maybe there's a hidden wisdom in those bare boned expressions of grief, the kind I fought knowing; but feelings have a way of showing up when we cue them. I never wanted to indulge them. Yet, emotional memories are real, even the ones we've never made, but exist as extensions we stumble upon. Evidence that exposes a broken heart is as real as the evidence found in a crime scene. More so, we can sense seamline stitches of a loved one's making. Things, mere objects we've never seen, are able to connect us to the other and prompt an immediate emotional response. I can testify to that fact. It was hard. I didn't want to repeat it.

After my visit, I heard news that the last fresh flowers were taken to the Stickers; the vases, at long last, stored away in a box and tucked on a lower shelf in a cabinet; and all the tacks, holding the planes in place, plucked from the wooden ceiling, all but one. The balsa models were given to children in the community or to the elderly to hang on some future Christmas tree. Everything was tidied up, boarded up, and loved up till the last parting breath that touched the chilling air vanished in the warmth of a departing car. The life of the living overtook the homage of the dead in the community, once again. Scott and I, especially Scott, took priority. He had to be loved back to his full stature, given time to take his journey. We all knew his well-being was crucial to us as a community, but no one spoke the thought. We just acted upon it.

Seeing Scott, took my breath away, more so than the miniatures of the Ryan. His hair had grown darker, a darker blond, and it had been left to grow, one length, to the bottom of his chin. It looked good on him. His skin was pale from being indoors too long. His facial hair, also, left to grow freely the last two years of his coma, had been clipped shorter, I was told, a week before he awakened. It was a light brown that matched his eyes. In fact it softened his eyes. I think Samantha would have thought the beard, handsome; but Scott didn't want it. He wanted it off.

The first thing he said upon hearing I was present was, "Robyn, would you shave this bear face?" For some reason, his first words startled me. I didn't think they'd be about his appearance. When he said, "It's what Samantha would have wanted," the tightness in my chest flipped, making me feel even stranger. How could he possibly know what she would have wanted, concerning a beard she had never seen, and would have adored from my estimation? The old intruding doubt about Scott crept back into my heart, again—that barrier I knew all too well, which stood between me, and the Samantha I loved, the barrier I never wanted to see again.

Without thinking, I said to him, "Prudence could probably do a way better job than I could, Scott." I had to get my opinion in, which I regretted, immediately. The look in his unseeing eyes hit hard and unexpectedly. I was the first to reject him. "I'm so sorry, Scott," I said. "Hey, I'll try. No promises you'll turn out looking good, though." He offered a token laugh to buoy my joke.

I took the scissors in my hands, but inside I resented the fact that I had been corralled into the silver planes room and, now, before the air of the mountain had circulated through my lungs, twenty-four hours, I stood over Scott, clipping away at his past. Prudence called out, "Clip as much off as possible, first, before shaving."

"Got it," I responded.

I clipped, gritting my teeth. Scott didn't sense my anxiety. He was too wrapped up in his own feelings. Next, I plopped shaving cream onto my palms and pat both sides of his face. When I picked up his Paw's straight edge, I sighed, feeling like I held a lethal weapon. He took note of my action, and, apparently my hesitancy, because when I drew near to take my first swipe, he said, "Don't worry if the blade slips. I'll be fine. Really, Robyn." His tone was soft, almost filled with a melancholic plea.

The words, their tone, and the look on his face, caused me to pause, completely. I lowered the razor and asked, just to make sure I hadn't misinterpreted the voice of grief incorrectly. "Scott, why do you want me to shave you?" He lowered his head and didn't respond. "Did you think I'd botch it, make a fatal error?" He still didn't respond. At that moment I stood between wanting to hug him and wanting to whack him across all the fluffy white I'd just applied.

Finally, he said, "I don't know what you're talking about." I had seen enough cover-ups in LA to detect the whopper going down before my face. "Prudence," I called out.

"What cha need, Robyn?" I heard her say.

Scott grabbed my arm forcefully, perhaps not knowing how near I was to him when he began waving his hand about in search of its target. "Don't say anything to my Maw," he said in a voice I'd never heard him use.

"Prudence," I said, as I swung my arm free of his grasp, "would you take over for me? Turns out, I'm definitely not the person Scott thought I'd be for this job."

"Oh, sure, hon," she called out from the other room.

I walked home, stunned. My mind refused to grapple with what had happened, but my heart, somehow, drifted to the pain behind it. Glimmers of his reality punctured the evening sky, opening new pinpoints of light in the already star-studded darkness. Not only had Scott lost Samantha and his eyesight in the same day, living with those losses, practically speaking, made him lose his will to live. I corrected my foolish ramblings. *No, the first loss would have been enough to make him cast away his heart as a burdensome stone, cause I'm sure it no longer beats under his chest bones.* With that mammoth loss, Scott had an Everest before him, but climbing it *blind* without her must have thundered across his soul like stampeding horses on some wilderness terrain, kicking up a dark cloud—like another kind of blindness.

And as my eyes grew weary, trying to stay open to see a world that looked fairly dark and unrelenting in those moments of reflection, I pondered another reality Scott faced: No one had told him that he'd lost three and a half years of his youth. To him, his coma seemed like a brief blackout of months. None of us could bring that third loss into focus, hand it to him atop everything else. It seemed cruel. Everyone wanted him to rest and grow strong; yet with all the good intentions being poured out around him, we couldn't read what was going on in his heart or head. Perhaps our own goodwill afflicted him, as an out-of-place thorn in his grief. Our eyes were filled with happiness at his return. We had gone through our years of processing Samantha's death. He had just learned of it. We weren't prepared to go backwards, join him at the starting line after we'd run our race of endurance, even though we knew we must, if only to take his hand while he walked it out.

He said the strangest thing when he learned of Samantha's death in the Ryan. It made his parents aware of something. He wasn't ready for any more facts that cut life from him. He said, "That can't be. She talked to me on the ground." The family gave him ample room for any incoherent thoughts he might have. No one corrected him. Ma Sticker told me about it the day I arrived. She had a feeling Scott needed to say more about how he saw, and remembered, the accident. She put the extraction in my care. I didn't want the responsibility, but she insisted. "Be gentle with him, Robyn," is all she said. No one knew at that point that Scott blamed himself for Samantha's death. The Ryan, after all, was his desire, he figured, long before any excitement formed in her. No one else blamed him, though, not even me, not anymore.

The next morning in Elgin I bought an electric shaver and surprised myself for remembering his favorite flavor of ice cream. I, also, found a single CD player, headphones, and some spiritual-sounding tunes by Sinead O'Connors. I dropped Bolton's 'Soul Provider' into my cart before leaving the aisle. I took great care to make sure the music's timeline matched Scott's reality of time.

On the way to the register I picked up a new feather pillow and Charmeuse silk pillowcases. They were meager attempts to provide sensate experiences that didn't require vision. By the time I got to my car, it all felt pretty lame; but I lugged everything up to his front door, nonetheless. I figured, whatever I do for Scott would end up feeling dumb to me, so I might as well get on with it, because, like it or not, I was part of his recovery program. That was my attitude when it came to Scott. I assumed the role of perennial complainer. I sighed and knocked. Prudence waved me in. Scott had taken a drive with his Pa up the hill to the cabin. "They'll be home soon, Robyn. Come, sit with me."

"How is he, today?" I asked.

"Oh, the same. He seems totally lost, hon. Breaks my heart to watch. What's worse, I think my concerns burden him. He's not eatin' much, either."

"Oh! That reminds me," I blurted out, breaking the seriousness of the moment, rather awkwardly. "This might help him get his appetite back." I whipped out the chocolate ice cream, and headed toward the freezer. Prudence didn't say a word. Two other containers stood front and center and felt heavy when I moved them to make more room.

"Unopened chocolate ice cream?" I asked.

"Maybe he'll like your brand better. I know he'll be glad seein' you, though. Oh, gosh, that didn't come out right."

"I know what you mean, Prudence. It's okay. How have you been lately?"

"Oh, as of late, really good. Winters are easier on me. No one's out sprayin' the highways or forests. This trial is showin' me things I never thought of, like how connected the body is to the soul; but compared to what Scott's goin' through, 'tain't nothin'.'"

"Don't compare," I said. "I'm sure your hard is hard."

She took hold of my hand and nodded. "It's been a life changer," she said. "But gotta keep trustin'," she said.

I wondered about her take on the word *soul*, and what she was trusting in—the process, I supposed—but didn't ask. I assumed soul meant emotions, like soul music or soul food that's comforting. That's when I heard the Cherokee pull up. I got up to peek out the window, and it hit me as soon as I stood near it. I was watching Scott without him knowing, just the way I had watched Samantha years before, but on the other side of the same window. Something was off. A strange tension filled Scott's face.

He pushed through the door. His pa followed. "What do you mean it's a '94 Cherokee, Pa? That makes no sense!"

"You asked how come it had the new car smell, Scott. Alls I said was, it's practically brand new, a '94." I bit my lower lip. Prudence looked at her husband with a startled expression, and right then, Mr. Farley realized he'd unscrewed the lid on a closed jar. The news of the unfortunate timeline, the last robbery, had collided into Scott. Time's constant variable splintered, ruptured into a catastrophic warp the moment that innocent comment pierced his ears. The new '94 Cherokee was, indeed, purchased in October, 1993, four months before Scott awakened. He figured the last two months of 1990 had passed him by, bringing him into his present, February 1991, but then, that reality vanished.

"What's the date, Maw?" Scott asked. Prudence stared at him wide-eyed. I stepped up and took his hand. Immediately, he drew back, not knowing I had been in the room.

"Scott, it's me. It's 1994, Scott. I'm eighteen. You're still three years older than me, minus a month. I'll never catch up with you, Scott. You're just going to have to face that fact," I said, trying to make the situation a tad lighter, but failing miserably. I rubbed his hands in mine, the way I had seen Samantha rub Bessie Jane's.

Scott cried out. A whimpering groan filled the room. I could tell he wanted to run, but couldn't, not knowing how or where. His eyes darted back and forth, like a frightened critter searching for an escape route. Finally, he tilted his head backwards, casting his eyes upward in search of answers, all of them. He wanted a way out of the confusion. Once again, he groaned. It looked as if he were hoping for a rescue, a divine hand to reach down and lift him to his bride. He shook his head, as if he read my mind, and called out her name. She was his anchor, his heart, his newly beloved. His faith believed her to be in another world, but his soul insisted they still should be together. When she didn't appear, when he didn't sense her presence, all the energy within his body dissipated. He slumped up against the wall. "Scott," I said.

"I'm tired, Robyn," he said. "It's been a long day. Just go home." With that declaration, he stumbled toward his bedroom. "I'm alright, Maw," he said, knowing Prudence was moving in his direction to steady him. "Please, go, Robyn."

The day had not gone the way I had planned, but that wasn't

new to me. None of them ever did on the mountain. I wondered if that would change.

I awoke the next morning within the soft translucent glow of the morning sun. My thoughts slid back to the days of concocting breakfasts with Mother under the same streams of light, and the same comforter. I wondered if she had convinced Dad to play the breakfast game with her. That memory linked into a desire to see the family photo album Mother had begun upon my departure from New York. I slipped downstairs in my bulky robe to retrieve the album and then scurry back to bed

White sunlight arrowed its way into the great room in piercingly broad strokes. Rows of filtered light streamed in, covering the floor, but more. The near parallel beams rose upward, almost to the ceiling, making the room much too bright to see what lay before me until I faced the floor-to-ceiling bookcase. A movement in the room drew my attention from my task. I turned, knowing Mother's morning plans involved puttering about in her greenhouse, and Dad's would take him to the local Rotary Club. I knew I wasn't alone, but couldn't see who or what had made the noise. Was it man or beast?

Looking up, my eyes were flooded with the intense blinding light. I had to squint and raise my arm over my head for some relief. I saw a figure approach. From where I squatted the shape loomed over me, large in stature. When I stood up, it still seemed taller than me. "Dad," I said, "Is that you?" I didn't know anyone taller than me in the mountains.

"No, it's me, Robyn," said the voice. A smile spread across my face. When I stepped closer into the person's protective shadow, my eyes could see again. They rested upon a man with a healthy tan. Dark hair draped across his eyes and upper cheekbones in wisps. It merged with his trimmed black beard. Even with all the hair trails happening, he was unable to cover the smile that cropped up behind it.

What I noticed, and what disarmed me most wasn't his height, at least six-four, as I calculated. It was his eyes, looking insanely like his sister's, even to the point of pouring out love in my direction, exactly as she would. "Richard!" I cried out.

My next movement was sheer impulse. It overtook me the way a wave in the Atlantic once had, when a girl. I helplessly surrendered to it, then. Now, I leapt into its force and found myself flying into his arms. I'd never done anything as bold, before or since, and felt no awkwardness in the doing. Such overwhelming pleasure filled me as he greeted my gesture with a tender embrace. He wrapped his arms around me, tightly, and laughed a laugh I'll never forget. Hearing it, while tucked in his warmth, I felt home surround me entirely; yet I checked myself, not wanting to misread the feeling of his embrace, not wanting to want something I would never have, as usual. Perhaps, like those sisterly hip bumps he bestowed upon Samantha, and, once, on me as 'the little neighbor girl,' this hug was nothing more than a friendly reception after a long absence. And, perhaps, the thrill, pulsing through me, was due to actually seeing the man I had wanted to visit so many times in California, but never found the courage or the time to pursue it —since the man connected me so much to home.

I lingered, not wanting to depart from the closeness, not wanting to see his face, maybe change, or hear any words that would tell me to stand apart, so I thought I should be the first one to break free of the embrace. At least that's what I intended to do; but when he enveloped me, I couldn't move. It was as if he were built to hold me. Suddenly, I knew the fullest meaning of the word soul. My will, my everything yielded to the moment. I yearned to remain captured in his embrace, and the impulse that prompted it only grew. My mind in bursts of whispers told me to shut the door on the feelings. I laughed inside my head at the mere thought of shutting Richard out. I backtracked in my mind to assess the reality, and realized that voice wasn't my thoughts talking. It was fear, and it lived apart from me, an unwelcome intruder upon my thoughts, even though no stranger over the years.

While embracing the present reality, however, it dawned on me how painful it would be, if he shut the door on me. I couldn't bear another Sticker heartbreak. So, when I did look up to see his smile widen even more, radiating a softness I'd never seen on a man's face, I knew, inside, he felt the same inexplicable attraction. Still, I waited to hear his voice.

"You've grown up," he said softly.

"You've grown, too," I said, thinking it the stupidest thing I'd ever spoken. We both laughed. Our faces almost touched. I could smell the mint on his breath, and a sweet fragrance rising from his warm skin beneath his opened parka.

"This is unbelievable," he said to me.

"Absolutely unbelievable," I uttered.

"Do you know how long I've wondered about holding you?" he asked.

"I haven't a clue," I said.

"A long time," he whispered.

Richard pressed his warm mouth onto mine. I actually had to tilt my head back, which resurrected a scene from a dream. I felt him bend forward, just a bit too, which caused me to inhale deeply within the thrill. Feeling him move toward me, like that, melted every barrier I'd ever constructed around my heart. Even when Mark's lips landed, briefly, on mine, long ago on that night in California, I had never kissed him back. I couldn't imagine any kiss surpassing the one Richard and I shared under that pristine light. He captured my heart. "Richard," I gasped.

"I know," he said, pulling away some. "Too fast."

"No," I said, "too wonderful."

That's when Mother entered the room, and even though Richard's soft warm lips switched gears to carry out a polite discourse with his neighbor, who stood in utter surprise after stumbling upon our encounter, he and I maintained that uncanny sense of unity we'd begun, as if we'd been together forever. We held hands, while talking about something so bizarre—us! It even felt odd for us to express the sense of relationship we felt, aloud, at that point; yet we did, since it was Mother's desire to pursue the back-story of what she'd witnessed. "Inception point?" she asked.

After a few minutes of exchange, she said, "You mean you never expressed interest before this morning?" Mother asked Richard, first, and then me. We both shook our heads, no. She smiled a goofy, yet lovable smile, fully pleased, and headed for the kitchen. "Coffee, anyone?" she asked.

KNOWING

The next day Richard arrived early. Nothing was as I expected. He came to let me know his mind. There was no tender embrace, no kiss. He greeted me with a hug, a quick one, and I could see in his eyes, even though lovely and warm, something troubled him through the night, maybe even kept him awake. He looked tired, not wearing the same face I looked upon yesterday. Even his body language changed. He stood apart, still gentle, but resolute, rather like a bulldog I'd met once.

Apparently, he and Dad had a conversation the afternoon prior in the barn. It prompted Richard to head home to pray. I didn't know about the conversation for a long time. It went something like this:

"I'm pleased to hear of your feelings for Robyn, Richard. You know I think highly of you."

"Thank you, sir. That means a lot."

"Ah, I've been elevated back to sir, have I?"

"You've always been there in my book, Mr. Thomas. Just never knew how much."

"Feel free to call me Ed or Edward. I know you respect your elders, Richard. Your parents raised you right."

"Thank you, sir. I mean, Ed; but I respect you for more 'an just bein' older than me. The way you took to changin' things in your life for your family—that's what impressed me, Mr. Thomas. Ed!"

"Well, that's good to hear, because I'm about to let loose some hard words involving change, Richard. I hear you and Robyn are at a crucial point, and I owe you this angle. She . . . well, she hasn't come to believe in Christ, yet. Do you know that?"

"I s'pected it in the past, but wasn't sure. I was hopin' to talk with her 'bout it."

"Here's the thing. I'd rather you not. I don't want her to convert for ulterior motives. Do you understand how that can happen? I don't want her to become your missionary-dating project either."

"I understand."

"I'd like you to pray in earnest over this new development in your relationship with Robyn. Elizabeth tells me it's mutual."

"It seems so; and I will. I'll be prayin' and fastin'."

Dad said he'd join him in the fast and thanked Richard for being so willing to do what was right in God's sight. That was that. Not knowing about that conversation, when it rolled into place, was a good thing, because I would have raised hell right out of its domain and into ours.

Instead, that morning, Richard sat with me on the sofa and took my hands in his. He said, "Robyn, I haven't been able to share with you why I'm home."

"No," I said, "we didn't get much time to talk, yesterday. I just assumed it was similar to mine—Scott."

"Yeah. That's right. What he's facin' is the worst. In my book, he's still my brother-in-law, and he's definitely my brother-in-Christ, who's hurtin'."

"Okay," I said. "Well, all I can claim is something of a friend-ship, I suppose; but I still feel the pull to be here for him."

"Oh, definitely. I didn't mean . . . oh, gosh, I'm sorry. I didn't mean to slight your motives any. I tossed lots last night, so my words are goin' through a sieve, rather than a brain. Did I sound one-up-on-ya? Didn't mean to, Robyn." Richard craned his neck, trying to release the tension he held. What he wanted to do was lay his head on my lap and allow his tiredness to take over, but he couldn't. He had to present a stand that proved as hard as he imagined it would be during his sleepless night. While his heart ached, thinking he might be blowing the precious unfolding we experienced yesterday, I began wondering if sabotage were afoot.

What Richard didn't say that day was, when volunteering as a youth leader at a fellowship in southern California, a thought floated through his mind, one that alluded to a marriage between the two of us. Uncertain of the thought's origin, whether God, a hidden desire of his heart, or the giant burrito he'd just eaten, he left it with God.

It wasn't until the sense of urgency to help Scott pressed in on him that that thought struck his heart with a greater intensity. He didn't understand the timing, or even if we'd see each other, let alone mutually consider being together. What he felt when he saw me, though, left no room for doubt as to his part in the connection; but then, Dad entered the picture and Richard put on the brakes as requested. He respected my dad and, more so, the Scriptures they both knew.

What I felt was a distancing from the man who drew me in, and I didn't know why. Simple female confusion. There was no way I'd have known about being 'equally or unequally yoked.' That stuff lay in Dad's chosen domain. He was the Bible reader. Mother and I left those particulars up to him. But I learned, that's not how it works.

We didn't stop talking or acting like friends. We did acknowledge something had happened between us, but something else was happening, too. I couldn't peg it. Seeing him around didn't stop me from feeling wonderful; and he seemed glad to see me, yet . . . .

When Mother let slip that Richard had never seen any of my films or ads, my feelings for him surged. I realized that first kiss, in his mind, was with his goofy, grown up neighbor, not the movie star or model others thought they knew. I wasn't sure I liked or could manage the increased feelings Mother's revelation released in me, since I'd nowhere to put them. They made me want to be with him all the more, when he, obviously, had other plans that didn't include me.

Richard told me about the day when he knew he'd be coming back to the mountain. He said he was stalled in traffic, when a foreboding sense about Scott fell over him. He prayed immediately, knowing then and there, he had to arrange for his departure from his architectural firm and church. Not wanting to leave either his boss or pastor in the lurch, he started making plans as soon as he reached his apartment. That's when I told him about the razor. His eyebrows shot up. "When was that?" he asked. When I recalled the day and told him, his eyes widened. A puzzled stare lingered on his face for a long minute, as his brain jumped through loops. His eyes remained lowered, shifting, He said, afterwards, how the hand of God moved that day, for the good of His children. "That's the day I was in the traffic I mentioned," he said. "What's more amazin', Robyn, if'n you consider the time zones, it wasn't just the same day, it was the same hour!" He told me how he had no clue I was home until he saw me that special morning, bathed in glorious sunlight. The memory of it made him smile that warm and wonderful smile I'd missed and already felt was mine.

So, I reconciled myself to the fact that Richard had come home for Scott, just as I had, and that we should leave it at that, so our focus wouldn't be blurred. He might not have come home for me, but I came home for me, indirectly; and I didn't want to complicate matters with wanting another Sticker in my life and not getting the second one either. He considered his return a God-thing, whereas mine, well, I wasn't sure what it was or why I came. The only two things I knew for sure were, I felt drawn to be home, and being home felt wonderful. That was enough for me. I, also, knew I felt relief with Richard onboard. Scott would be covered, when I failed him; and I was sure I would.

The familiar wrapped itself around me like a worn out, but favorite sweater; even the tension I felt around Scott seemed normal. I came to appreciate how he was an integral part of my childhood and current life, whether I liked it or not. I thought, maybe someday, being here would help me understand how we fit together, whereas, if I stayed away, that wouldn't happen. I was glad to be home.

I began noticing how the tension between Scott and myself eased up at various turns. Richard's presence served as a buffer for me. It changed the social dynamics and took the edge off being around Scott, just like Dad's influence had in other social settings. I felt lifted out of the self-imposed position I assumed—thinking I'd be the bridge over some unnamed gap, as if I were the only responsible peer in Scott's life. I could breathe, finally, and see him as a friend, again, like I had when he and Richard worked on the barn project with us.

Scott's Paw did a little jig, a slight one, when Richard suggested a weekly study in his home. "It'll be like in the old days," he said. Mr. Farley said, "Our home's always open for sharin' the Good Book; but Richard, the teachin' baton, it's headin' your way, son." He told Richard he was "fully equipped to undertake the task," whatever that meant. I continued to remain wary of all the God talk.

Richard did ask Scott if he'd attend the studies. Scott said, "Shucks, even if I stayed in my room, I 'spect I'd hear that boomin' voice of yours." The way he said it, sounded ominous, as if it were a rejection, but then he added, "So, I might as well set my aged carcass in front of your ugly face and listen." Then one of his big smiles followed. All those amazing white teeth, which I once criticized as being too big for his face, burst into full view, lighting up everyone's facial features with smiles. It was good seeing those two tease each other, again. Richard brought a certain Sticker-disposition back into Scott's life. He carried so much of Samantha within him. He was the brother she most loved, after all. She must have told Scott about that emotional attachment; or he, being Scott, just sensed it. Love has a way of crossing boundaries, midstream like that. Either way, Richard was a balm for his soul. We all felt it.

The next week I got an unexpected call from Pearl. She tried my number in California and discovered the disconnect. That led her to the library and the West Virginia White Pages. Spring break was coming up and she, never wanting to do the typical college-minded-party-thing on a bunch of hot sand, smelling of alcohol, decided to find me instead. She suggested doing something sane, but different. I was thrilled. "Oh, yes!! Come. Please! That'll be perfect."

Was Mother elated with all the incoming adult children at her door? Do teary eyes count? She even told me how she would be forever in debt to Pearl's parents for taking me when they had. I said, "I doubt if they feel you owe them anything, but I understand." Mother gave me a curious look, as if to say, you could have gone with 'I understand,' and left it at that; and she was right. It seemed I still wanted to have the final word with her, something I yearned to leave behind, with all my other childhood diseases; but there it was again.

Pearl came and we played three whole days together: board games with and without my parents, hikes, horseback rides, trips to town, and at the close of the third day, I took her up to meet Scott for something *different* to do; but instead of different, unusual showed its face.

I've seen Pearl around a lot of boys. She maneuvers that territory well. She never failed to walk in her self-control zone with dignity; but when she gazed upon Scott, the look that entered her eyes was the same that cropped up in Samantha's when she saw Scott's twinkle. Scott wasn't putting out any twinkle that day, but I still bit my lip, stepped back a bit for a better view, and hoped I was reading her incorrectly. I waited and continued watching, as my sober and wise friend turned into a giddy girl in his presence. *Oy vey!* I thought.

Even though Scott couldn't see her touching her hair and pulling her sweater neatly down around her hips, I wondered if he could sense what was going on in the room. Scott was in one of his better moods. He entered conversation in his typically limited way. Pearl went back to school the next day, and that was that.

The next week Scott phoned to ask if I could pop up, sooner than later. He had something he'd been holding onto that he wanted to set free. "By myself?" I asked.

"If'n that's alright with you?"

"Sure. I'll be up in the hour. Is that good?"

"Way good," he said.

When I got there, no one else was home, which he probably wanted. I could tell he'd been crying. It's difficult for me to see someone cry, especially a man, but there's something wonderful about crying if it captures beauty and does justice to a cherished one's ending. It's like the ending note of a song. That one note must be executed with an earnest desire to reach perfection, otherwise the whole song could fall flat, lose its strength. Every impression we encounter in a long stretch of beauty will sour, if that one final note gets raspy in a throat bent only on self. We never know when our own endnote will arrive. Singing well, all the way through our song's journey, is vital.

Samantha once said there are two kinds of tears, the good ones and the bad ones. The bad ones drown us in self-pity; whereas, the good ones water the seed of life within the crevice of a broken heart. The good crying helps bring life out of pain; the bad only causes the brokenness to linger and widen. Drowning the earth destroys life, but a well-watered, tender sprout can grow into a forest.

I sat near Scott on the couch. "I ain't breathed out this story t'nobody, 'bout that day, I mean . . . when . . . when it all happened." I sat stunned and transfixed that those words were aimed at me. How could he want me to hear the story, first? His hands brushed his cheeks and continued up the sides of his head, disrupting his hair in an endearing way. I cringed for a moment, not knowing if I could hear what was resting on his heart. When I rested my hand on his arm, however, I knew I could. I felt safe. Scott would be my anchor. His tears were good ones.

"Robyn, when I couldn't pull up the Ryan's nose, and knew we were goin' down, I cursed myself for lettin' Samantha sit behind me on that maiden voyage. But, I couldn't stop my wife, when she laid down the Ruth-argument, ya know." I didn't know. I had no idea what he was talking about, but I nodded, not even thinking of his blindness.

"When I saw the mountain up 'head, my heart sunk. That's when I used every ounce of my strength to turn the Ryan into the trees, and by God's grace I was able to shift direction, just 'nough. I thought, if'n I could hit the most bendable parts of some trees to lessen the impact, there might be a chance for us, at least for her. That's when I unbuckled my seat belt to throw myself over her. I wanted to cushion her. I didn't care 'bout dyin'. My only thought was to be as near to her as I could. I wanted to protect her, some-how, and God only knows how I wanted to hold her, one more time.

"She didn't like that one bit, though. You should've seen her face, Robyn. You wouldn't 'ave recognized her. I ain't never heard her so upset. The whole time she was quiet, till then. She knew the thick of it was comin', and when I turned to face her, she cried out, "Scott Farley, you get that seat belt back on you right now!" Then she started cryin'. She cried for me, not for herself. I scared her, see? She wasn't scared of doin' 'nythin' with me, not even dyin'. She was worried 'bout me, 'cause . . . we weren't doin' the same thing with the seat belts. So, she grabbed me and held onto me. And, I told her I was sorry. She said, 'Scott . . .'"

He stopped talking. His chest heaved with uncontrollable sobbing. It was hard for him to draw sufficient breath, but what did reach his lungs came by way of a labored, muffled sound, like that of a bellow fueling a flame about to be extinguished in a reservoir of ice. Tears streaked his face, fat rolling drops that seemed to have no end. It was as if a well of pain had been tapped, one that hadn't been given the opportunity to drain. Now that it had, it poured out in violent spurts. I felt more compassion for Scott in that moment, than anyone I'd ever known. I didn't know what to do, other than hold his arm tighter.

"Right 'fore the plane hit," he continued between breaths, "she whispered she loved me." He stopped, again, and then I slipped my arms around his head and drew him closer, wanting to soak up his tears, because they were part of Samantha. Scott had given me the greatest gift—her last words, or so I thought.

I heard, "I have to finish, Robyn," rising up from the cavity of my embrace. I sat back down, as close to him as I could. He cleared his throat and wiped his eyes and ran his sleeve across his nose. "This is important. I want you to know this part."

"Okay," I said, wiping my eyes, too.

"I felt myself bein' ripped from her arms, but not for long. That rentin' lasted a second or two, 'cause she was there, again, with me, in the blink of an eye, holdin' on tighter than I ever imagine possible. Robyn, we fell together. I tried flippin' us 'round, so I'd be the one to hit the limbs and the ground first, but I couldn't. I tried hard. I couldn't figure out how she got herself in that position, since I fell first, or how she kept it strong all the way down." Scott's voice quivered. I squeezed his arm again. "In that struggle and concern for her, I felt the strangest peace surroundin' us. There wasn't a lick of fear on her face. I never felt the blows of the limbs on my body, not a one; and it didn't seem like she did either. I only felt her warmth, holdin' me, her love all 'round me. I don't remember hittin' ground." Scott took a deep breath and released it in a quiet sob, and then his body went limp.

Suddenly, the angels Samantha had introduced to me came to mind—the ones inhabiting and guarding the forest around our

Sun Bowl. When Scott began speaking, again, that thought burst like a bubble, receding back into the invisible world.

"But right off, when I opened my eyes, there on the cold ground, I saw her clear as day, sittin' with me, rockin' me in her lap, smilin' that smile in her eyes, ya know. She was brushin' my hair back with her warm soft hands. How, I thought. How could she be okay? But, her smile wiped away my questions. You remember how that smile could raise the dead, right? So in my confusion, I thought, maybe that's what's happening; but still, none of it made any sense. Not a lick.

"She began singin' a little song, sayin' all was fine, that I shouldn't worry, said everythin' would come 'round right. Those were her exact words, "come 'round right." She said I could close my eyes and rest; help was on its way. She told me she'd be with me, called me her love. Robyn, she kept me warm, kept me wantin' to live for her. She never left, all through the coma. We talked every day.

"Towards the end, she kept sayin', 'It's time for you to wake up, Scott. It's okay to wake up, my love.' I didn't know what she meant, 'cause I felt perfectly awake, enjoyin' every minute with her. I didn't want to blink myself awake, but then she began tellin' me it was time again in that same voice she used when she wanted me to buckle that dang seat belt. So, this time I finally said, okay, and I woke up. And, I admit, Robyn, after hearin' she was gone, I wished I hadn't lived; and I . . . I did want to die right off after comin' home. You were right, but that's gone. It's not what she'd want. Nope. Not at all. So, I'm askin' your forgiveness for sayin' that foul thing in her name, and for usin' that lie to try 'n' draw you into my crazies."

At that point my tears fell and I didn't hide them. "Of course, I forgive you, Scott." I wiped my face, and felt a glowing love for him enter my being for the first time. Everything tumbled into place, like my inner combination had been turned successfully, and my lock opened wide. It felt like I had this love inside me that wasn't mine, and it was all falling on Scott. In it, not only did I utterly care for his well-being, I felt completely laid bare and known by the same engulfing love.

I searched for an unsearchable reason. In hearing what had happened in the crisp waves of that autumn descent, I had been made privy to a miracle, given freely to a boy I'd seen as an intruder. Finally, I saw all the hiding places I had formed within my own mind, as if a floodlight had been turned on inside me. Is that what goodness does, I asked myself.

In that openness, I sensed a major, undefined shift rearranging my reality. I didn't know what it meant, but an unusual joy surrounded it. I had a sudden urge to read my dad's Book, but knew my time with Scott wasn't over. I found it uncanny how I actually wanted to be with Scott, to sit with him. I wondered what Dad would say, and then I wondered what Mother would think, because I knew she wouldn't *say* anything, not on this topic. And then, I wondered if the shift that fell upon me was the first part of more to come. I remember thinking, *Is this love the way, the way into God?* Finally, I understood why I couldn't understand Samantha or Dad. They lived in another world—a totally different perspective created their view.

"Scott, what you've shared will fill my life forever. It's brought a whole new—everything! It's life and love. Celebrate them, Scott. What happened to you and Samantha will never happen to anyone else in the whole world. Don't you think she's up there, giddy with laughter? Oh, I do. Why do I?"

Scott gasped with relief. "You believe me? I hoped so hard you'd believe me," he said.

"Believe you! What you've shared is more real than anything I've heard in my whole life. Well, that's not entirely true," I said, pausing. "At least my ears heard, when Samantha shared things like this. It's the world she occupied when I followed her like a lost puppy. Clueless me. Oh, Scott! I was so bound up in myself. I'm so sorry. No more. I didn't hear with just my ears!" That's when he straightened up and looked at me. I mean, it seemed as if he saw me more clearly than any sighted person could. I told him, "Does this mean God's got hold of me? 'Cause I'm not squirming, Scott. Fact is, I like being with you—a lot."

He wept. We wept. I asked why he was crying again, since his tears seemed different. He said, "It's joy." And then, he said, "Robyn, ya gotta get this, 'cause I do! I see the evidence of the hope Samantha anchored in her heart from the first day we met you. Not everyone can connect those dots. I can, now! You're livin' proof. We're livin' proof. The victory banner is flyin' over our heads; and it's all connected to her, because she rested under it." Good tears showed up, again. I could tell there was a shift occurring in his soul, too.

I didn't understand his reference to a victory banner, but he said, I would in time. I wondered something, but didn't have to wonder for long. What would Richard say?

When I told him up in the hayloft, he exclaimed, "Holy catfish! Ain't God the most amazin'!" And then he ran around the loft with his pitchfork raised to heaven, shouting, "Thank you, Jesus!" I thought the irony of that scene couldn't be more perfect. There he was, my sweetheart in an old red shirt with hay hanging from it, thanking God, as he waved the only image I picked up from a cartoon I once saw as a child of a devil. Irony or God's humor. Take your pick. Finally, Richard lifted my hand into his and said, "Oh, I'm so hungry! Let's pick up a bunch of steaks, and fire up the grill." I think the man was petitioned-starved. He told me every churn and grumble of his stomach was well worth hearing my good news.

* * *

WHEN I LOOK BACK ON MY CHILDHOOD ON THE mountain my heart zooms in on Samantha every time. She led me with a generosity of spirit few find in another. Her friendship was genuine. She lived it. I walked away from her in the darkness I carried, but she never stopped loving or being herself. Our days together existed within a measured beat of time and space. They lay poised for two souls to unite as friends.

The faith that sent her into her everlasting life never stopped nudging me onward, even after her earthly end—all because she believed with her whole heart, mind, and strength, and waited upon the God who places angels in trees to make all things fall gracefully well for those she loved. I wrote this poem in the wee hours of my new life after reading the Book of John. Scott had suggested I start my journey there.

> *We settle down in grassy sward,*
> *As single kernels under guard.*
> *We lie sealed under sun and rain,*
> *Not knowing of our Savior's gain,*
> *And then His Spirit ruptures us.*
> *For what is seen is seen in part,*
> *Until Love's sown within our heart.*

It all comes down to an immense simplicity. When we turn into the light, darkness vanishes. Poof. That's it. That's all, as in everything.

Everything clicked that day and night. Samantha's words, oh, the words, the words, her words, those simple turns into life that sprang from her heart. I shall retain her words forever; but space has opened all around them for more words. It's what she wanted for me—to rejoice in the Word that made the stars and shone through them into the hearts and minds of man, the twinkling stories eventually printed on pages, each teeming with life, more so than the trees with all their angels.

After that day, Scott and I held the precious secret of the miraculous deliverance in confidence, only sharing it with a few others; but my secret, well, it was broadcast far and wide. The love between Richard and me surged, as if the relational cord that bound us had been plugged into a 220 outlet. Dad smiled a lot. Mother wondered at all the infectious joy. She was at the top of our prayer list.

Scott's spiritual vision grew stronger than ever. He and Richard study regularly together; and, something else, Scott's physical sight improved to the point of being able to see shadows after his first surgery. We wait to see what the next intervention brings.

I thoroughly love my mother, these days. She's the perennial trooper of goodwill toward man. I was baptized in the Sun Bowl, that first glorious summer, once the water warmed. I wore a dress I made from material I couldn't pass up. I bought the whole bolt, so that I could sew gifts to disperse far and wide. It's pure white cotton with small, colorful dragonflies zigzagging in every direction. I can almost hear them, those frail beings enjoying new life; and I could almost feel you, Samantha, wanting to jump into the water with me, or was that the angels showing me your heart's desire. Scott hadn't been the only one who saw more clearly that year. Dad said he knew Mother would eventually come around. He didn't say when, because no one knows God's timing for births, or deaths, or being born again.

Friends threw 'the mountain lovebirds' an engagement party before I left to join Pearl at her campus apartment that fall. Is that too much information in one sentence? Yes, Richard and I got engaged a week after my baptism, and I returned to school, as a sophomore. Finally, I was on track with my age, when it came to school. What an oddity that felt so right. I was a nineteen-year-old sophomore. The only thing truly odd about me, at that point, according to the student population, was that I was an engaged virgin. Call me silly, but I think it's wonderful, keeping promises and covenants and finally knowing why. I have no doubt Samantha would be nodding in approval, if she were here.

I close this story, now, with a series of confessions to you,

Samantha, my dearest friend. Yes, when I think of you, sorrow no longer pierces my heart. Joy has taken its place. Most of the time I accept the grace as it washes over me. Yet, and even so, I still fall upon a certain yearning that crops up, occasionally. And sure, I embrace it for a few moments, because I still get fooled into thinking I'm embracing you, but I'm not. I'm learning that truth more each day. It's sticking.

My unrealistic desire runs this way: I have a wish. I wish I could share with you at this time in my life, in an even keel, give-and-take way. I actually believe I might be able to pull it off, this time. Then I pause, wondering if it's just my pride rearing its head again, or if it's Christ in me confirming the new creation's ability to love as a true friend. That lack of knowing makes me cringe a bit; and then, I let go of the thought and breathe in the air, because there's nowhere to go with it and it makes my heart hurt a bit.

Richard reminds me, when that thought pops up that I need to remember just how strongly God was there for you at the end. I know that's true from Scott's confession. He, also, repeats the truth that, someday, we will live together in unsullied love, balanced and whole, without tears or fears, forever—all of us. No cringing doubts, no worrying, no jealousy, just loving and sharing. I want to say, *Imagine* that one, John Lennon, but since he has long gone to dust, wanting nothing of its reality, as proclaimed in his song, I will proclaim, under the banner of love, that it surely does exist. Even within me now, it expands.

There have been times, too, when I've longed for another miraculous friendship. Could there be another brightly lit star who challenges my thoughts and fills me to overflowing? I suppose I want to prove to you, Samantha, and to myself that I could be a better friend; but I've found that's not happening, and that hurts a bit, too, knowing I won't get that opportunity. Most of the time, though, I smile when I think of you. I really do. God's mercies are strong. I mean He gave me *your* Richard to love.

I'm happy with my life. I've made a few good friends at school and church. Pearl remains a constant source of appreciation. She's a great housemate, and I love her; but she's not you. No one is. I know that sounds elementary, but I'm gaining insight into how we're all so different, for unique reasons. Pearl's becoming better friends with Scott. She's more herself, now. I think you'd approve. I know you would. Scott keeps her at a proper distance and prays for her everyday.

Another thing, dearest one, something I've wanted to say for so long: Congratulations on your takeoff—the real one! It must have been glorious!

Sometimes, when I'm alone, with no paper due the next day or places to go, for one reason or another I go inside myself. You rise up from my heart as a feeling I cherish. Sometimes I think, if I asked you a question, you'd answer me; but then I turn from that thought, knowing I must wait for that joy to happen, wait for the day when I'll reach out to you, and you'll be there, for real. I wonder what my first question to you will be; but then I correct myself. Yes, I still do that. This correction is important to know, now, for when we see each other again, then, we will be known, fully, all of us, as we are known by Christ, for we will be as He, when we see His face. I'll have no more questions for you, then, even though you bore them all so well.

I laugh at myself, too, because when I'm feeling a bit mischievous I truly can imagine myself colluding with you in designing a foolproof prank to pull on Richard, one that would make him laugh till he fell to the ground; and then I can picture us both jumping on him at the same time.

Then, there's the image that keeps popping into my head. Maybe it's connected to our day at Bessie Jane's. It seems so real. I see myself, somewhere in my late eighties, having lived an abundant life. I'm content and thankful for every turn that's led me to that age and place. I see myself on the mountain, not at Bessie's but my own well-loved dwelling. There are notches on a hallway doorjamb, some as low as three feet—measurements of loved ones with names that sort of sound like Ricky, Sam, Frieda, and, of course, Scottie. It's a home nestled near the site of your crash and miraculous departure.

On that particular day, I'm comfortably folded in my rocker on a familiar deck. Eternity might even be tugging at my soul, telling my body it's time to let go. I draw another breath, and then I look up to see a young girl of Olympian stature (correction: godly stature) racing toward me, her blue-black hair, flipping endlessly in a flurry of ceaseless motion. She's smiling and laughing with the love of her life--not me—Scott Farley; and I feel no jealousy.

I stare at the two of them, as they glide like the wind towards me. A feeling of immense pleasure wells up within my heart at seeing the amazing duo, heading my way once again. I step toward them and in the peal of my laughter, I'm ten, again—just a better version.

And here is where I give Samantha the final word. I asked her, once, to define the word, *after*. She said, "It's sometimes sweet, 'n' sometimes painful. Depends on what comes 'fore and how you set your mind to bearin' what spills out of it."

OTHER BOOKS AND BOOK REVIEWS

A short, chapter addendum to *Beyond the Cradle* can be found on Amazon, as a Kindle eBook. It's a small but powerful chapter titled: *A Sampling of Samantha Sticker's Inexhaustible Mind*.

The Begins of Into was published late in 2022. Its newest edition, the Green Edition, emerged in February 2024. Think fantasy without witches, sorcerers—without any magic whatsoever. Think Biblical realities. This story explores God's mysterious ways and the spiritual dimension found in two kingdoms with humans in the middle. That approach leaves *the magical* in the dust. The realm of magic is a kingdom I will not promote in my stories, other than to mention it as a passing misstep toward darkness. Focusing on the larger picture of truth, as revealed in Scripture, provides an ample platform to rest stories upon.

    I've come to regard *The Begins of Into* as a faith primer set within an entertaining tale. It creates easy access for young readers to consider their faith journey in this world. It's ideal for pre-teens, teens, new believers, and parents who desire to come alongside their children and discuss what it means to be a stranger and a pilgrim in this world. Its sequel, *The Crèche Catcher*, will appear later in 2024. It's a supernatural fiction that tackles the topic of sanctification, while revealing the heart of God toward children-in-the-womb.

Dear Readers~

I'm thankful for the time you've spent reading *Beyond the Cradle*. It brings me joy, knowing the characters I've come to love have been embraced by you, too.

You might not realize this fact, but we indie authors really need help exposing our novels. We are typically lame at marketing; plus, we're usually on a shoestring budget.

Writing an honest review on Amazon for a book you've read ties the circle of sharing up with a precious bow. It's really special to us.

Would you consider leaving stars and your honest opinion in a review after reading one of my books? Whether the review length is short, long, or in-between, doesn't matter. It just really helps.

Thank you so much! Anne

ACKNOWLEDGMENTS

Special thoughts of Lee Hough, who read and loved this story, when it was a novella, many decades ago. He was a senior acquisition editor at the time. Lee has since gone home to be with the Lord. I cannot call to tell him *Beyond the Cradle* has become a novel, like he asked me to do when it happened. This is my way of celebrating his influence on me. His encouragement has always been a part of this story.

A shout out to K. Craytor for being the first person to read the entire fuller draft, while still in its less-than-fully-edited form, and still being amazingly enthusiastic about what she read.

Special mention: The sweet poem attributed to Scott, *Did A Child*, was written by my son when he was nine.

ABOUT THE AUTHOR

Anne Stanton's writing has appeared in various publications from literary journals to a national children's magazine and various city newspapers. This is her debut novel.

She lived in one house until nineteen, leaving home as a sophomore to attend college in Columbia, Missouri. After graduation she relocated out West, where she was born again. As a certified teacher she rallied round the homeschool movement, helping parents in her church to launch with confidence. When a mom, she joined the rank and file lifestyle of home-education, loving everything about it. This story's first sentence was written on a deck, raised above rattlesnake ground in sunny Northern California, while her firstborn, sitting nearby, practiced writing her ABCs. Anne now lives in the Pacific Northwest.

Follow Anne on Instagram @anne.j.stanton